the Diplomat

SOPHIA FRENCH

Bella
BOOKS

2015

Bella Books, Inc.
P.O. Box 10543
Tallahassee, FL 32302

Printed in the United States of America on acid-free paper.

First Bella Books Edition 2015

Editor: Shelly Rafferty
Cover Designer: Judith Fellows

ISBN: 978-1-59493-437-7

About the Author

Sophia French lives in Hobart, Tasmania. *The Diplomat* is her first novel.

Dedication

for Li

CHAPTER ONE

Rema loved every weave and fiber of her uniform, but most of all she enjoyed tightening the silver clasp that sealed its high collar. Even after thirteen years, the triumphant final touch still evoked her pride at becoming the first female diplomat in the history of the Empire.

She admired her reflection in the cabin's mirror. The trousers still fit snugly about her narrow hips, and the coat, which shone a vibrant purple in the morning light, added length to her shoulders and drew tight at her waist. She swept her bangs from her eyes and ran a comb through the tangles of her dark red hair. It had grown over the journey to rest just above the collar. Time soon for a trim.

With a dampened cloth, she wiped her face clean while feeling the sharp curve of her cheekbones. A woman in trousers was an oddity, and Rema's angular features and boyish figure often caused her to be mistaken for a beautiful young man. Fortunately, she enjoyed the attention.

Three short raps sounded on the cabin door. "Come in," Rema said, adjusting her collar.

The door opened to reveal the sweat-soaked face of the first mate. "My lady, we've docked."

"Evidently." Rema gestured to the window. Beyond its wooden frame, the city was visible, a sprawl of stone buildings beneath plumes of chimney smoke.

"You'll be wanting an escort to the royal palace. This is a rough city, especially for a woman on her own."

"I have diplomatic immunity. Surely the muggers and rapists will respect the authority of our Emperor."

The sailor tilted his head. "Are you joking, my lady?"

Rema smiled. "If you want to send some of the crew with me, it would be appreciated."

He nodded, gave her an inexpert salute and left. Despite their initial reservations, the crew had warmed to Rema over the voyage. She had won over harder hearts than those of a few cranky seamen, and despite being a woman alone among men, she'd never felt threatened. Diplomatic immunity might be worth little on foreign streets, but these men had family in Arann, the imperial capital.

Rema waited, her gaze on the city, until three large sailors arrived in her cabin, their heads bowed in bashful reverence. No doubt they had been chosen for the terrifying tattoos on their forearms, one of which featured a skull devouring a snake—surely an uncommon occurrence.

One of the sailors reached for her luggage, and she raised her hand. "No, that's fine. I can manage it myself." She took the handle of her ornate wooden trunk, which had seen most of the world with her. It was a unique and inventive design—a chest with wheels attached and a long handle, perfect for a roaming emissary. Though its polish had long worn off and each wheel had been replaced at least twice, the chest remained intact, and Rema was convinced that if anyone else touched it, it would immediately fall apart.

She followed the sailors through the narrow halls of the lower deck, trundling the luggage behind her. As she ascended onto the deck, the stench of the docks pried open her nostrils and settled in her stomach. It was a rancid mixture of decaying fish, sweat and city sewage, the characteristic perfume of dockyards everywhere.

The sun gleamed bright against the water, forcing Rema to squint as she gazed toward the docks. Innumerable small boats and large ships cluttered the crescent sweep of the bay. Upon the cobbled shore, men and women dragged crates and pulled squirming nets. A breeze swept across the deck, and Rema shivered. She'd never become accustomed to these eastern chills.

The captain marched across deck. "My lady. A good journey, wouldn't you agree?"

"I've had many worse. My thanks to you and your crew."

"We'll be here for the week." He scratched through his beard and flicked a wiggling insect from his fingernail. "If that's not long enough, another ship'll be here in fifteen days."

"That's more than enough time. Thank you."

The captain walked away still digging at his whiskers. Rema gestured to her escorts, crossed the creaking deck and followed the thin gangplank to the shore. The sailors whispered behind her, impressed, it seemed, by her balance. The wheels of her luggage hit the cobblestones with a shudder, and she weaved immediately to avoid a pile of fish guts drying in the sun. One of the sailors wasn't as vigilant, and she smiled as he let loose a stream of profanities.

"Excuse him, my lady," said another of the sailors, who had a dolphin tattooed on his cheek. "He shouldn't use language like that in front of you."

Rema laughed. "If there's a sailor's cuss I haven't yet heard, I'd like to know about it."

The docks were crowded, and Rema moved cautiously to avoid heavy crates and jutting elbows. As she passed through the tumult, the dock workers stared at her. "That's a bloody woman," said a squat man gutting a fish, heedless that he was spilling the mess on himself. "Look, she's dressed as a man."

Rema paused in her march. "It's better than being clad in fish guts. You should take more care with your work." She resumed her measured pace, leaving the fisherman speechless.

The dolphin-tattooed sailor walked beside her. "Be careful. It might not be wise to talk back to folks like that. Some's pretty rough."

"If I didn't talk back, I wouldn't be much good at my job." As Rema spoke, a woman sorting fish heads cast an admiring glance up Rema's body. She blushed as their eyes met. Rema winked, and the woman found an intensified interest in her work.

The group continued through the city streets, leaving the salty stench behind them. A crowd pressed close, composed of slow-moving travelers, impatient merchants and lumbering wagons. Swarms of children menaced travelers by running about their feet. Even the houses lining the streets were tightly clustered, and their thatch and slate roofs competed for space.

A horse strutted by while relaxing its bowels, and the unfortunate sailor who had trodden in the fish guts managed to further ruin his boots. His curses withered the air. "How I'd missed dry land," said Rema.

"This is one of the poorest capitals on the continent," said the sailor with the dolphin. "What's a fancy diplomat like you doing here?"

"Fancy diplomacy." Rema waved to three farmers who had dropped their bundles in the street to stare at her. "Are you interested in hearing about it?"

"You can talk all you like," he said, and Rema chuckled. No doubt the sailor was only interested in the sound of her voice, which was low, smooth and accentuated with lyrical subtleties. A diplomat's voice was her weapon, and Rema's was lethally honed.

"Danosha is a backward kingdom, ruled by a King and Queen born with the proper blood but not much imagination. I doubt there's been an agricultural or military innovation here in centuries." Rema stepped over a wandering cat. "They're presently at war with Lyorn, a plutocratic realm that's rich, expansive, well-armed and with no shortage of fine military minds."

"Right."

Probably she'd lost him at "agricultural," but Rema pressed on regardless. "As you might expect, Danosha is losing very badly." She ducked beneath a line of washing. "This is where things get interesting, so pay attention."

"I am." The sailor glanced at her chest before returning his serious gaze to her face. "Go on."

"If Lyorn conquers Danosha, it will become rather more formidable. Lyorn has close ties with our enemies, and the stronger they become, the more we have to worry about our vulnerable eastern shore."

The sailor nodded. "Vulnerable."

Their approach startled a woman drenching clothes in a bucket, which she knocked over, flooding the street with rivulets of soapy water. "Is it always like this?" said the sailor. "People staring at you?"

"Very often. I was in Urandal three months ago, and you should have seen the trail of blushing, bewildered women I left behind me."

"That doesn't bother you?"

"Quite the contrary. Anyway, back to our conversation. I'm here to offer Danosha the military support it needs to bring the war to a stalemate. Lyorn bleeds itself on our superior armies, agrees to a ceasefire and a future crisis is averted."

"Averted. Sounds good."

Rema and the sailors reached the edge of a marketplace teeming with aggressive hawkers. They passed through the stalls, avoiding eye contact. Just as Rema thought she was safe, a merchant ran up to her and bellowed in her ear. "No," she said. "I don't want any oranges. Thank you." The man retreated, still brandishing the unwanted fruit.

"So you're here to save these foreigners from being destroyed," said the sailor, who had himself barely avoided being sold a pineapple. "Sounds like an easy job to me."

"You'd be surprised." Rema stretched her arms toward the sun, releasing the tension in her shoulders. It was best to enjoy the open air while she could. Soon she'd be stuck in the stuffy confines of the palace, listening to the mumblings of orderlies and bureaucrats.

The streets widened, and the crude dwellings gave way to sturdy, multistoried houses. A large smithy came into view, its chimney puffing dark clouds of smoke. A scarred man worked a grindstone in its yard. He lifted his head and scowled at Rema. "What are you looking at, you cocksucking pretty-boy?"

"Good morning to you too," said Rema. "I hope your craftwork is finer than your manners."

The man's face purpled. "You're a woman?"

"Am I the first you've seen? No wonder you're surprised."

"You're wearing long trousers." The man's expression grew sullen. "That's perverse."

"And imagine how perverse I would be if I took them off." Rema treated the man to her most winning smile. "Have a good day."

She left the man at his grindstone, his face twitching in slow and reluctant thought. Her conversation partner frowned. "You've got some courage," he said.

"Why, because I'm not afraid of an ill-tempered blacksmith?" Rema yanked her luggage over a high cobblestone. "Come on, it grows late. Let's pick up the pace."

It was midafternoon when they arrived at the wide road leading up to the palace, which sat on a small hill in the center of the city. Its tired walls seemed a gesture to tradition rather than an obstacle that might seriously keep out an invading army. The road continued beneath a raised portcullis, and a stream of travelers wandered to and from the palace, most of them miserable-looking peasants. Presumably, the rulers held audiences for their stricken people to placate them with royal gestures and mumbles.

Rema brought the sailors to a stop amid the drifting crowd. "You three had best go back to your ship. I'll be safe now. Thank you for the courtesy of your escort."

"You didn't need us at all," said the tattooed sailor. "If a mugger came at you, you'd just talk at him until he apologized and ran away."

Rema accepted the compliment with a graceful tilt of her head. "Go on, before it gets dark. Here." She counted out several coins from her purse. "Try not to drink it all."

The money disappeared into the sailor's big hand. "You're a jewel of the Empire, my lady. Have fun with the fancy diplomacy."

"Enjoy your evening." Rema arched an eyebrow. "And advise your friend to tread more carefully."

She left the sailors counting their wealth and proceeded toward the palace entrance. A guardsman separated from the brickwork and stepped into her path. He looked her up and down, opened his mouth to speak, hesitated and inspected her one more time to be sure. "Miss," he said finally. "May I help you?"

"Good afternoon." Rema performed a modest bow. "My name is Remela. I'm an emissary from Emperor Ormun of the Pale Plains, Heir to the Wide Realms, Lord Master of the City States of Urandal, King of the Lastar, Lord of Goronba and so on. Please don't make me say the rest."

The guard began to laugh and quickly turned the sound into a cough. "Well, looking at you, I can see you're not some peasant come to shovel muck at the feet of the king. I'll wave you on through and ask someone to give a shout to the steward. Just loiter around in the front court."

"I'm excellent at loitering. Enjoy a safe watch."

"Aye, thank you." The guard grinned under his mustache and wandered back to his post.

Rema tugged her luggage through the portcullis and into the din of the courtyard. Guards clanked across the cobblestones, horses grumbled in their stables and peasants raised their voices in complaint as they pushed toward the palace doors. Rema fought her way through the chaos and into the relative quiet of a wide, high-ceilinged front court. Windows above the door admitted the afternoon's light and warmth, and archways about the walls opened into numerous palace corridors.

A series of stone benches lined the walls, most occupied by slumped visitors waiting for guards to lead them to the audience chamber. Rema pulled her trunk next to an empty bench and sat with her feet crossed, her eyes closed and her face lifted toward the sun. After a stretch of pleasant idleness, a cleared throat summoned her attention.

Before her stood a middle-aged, balding man in white robes. Like all native-born Danoshans, his skin was lily-white. Deep creases lined his face, and his eyes were heavily pouched as if he rarely slept. "By that weary face, I'd say you must be the steward," Rema said.

"I'm Yorin. You must be the emissary." Yorin began to extend his hand, but hesitated.

"Yes, I can shake your hand. You don't have to serenade me first."

Yorin gave her a furtive handshake. "Not to insult you, but I've never had to deal with a woman diplomat before. And to have one come from your Emperor is a bigger surprise still."

"I obtained my position while his father was still in power. Ormun decided to keep me. My name is Remela, but please call me Rema."

"Rema it is. You should be aware that the Queen dislikes Emperor Ormun very much."

"Any sensible woman would," said Rema. Yorin's eyebrows jumped, and she laughed. "Don't look so shocked. So long as I get the results he wants, Ormun doesn't care what I say about him."

"Let's get you out of this filthy court." Yorin spoke with a new touch of warmth. "This palace must seem a hovel to you."

"After three weeks at sea, anywhere is home."

Yorin's lips moved in the barest beginnings of a smile. He drew his robes around him and beckoned Rema to follow. "Very well. Come, then, and keep your wits about you. Some of these idiot servants will knock you over without a word of warning." He trudged across the court, and Rema followed, her mood brightened by the prospect of a challenge. Whatever these people thought they knew of diplomats, they were soon to be surprised.

CHAPTER TWO

Rema pursued Yorin down a wide, torch-lit corridor. Immense wooden beams supported the ceiling, all of them dark and swollen with rot. Yorin stopped before an open door and motioned to the bedchamber beyond it. "We'll settle you in here for now."

The room was constructed of meager stone and furnished with a simple bed. Its one interior window overlooked an inner courtyard. Certainly less luxurious than her usual lodgings. Most monarchs feared that if an imperial diplomat slept poorly, the Emperor might take grave offense, and consequently Rema had slept on more silken sheets than she could count. Yet given the condition of the palace, this might well be the best Yorin had to offer.

Rema pushed her luggage against the wall and returned her attention to Yorin, who was playing with his sleeve. Its fabric was worn and stretched—the sign of a man with many worries. "Who do I deal with here? Yourself? An ambassador?"

"King Cedrin and Queen Talitha themselves. You've come at a dire time for us, and they'll hang on your every word. The King is in session, but the Queen is in her private chambers. I'm going to take you there now."

"How gracious." Rema dusted some dirt from the hem of her coat. "I usually have to deal with functionaries."

"All we have around here are disfunctionaries," said Yorin without smiling. "This way."

He led her back to the court and directed her to a high stairway in the corner. As they climbed, Rema looked down at the heads of the people below her. "Are they all here for an audience with the King and Queen?"

"Indeed, although only the King gives audiences." Yorin proceeded slowly with one hand on the balustrade. "The peasants need some assurance in times like this."

"And who is actually governing?"

"Well, my official response is that the King and Queen are." A conspiratorial note entered Yorin's voice. "You seem like a canny woman, however, so let's just say that I have the authority to handle many affairs. Prince Calan interferes where he can, and Elise likewise does her best to make my job difficult."

"Elise. That must be our ill-fated princess."

The stairs ended at the junction of three corridors. A faded black-and-purple carpet ran down their lengths, and a painted mural decorated one of the cracked stone walls. Rema peered at its peeling design, a hunt scene, although the hounds were so faded that they might have been sausages for all she knew.

Yorin drew Rema away from the stairs. "Understand that Elise doesn't like being called a princess. She's our court enchantress and skilled at her art. She's also very displeased with Ormun's terms, as you might imagine."

"An enchantress?"

"You don't believe in magic?"

"I once was sent to parley with the so-called Wizard Kings of… no, I can't even remember the name of their territory; there were simply too many vowels. It turned out their feared sorcerous army was regular armor covered in pitch and set alight. It had something of the effect of flaming warriors, if an enemy didn't think to look closely."

"A few charlatans. Sometimes a farmer sells you a bad egg, but you don't give up on eggs."

"You might, if the egg were bad enough." Rema shook her head. "I don't discount there's an odd thread of enchantment in our world, especially in the south. Even Ormun has a court magician. But in my experience the majority of magicians are little more than clever frauds."

"Elise is genuine. I've seen her accomplish some remarkable things."

"Such as avoiding marriage until the age of twenty-six. Not that I can blame her."

Yorin's expression became even more grim. "Let's not keep the Queen waiting."

He led Rema to an unassuming wooden door and knocked twice. The handle rattled, the door cracked open and a small girl peered through the gap. After a second of blinking incomprehension, she opened the door wide and smiled in earnest terror.

"Thank you, Alys," said Yorin. "You can go make yourself useful in the kitchen."

Alys nodded. She looked at Rema, and her eyes grew huge with wonder. "M'lady, you're wearing trousers!"

"Alys!" Yorin scowled at her. "Off to the scullery."

"Yes, Master." Alys gave Rema a final amazed look before darting back down the hallway. Rema smiled to herself. Given the task ahead, a touch of levity was welcome.

Yorin gestured to the open door. "Talitha wants you alone. I'll close the door after you."

Despite numerous flickering candles, a drab gloominess pervaded the Queen's chamber. No surprise there—palaces of this kind were commonly grim, as if shadows seeped from their walls. Rema crossed the threadbare carpet and stood in the center of the room. Talitha sat in a tall wooden chair, her wrinkled hands upon a closed book on her lap. Bookshelves were stacked high on the walls about her, and a writing desk took up an entire corner. A literate woman. In usual circumstances Rema would be pleased, but it was much harder to outwit the well-read.

Talitha turned her deep-set eyes toward Rema and squinted. She seemed to be in her late fifties, but worn by the demands of rule and motherhood. Her handsome face was sunken amid flabby folds, and an enormous purple gown concealed her body.

"Your Grace, my name is Remela." Rema made a low bow. "I have been sent to you by Emperor Ormun of the Pale Plains, Heir to the Wide Realms, Lord Master of the City States of Urandal, King of the Lastar and shall we skip the rest and get to the point?"

Talitha gave a brittle laugh. "Indeed." She bent forward, her chair creaking as her weight shifted. "You sound very young for a diplomat."

Rema stepped further into the light. "I'm thirty years old, Your Grace."

"I'll be damned!" Talitha leaned nearer still, and her chair groaned again—might the Gods keep it intact. "You're a woman."

"So I've been told."

Talitha scratched her thinning scalp. "It's inconceivable. The great barbarian Ormun, capturer and plunderer of women, employs a female diplomat in his service. What's next, a butcher marrying a pig?"

"I was appointed by his father. Ormun spared me after the coup."

"Not many survived that incident." Talitha puckered her lips as her gaze followed the lines of Rema's uniform. "You must be very good at your job."

"I'm sure you'll test me to my limits, Your Grace."

"Sit opposite me, girl. Don't call me 'Your Grace.' My name is Talitha, and I've no patience for groveling."

Rema settled into a neighboring chair so well-padded it seemed possible it might swallow her. "If we're to be informal, please call me Rema. I don't much like my full name."

"Strange. I thought it pretty." Talitha ran a crooked finger across her chin. "So, a female diplomat. You wear your uniform well."

"I know."

"And you've a bit of sass in you too. You're a striking creature, Rema. Articulate, handsome and with a touch of your own fire." Talitha's eyes glittered in the candlelight. "A diplomat who speaks without servility is a very rare thing. I'd venture that you're one of the Empire's best."

"Possibly. I'm certainly the most attractive."

"Three weeks to get here. Three weeks to get back. Are we really so important as to deserve a diplomat of your caliber?" Talitha reclined, and her body moved mysteriously beneath her gown. "It's as if the Emperor thinks we might refuse."

"The Emperor rarely thinks. For my part, I'm very sure that you're planning to refuse. That's why I'm here."

"Oh? We are a beleaguered little kingdom, and the most powerful man in the world is offering to save us. So tell me, why are you so very sure that I'm not receptive to your generous offer of help?"

"Ormun demands your unwed daughter." Rema looked into Talitha's faded blue eyes and found the admiration she'd hoped for. "Had you betrothed her to a Lyornan merchant-king, you could have ended this war already. Clearly she doesn't want to marry, and you're perfectly content to keep her."

"Well, well. I was certain some belligerent emissary would swagger through the door and, with idiot confidence, demand to put my Elise on a cargo ship."

"I know she isn't chattel. Ormun has made you a cruel demand, crueler than most men could realize. To have clawed off marriage for so long, she must be a fiercely independent woman."

"I had five daughters." Talitha's tone grew distant. "Three sons, two still living, so there's someone guaranteed to inherit our mess. Four of the girls were packed off. In return, a little land, some respite from war and grandchildren I've never seen. Never will."

"I understand."

"Now, Elise." A fond smile brightened Talitha's face. "My third daughter. When she reached the age of eight, my husband wanted to marry her to some distant prince in order to secure safer sea trade. Sea trade! Can you believe it? Fortunately, little Elise hid for two months in the palace towers and thus escaped her fate. And it was always the same ever after. My husband kept trying to marry her off, and she'd vanish until the suitor would write back, fed up, to call off the wedding."

Rema laughed. "How did the King handle it?"

"Poorly," said Talitha, grinning. "When she was seventeen, a magician visited us at court, in search of our patronage. My husband was unimpressed. Elise, however, was fascinated. She convinced the wizard to sell her a few old books and some odds and ends from his pack. For the next year we hardly saw her, locked away as she was reading those books."

"A magician?"

"Hush! I'm telling the tale. Now listen. The next year, Cedrin suffered terribly from gout. Elise brought him some foul-smelling remedy she'd mixed. In the morning, he'd never felt better, and, after eighteen years of wanting nothing more than to be rid of her, my husband decided she was worth keeping."

"She taught herself how to heal gout?"

"Oh, and more. She found her escape, bless her heart, and since then she has served as an official at my court." Talitha's eyes grew smoky with affection. "As you may have discerned, I love Elise fiercely. The idea of Ormun snatching her away does not sit well with me in the least."

Rema remained silent. There'd been no doubt the woman would be difficult to extract, but she'd never expected her to be an enchantress, of all things.

"Oh, I see you thinking," said Talitha. "You're determined to pry her away from us. It's your duty, and you're such a surprise that I can't bring myself to detest you for it. But mark my words, this war will be over before you convince me to surrender her to that marauding rapist you call an Emperor. How many wives does he have now?"

"Nineteen."

Sarcasm darkened Talitha's voice. "I'm sure he treats them all with care and respect."

"I share your reservations, but don't forget that your kingdom needs our help. There are many more lives at stake here." Sensing that the conversation was over, Rema rose to her feet and straightened her coat. "I appreciate having had the privilege of your attention."

"Yes, yes. Yorin will arrange all the comforts you require, or rather all that we can offer. Don't expect to drink from cups of pearl. My husband will see you this evening, and you can tell him about how terrible the war is and how badly we need your soldiers, and so on." Talitha gave an exasperated sigh. "If you truly want to help us, why not take your coaxing little voice to Lyorn and tell them to leave us be?"

Rema bowed her head. "They're on the cusp of victory. Keeping them from their kill would take a better diplomat than I."

"Well, if you find one, send him my way." Talitha opened her book again. "Or her! Of all the unexpected things…"

Rema left the chamber and closed the door quietly behind her. Yorin was fidgeting in the corridor outside. "I'm surprised," he said. "I'd expected her to evict you much sooner."

Rema returned his questioning stare. "You must understand this trade is necessary. The war will destroy you without our help."

"Any fool can see that. And while Elise is well-loved at court, not least by me, she is also a source of conflict." One of Yorin's mobile eyebrows crept upward. "A lifetime of unruliness has shaped her character in a wild direction."

"Ormun has a talent for subduing unruly wives." A familiar ache crept into Rema's chest, and she took a moment to steady her breath. "This isn't my finest moment as a diplomat, Yorin."

Sympathy softened Yorin's tired eyes. "Ah, well. That's monarchs for you. Despite our wiser heads, they all do what they want in the end." He motioned for them to walk. "Come. Let's not chat in front of the door. She may be old, but her hearing can be sharp when you'd least like it to be."

Yorin's cloth sandals padded softly, a gentle accompaniment to the sharp clicking of Rema's high leather boots. Just as her uniform was intended to convey the wealth of the Empire, Yorin's simple garb said as much about the poverty of Danosha. A lesser diplomat would have drawn pleasure from the difference, but Rema knew better. This struggling kingdom needed all the help she could give.

Before they could reach the stairs, a young woman emerged from the stairwell. Her pale, rounded face was obscured by a tangle of waist-length black hair. Behind the untidy locks, her eyes shone an intense silver-grey, and her full lips were turned in a pout. The cut of her red dress exposed one of her shoulders. As she walked toward Rema and Yorin, the scarlet fabric tightened against the curve of her ample thigh, and Rema's pulse stirred.

"Elise," said Yorin, nodding to the arrival. "This is Remela, the Emperor's emissary."

"My lady." Rema gave only a small bow. If this woman objected to being labeled a princess, then it seemed fair to spare her the deep bow Rema reserved for royalty. "It's a pleasure to meet you. Please call me Rema."

Elise examined Rema with a puzzled tilt of her head. She gave a deep, rich laugh, and the sullen look cleared from her face. "I don't believe it. You're a woman!" She took a step closer. "And a pretty one too. I was expecting some imperial toad with mustaches."

Rema rubbed her upper lip. "I shaved my mustaches this morning. I'm sorry to disappoint you."

"You're amusing too." Elise's voice warmed with pleasure. "I've never seen a woman in trousers. They're very becoming on you."

"They certainly drew attention in the city." Rema smiled, and Elise's cheeks pinked. "But I'm used to it."

"Well, this is a problem." Elise folded her arms. "I was expecting you to be loathsome. How am I going to hate you now?" With her lips parted in appreciation, she gave Rema a second lingering inspection. "How did you do it? I've never seen a woman diplomat."

"That's a long story." As enjoyable as Elise's interest was, indulging it would only make matters more difficult. "I'm sure we don't have time."

"Oh, are you in that much of a hurry to abduct me?" Elise pouted again. "To take me to that famous gentleman Ormun of the Pale Plains, who will hold me tenderly and stroke my hair as I fall asleep?" Temper flashed behind her eyes, and she put a hand on her hip. "I'll never allow it."

"I think you'll find that I'm very persuasive."

Elise lowered her lashes. "I imagine a job like yours requires a talented tongue."

"I've been told mine is exceptional." Damn those silver eyes.

Elise's breath quickened, and more color rose in her cheeks. "You're fascinating. I need to know all about you." She turned to Yorin. "What are the dinner arrangements?"

"I don't know for certain." Yorin spoke with obvious irritation. "I expect she'll dine with your parents."

"What a shame. Rema, will you join me in my tower tonight for dessert? I'll be a welcome relief from my dull parents, I promise."

"It would be my pleasure," said Rema.

"Oh, the pleasure will be mutual. Yorin, see she's well taken care of in the meanwhile."

"Of course she will be," said Yorin, his brows dragging almost to his nose. "What do you take me for?"

"I shan't answer that." Elise winked at Rema. "By the way, don't get too excited when my father leaps at the chance to sell me into slavery. Until you persuade my mother, you'll never get anywhere. And even then, I'll never go. Is your Emperor a patient man?"

"Far from it," said Rema.

"Then you're in trouble, aren't you?" As Elise walked off, her large hips moved suggestively beneath her dress, and it took some effort for Rema to look away.

"She's off to her tower," said Yorin. "If you're unlucky, she'll put a hex on you and make your job harder than it already is."

"I think I'm hexed already. That dress…"

Yorin's eyebrows twitched. "Yes, it was obvious you two enjoyed each other's company a little more than was natural. If you want to stay in the King's good graces, don't remind him why his daughter is so determined to stay unmarried."

Even Rema, expert diplomat though she was, couldn't hold back a smile. "I'm sure I don't know what you mean."

"Take my advice. Keep away from her altogether and focus on his grace. I'll put the right words in his ear, and then all three of us will persuade the Queen. She'll see the necessity eventually." Yorin's voice strengthened with urgency. "This war goes very badly, Rema. Hundreds die every day. If you're half the diplomat you ought to be, then you'll focus on what matters."

Rema's good mood faltered. "There's no such thing as a war that goes well." She met Yorin's somber eyes. "Don't worry. My head isn't easily turned. My purpose here is to see peace between you and your enemies."

Yorin's lips knitted together as he brooded for several seconds. "So be it," he said. "Your meeting with his grace is a way off. Are you hungry? I can arrange your lunch."

"Please do. Something simple."

Yorin's chuckle proved every bit as gloomy as the man himself. "You'll find little around here that isn't simple. Well, except for Elise, but I think you're a match for her. Come along, then."

CHAPTER THREE

The red-bricked kitchen swarmed with servants, many of whom stood between long wooden counters kneading dough, sifting flour and pouring batter into trays. They stopped their work to stare at Rema. Yorin shook his fist at them, scaring them back to their duties. He led her past the ovens and into a low room containing several rough-hewn tables. "Take a seat, and I'll bring you some food," he said.

Rema chose a seat against the wall and pressed her back to the warm stone, which had been heated by the ovens on the other side. She relaxed, the heat moving through her muscles, and was on the verge of dozing by the time Yorin returned with a platter of food. "Thank you," said Rema, eyeing the meal: a mug of water, a dark-crusted lump of bread, a flat wheel of cheese and an unhappy apple. Not quite a banquet.

"Enjoy the feast," said Yorin without a hint of irony. He nodded farewell and left the room still tugging at his sleeve.

Rema gnawed at the edge of the cheese. As she ate, curious heads popped through the archways that connected the room to the kitchen, accompanied by muffled giggling and conversation. Ignoring the servants, she tasted the water and gazed at the plain stone wall in front of her. Her meetings with Talitha and especially Elise remained vivid in her memory. Two powerful women, both tied by their circumstances. Would the King offer any further surprises?

A polite cough preceded the entry of a young man, who looked to be in his late teens. Judging by his shaggy mop of black hair and the silver shimmer of his gaze, he was one of the two surviving royal sons. His beautiful eyes and arched lips contrasted painfully with the rash of pimples along his jaw and the gangliness of his young body. He'd probably grow to be attractive, but he had some adolescence to pass through yet.

As he wandered into the room, his eyes lit with humor. "So this is the famous diplomat! You have the servants in an uproar. The head waitress has been telling all her girls about the handsome young man who arrived today. Now she can't look anyone in the face."

Rema brushed her bangs from her eyes. "I have that effect. Would you care to join me, Prince?"

"Prince. Ugh. Just call me Loric." Loric dragged a chair to her table and lolled on it with the inelegant laziness of someone used to spreading themselves across furniture. "And what do I call you besides divine?"

"Just call me Rema." Rema offered him a piece of cheese, but he waved his hand.

"I think I'd lose a tooth on that thing." Loric grinned as he scrutinized Rema's face. "Our Elsie's going to adore you."

"We've met already. She had no complaints. Does she prefer to be called Elsie?"

"Oh, it's only me who calls her that. It's my duty as a little brother." Loric laughed, sounding uncannily like his sister. "She's spent weeks ranting about her intention to tear the imperial ambassador apart the moment he arrived. I'll bet you dazzled her. God, does everyone look like you where you come from?"

"Exactly like me." Rema sipped her water. "The confusion is tremendous."

Loric laughed again, this time with even more enthusiasm. "You're going to charm the sandals off everyone here, aren't you? And it's not going to help you one bit."

"You really ought to hope that I succeed." Rema lowered her mug and stared at him over its rim. "That's if you want a kingdom left to inherit."

"Inherit! My least favorite word. It's a terrible dilemma for me, you know. If my elder brother Calan manages to get himself killed on the battlefield, I'll have to become king someday. Heaven forbid."

Loric locked his hands behind his head and swung his feet onto the table. "On the other hand, if my brother manages to get himself killed, huzzah, huzzah! He's a devil."

"Perhaps you should be more worried about the soldiers dying in their dozens."

"Yes, well. I care about the people being killed, really, but what I care most about is Elsie. You might be able to convince my father that she needs to go. You'll certainly not have any resistance from Calan, who hates her. But my mother loves Elsie, and so do I, most of all." Loric's silver eyes were calm but pleading. "I don't want to lose my sister, Rema."

"I don't want to take her from you. But I do want to save you and your people. Diplomacy isn't easy."

Loric sighed. "Tell me about Arann. Is it as big as they say?"

"Bigger. They haven't invented words large enough to do it justice. Each day it grows larger, a city of white stone spread across the Pale Plains. At night its torches seem to outnumber the stars."

A childlike glow of excitement crept into Loric's eyes. "They say the imperial palace is one of the biggest buildings in the world. Is it really so large?"

"It's seen better days. Even so it's impressive. Columns of gold and jade, tapestries embroidered with silver and candelabras studded with rubies." Rema smiled at the youthful wonder spreading across his face. "The gardens are especially beautiful. The air is as intoxicating as perfume, and there are trees, fruits and flowers from every country in the world."

"So what do we get in exchange for Elsie? Seven-foot men with swords of diamond? A sapphire ship that shoots molten gold from its cannons?"

"No. We don't loan those out. Just soldiers and supplies that'll win your war."

"I don't know. Lyorn's rich. They say that when their soldiers march, their spears blot out the sun."

"They say that about every large army. Me, I've never seen a spear tall enough to do that. The reality is that Ormun has more soldiers than any ruler alive."

"He's committed more atrocities too."

"Not least the murder of his own father."

"So you admit it then!" Loric straightened in his seat. "You admit that he's a monster!"

"Of course he's a monster. He's a brutal, savage tyrant who crushes his enemies without remorse. It's hardly the sort of thing that we can keep secret."

Loric clutched his head. "I didn't expect you to be so frank. God. Is there any wine down here? How can you just drink water?"

"I'm not touching a drop until I've dealt with your father." Rema leaned forward. "Will you tell me about your sister?"

Loric scratched at his pimples, and Rema struggled not to wince. "Well, you say you've already met her. A few seconds with Elsie and you know what you're in for. She's got a temper and she sulks, but she has a good heart. Unlike some others around here."

Someone sniggered, and Rema turned in time to see the pudgy face of a pageboy, who squeaked and darted out of sight. "It's my clothes, isn't it?"

"It's everything. The way you talk. Your stunning golden skin. I'm in love."

"Then you'll want to answer my every question to win my affection. Tell me about the people here who don't have good hearts."

"Calan." Loric's spotted skin flushed dark. "He's determined to win this war no matter how much blood is spilled on either side. He commits atrocities on our enemies, and he forever rages about how he'll cut apart every Lyorn general who's beaten him in the past. He details it all for us, limb by limb."

Rema kept her face composed, but unease stirred within her. A familiar-sounding variety of man, and not the kind to respond well to diplomacy. "And he doesn't like your sister?"

"Calan doesn't like women with opinions and especially not women who express them. Elsie has definite opinions about Calan and makes them clearly known. Needless to say, they don't get along."

Rema gave a noncommittal nod. "Tell me about your father."

"He's a decent man."

"I hear that often. It usually means the speaker is too polite to say what they really think."

"He really is!" Loric laughed. "He's just indecisive. He thinks our problems will solve themselves. He waves his hands over the peasants and believes he's actually helping the sorry bastards. Worst of all, he doesn't listen to anyone except Calan, who rides roughshod over him. He's afraid of my brother. We all are, except Elsie, even though she has more reason to fear him than anyone."

"So your father doesn't listen to Yorin?"

"My parents overrule him more than they should. I think he tries to get things done behind their backs. Yorin doesn't much get along with Elsie either, but to be fair, she's terribly cheeky to him."

"He wants this deal to work. Why not take his advice and support what's best for you?"

"Because I don't want what's best for us." Loric's smile faded. "I want to keep my sister. She's the only beautiful thing in this moldy palace. You'll understand if you get to know her."

Rema drained the last of her water. "Thank you for your honesty."

"I didn't have much choice. I'm terrible at lying." Loric gave her a rueful look. "You're not like any of the diplomats we usually get. They're fat and gruff and slam their fists on the table."

"I can easily slam my fist on the table, and if I finish this cheese, I'll be fat. Gruff is something I'll work on."

Loric rested his head in his hands. "Why does the Emperor want her? It seems like such a pointless addition to your demands." His voice cracked. "Why our Elsie?"

"Because Ormun is an obsessive tyrant who won't be happy until he has a wife plucked from every region of the world."

"What does that make you, then?"

"A diplomat." Rema met Loric's accusing gaze. "I arrange for peace before he sacks the cities. I persuade rulers to surrender rather than fight a battle they can't win. I prevent kingdoms like yours from becoming consumed by their neighbors." She raised her empty mug. "That's how I justify my career. A thankless job, but the uniform is attractive."

"You're not going to give up, are you?"

"I hate to say it, but no." As Rema stood and gazed down at the defeated prince, compassion gripped her heart. If only these people hadn't proven so decent. "Where might I find Yorin now?"

"Out in the court, trying to get the guards to do as they're told." Loric managed a feeble smile. "Even though you're going to ruin our lives, it's nice to have met you."

"We'll talk again soon. I'm sure I haven't satisfied your curiosity about the sights of the world." As Rema moved to the door, Loric stared at the half-eaten cheese, his face so glum she could scarcely bear to look upon it.

In Rema's absence, the kitchen had grown even more hectic. Cooks shoveled food into ovens while serving boys ran to and from the cellars. Amid the chaos, a broad-chested woman shouted orders to the other servants. As Rema neared her, an atmosphere of joyful, expectant malice became palpable from the crowd. Surely this was the head waitress who had so embarrassed herself, a fact confirmed by the woman's slack-faced horror as her gaze rested upon Rema.

"My lady, I heard tell of your flattery." With exaggerated grace, Rema took the stunned woman's hand and kissed it. "My fondest regards." The kitchen fell into disorder, and the laughter of the servants remained audible even after Rema had entered the cool hallway outside.

The corridor bent twice and rejoined the front court. The twilight beyond the windows indicated it was late evening, and the wide space was empty of peasantry. Instead the court was occupied by harassed guards, who marched in ragged lines while Yorin reprimanded them. As Rema watched the parade, she learned from Yorin's abuse that their uniforms were dirty, their swords were held at the wrong angle and that they had insolent jaws.

She touched Yorin's sleeve. "You're a hard master. What exactly is an insolent jaw?"

"You've got one yourself," said Yorin. "To be honest, I don't give a damn about their uniforms, but if they knew that, they wouldn't bother to wear them."

"I just met Loric. He spoke well of you."

"Loric?" Yorin's brows wriggled, leaving Rema no clearer as to what emotion they were intended to signify. "He's a good lad, but he's not worth your time. He has no influence here, and he's hopelessly devoted to his sister."

"My time was far from wasted. Now, King Cedrin. How long until I get to see him?"

"You may as well see him now. If you go through the big archway behind us, you'll find the corridor runs straight to the throne room. Identify yourself to the guard."

"He's going to talk to me from his throne? That's not wise for a monarch in need. It seems aggressive."

"I told him as much. But it's all he's ever done, and his mind works in well-worn tracks. Hurry off with you. I've got to berate that man for having his jacket on inside out."

"In my court, that crime is punishable by death." Rema left Yorin shuffling his brows, apparently unsure as to whether she had been joking, and walked through the colonnaded corridor to the throne room.

Her journey ended at a broad double door with curling ornamental hinges. A single guard was standing before it, his halberd propped behind him and his eyes vacant behind his coif. Rema tapped her heel, and the guard leapt to attention. "May I help you, sir?" he said, resting one hand on his halberd.

"Will you tell his majesty that the Emperor's diplomat is here?"

The guard turned crimson. "I beg your pardon, my lady. I meant no offense."

"Actually, I quite like being called 'sir.' Whenever someone says 'my lady,' I feel like I'm expected to curtsey and simper."

The guard rubbed his chin. "I, uh…I'll let them know you're here." He pushed the doors ajar and whispered through the gap. A voice muttered in assent. Rema waited, her hands folded before her, until the door opened wider and another guard called her through.

The throne room conformed well to the general aesthetic of the palace—that is to say, it was grim. Numerous lanterns were fastened to the walls, but they were losing their battle against the shadows, and much of the open space was shrouded in darkness. The room itself was bare, and even the floor was uncarpeted. Mud and grass smeared the worn stone and clung between the slabs. At the far end of the room, a simple wooden throne sat on a plinth. A large man was slumped upon it, his eyes on Rema. A king, it appeared, and not the jolly sort beloved by bards and poets.

As Rema approached, Cedrin gestured to the guards. They retreated into the darkness, leaving nothing in sight but the gleam of their swords. Rema strode across the room, her footsteps echoing, and stopped at a respectful distance from the throne. Cedrin continued to stare at her, his hand massaging his clean-shaven chin. His eyes contained the same silver as his children's, but their steel was dulled by age and worry. The slump to his bowed lips seemed permanent.

Rema bowed. "Your majesty. I am Remela. I have been sent by Emperor Ormun of the Pale Plains—"

"Heir to the Wide Realms, Lord Master of the City States of Urandal, King of the Lastar, Lord of Goronba, Tyrant of Dujandal." Cedrin took a breath. "Emperor of Molon, Ruler of Ulat Province and Lord of the Tahdeeni."

"I'm impressed. I usually stop at about four."

"It was all on the letter. I think it took up half the missive." Cedrin touched a finger to his temple. "Why has Ormun sent me a woman? I had hoped to discuss strategy."

"I doubt discussing it with a woman could cause you to fare any worse in battle than you already are."

Cedrin's eyes widened, exposing creeping red veins. "You are impertinent for a diplomat."

"On the contrary, I'm very pertinent. Without my help you'll lose this war and your kingdom. A good reason to watch your tone." Rema watched his face as it passed through irritation and doubt to arrive at grudging admiration—a transformation she had witnessed many times before.

"God, but you're well-forged, aren't you? I suppose women are different where you come from. Here they would never be trusted with matters of war or treaty. They don't have the right heads for it."

"After meeting your wife and daughter, I find that hard to believe."

Cedrin chuckled, his broad shoulders heaving with the effort. He was unwell, then, perhaps not sick with any ailment but nonetheless suffering the decline common to monarchs. If his body had once been muscular, it had long since gone to flab, and the damp palace air seemed to have affected his lungs. "I'll concede that some women have a spark of manhood in them. Like yourself, for instance."

"If that's so, I must have it removed." Rema took a step closer, deliberately shifting from a conciliatory distance to a more aggressive one. "Did you understand the terms of our proposal?"

"You'll give us material and martial aid. Soldiers and supplies by sea. In return, we promise not to take any more territory from Lyorn than that which we've already lost."

"And?"

"And my unwed daughter in marriage." Cedrin pinched his brows together. "Which is clearly an unnecessary and provocative addition to your requirements."

"Ormun insists upon it. He would like your families to be closer." It was disconcerting how easily the diplomatic language skipped from her tongue, how sincere it seemed.

"If he hadn't already married so many times before, that argument might hold weight. The treaty is fair without giving up Elise. She's invaluable to us. She heals the sick. She augurs the future. She bedevils our enemies."

"Oh?" Rema spoke with calculated irony. "Then she'd better work harder on the bedeviling. You're losing provinces at an alarming rate."

"I can assure you that my Elise's abilities are beyond doubting."

"I came not to spread doubt, Your Grace, but to bring you to resolution." Rema clasped her hands together. "Your daughter or your kingdom. Choose."

"Now I see why Ormun sent a woman." Cedrin drew himself upright. "Only they can be so cold-hearted."

It was too tragic a remark even to provoke laughter. "Yes, we are a cruel sex. Always waging wars, pillaging cities and raping defenseless men."

Cedrin groaned and pushed at the flesh of his forehead. "You sound overmuch like my daughter. The last thing I need is two unruly women at court."

"Remember what I said about insulting the diplomat."

They stared at each other. "Very well," he said, with strained cordiality. "But we need to discuss the specifics of this aid. I need to know how much and how many. Where and when."

"I have all the information you need."

"Fine. I'll need to talk to my boy too. He'll be back in a few days. He was very excited at the prospect of meeting an imperial ambassador. I suspect he'll be in for an unhappy surprise."

"I'll be sure to apologize for being so inappropriately female."

"Don't lay the fault on me, diplomat. You'll dine tonight with my wife and me. The table is being laid even as we speak. Go now and find Yorin, wherever he's hiding, and get him to escort you there." Cedrin exhaled a long, rattling breath. "I politely dismiss you."

"It has been a pleasure and an honor." Rema bowed with exaggerated reverence, turned her back on the throne and walked to the door. The guards stared at her as she passed by, and she resisted the impulse to thumb her nose at them. There was nothing like a royal audience to put her in a rebellious mood.

Yorin was waiting in the corridor, his forehead rumpled. "Poor Yorin," said Rema. "You're going to fret yourself into the grave."

"At least that'd give me the opportunity to rest. Did His Majesty agree?"

"He hoped to bluff and found himself up against a woman immune to bluffing. He still wants to talk war first, however. It seems to me he's stalling."

"Never mind that." Yorin worked his eyebrows in what seemed to be encouragement. "You've accomplished more than you know. The Queen had ordered him to reject you outright unless you agreed to let Elise stay. By reneging on his promise to her, he's as good as conceded."

"Ah. Dinner will be tense, then."

"With those two, it very often is. Consider it a test of your diplomacy."

"If they dine alone, where do the others eat?"

"Elise and Loric always dine together, usually in her tower. I eat with the servants."

Rema considered Yorin's tattered robe and gaunt features. Did his exhaustive service come with any compensation at all? "I've visited palaces where stewards feast beside their monarchs. Perhaps it's time to consider a change of courts. I can put in a good word for you."

"It's by choice. I can't stand their bickering." Yorin's eyebrows performed another inscrutable motion. "Anyway, I've no time to keep up with your endless chatter. You know the way to the kitchen already. Take the door on the left just before you reach the archway. That's where they dine, and the Queen should already be there."

Rema wished him a good night before wandering back into the increasingly familiar palace. With the arrival of evening, more servants had emerged into the corridors, cleaning the floors, replacing torches and dragging linen about in overstuffed baskets.

As she neared the kitchen, she came across a woman shaking out a tapestry. "Good evening, my lady," the servant said. "Won't you pause to kiss my hand as well?"

"Only your hand?" said Rema, and the woman reddened and returned to beating her tapestry, a thoughtful smile curling her lips. Rema continued on her way, her mood lifted by the exchange. No matter where she stood upon the world, one thing had always proven true: women blushed in her presence as their knees failed them. There was some solace in that. Of course, she needed to ensure her talent didn't get her into any trouble, given the presence of the alluring Elise.

Rema reached the door of the dining chamber and paused for a moment to gather her thoughts. Should she knock? No—Talitha would respect it more if she simply entered. She opened the door and stepped inside.

CHAPTER FOUR

The dining room was modest, set for private feasting rather than banqueting. A sturdy, attractive table with a rich cloth took up most of the space. The paintings and tapestries on the walls were forgettable but for a remarkable oil painting of an archer. So realistic was the depiction, it was possible to believe the muscles in his arms were tensing.

"Good evening," said Talitha. She sat alone at the farthest end of the table, her hands folded before her. Her face bore the same contemplative squint as before. "Please sit beside me."

Rema bowed and took her place. "How has the day treated you?"

"No worse than usual. Incidentally, it'll be easier if you go back to bowing and scraping while we're at dinner. He's bound to sulk about it afterward if you don't."

"I don't think he expects me to do much of either. I've just come from talking with him."

"Hah!" Talitha gripped Rema's shoulder. "I'd say 'you poor girl,' but I expect you gave him a hiding. I wish I could've been there."

They waited in amiable silence. After several minutes, Cedrin shambled in and squeezed into a seat at the opposite end of the table, leaving a significant distance between himself and the women. "Good evening to you both."

"Why so far away?" said Talitha. "Does our guest have the plague?"

"I always sit here, and you always sit there. Let's not upset a court tradition."

As they waited for their food, Rema admired the tension rising in Cedrin's face. His fingers tapped without rest against the table, and a cord of muscle at his jaw tightened as he ground his teeth. "Look at him," said Talitha, leaning over to whisper in Rema's ear. "He's utterly infuriated."

The door opened to admit three servants with platters. "Thank God," said Cedrin. "What took them so long?"

The servants struggled not to stare at Rema as they spread the dinner across the table. Among them was Alys, the young girl who had earlier attended the Queen. Rema smiled at her, and Alys, instantly befuddled, dropped her cutlery and earned a deadly look from Talitha.

The moment the servants had left, Cedrin speared a rubbery steak with his fork and began to eat. Talitha poured herself a glass of wine and turned to Rema. "The servants have been talking about you all day. Do you always create such a stir?"

"Often," said Rema. "Once, however, I arrived at court at the same time as a troupe of dancing crocodiles. Very few people noticed me."

"You have a knack for inoffensively nonsensical responses." Talitha tilted her wineglass, shifting the sediment. "You claimed to be thirty years old, I recall."

"I've worked four years for Ormun. Nine years for his father."

"Thirteen years. A diplomat since the age of seventeen. Little wonder you're good. And how does a woman enter such an unlikely career?"

"I decided upon it when I was fifteen. At that time, I could write and speak in five languages, which helped convince the diplomatic college to take me seriously."

"What manner of girl has such ambitions and talents?"

It was a pleasant subject, and Rema let herself warm to it. "I was the child of traders. My mother was an eccentric obsessed with finding the perfect trade route. By land, by sea, over mountains, she didn't care. My father was just as mad. He encouraged her because he believed the travel was good for his poetry." Rema raised a goblet of wine to her lips. "My father spoke Ajulai, my mother Nastil, and of course we all spoke Annari too. I learned Ulat and Tahdi as we traded across Amantis. A reasonable repertoire at fifteen."

"I take it then that your father was Ajulese and your mother a Nastine. Parents from different continents. How uncommonly romantic. No wonder you have such curious features."

Rema smiled. How quaint that these people imagined their pale, broad faces to be the standard of ordinary humanity. "Our life was romantic too. Sometimes we'd lose all our money and have to live in some forgotten kingdom until my parents earned enough to get us moving again. It taught me a little about the world."

"That's a very colorful childhood. But it doesn't explain how or why you became a diplomat, does it?"

"She's a good-looking woman," said Cedrin, exposing teeth greasy with food. "I'm sure we can guess how she did it, if not why."

The comment was too banal to incite any real indignation in Rema, but Talitha narrowed her eyes. "You're drunk already. Apologize to our guest."

"I think she can take care of herself." Cedrin lifted his fork and shook the ragged piece of meat that hung from its end. "I meant it only as a joke."

"Have no fear," said Rema. "I've heard that insinuation so often that it's ceased to shock me. And it's not how I earned my position, no."

"Well." Talitha chewed a trembling piece of pudding until its dark juices ran out of the corner of her mouth. "I won't ask you to tell me everything yet. You can do so later with the breath you haven't wasted trying to persuade us to accept your ridiculous terms."

"I already accepted her terms." Cedrin stared into his mug as he spoke. "All that remains is to ensure the military provisions are sufficient."

"You did what?" Talitha dropped her fork. A metallic shiver rang out across the table, and Cedrin lowered his napkin, revealing the sour cast to his lips. "You agreed to give up Elise? Are you mad?"

"Are you? We can't last another month, Talitha!"

"You won't last another week unless you recant immediately." Talitha trembled with anger; how ironic that her fury was directed at her husband and not the diplomat who had arranged the misfortune. "You idiot, do you know what will happen to her over there?"

"Perhaps she'll have some sense knocked into her. Get a few children into the world before she's barren."

"Disgusting!" Talitha's complexion approached a dramatic shade of purple. "You sound like Calan. I doubt you even believe those foul words yourself. You're just trying to escape into piggish denial."

This was clearly a long-running quarrel, best left to those most practiced in it. "Perhaps I should excuse myself," said Rema.

Talitha pressed her leathery fingertips to Rema's hand. "Yes, that would be best. I have some very strong words for my husband."

Cedrin poured himself a deep goblet of wine. "It'll be a long night."

Rema bowed quickly before closing the door on Talitha's heated tirade. She walked back to the front court, her coat keeping out little of the nocturnal chill, and stretched flat on one of the benches. The ceiling above her was wreathed in shadow, and as she stared at it, her tension subsided. It was quiet but for a few servants shuffling through the court and the echoing tread of guards in the hallways. One could almost imagine sleeping here.

She closed her eyes and focused on her breathing, and her thoughts drifted to Elise. A provincial pit like Danosha was no place for an assertive, ambitious woman, especially one attracted to her own sex. There were few things more despicable than these cruel eastern kingdoms, some of which even imposed death upon women for loving one another. What relief was in sight for this defiant princess, for whom even loneliness would be better than a life under Ormun's cruelty?

The sound of footsteps roused her, and she sat up. Loric smiled shyly as he approached. "Yorin did arrange you a proper bedroom, didn't he?"

"I was just taking a moment to rest. I've come from dinner with your parents."

Loric sat on the bench beside her. "And I've come from dinner with my sister. She's tremendously excited and nervous, almost like a child. It's very unlike her."

"Then I hope she composes herself soon. She's invited me for dessert."

"I know that! Why do you think she's so worked up? She wouldn't stop talking about you. We don't get female visitors to the court, least of all ones like you." Loric stretched his long legs and looked at his boots. "You're very clever. Here we are, both delighted to have you staying, and yet you're working as hard as you can to make us both unhappy. And I still can't hate you for it."

"That's diplomacy for you." Rema gave him a sympathetic smile. "I'm something of an enchantress myself."

"I'll say." Loric chewed his lip for a moment, then stood. "Come along. I'll show you where her tower is."

"That's very kind of you." Rema's knees ached as she rose from the bench, but she kept the grimace from her face. It was an old affliction, a worrying one, and the chill only made it worse.

Loric led her up the stairs, through an archway and down a short corridor that ended in a narrow, circular stairwell. "Up there," he said with an unnecessary gesture. "Quite a few steps! Don't worry, though, she's in there. You'll be a little earlier than she's expecting, but I can't imagine she'd be unhappy about it."

"Thank you."

"You should know that, uh, my sister..." Loric ran his hands through his hair. "She's not like most women. She'll find you very attractive. She might, um, she might...express certain desires or intentions. If that makes you uncomfortable, you should probably find an excuse not to attend."

"I think I can handle her," said Rema, hiding her amusement. "Have a good night, Loric."

"You too." Loric scratched his head, opened his mouth and closed it abruptly. After hesitating for a second in helpless silence, he blushed and walked away.

The circular steps of the staircase were closely packed, forcing Rema to tread slowly. The stairwell featured several narrow windows, but breathing the night air did nothing to cleanse the apprehension in her heart. The stairs ended at a low wooden door. Rema tapped once.

The door opened immediately, spilling warm light into the stairwell. Elise stood in the doorway, one hand against the frame, and lowered her eyes to take in the full length of Rema's body. A mellow perfume drifted around her, a scent not present on their first meeting, and on closer inspection, it was clear she had gone to some effort to embellish her eyelids with dark shadow. The contrast with her silver eyes was striking.

"Look at you," Elise said. "You're so impressive and composed. And even after spending the evening with my parents."

"Your parents are amateurs. At some courts it's a miracle if dinner ends and nobody has been killed."

Elise beckoned. "You're wonderful. Come in, hurry. It's cold out here."

The tower was almost stifling, though it wasn't clear why; the countless wavering candles that illuminated it could hardly account for the heat. Every part of the room was cluttered with books and paraphernalia: a small alembic, several baskets filled with herbs, more strings of herbs hanging low from the ceiling, a vibrant green flower in a mortar and pestle, vials of powders and crystals, and even a cauldron in one corner. Rema peered into the cauldron—what horrors lay within?—only to find it filled with clothes.

"I use it to hold my washing," said Elise, following Rema's gaze.

Somewhere among the mess was a small bed, piled high with blankets and pillows. A little table covered in dirty plates was pressed against the wall. "A servant should be along soon. In the meantime, I'll just place these over here." Elise moved the dishes onto a stack of tomes, which wobbled terrifyingly, and Rema held her breath. "Don't fear. They've never fallen before."

"You've also never seen a woman in trousers before. Don't tempt fate."

"It's not fate I plan on tempting." Elise gestured to the table. "Please sit!"

Rema was barely able to pull the chair back far enough to squeeze her legs underneath. Elise rested her elbows on the table and propped her head upon her hands. "How was your dinner?"

"I didn't have a chance to eat anything. Your parents began their argument too early."

"No wonder you're so slim." Elise fidgeted. Though she wore a serene smile, it did little to disguise her agitation. "You'll have to fill yourself on dessert."

"I'll gorge until I explode. By the way, I notice you're wearing a perfume. It's most evocative."

Elise laughed nervously and looked away. "I make all my own scents and cosmetics. I'm afraid we don't get many merchants this way." She tilted her face back to Rema, and her expression became coy. "How do you like my fingernails?"

She extended her hand. Her nails had been painted a shade of deep azure flecked with silver. "I know merchants who would pay well for a polish like this," said Rema. "And you've trimmed them so nicely."

Elise flushed as she toyed with her long jet earrings. "I think it's nicer to have short nails. Don't you?"

Their eyes met. There was a familiar heat in that silver gaze, and a tangled mixture of amusement, pity and pleasure swept through Rema's body. Was Elise attracted to both sexes or only interested in women? In either case, how unfortunate for her that she had been born in Danosha, where the laws and customs did everything they could to punish women who followed their hearts.

A knock at the door made them both turn. Alys tottered in with two trays—that she had carried them up the stairwell without falling seemed nothing short of a miracle—and gave as much of a bow as she could muster under her burden. "Mistress, as you ordered, wine and a fruit custard."

"Thank you, Alys," said Elise. "Please set them down."

Alys placed the trays before them and hesitated before turning to Rema, her entire body animated by an impulse of bravery. "Can I just say, my lady, that I think you look very impressive in your wonderful clothes," she said in one long, frightened exhale.

Rema laughed. "Thank you, Alys. Please call me Rema."

"Yes, my lady. I mean, Rema!" Alys skipped from the room, so overjoyed that she forgot to close the door behind her. A moment later she dashed back up and pulled it shut, mumbling apologies.

"She's a funny thing," said Elise as she lifted a glass. Her eyes seemed to have grown brighter than the candles around them. "You're quite an inspiration, a woman in your position."

"You're doing very well yourself. I've met a lot of court enchanters, but they're always surly men with sticks in their beards. I've never seen an enchantress."

"It's not easy to get ahead in this male world, as I'm sure you know." Elise ran a finger around the edge of her wineglass. "You know, we were talking about you at dinner. My brother is completely in love with you."

"He's a nice boy, but not my kind of lover."

"I wouldn't have imagined he was. But tell me, who is your kind of lover?"

Rema only smiled and sipped at the wine. It was sweet with a mere hint of bitterness, just as she liked it. "This is very good."

"Is it? I know nothing about it. I just ask for wine." Elise glanced at Rema's hands. "I've heard a great deal of talk about getting me married. But are you married?"

"No."

"And how old are you?"

"Thirty."

"And they say I'm irresponsible for not marrying by twenty-six! Thirty. You look younger."

"There's a balm I stock up on when I'm in Arann. It keeps the moisture in my skin."

"May I?" Elise stroked a fingertip across Rema's face. "You're soft indeed." Her voice had lowered to a murmur, and the first signs of a blush burned in her round cheeks. "You'll have to get me the recipe. I'm afraid I'll be a hag by the time I'm your age."

"You could never be a hag." Rema drew the custard closer and tasted a spoonful. It was pleasant enough. She lifted another spoonful, but paused before it met her lips. "Do you really want to stay here your entire life?"

"Of course not. But it's better to be a free woman here than to be trapped in glorious Arann as one of Ormun's sorry wives."

"Yes. It is."

They remained silent as Rema dug through her custard and Elise tasted her wine. A gust of wind struck the tower, stretching the flames of the candles and ruffling the pages of an open book, and as if broken from some spell, Elise looked up. "Let's play a game."

Rema raised an eyebrow. "Tell me the rules."

"I ask you questions and you answer yes or no. But the answer must only be the truth." Elise bit the edge of her glass. Her mounting nervousness was increasingly amusing, but Rema had more compassion than to laugh. "You can also confess you don't know if you honestly don't."

"Can't you already tell if I'm lying with your sorcery?"

Elise giggled, her eyes shining and her cheeks flushed, and guilt tugged at Rema's heart. "I wish. I'd love to know what goes on in your head. You seem to say what you mean precisely and not one word more. Unlike me, babbling and making a fool of myself."

"I enjoy your babbling. Very well, I'll play your game, even though it seems designed to trick diplomats into admitting their secrets."

Elise lowered her lashes, concealing the silver circles of her eyes. "Do you have any secret orders from the Emperor?"

"No." Rema laughed. How unexpectedly childish a question, though endearingly so. "I feel like I'm being interrogated."

"You are! Let's see. Would I enjoy being married to the Emperor?"

"No."

"Is he as brutal as they say he is?"

"Yes."

Elise widened her eyes. "That's terrifying. Do you like being his diplomat?"

Rema hesitated. Now the questions were beginning to bite. "Yes and no. Is that allowed?"

"No! But I'll forgive it once. Did you think my father was foolish?"

Rema smiled. "Yes."

"Excellent! What about my mother?"

"I don't know."

The candles wavered, subtly shifting the radiance in Elise's eyes. "Are you really thirty?"

"Yes." It seemed Elise had lost her fuel already. "Surely you can ask harder questions than these."

Elise's breath came quick and shallow, and her scarlet glow had reached her neck. "Very well. Have you enjoyed my company?"

"Yes."

"Do you...think me attractive?"

Now this game was something Rema understood. "Yes."

Elise's face twitched, and she began to nervously stroke the stem of her glass. "Have you...have you..." She drew a quick breath. "Have you ever lain with a woman?"

"Yes." Rema was no longer able to keep the amusement from her voice. "When are you going to start the hard questions?"

"Those were the hard questions." Elise's voice shook and excitement shone in her eyes. "I'm blushing, aren't I?"

"You've been blushing all evening. I assumed it was normal for you."

"Don't tease me! Let's keep playing. It doesn't have to be the same game as before. There are all kinds of ways we might entertain ourselves."

Rema sighed. As thrilling as this little engagement had been, she had allowed it to go too far, and now it was time to escape with as much decorum as possible. "You should eat your custard. As for me, I think it's time for bed."

"To bed?" Elise traced a shape on the table with her fingertip. "You're leaving me already?"

"I'm afraid so." Rema pushed her bowl away. "I enjoyed our evening together. Thank you, Elsie."

Elise laughed and gave Rema a delighted look. "You've been talking with my brother! Only he calls me that."

"I think it's cute. Do you mind?"

"No." Elise continued to giggle. "Not at all."

Rema rose to her feet, bowed to Elise and took a few steps toward the door. "Wait," said Elise, hurrying to stand. She moved to a pile of papers and brushed them aside, revealing a small chest. She opened the chest and took out a long silver chain attached to a black stone, which was about the length of Rema's thumb and capped at either end with gold.

"I must be mad, but I'm going to give you this. Stand still." Elise moved close to Rema and undid the clasp of her collar. Elise's fingers trembled as she hooked the chain behind Rema's neck. "This stone will protect you. You're going to need it."

Rema arched an eyebrow as the black stone nestled against the curve of her collarbone. "If I'm in danger, you should tell me in detail."

"If I could, I would."

The surprises kept coming. Magic stones? Protection? But as curious as Rema was about the odd display, Elise has begun to stir certain emotions she didn't dare indulge. It was time to leave. "Well, thank you."

Elise parted her lips, and her tongue grazed against her teeth. There was no mistaking the desire in her eyes, and Rema's blood burned to match it. If she didn't leave now…"Goodnight," Rema said, retreating toward the door.

As she entered the cold stairwell, she was unable to resist one final look into the tower. Elise still stood where Rema had left her, a single finger pressed to her melancholy lips and her gaze fixed on the floor. Rema closed the door as softly as she could.

CHAPTER FIVE

Rema woke. The sound of activity outside her door implied the day had begun without her, which was no surprise; after a sea voyage, her body often wanted nothing more than to hibernate. She untangled from her blankets, removed her underclothes and unhooked Elise's pendant. In the corner of the room rested a basin of water with clean rags beside it, and she took the opportunity to wash herself.

After drying her invigorated body, Rema lifted the pendant and ran the chain through her fingers. Was it an enchanted spying glass, perhaps, that even now relayed her nakedness back to Elise? Now that would be a worthwhile application of magic. Rema took clean undergarments from her trunk, slipped them over her goose-pimpled body and redonned her uniform. The room's tiny mirror revealed that her hair hadn't survived the pillow, and she fixed it with a few fussy gestures. After a moment's consideration, she returned the pendant to her neck.

As she entered the corridor, Rema almost lost her head to a pair of servants wobbling by under the weight of a large barrel. "Sorry, my lady!" one said.

"Sorry, my lord!" added the other.

Rema wagged her finger at them before continuing to the front court, where she smiled as sunlight permeated her skin. At least the sun was still capable of warmth in the East. The doors weren't yet open to the peasantry, but the court was crowded nonetheless with rushing servants.

Rema looked through the throng and spotted Alys's pinched face. "Alys," she said, her voice raised above the hubbub.

The servant girl jumped as if scolded. "My lady Rema. I hope you had a lovely sleep!"

"A little too much of it. Is Yorin about?"

"I don't know where he is. I'm supposed to go clean out the ovens. I'll be black as charcoal."

The girl seemed no older than ten, but she could have been an undernourished teenager. Either way, the thought of someone so youthful crawling about in ovens had little appeal. "There'll be no dirty hands for you today. You're going to spend the morning showing me the palace."

"Really? But won't I get beaten?"

"If anyone tries to beat you, I'll beat them back."

Alys chuckled. "So long as you let Yorin know that I was only doing what you asked."

"I promise. And now I'd like to go for a walk. What's the nicest sight you have?"

"The gardens are out back. They're nice. Come along!"

Alys led Rema into a corridor decorated with wired suits of armor, decaying portraits and poorly-carved sculptures. Rema stopped, captivated by a hideous statue of a mother holding her infant. The child was so badly carved that it looked more like a pumpkin with feet.

Alys drew Rema's attention to an immense oil painting of a woman. Her eyes were nothing but swathes of black paint. "That was the Queen's grandmother," said Alys. "She scares the life out of me!"

Rema laughed. As they walked, Alys pointed out a few other items of interest: a suit of armor said to come alive each full moon and chase girls through the palace, a picture of a donkey painted by a blind man, and a cracked sculpture rumored to be inhabited by a thousand vengeful ghosts. "Sounds plausible to me," said Rema, touching its chipped face.

"Oh! Don't touch it!" Alys hopped on her feet. "Come on." She dragged Rema to the end of a corridor and heaved open a wooden door that bulged with rot. "This old door has to be replaced, but Yorin doesn't like to spend money on anything. Anyway, here we are!"

High walls shadowed the modest palace gardens, but plenty of sunlight still filtered through the trees and hedges. The flora had been arranged in neat harmony and orderly squares, and the grass was well tended. As they walked across the damp blades, the aroma of loamy dirt mingled with the fragrance of flowers in bloom.

"Let's go sit on the bench beneath that tree," said Rema.

Alys nodded and shyly took Rema's hand. As they walked by a flower bed, she snatched a rose to put in her hair. "You won't let me get beaten for that either," she said, grinning up at Rema.

They reached the bench. Rema ran a finger along its split surface. Fortunately, it was dry. In her vanity, she had a fear of ruining her uniform, and she'd only brought one spare. She sat and stretched her legs, feeling her knees loosen, while Alys stood twirling a blade of grass.

"I'm curious about the court, Alys. Tell me about the people who live here."

"Well. There's Master Yorin, who does everything and is grouchy because of it. Then there's Lady Elise, who we all love very much. She brings us potions and poultices when we're sick. She's very scary, though."

"Scary? Why do you say that?"

"She knows magic, and she has such an awful temper. I heard some servants calling her a witch once, but Yorin found out and gave them a hiding. Gossiping about Lady Elise is the surest way to get him angry!"

"What about the others?"

"Um." Alys folded her hands behind her back. "The King is benevolent. I don't know what that means, but Yorin told me it once. The Queen is forever reading in her chamber. Prince Loric doesn't do much of anything, but we don't mind because he's so sweet. Prince Calan is always off at war."

"Is there anyone else who visits here regularly?"

Alys lowered her voice. "I'm not going to get in trouble, am I?"

Rema pulled a leaf from the tree above her and flicked it at Alys. "Don't be silly."

"Well, there's a man who comes in all hooded and meets with Prince Calan. He has awful eyes. Even Yorin isn't sure who he is."

Rema tossed another leaf. Sinister hooded men with evil eyes, and just when she'd started to make sense of the situation. "Thank you, Alys."

"I'm happy to help! Have you had any breakfast?"

"Actually, no." Rema frowned and pressed her hands to her stomach. "I forget about food when I'm thinking."

"Would you like to stay here while I fetch you something from the kitchen?"

"That would be very considerate."

Alys saluted and dashed back toward the palace, nearly falling over in her enthusiasm. Rema brushed a stray blossom from her sleeve before resting her head against the bark of the tree, her face turned toward the warmth of the sun. Every good diplomat knew when to take advantage of a moment of tranquility, and who knew when she might be blessed with another?

"How strange," said a voice, and she opened her eyes. Loric was ambling across the garden toward her, his hands in the pockets of his plain white tunic. "We keep running into each other. I think fate is sending us a message."

"The only message I get is that you're following me."

"Don't be suspicious. I visit the garden every morning to think in the fresh air. I'm sure being in that stone box has rotted everyone else's lungs."

"It's not much of a garden." Rema tapped the bench to indicate he could sit beside her. "Ours has a waterfall. You can hardly hear for the roar of it."

"We have a hedge in the shape of a horse," said Loric, easing onto the bench and stretching his arm behind him. "Beat that."

"I can't. I concede. The Empire is yours."

Loric laughed as he picked a leaf from her hair. "You're gathering leaves. They must like you nearly as much as I do."

Rema couldn't resist a smile. Even if he hadn't grown into his looks, his wit served him well. "And they call *me* charming."

"With good cause." Loric inched closer, his eyes intense under his shaggy hair. "I've some interesting news for you."

"Oh?"

"Very early, just as the sun was rising, my parents and Elsie had a little conference. I was invited. Normally I'd not go, but such things are more exciting now that you're around."

"Excitement follows me. Tell me more."

"Well, it started dull. Father grumped at us, telling us we're going through with the deal, there's no way out of it, I'm the King, grr! Yorin nodded wisely all the while, and we all knew that the sly badger had put these words in Father's head. Then Mother drew herself up until she was as tall as those oaks over there. She insisted that you have to go, that they should have you on a ship by tomorrow morning."

Loric's smile grew. "Now, the fun part. Elsie had been listening this whole time with her sulkiest face on—and believe me, she does an excellent sulk. The moment Mother was done, Elsie leapt up and insisted that you must not be sent away. Which, of course, threw Mother into a complete fit of confusion. Father naturally asked if Elsie meant to say she's accepting her marriage, and Elsie said no, she wants both not to be married and also for you to stay. Cue pandemonium."

Rema laughed, and Loric smiled so widely that the ends of his mouth threatened to meet at the back of his head. "They thought Elsie had gone crazy," he said. "But anyone would go crazy for you."

"An amusing anecdote." Time to probe a little deeper. "What can you tell me about a man in a hood?"

"Where did that question come from?"

"All topics are connected. You know who I'm talking about."

"Yes." Loric's face became glum. "I don't know his name. All I know is that my brother uses him for his butcher's work. He's a torturer and assassin. My father knows all about him too."

They were interrupted by the return of Alys, who approached with slow and uncertain steps. She held a tray of food in her arms. "Hello, My Lord Prince Loric sir," she said, her lower lip hanging in dejection. "I only brought enough breakfast for one, because I thought Rema would still be alone."

"Oh, Alys," said Rema. "Thank you. Loric isn't here to eat but rather to bother me, isn't that right?"

Loric averted his eyes. "If I'm a bother, I'll leave."

"Don't be so sensitive. Alys, I'd like to see more of the castle later. Will you be around?"

"Yes, always," Alys said, smiling again. "Just leave the tray on the bench, I'll come get it later. Remember, tell Yorin that I wasn't troublemaking!" Her eyes widened to emphasize her final request, and she strolled away across the grass, humming to herself.

"That imp is quite devoted to you." Loric peered at the tray. "Two slices of bread with jam, an apple and a pastry! What a treat!"

Rema took an experimental bite of the bread. It was thick and floury, and the strawberry jam tingled on the tip of her tongue. "Now here's something I can't belittle."

"Just don't expect much from the pastry. I mourn for the pastry chef we lost a year ago. Strong men fell to their knees weeping just at the thought of her pies."

"You lost her?" Rema bit into the pastry. It was some kind of tart, dry and crumbly. The crumbs clung to her tongue and mouth—if only Alys had brought a drink as well. "What happened?"

"My father learned that she was spending a little too much time with my sister, so he sent her away." Loric blushed. "Poor Elsie. She really liked that one too."

Of course Elise had sought comfort in the servants. Forceful as she was, it was improbable she would never have tried to satisfy her desires before now. "Does that sort of thing happen often?"

"Not too often. Elsie knows she's gambling every time. Her dalliances are about the only thing that might convince our mother to pack her away. You're too tempting for her to resist, though." Loric plucked a blossom from his shoulder and frowned at it. "If you're not interested in her like that, I can ask her to stop chasing you."

The look in his eyes made clear that he wanted badly for Rema to ask exactly that. "Don't worry," she said, after an awkward pause. "It takes a great deal to make me uncomfortable."

"And what does make you uncomfortable?"

"Well, I once saw a man forced to eat himself from the feet up."

Loric opened his mouth, closed it and opened it again. "That isn't true, is it?"

Rema replied with her most inscrutable smile. "A diplomat never tells."

Shaking the leaves from his hair, Loric stood. "Thank you for an image that I'll carry with me all day. By the way, my brother is supposed to be back tomorrow. I desperately want to be there when you meet him. And I'd like to invite you to dinner with me and Elsie tonight, to spare you from my parents."

"That's a gracious offer. I accept. As for your brother, we'll see what happens."

"You may have seen some amazing things, but I bet you've never seen anything like a fight between Elsie and Calan." Loric glanced at Rema, not quite making eye contact. "Don't you feel bad about what you're doing?"

"I like you both. But I also have to save a kingdom."

"You know, mostly I've felt sorry for Elsie." Loric's lips tilted in a crooked smile. "But maybe I really ought to feel sorry for you."

A little too perceptive for comfort, this one. "I've an apple to finish, and I don't want to eat it in front of you. It's undignified."

"I'm tempted to stay now just to see what you look like when you're undignified." Loric ran his finger around his neck. He was blushing even under his collar, the poor boy. "Well, back to my hard day's labor." He disappeared into the hedgerows, casting a furtive glance backward.

Rema returned to her morning relaxation. A beetle crawled up her sleeve, and she peered with interest at its slick red carapace and seeking, spindly legs. With care she redirected it onto a crisp leaf, placed the leaf on the ground and watched the insect stumble into the grass. Loric's story was troubling. If Talitha was in a bad mood, then it would be wise to avoid her for a time. Better to wait for the return of Calan, who obviously held influence over his father.

Her thoughts crept, once again, to Elise. The barely-veiled desire in Elise's eyes had made clear Rema's mission was to be an especially painful one. At the court of Arann, she was known as a relentless advocate for the vulnerable: slaves, prostitutes, beggars, the crippled and uniquely-minded, those who refused the sex given at their birth, and, of course, people like herself and Elise—women constituted to love women, men constituted to love men. As a Danoshan, Elise would have been told throughout her life that her way of loving was some monstrous sin. If only Rema were free to demonstrate the beautiful truth that women could love one another—with as much passion and lust as they dared—and day would continue to burn into night, as it had always done.

She caught herself. Such thoughts could easily crush her. Far more productive to find Yorin and learn more about the imminent arrival of the eldest prince. Her knees ached as she stood from the bench, and she took a moment to shake the pain from her legs.

As she crossed the garden, she passed a group of servants beating compost out of tin drums. She caught, for a lingering moment, the eye of a young woman among the group, and received her reward: a nervous smile, a coy movement of long lashes. It was a fine thing to be Rema.

She found the front court once more crowded with peasants, their harried faces expressing countless miseries. As Rema stood near a wall, trying to see through the packed mass of heads, a tall man with a coiled purple mustache walked toward her. His tunic was dyed orange and red, and it had been wrapped several times around his body, causing him to puff at the waist. Judging by his absurd mustache, he was either a dye merchant or a dangerous lunatic.

The man's chapped lips lifted in a smile. "Fancy meeting a mouth of the Emperor in a dungheap like this," he said in Annari, the language of the Empire.

"Perhaps you'll bring a little color to it," Rema said in the same tongue. The man spoke with an accent, and it took her only a second to place it—he was an Ulati, from the far northern steppes of Amantis.

She switched to Ulat, which she enjoyed speaking for its melodic, rolling vowels. "You're a long way from home."

"A merchant is always far from home," he said, switching likewise to Ulat. "And your master has ensured my home is not what it used to be. I feel bound to note that when he conquered our province, he killed two of my brothers."

"If he'd had his way, he'd have killed everyone. I'm sorry I didn't end the war in time to save your brothers."

The Ulati tugged on his mustache, which sprang pertly back into position. "Anyone who speaks my language so sweetly can't be entirely rotten." He extended his hand, and she shook it. "My name is Muhan."

"Rema. I'm amazed. You still haven't made an astonished comment about my being a woman."

Muhan grinned, revealing teeth stained in countless colors. "I didn't want to be rude, and besides, it made a great deal of sense. My wife always settles disputes at home, so why shouldn't women be out settling them abroad?"

"I don't know if I like your analogy, but at least you're trying. Have you really come here to sell dye?"

Muhan gestured to his prismatic body. "Do I look as though I'm here to sell cabbage?"

"With leaves of particularly vivid green." Rema smiled. This meeting was precisely the antidote she needed to the dourness of this cold, superstitious kingdom. "It merely seems odd to offer luxury goods to a kingdom that's impoverished and on the wrong end of a war. You should be selling your goods in Lyorn."

"Such is my plan, but I thought I'd try my chances here before heading north. At the very least I can earn some coins exhibiting myself in the street."

Rema glanced at Muhan's hands. Each finger was stained a different color, and a vivid swirl ran up his dark forearms. "If you want to skip the queue, come with me. We need to find a man in a white robe, his forehead dragged somewhere down to his knees by the weight of the world."

"I will follow you like a puppy." Muhan returned to speaking Annari. "Where might this man be?"

"Let's find out." Rema stepped onto a bench and gazed over the heads of the crowd. "There he is! Hiding in the corner and shouting at a servant. Follow me."

Rema led Muhan toward Yorin, who was berating an unfortunate pageboy. As he noticed Rema's approach, Yorin's eyebrows made an intrepid attempt to reach the top of his head, and he waved the servant away. "You're lucky I don't make you a jester, you damn fool. Now go on, get."

"Yes, Master." The pageboy gave Rema a grateful look before scampering off.

"That idiot is more useless than an aphrodisiac in a monastery." Yorin exhaled a long, irate sigh. "Nevermind, nevermind. Who is your colorful friend, Rema?"

"Welcome, palace man of great dignity!" It seemed Danoshan was not one of Muhan's stronger languages. "I be known as a trader, Muhan." He clasped his hands together in a gesture of respect. "To where is the address of my honor?"

There was a moment of awkward silence, and Rema cleared her throat. "Yorin, can you speak Annari? It might help."

"Well enough," said Yorin in capable Annari. "Stop butchering my native tongue, Muhan. I'm Yorin, the king's steward. I suppose you're here to sell me something."

"Exotic dyes!" Muhan spread his arms wide. "Shades beyond even the comprehension of nature! If you don't mind me saying, your plain robe could be transformed into a spectacle of radiance with only a momentary soak."

"If we can't eat it, I'm not interested."

"What you do with the dye is none of my concern. For all I know, it may taste as spectacular as it looks."

"Give him a chance," said Rema. "Don't you think Elise and Loric might at least be curious to see him?"

"I suppose they might," said Yorin. "Especially Loric. The boy's too easily amused. And it'll give him a chance to practice his Annari." He scratched the tip of his nose. "You're fortunate that you found our persuasive friend to talk on your behalf, Muhan. I'll inform the court you're here." He retrieved an envelope from his robe. "And Rema, this is for you. I don't know why she didn't come to you directly."

Rema turned the envelope in her hands. It was unmarked, but she detected a familiar perfume. To her alarm, the scent provoked her heart to beat faster. "Thank you," she said, slipping the envelope into the pocket of her coat. "Shall I leave you two to get better acquainted?"

Yorin nodded, his mind clearly already on other things. Muhan grinned and twirled his mustache in her direction. "I appreciate your support, my lady of Arann. I look forward to meeting you again."

"I'm not hard to find. Just follow the giggling of the servants."

Rema returned to her chambers and closed the door behind her. It was cool within, and the room was dark enough that she paused to light a lamp at the bedside. She sat on the edge of her bed and tore the envelope open. The letter inside bore one of the strangest writing hands she'd ever seen; every letter seemed to have a new loop or flourish.

Sweetest R: You are beautiful and witty and I miss you already. Remember, there's trouble on the way. Be a wary little diplomat and don't forget to wear your present! Forever, E.

The intimacy of the letter was sweet, even touching—but its content was puzzling. If Rema were to list those people who had reason to see her harmed, Elise would be at the top, yet it was the enchantress herself sending her affectionate warnings. Yorin? He had the power to harm her, but he was the closest she had to a certain ally. Loric? Ridiculous. Cedrin and Talitha? No ruler would touch an imperial diplomat. What about Muhan? He had a personal motive to dislike the Empire, but Rema was a fair judge of character and found it hard to picture him as a brightly-daubed assassin. That left Calan and the mysterious hooded man.

It was too much to think about, and she was tired of this drab palace. Rema returned to the hallway and walked to the nearest guard. He eyed her nervously as she drew closer.

"Good morning, guardsman," she said. "Is there a tavern close by where the food is edible and the water clean?"

"The guards usually drink at the Bristled Sow." The guard stared at her trousers as if they were a wild animal. "If you go down the road from the gates, it's the first tavern on your right when you reach the big square with the fountain."

Rema saluted. "Thank you. Have a good watch."

"You too, sir. Uh, my lady. I mean, have a good day, my lady—"

Rema fought back laughter as she walked away. No matter where she visited, be there painted traders, rebellious enchantresses or sinister hooded men, she unfailingly remained the greatest novelty of them all. Well, except for that time with the crocodiles.

CHAPTER SIX

The courtyard behind the gate was in a state of confusion. A horse had leapt over its stall door, and several soldiers were in pursuit, attempting to subdue it before it kicked anyone. A child stood alone, staring at the twisting, rearing beast. He was too near those flying hooves for comfort. Rema took his hand and pulled him away from danger.

"Has someone lost a child?" she said, to no response. Frowning, she dragged the stray child over to a guardsman by the door. "Take this boy to Yorin. We can't have parentless children wandering the courtyard."

"It happens," said the guard. "They come to see the palace. Isn't that right, son?"

"I want to see the King," said the boy. "My father is sick and he won't get better." He couldn't have been more than eight years old, and his pudgy face showed a touching determination. Rema's compassion stirred—the poor thing was barefoot, and his feet were black and swollen.

"Forget about taking him to Yorin," she said. "Take him to Elise."

"My lady, while you are a valued guest, you aren't really allowed to give orders…"

Rema crossed her arms. "Are you defying me, guardsman?"

The guard blanched. "As you wish, my lady. Come on, boy." He took the boy's fat hand and led him toward the palace. Another guard sniggered, and Rema glared at him. He snapped back to a respectable composure.

After the horse was brought safely to rein, Rema left the courtyard and moved beneath the shadow of the portcullis. The morning remained pleasant, and the worst odors of the city were some distance off, though every now and then a whiff of sulfur or manure caused Rema's eyes to water. As she strolled down the road leading to the palace, her skin prickled beneath the stares of the city folk. Many looks were appreciative, others bewildered, and quite a few hostile— but such was to be expected when garbed in fine silk and scandalous trousers. Rema kept her head high. She had no illusions about the dangers of the city, but confidence was effective armor.

Despite her bravado, it was a relief nonetheless to reach the square. As promised, its center was dominated by a square fountain. A modest jet shot from its waters and broke into a glistening spray that crashed musically onto the surface of the pool. Children splashed in the waters while travelers passing by stopped to appreciate the sound. Several merchants roamed the square selling fruits and toys, and Rema moved quickly to avoid being sold a tin windmill.

The Bristled Sow proved warm and well-lit. The smell of alcohol had worked its way into every surface, true of taverns everywhere. Several off-duty guards were sitting together at the large central table, thumping the table, clinking their mugs together and braying with thin, drunken laughter. No doubt they were night watchmen to be drinking so heavily at noonday. Either that or they were shameless drunks, a not uncommon secondary occupation for guardsmen.

The guards paused in their revelry to look at Rema. They giggled in tipsy conference. "Hey!" one of them said. "Hello!"

"Hello to you too."

"I told you!" The guard knocked one of his companions on the back of the head. "It's a bloody woman!"

Drunken guardsmen, like bed lice, were the same the world over— an irritation. Rema took a seat at the next table. The guards continued to stare, and she stared back. "Do you lads ever chase criminals, or are you more interested in pursuing the bottom of your tankards?"

Several of the guards smirked. "You've got a pretty voice," said the one who'd had his head thumped, slurring and spilling his drink on himself. "Pretty little face too. Wouldn't mind spending a night or two with you."

"And yet a moment ago you thought I was a man. What does that tell you, lads?"

The guards cheered and clapped their chastened friend on the back. Rema couldn't resist laughing with them, and the tension in the room dissolved. Satisfied with their fun, the guards returned to their bantering.

A servant took the opportunity to duck over to Rema's table. "Morning, miss," he said. "May I get you a drink or a meal or both or neither?"

"I'd be afraid to touch what they're having. I'll have a meal and some water. What do you serve here?"

"Our usual customers like it simple, which his fortunate, as simple is all we do. If you've money for it, there's meat. Otherwise, we can bring you a mash of vegetables, with a bit of butter if you like."

Rema had no desire to learn what passed for meat in Danosha. "I'll take the vegetables. And just a little butter." She took a coin from her purse and pressed it to the surprised servant's palm. "Keep whatever is left over."

"Yes, miss! We'll cook it extra quick, miss."

"No rush. Just bring the water first."

Rema crossed her legs and waited, and the servant soon returned with a mug of water. It tasted of tin but soothed her throat and cleared her head. As she put her purse away, a thought struck her: she might well be the wealthiest person in this kingdom. Ormun's father, Togun, had rewarded her exceptionally for her long service. She had one of the largest offices in the palace, and she owned a ten-room mansion by one of Arann's lukewarm bays, where the water always seemed to be the color of the sun. Her work kept her so busy that she was rarely able to visit it.

In a realm like this, it was hard not to grow nostalgic for the days of Togun. He had been a good Emperor, insofar as there could be such a thing. At Rema's urging, he had reformed the Empire and the great city of Arann, improving opportunities for women and ending slavery. In return, she'd brokered many of the foreign deals that had allowed him to consolidate his reign. If it hadn't been for Ormun's coup, the Empire today would be very different, and she wouldn't be crossing the world to abduct innocent women.

The meal landed in front of her, returning her to the moment. The mash was a terrifying brown and filled with haggard lumps. "What vegetables are these?" she said.

"All sorts, miss. Potatoes. Parsnip. Some other things."

"Why is it all so brown?" She tentatively tried a spoonful. It warmed her mouth and the taste was bearable, though the texture was mysteriously grainy. "It's not so bad. Thank you."

The servant bowed and trotted off to refill the guards' mugs. Rema tried another spoonful and discovered a potato skin. Spitting it out seemed impolite, so she began to chew it.

"That dead-eyed bastard is back in the city," said one of the guards, his voice amplified by ale. "I saw him this morning, skulking about."

Another laughed. "Better not fall asleep on the job, then, or Calan'll have him after you."

"I heard that he went into a Lyornan village at night, killed all the children. Can you imagine what it must feel like, seeing your little one's head on a pike?"

Her interest piqued, Rema shifted as if to make herself more comfortable, and in the process she inched a little closer to her neighbors.

"I've got two daughters," said a third guard. "I don't even want to think about it."

"He's not human. I don't know where Calan found him, but it weren't on this earth."

"Here's what troubles me," said the guard with the daughters. "War gets desperate, fair enough. I'm no cringing heart. But when you hit a man, it gives him license to hit you just the same. How long until Lyorn are putting the heads of our children on pikes?"

The guards fell into silence, each of them focused on his mug. "I'll tell you this," said one, breaking the quiet. "I fucking dread the day I get shifted into the army. They're dying like flies out there."

Rema finished her meal and pushed the bowl aside. It was about time she returned to the palace; the glow of morning had long been consumed by the steady light of afternoon, and it wouldn't do to miss anything important at court. She glanced at the guards as she left the tavern, but they had long lost interest in her—the solace of stupor was all they cared for now.

Her walk back was uneventful but for a boy who kept chasing her, hitting her legs with a stick. After enduring his foolery for several seconds, Rema snatched the stick from his hands and snapped it, and he ran away crying. She had little patience for unruly children, who never responded well to diplomacy.

Arriving at the palace, Rema found the flow of visitors as steady as before. As she escaped to the relative quiet of a corridor, three servants wobbled toward her with a mattress on their shoulders, and she flattened herself against the wall to let them by. Amid all this activity, what was there for her to do? Perhaps she might visit Elise and inquire about the well-being of the barefooted child—not merely as a pretext to see the beautiful enchantress again, of course, but in order to alleviate her concern for the boy.

In daylight, Elise's tower had become a well of radiance through which motes of dust capered. A quick tap at the door conjured the sound of muffled movement from within. The door cracked open, revealing Elise's delighted face. "You're very early for dinner," she said, opening the door and waving Rema in.

Rema stopped short at the edge of the room. The disarray was astonishing. Piles of soil and red trailing weeds covered the table, and a crucible was hissing on the windowsill. "What happened in here?"

"I was working on a remedy for that little boy's father." Elise dusted her hands. "It sounded like he had the red scabies, so I mixed up a little potion. And just in case it's not red scabies, an unguent to reduce itching."

"Who'd have known magic was such messy work?" Rema swept soil off a chair before sitting. "What exactly is the red scabies?"

"It's horrible, that's what it is." Elise sighed. "The guard mentioned that it was you who sent the boy my way. What am I to do with you, Rema? You're not just clever, funny and beautiful. You're kind as well."

Rema leaned back in her chair and admired Elise, who had been transformed by her art. Her hands were covered in soil, and she'd managed to transfer a streak of the dirt to her cheek. She wore no cosmetics, smelt like dirt and bitter roots, and had replaced her seductive dress with a brown smock that covered her shoulders and disguised her figure. Yet she appeared even more attractive than the night before. Her eyes seemed warmer, the curve of her lips more suggestive. Above all, she displayed none of the giddy nerves that had plagued her over wine and custard.

"Did Yorin pass on my letter?" Elise wiped her hands on her smock. "I hope you didn't mind my being cryptic."

"Diplomats love cryptic letters, but I wouldn't mind a little more explanation."

"I just have reason to worry for you, that's all." Elise twisted her hair around her finger, evidently forgetting about the dirt on her hands. "I suppose you came to ask about the boy, not to see me."

"Something of both. I'd heard you do a lot for the sick."

"Much more than my father. He genuinely believes he can make them better by passing his hands over their fevered heads." Elise stared at a long tangle of her hair, which was clumped together with soil. "Oh, no. Look what I've done."

Rema laughed. "I should have told you, but…"

"You're wicked as well. Perfect. I can't wait for our dinner. I know I made a fool of myself last night, but I hope you'll give me another chance."

"I enjoyed our evening. In truth, I should have stayed longer."

Elise veiled her eyes beneath her lashes. "Yes, you should have."

"Well." Rema stood, keeping her distance from the dirty table. "Now that I know the boy is fine, I should learn if Yorin has any news for me."

"Turn around," said Elise. Rema hesitated but obeyed. A moment later, a hand brushed across her behind. "You have soil on your trousers." Another brisk sweep followed, and Rema's pulse skipped as Elise's fingers lingered on the curve of her left buttock.

"That doesn't feel like brushing." Rema stared at the wall, too startled to move.

"Of course it was." Elise turned Rema to face her. "All gone now." Her hand remained on Rema's shoulder, and Rema became very aware of the closeness of their lips.

"I'll see you for dinner, then," she said.

Elise lifted her hand and stepped away, and the anxiety in Rema's chest eased. "Yes, you will. I'll have to get the servants to help me clear a space. They grumble about bringing the food upstairs, but surely the exercise is good for them." Elise tossed her hair. "Go on, then, Rema! Run along and diplomat somewhere else. You're keeping me from my work."

As Rema descended the tower, she brushed several times at the seat of her trousers. Perhaps Elise had invented the soil as an excuse for a covert caress. If so, it was a deception worthy of herself.

Only a few unhappy peasants remained in the front court, still waiting with dour patience to see their King. Yorin stood near a wall in agitated conversation with a tall, long-haired man whose tanned arms were encased in tight gold bracelets. His dark eyes betrayed no emotion and were divided by a striking high-ridged nose.

"I'm telling you," said Yorin. "Nobody mentioned your arrival."

"The letter was sent," said the man. Judging from his appearance and his glottal accent, he was from Narandor, a kingdom on the northern edge of the continent—one of the many prudent nations aligned with neither Danosha nor Lyorn, the better to keep their hands clean. "Would you be so foolish as to turn away aid merely because you misplaced a scrap of paper?"

Rema joined the two men and clasped her hands before her coat. "May I be of service here, Yorin?"

"Rema, thank God," said Yorin. "This man claims to be a diplomat from Narandor. He says he's come to discuss the war and offer an alliance. But we have no message from the Narandane to prove what he's saying."

Most Narandane could speak Huzi, a dialect common in the northern regions of the continent. It wasn't Rema's most fluent tongue, but she knew enough to test the man. "My friend tells me you claim to be from Narandor," she said, switching languages.

"Is that not obvious?" said the man in perfect Huzi. "You are an imperial diplomat. You know very well that letters do not always arrive intact."

Rema also knew very well that few diplomats would risk a long journey without some written confirmation they wouldn't be returned home in several boxes. "If you're truly a diplomat, you understand none of us travel without some seal of authority."

"I am not here to parley with Emperor Ormun, who has not even seen fit to grace us with the humblest trade agreement. Do not annoy me with talk of documentation you have no authority to demand."

Rema smiled and returned to speaking Danoshan. "He may or may not be a diplomat, Yorin, but he's certainly as tough as one."

"God preserve me." Yorin threw his hands up in frustration. "I suppose I have no choice but to let you stay, but this is very irregular. A message will go out immediately to confirm your claim. You can see the King this evening, and I'll find you a room."

"That is well," said the Narandane. "My personal servants will see to moving my luggage."

"If you prefer." Yorin raised his voice. "Alys!" The girl approached with her hands full of washing. "Take Lord Domyr to those vacant chambers near the bathing room. One for him, one for his servants."

Domyr's personal servants, a group of two women and a man all grim as their master, stepped forward bearing wooden trunks. Alys gave the company a terrified smile—perhaps she fancied the trunks were stuffed with naughty children—and directed them through one of the archways.

Yorin watched them leave before turning to Rema, his brow a scaffold of worry. "That's four rooms gone today. Can you believe that Loric demanded we let the dye merchant stay with us? He can juggle, it seems, and do conjuring tricks. So now he's in my palace taking up precious space."

"Your palace?" Rema raised an eyebrow. "Hmm. Muhan, Domyr and his servants. That's three rooms. Who took the fourth?"

"A fourth? I must have misspoken."

"You don't have to lie to me. Let me guess. It's a hooded man with nasty eyes and an unsavory reputation, and Calan and the King have insisted you tell no one about him."

Yorin looked away, but not before the twitch of his lips exposed his guilt. "Why am I not supposed to know about this man?" said Rema.

"Presumably for the reason I know nothing about him myself. Rema, listen to me. If you see him around, I beg you to leave him alone."

"Rest easy. I won't get you into any trouble."

"I'm not worried for myself." Yorin lowered his voice. "I'm worried for you! Don't cross that man. Don't even look at him. If it ever comes that you need to know something, I'll be sure that you do."

"As you say." Though her interest hadn't been satisfied, the candor of Yorin's reply suggested Rema might win his total confidence yet. It was a prospect worth pursuing. "To be honest, I've run out of errands for the day. Is there any paperwork you need help with?"

"Are you serious?" Yorin grasped her arm, and his eyes widened with frantic hope. "Tell me you're serious."

"I'm serious." Rema laughed as she freed her captive limb. "Take me to the paperwork."

She'd never yet seen that glum face produce a smile so heartfelt. "I'll have to arrange you a softer mattress," Yorin said as he led her out of the court. "And I take back all the uncharitable things I've said about imperial diplomats. You're the finest people in the world."

"Don't get carried away. The next diplomat who comes from the Empire may well be the unpleasant sort Elise is eager to roast over an open fire."

Yorin chuckled, while Rema allowed herself a contented smile. If it meant securing the man's loyalty, a little paperwork was no ordeal. After all, how much work could it be?

CHAPTER SEVEN

The bureaucrats of Arann had a saying: first the Gods sent locusts, then boils, and finally the paperwork. Yorin had given Rema three kitchen inventories, one for each of the three months past, and asked her to calculate how rapidly supplies were being consumed. He'd explained a grand scheme to predict exactly how much food he would need to sustain the palace for the next two years, and he had become so excited describing the idea that he had knocked over an inkwell.

The resulting work was enough to occupy an entire squadron of scribes, but Rema enjoyed the quiet scratch of the quill and the diversion from her guilty feelings. It was worth each tiresome stroke if it meant further developing the camaraderie between Yorin and herself. He controlled the servants and guards and knew the intimacies of the court, and that made him both an essential ally and a dangerous enemy.

The man himself entered the room, rousing her from a whirl of numbers. "You've been at that for hours," Yorin said. "You're not here to slave for me. Put an end to it for the day."

Rema flexed her cramped hand. "Once I get a quill in my hand, I have trouble stopping."

"I spoke to Alys on the way here." Yorin took some of her paperwork and peered at the long list of numbers. "She was frightened she might be in trouble, and was relieved to learn that you'd informed me of your morning's escapade to the gardens. That relief made her bold enough to request a pair of trousers, if you can believe it."

"A hundred years from now, every woman in Danosha will be wearing them." Rema stood and winced at the agonizing stiffness in her knees.

"You're grimacing."

"It's nothing. I'd better get to dinner. Loric and Elise are expecting me."

Yorin scratched his balding pate. "I can't begin to imagine what you three have to talk about. Don't lose sight of your mission."

Normally Rema might bridle at the suggestion she was losing her focus, but for once, she wasn't so certain herself. "They're not my enemies. If anything, they're my victims."

"You scourge yourself too much over this." Yorin slid another sheet of paperwork across the table and squinted, clearly disapproving of some figure. "In jobs like ours, we have to accept that our own principles can be overruled."

"I've been letting Ormun overrule my principles for four years. It never gets any easier." Rema shook her head. "I'll be on my way. Have a good night."

"Sleep well." Yorin settled himself before the desk and began to continue the work Rema had started. Did he ever rest from his duties?

Rema navigated the palace until she reached the foot of Elise's tower. The sun had melted deep and red, and beyond the stairwell's windows the first stars had revealed themselves. As she climbed, dread worried at her stomach, and each successive step felt higher than the last. Yorin was right—nothing good could come of this.

The door was already open and held that way by a stack of books. Inside the tower, Loric helped a servant clear space while Elise worked on stuffing books back into their shelves. The siblings turned and smiled together.

"Rema!" said Loric, interrupting Elise as she opened her mouth. "We're making room for you. Elsie lives in squalor, so it's quite a task."

"Squalor?" said Elise. "You should see his room."

"If she'd like me to show her, I wouldn't refuse." Loric grinned, and Elise pinched him. He leapt away laughing. It seemed that in his sister's presence, Loric became a different man; the gloom was gone from his eyes, replaced with a clear, animated look of happiness.

"Mind yourself, little boy." Elise frowned at the table, which was smothered by papers. "Rema, we're having trouble finding space for a third chair. You may have to sit on my lap."

"It would be difficult for you to dine that way," said Rema. "Perhaps I should come back later."

"No, I think we almost have enough space here," said Loric. "We'll just need to move this thing." He stared at something Rema was unable to see from her position in the doorway. "What is it, anyway?"

"A mysterious and powerful device that I'm forbidden to tell you about," said Elise. "Throw it in the corner there."

Loric hurled the unseen object across the room and dropped a chair into place. "Success! We've conquered Elsie's sprawling mess."

"I'll fetch the meal now, my lord and lady," said the servant, keeping his blond head low.

"Thank you," said Elise. "Careful on those stairs." Rema stepped aside to allow the servant through. He hurried down the stairs, his head still bowed, and his stumbling steps echoed up the stairwell.

"Now, get in here before I drag you in," said Elise, beckoning. "Oh, careful! Don't step on that!"

Rema pulled her foot back from the vial she had nearly trodden on. "Well, don't leave it on the floor if it's so fragile."

"That's what I always tell her." Loric folded himself into his narrow seat. Elise settled gracefully into the seat beside him and deliberately pulled the remaining chair closer to her.

"Come on, Rema." Elise patted the chair. "Cuddle up to me and we can talk while we wait for our meals to arrive."

Keeping a careful eye on the floor as she walked, Rema took her place. "So what have you been doing today?" said Loric. "More beguiling, I presume?"

"I've been stooped over a desk for hours." Rema marveled at the variety of Elise's belongings. "Why do you have an octopus in a jar?" It was a hideous thing, a whorl of suckers and glistening tubes curled inward on itself.

"Because if it wasn't in the jar, I would lose it." Shifting closer, Elise fussed with a wayward strand of Rema's hair. It was an unexpectedly intimate gesture; fortunately, it took more than a little flirtatious play to set loose Rema's well-controlled desires. "Your hair is such a lovely shade of red. Loric, what do you think?"

"I wouldn't say just lovely," Loric said. "Her hair is beautiful. Like the tapering flame of a sunset."

"Well, aren't you poetic. What about her eyes? They have such marvelous lids, not like our eyes at all."

Loric inspected Rema more closely. It was the first time he had looked directly at her without blushing. "They're lustrous, captivating amber. Like...uh. Like the radiant gold of the sun."

"You already used a sun-related metaphor for her hair. How fantastically lazy of you."

"At least I didn't just say her hair was lovely! Given your poor performance at poetic courtship, I think it only fair that Rema's chair be moved next to me and you sit alone all night."

Before Elise could respond, a servant waddled in beneath several trays of food. "Oh, excellent," said Loric. "That was very quick."

"Yorin demanded we work extra fast to bring this to you," said the servant. "He even told us to give you extra wine."

The trays contained too much food for the table. The servants unpacked it as best they could, but almost half of it ended up on a nearby stack of books. "Look at this feast," said Elise. "Have you enraptured Yorin's grouchy heart as well as ours? You continue to amaze me, Remela."

"If you call me Remela, I'll call you princess," Rema said, watching as the servant carefully navigated her way out of the room. No doubt the inhabitants of the palace lived in terror of disturbing whatever magic might lurk here.

"Speaking of princesses, how many others have you uncaringly snatched away from their parents?"

Rema stared at Elise, shocked out of her pleasant relaxation. Even Loric seemed taken aback.

"I couldn't say." Rema's appetite had vanished, replaced with a coiling uneasiness. "Marriage arrangements are usually handled by less-experienced diplomats."

"I remember when I first learned what it meant to be a princess. When I first learned that my family would only be mine until they decided to give me away." Elise's silver eyes smoldered, an effect both frightening and alluring. "When I learned there's no point falling in love, as it's already decided you have to go to some fat aristocrat whose breath stinks of eels."

"Yes, it's unfair." Rema tried to master her voice. "But perhaps it's no more unfair than life is for your peasants, who toil without reward to keep your family in power."

"So you're saying we all have to suffer in our own way? They will work in the fields, Loric will get hangovers from too much merriment, and I will marry a man who plans to rape me until I die in childbirth. How fair it all sounds!"

"Elsie," said Loric, taking her hand. "I thought we were going to enjoy dinner before we discussed this."

"I suddenly didn't feel like waiting." Elise narrowed her glittering eyes. "Justify it to me, Rema. Go on. You're so very clever."

There seemed no adequate response but the truth. "It's unjustifiable," said Rema. "Like so much else in the world. Your father and mother ruling over these people is unjustifiable. Ormun conquering kingdom after kingdom is unjustifiable. That we are having wine and good food while the people outside eat straw and dirt is unjustifiable."

"So you have no desire to remedy injustice. You think it's natural and should continue."

"The reality is that tens of thousands will die in this war." Rema found it impossible to match Elise's furious stare. Where was the lovesick innocent of the night before? "You know what suffering awaits the people of this kingdom if your parents don't accept my offer."

Elise gave a short, bitter laugh. "So now you make it seem like I'm selfish! It's actually my fault people are dying, and I should stop tormenting everyone and accept my fate. How wicked of me to resist my persecution!"

"No." Rema's heart ached. She'd never met a woman more beautiful in her indignation, and to be the cause of that outrage was more than she could bear. "The blame here is entirely Ormun's. The world is strewn with his victims. Some alive, some dead, and some so numb they can hardly tell the difference."

"You can do something about it," said Loric, his voice wavering with agitation. "Ask him to change the terms so that we can keep Elsie. That's all it would take."

"Ormun takes my advice on many things. But not on this. You two have every right to hate me, but I swear to you, I'd help you if I could."

"You could fail your mission. Concede that we won't give her up. Maybe then the Emperor will change the terms."

"Don't bother, Lor," said Elise with such resignation that Rema's stomach twisted. "She's not going to change her mind." She poked at something glistening on her plate. "Shall we eat?"

The meal proved tense. Elise focused all her attention on her food, her gaze never leaving her plate, while Rema toyed with her meal, eating little. Loric glanced often between Rema and Elise, obviously wanting to break the tension but unsure how to do so. Finally, Elise finished eating and put down her cutlery.

"So," Elise said, turning her attention back to Rema. "Let's learn more about the wonderful enigma that is you."

"Ask away," said Rema. Wary as she was, the return of conversation was welcome.

"You must have seen a lot of this world. What places haven't you been to?"

"Well, until yesterday, I'd never been here." Rema ventured a smile, and to her relief, Elise smiled back. A volatile temper, then, but also a capricious one. "It's the southern continent, Tamalan, that I'm most unfamiliar with. I once visited Alumbra, the kingdom said to be the birthplace of all sorcery, but that is all."

"Mmm." A dreamy look stole over Elise's face. "I've often dreamed of visiting Tamalan. They say the very air there is enchanted."

"Yes, but it's dangerous too. On its eastern edge is the Darmoor, which is home to nothing but savage beasts, though it must be amazing to see them. Some of them are said to be as tall as ten men. There's also reportedly an empire off the coast of Kahydeer, but the jungles are so wild that nobody can make contact."

"If I were you, I'd never rest until I saw all those exciting places." The resentful tone had returned to Elise's voice, though her eyes remained wistful. "You have money and power. You can live whatever life you choose. Why are you wasting your life running errands for the cruelest man in the world?"

"Despite everything, I believe in what I do. I'm the closest thing Ormun has to a conscience." Rema stared into her soup as a shadow moved over her thoughts, blotting what cheer she had left. "You don't know how dark-minded he's become. I sacrifice some of myself every day in his service. But I don't do it for the money or the power. I do it because I know what he's capable of without me." She looked at Loric and Elise in turn. "I don't expect your forgiveness, but I'd hoped at least to avoid your hatred."

Elise bit her lip and turned to her brother. "Loric, would you mind leaving me with Rema?"

"But we haven't even started the wine," Loric said. "Come on, Elsie."

"Let's not get started on wine. In the mood we're in, nobody will stop." Elise tugged his hand. "Please, Lor."

"I don't see why." Loric stood, untangling himself from the furniture. "I was looking forward to the evening."

"Take the bottles with you. You can drink yourself to sleep."

"And now you make me sound like a drunkard." Loric walked to the door and gave Rema a tragic wave. The door shut firmly behind him.

The moment the door had closed, Elise placed a hand upon Rema's thigh. Rema became very still, but for the wild rhythm of her heart. "You handsome, troubled woman," said Elise, cupping Rema's face with her other hand. The feel of her palm was soft, warm, distracting. "I'm so worried for you. There are people here that mean to do you harm."

"If I came to harm, it would save you from marriage. Isn't that what you want?"

"What I want is you." Elise pulled Rema's face toward her own.

Before their mouths could meet, Rema put a hand on Elise's shoulder and gently pushed them apart. "Elise, this isn't going to happen."

"It's happening right now." Elise drew Rema close once more. Rema turned her head away, escaping the kiss, and stopped Elise's hand as it slid toward Rema's inner thigh.

"Damn it!" said Elise. "I couldn't sleep last night for thinking about you. All I want is for you to desire me too, yet I have no idea how to begin to seduce you. I'm pathetic."

"You're not pathetic." If only Rema could touch her, reassure her somehow, but to encourage Elise further would only lead to catastrophe. "You're intelligent, charming and attractive, but it's impossible for us to be any closer."

"Can't you see how cruel this is? You're like something born from my dreams. The kind of woman I never dared imagine might exist. At least kiss me goodnight before leaving."

"That would depend on where you expected me to kiss you."

Scarlet bloomed in Elise's cheeks. "Anyplace you want to."

Rema looked away. She'd been such a fool. Why had she expected anything but heartbreak to come of this meeting? "I don't mean to do this to you. It'd be easier if you just hated me."

"I might be able to hate you yet, if you leave me feeling this way." Elise tried once more to bring Rema close, but Rema twisted out of her grasp and returned to her feet. Elise remained seated, her face crimson, her lips parted as if still anticipating a kiss.

"Elsie, I'm going to bed now."

Elise covered her face with her hands. "Be careful," she said in a wretched mumble. "When I said it was dangerous for you, I meant it."

"Don't worry about me." Rema moved to the door, not even paying attention to the placement of her feet amid the litter.

"Damn you, Rema." Hearing the anger in Elise's voice, Rema hesitated, her stomach in convulsions. "I'm begging you not to walk away. I need you. I'm on the edge of oblivion, and you're the one thing that might bring me back."

Only a cold heart could ignore such a plea—a cold heart, or one forced into coldness. Rema closed the door and descended the stairs. Halfway down, she began trembling, and she paused at a window to inhale the night air.

Why was this so difficult? As much as Rema enjoyed flirting, she took her duties seriously and was used to fending off inopportune advances. Usually the offenders were men, who were easy to resist, but she had many times been propositioned by women—in one memorable case, by a particularly pushy queen. In every case, Rema had remained resolute in her duty. Turning her back on Elise, however, had stung in a way she'd never before known. It was that fierce independence of hers, that beguiling mixture of temper and sweetness.

Arriving at the door of her chamber, she composed herself with a deep breath before reaching for the handle. "Rema, wait." Loric spoke from behind her, nasal from drink. He walked without difficulty, but she could smell the wine on his breath.

"Loric." Rema looked into his eyes and was relieved to find the same gentle, helplessly-smitten young man she remembered. "I'm sorry the evening didn't go as you hoped."

"Don't break her heart." Tears wavered in Loric's silver eyes. "You don't understand how terrible things are for her. You haven't met my brother." He placed an unsteady hand on Rema's shoulder. "Elsie has told me that you're the same kind of woman she is. Go back to her. She's been so lonely for so long."

"I can't help her."

"Why don't you just do what you want instead of what you're told? You're so much better than the person you're pretending to be."

Rema rarely found herself at a loss for words, but this was just such a moment. She opened her mouth and waited. Nothing came to her. She blinked several times and reached again for the door. "I really can't help her. Good night, Loric."

"Maybe you're just a coward."

Rema paused, her fingers on the iron handle, her breath coming through a hard knot in her throat. "Ormun's first wife was taken in the conquest of Tahdeen. The queen of the Tahdeeni had eleven children. Ten sons, one daughter. Ormun had killed all her male children, and the daughter was all she had. The child was sixteen years old and terrified." Her anger at the memory broke the knot, and the power returned to her voice. "Ormun said that he would kill everyone in the city unless the princess was given to him. The queen asked if the girl would be treated with respect. Ormun said that he would love her when he chose and where he chose. If he ever grew tired of her, he said, he would give her to his soldiers."

Loric steadied himself against the wall, his face pale. "God…"

"I was there when he said it, and I hadn't yet realized he was beyond redemption. I intervened. I told him our victory was enough, that to take a wife in this way was untold barbarism. Ormun calmly ordered me stripped and beaten in front of the entire room. And then I had to continue negotiations as if nothing had happened. Loric, I mean it with grief and sincerity when I tell you that I cannot help Elise."

"I'm sorry. I didn't know."

The sincerity of regret was etched on his adolescent features. Rema smiled at him and touched his sleeve. "How could you? I'm going to sleep now. It sounds like I'll need a good rest before I deal with this brother of yours."

"Calan. I'd forgotten." Loric rested his head against the wall and exhaled a bitter sigh. "He beats Elsie when he's angry. Goes up to her tower and pushes her around. The son of a bitch. My father knows and does nothing. My mother won't believe it."

Rema's stomach churned. "Can nothing be done?"

"Yorin tried. He had guards visit her room when he thought my brother might be there. Calan just orders them to leave. He's shameless. I tried to stop him once myself, and I was coughing blood for a week." Loric gave a weak smile. "Every night I pray that he's been killed in battle. One of these days, maybe my message will get through."

"Your brother may think he can intimidate women. He hasn't met me."

Loric shook his shaggy head. "You're tough and smart, Rema, but so is my sister. When she's angry, she's every bit as magnificent as you. But all the courage and wit in the world can't stop a brute, and they don't get more brutal than Calan. Goodnight." He lowered his head and stalked back down the corridor, his body shifting listlessly.

Rema entered her chamber, undressed as quickly as she could and threw herself under the blankets. At first, it seemed as if sleep would never come, but finally she was tossed into slumber. She awoke from scattered nightmares, a single tear drying on her cheek.

CHAPTER EIGHT

Rema washed without enthusiasm before donning her spare uniform. For once, the dressing ritual gave her little pleasure; she was caught in a swirl of unexamined emotions, and her heart was smothered by feelings too dangerous to contemplate. When finally she emerged into the corridor, however, her face was calm. A diplomat's exterior rarely expressed her feelings.

She passed through the front court, where a few servants swept while a lone guard patrolled without energy, and made her way to the kitchen. The pantry was unsecured. She liberated some bread and fruit—surely Yorin would consider it a just reward for all her paperwork.

Several servants were eating in the small dining chamber, and they looked up in surprise as Rema entered. Alys was among them, pecking at a piece of bread barely larger than a crumb. "You're up early, my lady Rema," she said.

Rema took a seat beside her. "I didn't sleep very well. Is Yorin about?"

Alys nipped at her breakfast again before answering. "Of course. I don't think he sleeps at all! He's having Prince Calan's bedroom cleaned out now, I think."

"How are the other guests?"

"Well, the painted man was quite happy with his dinner last night. He impressed the King with a conjuring trick, and he's going to give us all a show in the banquet hall today. Also, the head maid used all her savings to buy one of his pink scarves. I thought it very frivolous of her."

Rema swallowed a mouthful of bread. By the Gods, it was dry. "And the Narandane?"

"Their scary leader talked with the King. He came out looking very satisfied with himself. He dined with the King and Queen too, and we didn't hear the sound of plates breaking or raised voices, so it must have gone well."

"And the hooded man you don't like?"

"He slept upstairs in a chamber near the King's. We're not allowed to help him move his possessions or clean his room. I don't know where he goes for dinner either. For all I know he stalks the halls at night and drinks people's blood."

"Do you know where he might be now?"

"He's not supposed to leave the palace until the Prince rides out in a few days, so he must be near. Perhaps he breaks his fast in the gardens. He's been seen skulking there before."

Nothing good ever came from a person with a reputation for skulking. Rema consumed her last mouthful and swept crumbs from the table. "Thank you, Alys. Can you tell me where Yorin is?"

"You've so many questions for me!" Alys beamed. "You make me feel clever. Anyway, we're both done eating, so I'll take you to him." She skipped to her feet. "Come on!"

Rema followed the lively Alys through the court, up the stairs and down a long corridor filled with unhappy servants. Yorin was standing before an open door, shouting and waving his arms.

"Never a moment's rest," said Rema, putting a hand on his shoulder.

Yorin's irritated look softened. "Good morning, Rema. Alys, now that you're here, go get those cobwebs." He shook his head as Alys darted through the door. "That room is filthy. Calan will go wild if we don't get it clean. He seizes any excuse to berate us."

"I'll need to talk to him later. I was wondering if you could tell me more about the man."

A servant approached Yorin with a flask of water. "About time," he said, gulping from the flask. "Sorry, it's just the dust, it plays havoc on the throat...so, you're curious about Calan. I suspect you know quite a bit about him already."

"I'd like to know your point of view."

Yorin wiped his lips and shook the empty flask. "I've known the royal children from birth. Elise and I may not get along, but I respect her. She's endured a great deal with dignity. Loric's a good boy, always has been. Calan, on the other hand, is a difficult man to like."

"He tormented Elise growing up, I assume."

"The day he turned fifteen, he tried to kill one of Elise's kittens. When I went to flog him, he said that he was a man now, that if I tried to punish him he'd order me beaten instead. That was the last time anyone dared raise a hand to him, and his cruelty has only increased with age. He should arrive around midafternoon. You'll know he's here, believe me."

Rema shifted to make way for a frantic servant waving a broom. "I wonder what he'll think of me."

"Speaking frankly, he'll despise you. That's if he doesn't just ignore you. You have diplomatic immunity, but you may not want to be alone with him all the same. Like his sister, he has a temper. Unlike his sister, he doesn't loose his fury with words alone."

"I'll not be bullied by some arrogant prince. He'll be shown where he truly stands in the court of the world."

"You're too brave for your own good. If you do talk to him, be on your guard. And now, if you don't mind, I have to find out what the hell that man is doing with his mop…"

Rema left Yorin to his affairs, returned down the hallway and stood in a quiet alcove, running her fingers absently through her hair. Her tongue was still musty from the dust she had inhaled outside Calan's room. Some fresh air seemed called for. To the garden, then.

The air outside proved cool and damp, and a sheet of dark clouds extending to the horizon signaled an approaching storm. Rema walked across the grass, weaving between the hedges. Muhan was standing behind a hedgerow, peeling an orange, and Rema headed toward him.

"Good morning, Muhan," she said in Ulat as she clasped her hands in welcome.

Muhan returned the gesture, his mustache bobbing as he smiled. "Rema. A fine morning to you. I'm curious, how many languages do you speak?"

"More than twenty. At a certain point, you stop counting them and just start speaking them."

Muhan stripped the orange and dropped the peel into the grass. "I wouldn't think your Emperor had need of any language but the sword."

"I first served his father."

"A different man. Of course, from the perspective of an Ulati, the difference was not so great. But measured in lakes of blood and mountains of skulls, well…" He bit into the orange, spraying juice, and his eyes crinkled. "A tremendous flavor. You can always trust a fruit named for its color."

Rema chuckled as her nerves eased. It was pleasant to hear a poetic language of the West spoken here in the East, where even the birdsong sounded less lyrical. "Is it true that you'll be holding a performance today?"

"Indeed. Yorin told me to be sure that I did it before this crown prince arrives. I gather he's not one for joy and wonder."

"I've heard nothing good about him." As she watched Muhan eating, Rema's stomach growled. She should have stolen more from the pantry. "By all accounts, he's a violent and unpleasant man."

"On the subject of unpleasant men," said Muhan, his voice wet with orange pulp, "there's someone else in the gardens with us. I greeted him and he gave me a look like something out of the grave."

"Oh?" So the time had finally come to meet this fabled apparition. "Where did you see him?"

"See that dark corner over there, where the trees tangle together into a little grove?" Muhan nodded toward it. "He slunk back into there. The gloominess suits him."

Rema stared at the sinister grove. It was impossible to see through the tightly-woven branches to determine if anyone was still inside. "I'm going to talk to him. If I don't come out, fetch the guards."

"You might ask him if he's interested in dye. Be sure he knows that I have every color under the sun!"

Rema laughed and crossed the garden to the knotted clump of trees. Their roots tore the earth and snaked together, and their close-knit branches formed gnarled walls. It would have been a perfect place for clandestine meetings if it weren't so obvious. She pushed aside the dark foliage and moved into the clearing.

A man stood among the trees, tearing at a hunk of jerky. His hood rested low against his shoulders, exposing a head of thin blond hair. "Good morning," said Rema.

The man lifted his face. His eyes had earned their fearsome reputation. They seemed too large for his face, and their swollen whites were stark: hungry, patient eyes, better suited to some scaled beast living in a shadowed crevice. Otherwise he appeared unremarkable. He was broad-shouldered, about Rema's height, and muscular. His face was broad and wide-jawed, and if not for his eyes he could even have been handsome.

"So you're the imperial diplomat." Instead of the monstrous rasp she'd expected, he spoke in a pleasant baritone. "Calan's in for a shock."

"My name is Rema." Rema took a step closer. "And your name is?"

"Look at you, creeping up like a mouse. Don't worry, though, I'm used to it. My name's Bannon."

As it appeared unlikely he planned to leap at her and drain her blood, Rema strode to stand before him. Up close, his eyes were even more unsettling. He rarely blinked, and it seemed as if he were looking through her. "You work for Calan, don't you?"

"That man has a lot of problems. Sensibly, he's employed me to handle them."

"Did you really kill children and put their heads on pikes?"

"You shouldn't listen to rumor." Bannon winked. "On the other hand, if the situation called for it..."

"So you don't deny that you're a butcher?"

"Why should I? Word is your Emperor staked two thousand men, women and children during the siege of Molon. We should be bosom companions, you and me."

Contempt constricted around Rema's heart. "We are nothing alike."

"True. For one, you're prettier." Bannon's smirk widened. "Tell me, diplomat, why are you talking to me if your heart quails from dark things?"

"You have a notorious reputation. I wanted to see if any of it was true."

Bannon glanced down at her body, but she saw little lust in his pallid eyes. "So you've heard all the stories, yet you still sauntered right up to me, that cocksure look on your face."

"I don't frighten easily."

"I can see that." Bannon tugged a string of meat from his teeth. "Take some advice from a man well-situated to give it. Wrap up this business and get on your way. You've come to the wrong place at the wrong time." He tossed the remaining jerky to the ground, pulled down his hood and pushed past her, moving with the measured balance of a practiced swordsman.

Rema stayed in the thick, shaded grove long enough to arrange her thoughts. She was interrupted by Muhan, who poked his lurid mustache through a gap in the branches and peered at her. "Rema. The Gods are generous. You're alive."

"So it seems."

"I saw him slink away like a satisfied spider and was concerned when you didn't emerge."

"Sorry. I needed time to think. He's an unsettling character."

"Surely you've met many in your time." Muhan clasped his hands. "I have to prepare for my show. It's in the banquet hall, if you hadn't heard. Will you be in attendance?"

"I'll do my best." Rema gestured in return, and Muhan departed, his colorful tunic streaming behind him.

What to make of this unnerving meeting? First Elise had given her a warning, and now Bannon. Could they be referring to the same threat? It was hard to imagine any connection between the white-eyed killer and the silver-eyed enchantress. Elise's parting plea still echoed in Rema's thoughts, accompanied by a deep and impossible desire to offer consolation. But when the price was a kingdom...

She took her time walking to the banquet hall, pausing to chat in the corridor with bored servant women. They griped about their work, their husbands and the antics of their children, and she returned half-formed advice that they clung to as if it were divinely inspired. The stories of their lives provided a welcome distraction from her worries, and by the time she arrived at the banquet hall, Rema had managed to put behind her the memories of Bannon's unearthly eyes and Elise's unhappy ones.

A small group of lucky servants sat on stools just inside the banquet hall. The ever-present Alys was among them. Yorin stood beside her, his arms folded. "I'm surprised," Rema said. "You're letting servants take time off?"

"It's a reward to those that have worked hard," said Yorin. "Save for Alys, who is a lazy little creature. She's only here because I know you're fond of her."

"Lucky Alys. I suppose you want me to repay you with more paperwork."

Yorin ran his fingers over his face, disarranging the leathery folds under his eyes. "Don't say that accursed word. I feel I need to be sanctified every time I hear it."

Rema turned her attention to the banquet hall. At its far end was a wooden stage meant for entertainers. Muhan busied himself upon it, arranging boxes and erecting colored banners. Cedrin and Talitha sat together at one of the banquet tables, and Loric hunched before a table closer to the stage, his head resting on his fists. Elise, however, was nowhere to be seen. The fact caused Rema pain, but why? Why did that absence disappoint so deeply?

She crossed the hall and tapped Loric on the shoulder. He raised his head and smiled. "This should be fun," he said. "He juggles and conjures, apparently."

"Is Elsie not coming?"

"I wanted her to, but she wouldn't. She said she didn't need to see fake magic, and also that she had a headache, and also that conjuring was childish. In other words, she thought you might be here, and she can't handle seeing you right now."

"It's that bad?"

"You can't imagine." Loric lowered his voice to a whisper. "Late last night, she knocked on my door, choked with tears. I'd never seen her weep that way before. She kept telling me how she'd made a fool of herself again. She was so heartbroken that it was all I could do to keep from crying myself."

So Rema's necessary cruelty had reaped its harvest. She avoided Loric's reproachful stare. "Is it likely Calan will hurt her while he's here?"

"He hurts her whenever he feels like it. She should put a spell on the bastard."

"Why doesn't she?"

"She says that whenever a hex is cast, it hurts the wrong people. Rema, I don't understand why you're being so cold. She's starved for any indication of affection from you."

"If you could understand how much remorse I feel…"

"I'm sorry. I know she's being absurd. You've only been here a few days and she expects you to love her, when no doubt you already have some lover of your own back in glorious Arann. Yet I still wish you'd go to her. She's been lonely for so long. Perhaps you should tell her what Ormun did to you. It might help her understand."

"It's better that she doesn't know. And promise me that you won't tell her. After all, she might end up married to this man."

Loric closed his eyes. "Right."

Muhan clapped his hands, interrupting the conversations all about the room. "My royal majesties! Princes of the court, ambassadors from distant lands and noble servants of the realm! What you are about to see will amaze you unto the tenth generation." He began to pull a chain of ribbons from his sleeve, each one tied to the last and each a different color. By the time the fiftieth ribbon had emerged, even Rema was thrilled.

Muhan finished extracting the immense ribbon and flicked his wrist, sending its colorful tail high above his head. "Every color known to man is here. When they gather, they impart a mysterious power to their owner. Theirs is a magic known only to masters of the ancient art of color, like myself." He flicked the ribbons again and they unknotted, falling about his head in a drifting chromatic rain. The servants broke into applause, and Cedrin thumped his fist in appreciation.

"Now, behold!" Muhan took a ribbon from the ground. With a subtle movement of his hand, he wrapped it into a ball. He tossed the ball in the air, picked up a second ribbon and similarly balled it, and caught the first ball before it hit the ground. In this way, he began to juggle and fold the ribbons until he had no less than twenty such balls soaring above him, forming a dazzling arc of colors. The servants applauded again, and Cedrin hollered a throaty bravo. Affection touched Rema's heart as she noticed Loric leaning forward, enrapt as a child.

The ribbons fell with a light patter to Muhan's feet. He tugged on his mustache, winked and lifted his hands in fists. He opened his right hand to reveal a dove with red wings, which flew to the ceiling and perched on a beam. His left hand opened, and a blue-winged dove rose to join it. Rema clapped with the others. When had he performed that sleight of hand? His craft was excellent, worthy of a palace performer.

Rema looked over her shoulder, curious to know if Alys was enjoying herself, only to see Elise standing in the doorway. As their gazes met, Rema shivered. It would have been best to turn away, pretend not to notice, but Elise seemed so solemn, so sad…

Impelled by a surge of desires—to show affection, to demonstrate courage, to be forgiven—Rema held Elise's eyes as she blew a kiss, a warm whisper of air across her fingertips. Elise blushed and grasped the doorframe, looking as disoriented if she had been physically struck.

"You're missing the finale," said Loric. Rema spun, reeling from the realization of her own folly, to find that Muhan had revealed a box containing a monkey.

"Where did he find the monkey?" she said. Loric hushed her.

Muhan draped a multicolored patchwork blanket over the monkey's cage. He bowed three times, pulled on both ends of his mustache and whipped the blanket away. The monkey had vanished. The servants gasped, and Alys cried, "That poor creature!"

Shaking his head at the audience, Muhan flipped the blanket with a twist of his wrist and draped it again over the box. He bowed as before and lifted the blanket, revealing the monkey again. This time, however, its fur was dyed bright green. It glared at the audience, obviously unhappy to be part of the act.

The applause broke Rema's spell, and she turned in her seat. The doorway was empty. Rema hurried from the hall. A survey of the corridor confirmed the unhappy truth—Elise was gone. Rema stared into the distance, her thoughts incoherent and her heart unsteady, until a hand touched her shoulder and she gasped.

"Sorry!" said Loric, withdrawing his hand. "What's got you so nervous?"

"Elsie was…" Damn it all, she was falling to pieces. With effort, Rema regained her usual poise. "Your sister was watching the performance from back here."

"Really? I knew she couldn't resist a show. How do you think he does it?"

"I don't know, but I wouldn't want to be one of his stage animals." Rema glanced through the door toward the stage, where Muhan was accepting the applause with grace. "I'm glad his show went well. Your father seemed delighted, though your mother's expression never changed."

"She's amused. If she hadn't been, she would have left." Loric's smile became rueful. "It was good to have fun while we could. Soon Calan will be here, and we won't be laughing for quite some time. It's so nasty and dispiriting when he's about. I'm glad that all I have to do is sit around, read books, and drink wine; it distracts me from the horrors. And I know how feeble that makes me sound."

"You're far from feeble, Loric Danarian. Your passion in defense of your sister is rarer than you realize, as is the respect you show for the movings of her heart. Calan may be a fiend, but in you she has been blessed with a brother beyond all others. Hold yourself with pride."

Loric reddened and stared at his hands. He seemed about to respond when they were interrupted by the distant sound of a trumpet. "Speak of the devil. He's here."

Yorin joined them in the corridor, his face agitated. "Already! And why does he insist on announcing himself with those ridiculous trumpets? They frighten the horses. You lot in there!" He waved at the servants inside the hall. "Come on! One last check of the Prince's room!" The servants hurried past, the memory of the performance still radiant on their faces.

"Cheer up, lad." Yorin patted Loric on the back. "Let's go see your brother home. With any luck, he won't stay long."

"If luck were with us, he would be dead." Loric spoke with a savagery unsettling in such a gentle young man. "And even the worms would have better sense than to touch him. Yorin, if he lays a finger upon her…"

"I know." Yorin seemed to have aged into infirmity, and as he drew his robes around him, he fixed Rema with a look of immeasurable weariness. "You were curious about our eldest prince. Well, you'll not have to wait long now to see the measure of him. I only pray that he is able to see the measure of you."

CHAPTER NINE

A trumpet blared again, and Yorin pressed his hands to his ears. "God help us," he said as he, Loric and Rema hurried through the archway to the front court.

The peasants had been driven from the court, presumably by the two rows of guards who flanked the room at either side. They stood at attention as a man on a stallion rode through the open doors and into the court. A ragged soldier ran beside him, holding the dreaded instrument. He lifted it toward his lips, and Yorin cursed. "Someone ought to arrest that man." The note blew again, toneless and shrill.

Calan pulled his reins, and the animal whinnied in protest. It seemed that the character of each royal sibling was reflected in the subtle variations of their silver eyes: Elise's smoldered with temper, Loric's were soft with melancholy and Calan's were cold with arrogance. His dark hair was tamed close to his scalp, and he had the same tender lips and rounded features as his brother and sister. His nose was his mother's, broad along the bridge and upturned at the tip. Rema couldn't have thought him less handsome if his head were a mass of boils.

"This is a meager welcoming party," Calan said. "A threadbare steward, my fop of a brother and..." He stared at Rema. "What exactly are you?"

"This is the imperial diplomat, my lord," said Yorin. He held Rema's wrist, and she shifted uneasily. Apparently he wanted to guide the conversation.

"Truly?" Calan leaned over his saddle and scrutinized Rema. "But it's either a woman or the most absurd dandy I've ever seen."

"She is a woman, my lord. Her name is Remela."

Calan tugged on his horse's reins, causing the animal to snuff in irritation. "Just what this court needs. Another woman pretending to be a man."

"Better than a beast pretending to be a man." Elise's voice rang resonant and high, and every head turned toward her. She stood midway down the stairs with her hands on her hips, her hair wild and her eyes aflame with silver fury. Her black dress uncovered both shoulders and was slit on either leg, and as she descended, it moved to expose her considerable thighs. Rema drew a soft intake of breath—now this was beauty.

"Oh, sister," said Calan. "You know how I hate you wearing those sluttish dresses. We don't need to see your flabby body."

"The more you try to cover me, brother, the less I'll wear." Elise took another step, her head held high. "Perhaps one day you'll learn not to be frightened by female flesh."

"Perhaps one day you'll understand when a woman ought to speak." Calan was poor at hiding his emotions; he wanted to appear as if he were enjoying the contest with his sister, but irritation was evident in his narrow eyes and the twitching of his lips.

"So boast to us of your triumphs. I assume you slew plenty of dangerous infants and grandmothers. We're all so proud of your courage."

"If the war offends your sensibilities, you should use your magic to end it. Or perhaps you should return to the only thing you're good for and mix me a cream for my blisters."

"It's you that offends my sensibilities, Calan." Elise sniffed. "I notice your horse is fouling the courtyard. It seems you still enjoy spreading excrement through the palace, just as you did as a child."

Talitha's irate voice cut through the tension. "Enough, please," she said, moving into the court with Cedrin lumbering at her side. "Calan, must you bring that animal in here?"

"It's not my fault," said Calan. "She came down the stairs by herself."

"I expect you to show Elise her due respect."

"Oh, but I have." Calan's chuckle was deep and satisfied. "And there you are, Father, looking rounder than ever." He offered the King a mock salute, and Rema's blood chilled. An ambitious heir with no love for his parents was a dangerous thing, as she knew too well.

Calan dismounted, his boots colliding heavily with the flagstones. "Somebody take this horse away." He lifted a finger toward the guards. "And somebody else clean away this filth."

"There's no cleaning away your filth," said Elise. "You contaminate the air you breathe."

"I do believe I heard the horse whinny." Calan joined Cedrin and Talitha, looming over his bent parents by a full head. "My majestic parents. Tell me, has little Loric lost the power of speech? He's not even said hello."

Elise descended the stairs and put her arm around Loric, whose face was pinched in silent misery. "He knows better than to waste breath on you."

Calan laughed. "He needs his sister to stand up for him! Elise is more man than you, brother. But that's no surprise, given that she's fucked more women."

Talitha gasped, and her face flared crimson. "Calan, enough," said Cedrin, putting his hand on Calan's shoulder. "Tell me how the war goes."

"Things are on the mend." Calan tilted his head, arrogance written on his every feature. "We're outnumbered, true, but the Lyornans have become complacent. Like the rest of you, they foolishly assume victory is theirs. This week we gave them a few bloody wounds, reminding them that Danosha still has her claws."

"You mean you've been razing villages," said Elise. "Murdering travelers and torturing peasants."

"And what have you been doing for our family?" Calan's lips spread in a leer. "When they write the history of our triumph, historians will note that Calan fought and won the war while Elise was busy licking cunts."

"Calan!" Talitha glanced at Rema, shame hot in her eyes. "Not here!"

Elise walked up to her brother, her face charged with tightly-wielded fury. Calan towered above her in height, yet in her awe-inspiring indignation, Elise entirely overshadowed him. "Historians will note a monster," she said. "They will describe a man who shamed a kingdom with his atrocities. History will condemn you, Calan, and until then I shall condemn you, as everyone else here is too afraid to do."

Rema stared as if enchanted. Elise was sublime, fearless in her conviction, tempestuous in her outrage and defiant in her femininity. Rema had once challenged Ormun with as much spirit, decrying his excesses, challenging his cruelties and begging him to fight his growing darkness. The more she had been forced to comply with his will, the lower that torch of defiance had burned, until she barely felt it wavering. Watching Elise now, that old fire rekindled in Rema's heart—along with something more.

"Histories are written by men," said Calan. "Not whimpering women."

"I knew my letters at four years. I'm not convinced you can write even now."

"But I'd wager I claimed my first maidenhead sooner. How old were you when we first caught you rutting? Fifteen? Sixteen? The girl was older, I remember that much."

"You always come back to that, don't you?" Elise's eyes remained steady and unashamed, and Rema's cheeks heated. "You're so predictable when you're outmatched. First, you mock me for being a woman. Then you insult me for loving women—yes, Father, turn purple. I don't care who knows it. Finally you beat me until I can taste my own blood." Her lips twisted bitterly. "That part will escape the histories, for as you so rightly point out, they are written by men."

"Elise," said Cedrin, his voice harsh. "Do not speak of such things before the Emperor's emissary. Your personal shame belongs behind these walls."

Elise gazed at Rema as if challenging her to speak. Rema opened her mouth, and Yorin's hand tightened on her arm. Ah, yes—that little thing called diplomatic tact, an art she had once known so well. She remained silent, and Elise's lips trembled.

"All I want to do is love, and all he wants to do is hate," Elise said, her voice catching with emotion. "Yet you all think me the abomination." She turned and began to ascend the stairs.

Shame writhed through Rema's stomach, and she blinked away tears. As Elise reached the final step, Calan called out to her, his tone triumphant. "I'll have to pass by your room later. We have a lot of catching up to do." Elise paused, and her hand tightened on the balustrade. She flung back her hair and disappeared from sight.

"You can all go to hell," said Loric, and he followed his sister up the stairs. Yorin bowed his head, while the Queen and King stayed silent.

"Well, enough of this sideshow," said Calan, seemingly unaffected by the trouble he'd caused. "I must apprise you of the current situation, Father."

"Yes." Cedrin spoke as if his thoughts were returning to him from a distance. "And we must bring the imperial diplomat to talk with us. She has strategic information regarding the Emperor's contribution."

"Just be sure she doesn't try to arm my warriors with knitting needles."

"They could hardly fight more badly than they do now," said Rema. "Perhaps it would be an improvement."

Yorin's hand slipped from Rema's arm. "It speaks," said Calan, not turning to look at her. "And with a touch of venom. Not very diplomatic, but certainly very female."

"Not diplomatic? On the contrary. I held my tongue while you made a fool of yourself in front of this court."

Calan inclined his head in Rema's direction. "Is there a purpose to your interruption?"

"I'd like to talk to you. Privately."

"I'm sure you'd love to have me all to yourself." Calan surveyed the unsmiling faces around him and sighed. "God, I forgot what prigs you all are. Yes, fine. Let's get it out of the way so that I can have something to eat. Yorin, take us to my chambers."

"Yes, my lord." Yorin looked to Cedrin, who nodded, and Talitha, who looked away. Surely the Queen was mortified by the display between Elise and Calan, but Rema had no sympathy for her. Talitha had been so righteous in her condemnation of Ormun, yet had said nothing as her own son treated Elise with contempt…just as Rema herself had said nothing. Shame flooded her again, turning her stomach and tightening her throat.

Yorin directed Rema and Calan to the prince's chamber. Calan brushed past the steward without a word, his boots tracking mud onto the stone floor. As Rema made to follow him, Yorin caught her arm. "I'll be right outside. Don't test him." Rema nodded, and he released her. She stepped into the chamber and shut the door behind her.

Calan folded his arms and gave Rema a long examination. A trace of interest entered his cold eyes. "A woman with a man's job and a man's uniform. It's obscene, if you ask me."

"I didn't."

Calan's nostrils widened as he inhaled a quick breath. "I should warn you, I'm not used to women speaking to me in this way."

"I'm not surprised you're unused to women. A man like you is ever one of two things: a virgin or a rapist."

Calan's eyes showed as much surprise as if Rema had slapped him. "You're a sharp-tongued bitch, aren't you? I suppose that's how you try to compete with men."

"I wouldn't lower myself to compete with you."

"Get to your point."

"If you touch Elise again, the deal between you and the Emperor is over. Ormun wouldn't appreciate you beating his future wife."

"No doubt. Why deprive him of the fun of doing it himself?"

Rema flinched, and Calan's eyes lit. Damn it, he'd caught her off guard. "What else have you done to her?"

"I've never tried to fuck her, if that's what you mean. She disgusts me, the fat, mewling bitch." Calan moved closer to Rema, and she stepped back from the heat of his breath. "You, though. I've never had a woman in trousers."

"You've never been drawn and quartered either. Do I need to explain to you the concept of diplomatic immunity?"

He laughed, and she cringed as his spit flecked her cheek. "You vastly overestimate your position. Let me explain something to you. My parents are feeble, and my brother may as well have never been born. I am the power and authority here. Forget whatever deals you thought you'd struck in my absence. The man of the house has returned."

"Boast all you like. You're still losing your war."

"I'd like your Emperor's troops as much as any general would. I also want to be rid of my sister as much as any man would. But where you and I diverge, little diplomat, is your interpretation of the state of affairs." Calan leaned close enough that Rema was able to see the dark pores scattered upon his nose. "You believe I'm going to lose this war without help. So does my father, Yorin, everyone else. I know otherwise. I'm going to win it with or without you. The difference is only the quantity of blood spilt."

"What you believe is irrelevant. Your father already agreed to my terms."

"Did my mother agree? No? Then you have nothing." Calan sneered. "My father is a weakling who allows his woman to jointly rule. For once, that absurdity works in my favor. He remains free to change his mind as I see fit." He gestured dismissively. "You can leave now. When you join us later to pretend you understand the ways of war, I'll explain to you and my father what exactly is going to happen next."

Nobody dismissed her in such a fashion, least of all this cretin. Rema remained standing, her arms folded. "You're more foolish than I thought. We know the size of your army relative to your enemy. Not even Ormun himself could overcome such odds."

"Then Ormun is softer than I imagined. You're dismissed. Run off and console my sister if you want." Calan's smug smile became a leer. "Yes, I saw the way you were looking at her. I wonder what your master would make of that?"

Taken aback by the mention of Elise, Rema struggled to find a rejoinder. "Until we next meet," she said, and she closed the door on his laughter.

That had gone poorly, to say the least. Though she'd outwitted far shrewder men than Calan, she was distracted by the question gathering in her soul, one she was afraid to answer. To defeat this foolish prince, she would have to betray a woman who echoed every chord and matched every sentiment in her own heart. Gods, how she wanted to run to Elise and bask in the heat of her ardor, to confess to weakness and find passionate redemption...

"Rema," said Yorin. In her daze, she had forgotten he had been waiting in the corridor. "Are you listening?"

"I'm sorry." Rema pressed her fingers to her temples. "I wasn't at my best. He thinks he's winning the war and wants to conquer Lyorn, not come to terms with them."

Yorin glared at the door before taking Rema's arm and leading her further down the corridor. "If that's so, then who knows what madness he has in mind. I wouldn't be surprised if Calan never wants this war to end. He's reveled in the bloodshed ever since it began."

Rema smiled wryly. "I suppose approaching the Queen is bad idea right now."

"She'd be furious. Humiliated too. Angry at Calan and ashamed of Elise."

"And what about you? Are you ashamed of her?"

Yorin shook his head. "I'm an ordinary man with a wife and two sons. I go to our local church, for the good it does me. I know the prejudices I'm expected to hold. But Rema, I helped raise that girl. We may fight because of her damned temper, but she's grown into a brave and honest woman. She deserves to love as she wills." He sighed. "It hurts me to see her plight, I assure you. Nothing in this court goes unseen by me, but unbeknownst to her, whenever she gets entangled with some servant woman, I do my best to keep their union hidden. Her father always finds out eventually, but never from me."

Rema looked at him with a new appreciation. "Talk to Talitha for me, Yorin. Persuade her that after today she has no choice but to let Elise go."

"A clever thought." Yorin rested his hand on her shoulder. "You're not the confident woman you were when you arrived. Do you know why I stopped you there in the court, when you were about to speak up in her defense?"

"Because you didn't want me to offend anyone."

"No. Because you would have betrayed the secret that's clear already to those watching you closely."

Rema lowered her eyes. How could she deny his implication when her tongue would surely stumble on the falsehood?

"The King and Queen are inattentive. I'm not, and neither is Calan. You need to take your mind off her. Go have lunch. Muhan is taking lunch in the main kitchen, and if you hurry, you might catch him."

"Thank you." Rema pressed Yorin's wrinkled hand between both of her own. He shrugged his shoulders before stumbling down the corridor, hunched in thought.

The front court proved to be abandoned but for a servant woman on her hands and knees, scraping manure from the flagstones. As Rema strode toward the kitchen, she heard the sound of feet running and turned to see Alys rushing closer, flapping her small arms.

"Rema!" Alys wobbled to a sudden halt. "I have a letter from the lady Elise for you. Gosh! I ran so fast!" She shoved an envelope into Rema's hand and stood bent and panting.

"Thank you, Alys," said Rema. Alys gave her an exhausted smile, spun on her feet and ran off the way she'd come.

Rema opened the envelope where she stood. Elise's handwriting was as endearingly eccentric as before.

> *R. You are cruel. When you blew me that kiss in the banquet hall, I dared to hope...but then you abandoned me to Calan and my father. Despite everything, I still want so badly to believe that you're here to save me. You're a torment, R, an intoxicating torment. I hate you. Helplessly yours, E.*

Elise had ended the letter with a scarlet kiss, the pigment of her adorned lips pressed against the page in a full pout. Rema closed her eyes and pressed the letter to her chest. How could Elise expect her to abandon a diplomatic career that had spanned thirteen years and saved countless lives, all for the sake of a woman she didn't know? Yet Elise's frustration was sensible. After a lifetime of fighting for independence, she was doomed now to suffering submission, and to make matters worse, Rema had brought hope even as she delivered catastrophe.

She had consigned Elise to darkness while showing her a glimpse of impossible, unexpected light.

Rema put the letter in her coat pocket and walked blindly into the dining area. Muhan sat at a table, slicing into a pie. "Good afternoon, Rema," he said in Ulat. "Did you enjoy my performance?"

Rema managed to return his smile. Muhan was the only person in the palace who pronounced her name with the proper trill on the *r*, and trivial though it was, the effect evoked the memory of her home and the friends who awaited her there. Some of her anxiety departed, though her heart still trembled. "I felt sorry for your monkey. Or monkeys, as I suppose there must have been two."

Muhan pressed a finger to his lips. "Some secrets must remain so."

"So tell me. Are you a dye merchant or a conjuror?"

"There's little difference." Muhan impaled the pie with his fork, and purple juice oozed from its sides. "To sell dye is to sell a spectacle. Wherever I travel, I try to impress upon people the wonder that is living color. When I do, they are suddenly more inclined to purchase my wares." He winked. "You see, dye is not in itself a particularly useful thing. You won't be warmer in winter if your coat is red instead of white. But you may feel so if you come to believe that red means warmth."

"I've always liked you dye traders. You're an odd breed." Rema eyed a berry as it slid from his pie. "My parents were traders too. My father dealt in incense, but he was more interested in his poetry. I remember how as a child I'd fall asleep amid a haze of oak and velvet scents, listening to him reading poems aloud by lamplight."

"And your mother?"

"She had a merchant's blood. She adored haggling and making money, and she'd trade in most anything. She drew the line at slaves, but she did once get the notion to trade bears. That almost ended very badly."

"Perhaps it's a coincidence." Muhan stared into the distance, his brown eyes thoughtful. "I once stopped at a trade encampment somewhere in the north of Amantis. The plains were wide and the distant mountains broken. There I met a poet who smelt of roses and smoke. He sold incense, and he spoke often of a wife whom I never met." Muhan nodded. "Yes, a strange man. He was one of those poets who never break from their poetry even in daily speech."

Rema inhaled a wondering breath. Of all the chances..."That could have been him. My father was Ajulese. I take after him in my complexion and features."

"I can't remember his face very well." Muhan shrugged. "Perhaps he was Ajulese."

A warm, pleasant sensation spread through Rema's chest as her thoughts turned to her parents. "I loved them both intensely. I left them when I was fifteen, seeking to make my fortune in Arann, and they never questioned my decision. I only saw them four times more afterward. Three years ago, I learned that they'd died of the plague while traveling through Urandal. They were buried in each other's arms, just as they had always lived. I've never known two people more in love."

Muhan's face softened. "Go find some food. I'll wait here."

After giving Muhan a grateful nod, Rema went to the pantry and procured a wedge of cheese, a small pot of strawberry jam and a thick-crusted loaf. She returned to her seat and spread her bounty in front of her. "Will you be leaving us soon?" she asked as she sawed at her bread.

"Surprisingly, I have been asked to stay another night. Our young prince was so impressed that he insisted on seeing the performance again. I suspect he wishes to figure out how it was done."

Rema laughed. How enthralled Loric had been by that performance. "And have you sold much dye?"

"The people here can hardly afford my dye. It almost makes me feel guilty about taking their custom. But what merchant can refuse money?"

Rema watched his face as he talked. His flat, dark cheeks were deeply seamed, and the corners of his mouth were dimpled, giving him a perpetual expression of dry humor. It was reassuring to know that he would be staying in the palace longer. Their conversations in Ulat reminded her of Amantis, the great western continent to which she had been born, and the city of Arann, her home and a place of diverse traditions. How she hated Ostermund, this eastern patchwork of arrogant little feudal kingdoms, each incapable of expressing more than a single idea: one skin, one language, one angry god. She longed to wander between the tall and uneven stalls of Arann's marketplaces, to smell the sweetness of the palms, to sit in a circle of friends and eat rice from her hands, to look over the endless summer sea…

"I know those eyes," said Muhan. "I suppose even diplomats can become homesick. Tell me, is there a man awaiting you in Arann? A husband or a lover?"

Rema licked jam from her lips. "Not quite. My best friend will be missing me, and the gods know my heart yearns for her. We share everything, including our beds. She's a sweet, playful woman, a singer with a voice that angels envy."

Muhan's mustache twitched. "How interesting." He dabbed juice from his lips. "I must confess to being at a loss for words."

"I've been encountering that feeling myself. It's far from pleasant." Rema tested the corner of the cheese and grimaced as its thick skin resisted her teeth.

"I'm curious. A woman watched my performance from the doorway. Am I correct she was the princess you have come to abduct for Ormun? She had pale grey eyes and dark hair, the look so characteristic of this family."

"I never told you the purpose of my mission. You're as wantonly investigative as I am."

Muhan flashed his painted teeth. "You're not the only one who can charm servants, o great mouth of the Emperor."

"Yes, that was her. Elise."

"I noticed the little moment between you two. A look, a blown kiss. I would think a skilled diplomat might know better than to grow close to the woman she is supposed to wrap up and deliver to her master."

"I'm confident I can bring peace to this kingdom." Despite her training, Rema's voice betrayed a touch of nervousness.

Muhan fixed her with his compassionate gaze. "If you find yourself in need of a friend, remember me." He stood and clasped his hands. "Enjoy the rest of your meal. Perhaps my stay here will become longer still. In dark times people seek the presence of bright things, and who in this world is brighter than I?"

He left, his tread soundless on the stones. Rema finished her cheese and rested her head on her arms, staring at the stone wall. A spider trundled along a gap in the bricks, its legs feeling ahead with each step. Rema watched it until it tugged itself into a small hole in the masonry.

She would have to deal with Calan again that afternoon, and her insides slickened with apprehension at the thought. Something dark and bloody was unfolding in the court of Danosha, and at its center were Calan and that dead-eyed henchman of his. Yet there was unexpected beauty here too—the loyalty of Loric, the passion of Elise, the kindness of Yorin. In dark times, Muhan had said… but there was still light aplenty, and she would not allow such torches to be extinguished beneath the shadow of one man.

CHAPTER TEN

Rema stared at an immense battle-ax hanging on the wall. There were numerous deep notches in its blade, and it was a matter of guesswork as to whether they were from battle or from felling trees. As she turned to continue on her way, she spotted three tall figures moving in her direction—Domyr, the Narandane diplomat, and two of his servants.

"Good morning," she said, and Domyr paused in his march, his heavy brow lowering.

"We have not been properly introduced." His lips seemed incapable of forming anything other than a scowl. "I am Lord Domyr, ambassador to King Nazar Narandan."

"I'm Rema, ambassador to Ormun, of whom you may have heard." If the comment amused him, his face betrayed no trace of it. "Did your audience with King Cedrin go well?"

"From my point of view, yes. May I ask why you are here?"

He already knew why, but diplomats enjoyed their little games. "The Emperor wishes to assist Danosha in their war. I assume you've something similar in mind."

"I cannot say. I trust your own audiences with the King and Queen have been favorable."

"The situation is complicated." Rema made a noncommittal gesture. "Have you met the older prince? Calan? He's back today."

Domyr shook his head. "Should I?"

"If his boasts are to be believed."

"I will take it under consideration."

"If you care to bring the Empire in on your plans, feel free to do so." Rema peered into his black eyes, but there was no deciphering the thought in them. "If we both want to help these people, then we should do it together."

Domyr inclined his head. "Perhaps. Good day."

It was tempting to surreptitiously follow Domyr down the corridor, but she was a diplomat, not a spy. She returned instead to her stroll. She turned two corners, passed by a display case containing cheap gemstones, moved beneath a heavy archway and stopped short at the sight of Yorin bustling in her direction, his hands in his sleeves.

"There you are," he said. "His grace and Calan want to see you in the war room. It's an absurd room, just a table with some tiny iron soldiers and horses on it."

"Noblemen and their tiny iron soldiers. Will you take me there?"

Yorin nodded. He led her to the upper floor of the palace, navigating the maze of halls with the directness of someone who knew its every intersection, and into a hallway that ended in a large, half-open door. The voices of Calan and Cedrin were audible behind it.

"Good luck," said Yorin. "Don't let Calan get the better of you."

The war room was a wide, dust-choked space dominated by a single large table. A window on one wall permitted the waning afternoon light. Several faded charts hung on the walls, and a broad map of the continent lay spread across the table. Cedrin was hunched over the map, scrutinizing an arrangement of metal soldiers, while Calan lounged against a nearby support beam. He noticed Rema's entrance and grunted. "It's here," he said. "Finally, we can begin."

Rema adopted a pose of neutrality, drawing her feet together and resting her arms at her sides. "Your Grace, do you usually permit your son to be so impolite toward foreign dignitaries?"

Cedrin flushed and rubbed his forehead with his fist. "Yes, Calan, please. At least have the decency to call her by name."

"And what was its name again?"

"Remela," said Rema. "Not too many syllables for you, I hope."

"Very cute. I'll try to talk slowly so that you can keep up."

"Enough." Cedrin lifted his tired face to frown at his son. "She is an honored guest."

Calan marched to the door and kicked it shut. "Oh, spare me. Let's get to business. Remela, my father is old and absentminded. He accidentally accepted your terms when we both know that they need amending."

"You were fortunate to receive the terms you did," said Rema. "Ormun is pulling you out of a fire. Would you rather be left to burn?"

"Shut up until I'm done talking. Your proposal is that you'll give us troops and resources in exchange for two things. One is my sister. Fine, take the bitch. The other is that we agree not to regain any more land than we have already lost. In short, you want us to fight to a pointless stalemate." Calan bared his teeth. "In short, we gain nothing."

Rema stared at him. What manner of idiot had the royalty of Danosha brought into the world? "Peace is not nothing."

As Rema spoke, Cedrin's attention moved nervously between her and Calan. If this was any indication of his usual timidity before his son, serious trouble lay ahead.

"Here's what we'll do," said Calan. "We'll split Lyorn in two. We'll take the south and Ormun can have everything else. Isn't that what war is for? Conquest? Surely the Emperor would leap at the chance to command yet another plot of bloody soil."

"Ormun doesn't need Lyorn." Rema didn't keep the scorn from her voice. "How would he possibly hold it?"

"He holds many far-flung provinces. Don't be obtuse. Ormun could leave a standing army strong enough to repel any of Lyorn's neighbors. Do you really think Dantium or Kalanis are going to risk their necks against the Emperor of the Pale Plains?"

"You seem willing to, and you've far less at your disposal than either of those realms."

Calan gave Rema a look of focused contempt. "Those are our new terms, Diplomat. Accept them or leave."

"So let me be clear. You want Ormun to not only win a war for you but to give you half a kingdom. In return, you give him Elise."

"Isn't she worth it? She might be repulsive, but she's got an ample body. I'm sure Ormun will have many happy nights curing her perversion."

"Calan," said Cedrin without a trace of strength or authority. "Don't speak of your sister that way."

Calan spat on the stone floor. "I extend to her the same respect she shows me. Why do you indulge her? She's done nothing for us. She refuses to accept marriage, her natural lot in life. Instead she plays at being some kind of wizard and exhibits male appetites. She's an aberration."

"Your sister is confused on some matters, I'll grant you. But she's a valued advisor, and I wish you'd show her more respect."

"Leave Elise out of this," said Rema. "Calan's proposal is unacceptable. We're here to help you end this war, not to let you run rampant over this continent."

Calan gave a sharp laugh. "If you won't accept my terms, then we don't need your help. Isn't that so, Father?"

"Don't be rash," said Cedrin. "Those troops would be invaluable, Calan. And food is so scarce. Think of the lives we'll lose otherwise…"

"Think of the future we will gain!" Calan clenched his fist as an intensity of passion animated his face. "The only way for us to expand is north, through Lyorn's fattened belly. Peace? I call it impotence!"

Rema lifted one of the iron soldiers between her thumb and forefinger. "You have an army of five thousand. Perhaps less. Ormun will send you twenty thousand across the Sea of Red Winds. When your provinces are regained and Lyorn comes to the table, our soldiers will return, leaving not a single one behind."

"We will regain our mediocrity, and nothing more."

"You will keep your lives." Rema dropped the soldier to the table, and it landed upon its base. "The sooner you accept the offer, the sooner our troops will be here. If you agree now, I will return to Arann in three weeks to seal the agreement. The Minister of War is a friend of mine, and I can hurry the paperwork." She flicked away her bangs and stared into Cedrin's uncertain eyes. "Your Grace, in less than two months from now this war can be turned in your favor. In three, I predict it will be over and your soldiers returned to their families."

Cedrin stroked his chin. "These are hopeful tidings, Calan."

"Hopeful!" Calan struck his fist on the table, sending soldiers clattering. "And what will come of it if we march to our old borders and no farther? When these soldiers return home, Lyorn will strike again. Unless we bring our enemy to its knees, we will remain as weak as ever, a lamb among lions." His voice rose. "You will regret these terms, Father, and I will inherit nothing but ashes."

"You poor boy," said Rema. "You'd almost think you were the one being married to the Emperor, the way you whine."

"You're so softhearted for that whore. Not surprising, given the deficiency of your sex." Calan's tone harshened into a growl. "Consider this, Diplomat, if you so love peacemaking. If you don't help us win the war, I'll win it my way. Through death and blood. We'll crown ourselves in gore, and there won't be much to be said for innocence."

"Do you truly think Ormun, the Terror of Amantis, is deterred by promises of savagery from a mere pup?"

"No. But I think you are. You have the authority to negotiate, so negotiate. It doesn't have to even be half of Lyorn. Just some of their holdings. Enough to give us the edge. Enough to make this war worth fighting."

"Worth fighting? I've met many men like you, Calan Danarian. You crave war because on the battlefield, you can pretend that self-worth is measured by the number of lives you've ended. The tyrant in his castle is a hero on the field. In peacetime, however, people see your violence for what it really is."

"My lady," said Cedrin in a tremulous voice. "I might ask you also to temper your tongue. He is my heir and a prince of my blood."

"He is an idiot and a bully, and I won't negotiate with him any further." As Rema's tone hardened, Cedrin blanched and clutched his gown. He showed no trace of the authority he'd tried to wield over her in the throne room; in this match of wills, he was merely a bystander. "I came to negotiate with you, not your incompetent heir. The Empire of the Pale Plains does not deal with children waiting in the wings but with rightful rulers. This kingdom belongs to you and your wife. What is her position?"

"Her position is unclear."

"Then perhaps she should be present at the next meeting. Otherwise our time is only being wasted." Rema and Calan glared at each other, and a tight, angry vein writhed at his temple. "You know where I stand, Your Grace. You have my original terms or you have nothing. No ships, no soldiers, no supplies and no chance of victory. I serve a conqueror, and I can assure you that your son is no conqueror."

Calan's grimace exposed the fleshy darkness of his gums, but for once, he offered no rejoinder.

"He'd have you believe he's an expert on warfare," said Rema. "In truth, he's fought one war and he's losing it, whereas I have seen and concluded conflicts beyond count. Regardless of what the prince tells you after I have left this room, my words will remain wise and true, and his will remain impulsive and dangerous."

Cedrin remained as mute as the tin soldiers before him. "Enough," said Calan. "You've made yourself clear, so now leave us be. If you think my father will listen to you over his own son, you're stupider than I thought."

"If you think your father will take the advice of a belligerent whelp over that of the most decorated diplomat to serve the greatest empire the world has ever known, then you're the fool." Rema bowed to Cedrin. "Good day, Your Grace." Even after she closed the door behind her, she fancied she could still feel Calan's gaze on her back, hot with anger and suppressed violence.

Yorin was waiting further down the corridor, organizing a group of servants to clean mold from the brickwork. He scurried toward Rema, leaving the servants in undirected confusion. "Well? What happened?"

"Calan won't accept our terms unless we agree to let Danosha run roughshod over Lyorn. How can I accept that? Not only is it not in the interests of the Empire, but it means more death and suffering."

"The arrogant fool. Did the King listen to him or you?"

"I expressed myself forcefully. Whether he will listen, who can say?"

"I'll work on his grace, try to counteract some of Calan's poison. The King is timid in the presence of his son, but in private he'll come around to your way of thinking."

"I hope so." Rema blew out an unhappy breath. "But what if none of it matters? Calan doesn't seem the type to abide his parents' decisions."

"You think he'd make a move on the throne?" Yorin gnawed on his lower lip. "Yes, it's crossed my mind. He's acted like the lord of the court ever since the war began. He has a private killer installed right here in the palace."

"That man's name is Bannon, by the way." The day's emotion lay heavy in Rema's chest, and exhaustion filled her limbs. "I need to eat, and I don't have the energy to dine with anyone tonight. Can you have some food sent to my chambers?"

"I'll see to it. I'll have the food tested as well. Times like these, you can never be too cautious."

Yorin turned his head to watch a servant balancing on a tall stool. "That idiot's going to break his leg that way." As he spoke, Yorin's hands shook, and surely not with concern for the servant's well-being. She caught his shoulder and turned him to face her again.

"There's something else on your mind. Tell me."

Yorin hesitated before speaking in a voice thick with emotion. "My eldest boy is out there in the army. Calan intends to throw his life away for nothing."

"I will end this war, Yorin. Have no fear for your son. Tell me, how did your talk with the Queen go?"

"I observed to her that Calan and Elise plainly can't coexist. If Elise stayed with us, Calan might do any kind of evil to her once the crown came to him. And given a choice between a daughter and an heir, well. It's killing her, mind. Not only does she love Elise, she knows that

Loric would never forgive her. She'll lose her only two children worth loving."

"Loric will never forgive us either. Perhaps I'll never forgive myself."

"Cease those thoughts. You'll need to give Talitha the final push. She'll want some reassurance that Elise won't suffer too greatly, and you're going to have to lie, aren't you?"

"I don't know if I can." Rema stared at the mold as it fell away from the wall in dark chunks. "Not about that."

"You must. It's a truth that no parent wants to know." Yorin sighed. "I'm tired, Rema. I'll see to your dinner. Goodnight."

Rema was too numb to do more than nod in response. She had reached her day's limit, and it was time to seek rest.

To her surprise, the cool air in her chambers carried the light smell of sandalwood. Perhaps Yorin had ordered incense burned to make the room more pleasant. She sat on her bed and supported her head in her hands. The hanging scent reminded her of childhood, and her thoughts grew blurry with nostalgia.

After an immeasurable passage of time, occupied by memories of fiery sand and coiling smoke, there was a knock at the door. "Come in," she said, and a servant stepped through, holding a tray of food to his narrow chest. He looked around for a place to put it.

"Just leave it on the bed," said Rema. "I know it's a bad habit, but excuse it just this once."

"Yes, my lady. Your other uniform has been washed and should be dry tomorrow. It'll be placed on your bed tomorrow around midday."

"Very good. Enjoy your evening."

"Thank you, miss." The servant lowered his head in deference as he closed the door behind him.

Rema turned her attention to the tray. A feast awaited her—potatoes roasted in their skins, a length of pale fish, a bowl of colorful jelly and a half-bottle of wine. She ate her meal, careful to avoid spilling food on the bedclothes. Upon emptying the wine, a dizziness intruded upon her, and she rested her head upon the pillow. Her eyes closed and her thoughts scattered.

She awoke still exhausted, roused by a nagging anxiety. The incense hovered in the room, faint but distinct. Its lingering presence suggested she hadn't slept more than a few hours. Sitting upright, she tried to untangle the events of the day, but there seemed too many threads to follow. Was it possible this mission might fail? If Danosha fought alone, it would collapse within the year. Lyorn, swollen with power, would seek further gains by standing alongside Ormun's enemies. Countless soldiers would lay broken beneath the soil, and Rema would carry every death on her conscience.

In a terrible way, Calan had been right: she did have the power to negotiate. Ormun would disapprove of her giving in to the demands of some insignificant prince, but the prospect of a few new territories might placate him. She would despise herself, but that was inevitable in any case. After the suffering she had caused Elise, it would be more difficult than ever to convince herself that her work for Ormun did more good than bad.

She cast her mind back to the young, redheaded girl who had followed her parents across plains, sands and steppes. She'd lived a carefree life, playing with the donkey's tail, charming customers with her slender smile and sitting contented in her mother's lap as her father read his poetry. By some wonder, that girl had grown into a stubborn, ambitious young woman, one who had never let herself be daunted by the men around her but persevered until finally she stood above them. She had fought for peace, justice and equality, as her father would have wanted, and she had lived boldly and by her wit, as her mother had always done. She had ended wars, freed slaves and protected the weak, always sensing the nearness of her father's prophecy. But Ormun had destroyed that woman, his cruelty choking her faith and deadening her soul.

She took Elise's letter out of her pocket and stared at the curious handwriting. How she wanted to once more have the spirit of her convictions, to taste again the righteousness that Elise still breathed… With her fingertip, she traced the imprint of Elise's lips, and hot tears gathered in her eyes. In a chilling instant, Calan's threat to visit his sister flashed into her mind, and the blur of wine and sleep dissolved. That she could not allow.

Rema put the letter away, moved unsteadily to her feet and looked out into the corridor. A servant swept the hall, her long-handled straw broom whisking loudly across the stones. "Hello," said Rema.

"Can I help you, my lady?" the servant said, still sweeping as she spoke.

"What time is it? I fell asleep without meaning to."

"Night is upon us. Most of the court has dined and gone to bed."

Was it already too late? "I need someone to move my bedclothes. Can you do that?"

"If you command it, I can do it." The woman rested her broom against the wall. "But where on earth do you plan to sleep?"

"I'll lead you there."

They piled their arms with blankets and pillows, and Rema directed the woman through the palace to the foot of Elise's tower. The servant looked at Rema questioningly. "Just here," Rema said. "On the stairs."

"You want to sleep on the stairs, my lady? You'll be awfully uncomfortable."

"Humor me, please."

The servant settled the blankets and pillows in the entryway. The result was a pitiful bed, barely wide enough for a person to huddle in sleep. "Thank you," said Rema. "You may go now. Have a good evening."

After the woman had left, Rema began to ascend the stairs to the tower. She paused before a window to let the night wind trace her face. Those same stars hung over Arann, yet she had never felt further from home.

She reached the top step and pressed her ear to the door. Two voices were audible behind it, a man and a woman, and for a moment, anxiety gripped her chest. Then laughter—Loric, that distinctive chuckle—and her fear subsided. All was well.

Rema returned to her makeshift bed and wriggled into the mound of blankets. The stone slab under her body was cold and hard, and she rolled herself in bedding to gain as much padding as she could between herself and the floor. Content in the knowledge that Calan could not get by without waking her, she closed her eyes. The impressions of the day unfolded before finally blurring together into the usual incomprehensibility of dreams.

The sound of a footstep broke through her rest. She sat upright, cold and disoriented. "Don't come any closer," she said, squinting down the black hallway.

"Rema?" It was Loric, standing on the steps behind her. "What on earth are you doing?"

Rema pushed her fingers into the corners of the eyes, trying to banish the exhaustion that kept forcing them shut. "Waiting for Calan." Loric was little more than a shadow in the stairwell, but there was no mistaking that gentle voice and the silhouette of his unruly hair.

Loric knelt by her side and took her hand. His palm warmed her frozen fingers. "God. You're even more devoted to her than I am. I was just on my way to bed."

"Don't tell her I'm here. Please."

"Are you serious? She still thinks that you have no feelings for her. If she knew you were doing this…"

"Her knowing would cause nothing but trouble."

"You don't understand, Rema." Loric's voice was suffused with emotion. "You're the answer to the prayer she no longer has the faith to speak."

Rema freed her hand as delicately as she could. "Neither of you know anything about me. I'm just another diplomat trying to take advantage of her."

"Like hell you are. Look at what you're doing to protect her from my brother, even though we both know you couldn't do anything to stop him. If you really want to protect her, go up to that tower and hold her. If you could see how she's been weeping…"

"Please, Loric." Rema pressed her face to the pillow. "Just let me sleep."

Loric remained crouched for a moment, his breath slow and unhappy. Finally he grunted and rose to his feet. "I'm going. But don't ignore what your heart knows to be true."

"It's too late for your bad poetry." Rema squeezed her eyes shut. "Goodnight."

His footsteps receded down the hallway. Despite her exhaustion, it took some time for sleep to return. Dreams enveloped her, bringing a vision of Calan on horseback. The horse's head was a human skull, bleak and staring. Ormun stood nearby, his back to her. When he turned, she saw that his face was her own. The apparitions fled, and she dreamt of Elise, of bringing those unhappy lips to her own and kissing them until the world's end.

CHAPTER ELEVEN

"Get up, you damn fool."

Yorin. There was no mistaking that surly voice. Rema tried to rise, but the ache in her back and legs was unbearable, and her spine gave such a sharp twinge that she whimpered.

Yorin's angry expression softened into concern. "That's what you can expect sleeping on the floor. Take a second to unknot, but not too long. You're lucky the servants let me know you were here before someone else found you."

Rema caressed her suffering knees. "What time is it?"

"Just before sunrise. The clock in the front court says five hours after midnight, but who knows with that damn thing. So would you explain to me why you're sleeping in her doorway like a lover thrown out of bed?"

"I didn't want Calan to hurt her."

"Rema." Yorin sighed, his fingers on his brow. "I understand your frustration, but this is entirely improper behavior for an imperial diplomat, and you know it. Come on, we'll get you back to your chambers."

Rema stood and pressed her hand to her lower back. Yorin scooped as many blankets as he could into his arms. "Take the rest." She obeyed, her spine complaining every time she bent, and hobbled behind him. They returned to her room, where they tossed the blankets onto the bed. Yorin rearranged them with an expert's touch, leaving not a single wrinkled cover or loose sheet.

"You'd better lie down and stretch," he said. "Get those snarls out of your back."

"It wasn't just the floor. I've been having pains in my knees for months."

"I'm sure Elise has a remedy for that, but then again, I think you two have become more than close enough. You're lucky only a handful of servants spotted you."

"Don't forget, I've been charged with bringing her safely to Arann." As she spoke, Rema looked around the room with rising suspicion. Something was out of place, but exactly what eluded her. "Do you scold your night guards for standing sentry?"

"I would if they were making eyes at each other while doing it." Yorin gave a grudging smile. "I can't deny you were brave. It's exactly the kind of thing Elise would do. But it was still an utterly foolish gambit."

Rema opened her mouth to protest, only to be interrupted by a moment of insight into the source of her unease. "My luggage has been opened."

Yorin frowned at the trunk. "How can you possibly tell?"

"They couldn't get it to shut properly again. See how it's half-open at the clasp? It doesn't close unless you push it at the corners as well." Rema reached for the lid.

"Wait! What if an assassin hid a spider or snake in there?"

"I've been in this business a long time. I don't think anyone really tries to assassinate people that way." Rema opened the chest, revealing an untidy jumble of clothes, bottles and papers. "It doesn't look like anything was taken. Not a surprise, as there's nothing worth taking."

"None of these papers are important?"

"Of course not. I memorize sensitive information. I don't leave it sitting in unlocked bedchambers. These are just notes of names, dates and other things to help me remember."

Yorin pinched the flesh above his nose. "The person who opened the trunk may not have known that, however. Does it look in disarray?"

Rema gestured to the open trunk. "You can see for yourself it's in disarray. That's how I left it. Perhaps they just wanted to paw through my undergarments."

"Maybe Loric, then."

"If only it were so innocuous." Rema closed the luggage, this time securing the clasp completely. "For someone to come into my bedchamber, they must have known I wasn't here. That means they were creeping about at night, saw me sleeping before the tower and took their opportunity."

"Unless they came looking for you. Perhaps they expected you to be here. When you weren't, they went through your belongings."

"You really think someone wanted to assassinate me?"

"We're at war, Rema. Has anyone threatened your life while you've been here?"

Only enough times that she had nearly lost count. Rema touched the black pendant hidden beneath her clothes. "I've been given warnings. And I didn't make a winning impression on Calan."

"You need to start locking this door even when you're not in the room. I did give you the key, didn't I?"

"Of course." Rema fumbled in her coat and retrieved the broad iron key. "Are you sure you don't just have a light-fingered servant?"

"Who can say? You can't know someone's a thief until you've caught them once." Yorin scratched his cheek, his eyes lost in thought. "I'll see if the servants noticed anything. In the meanwhile, you watch yourself, and, please, stay away from Elise. If Calan can convince his father that you're in any way inappropriately involved with her, it'll be all over for you here."

"Yorin, really. You're reading far too much into my affection for her."

"Say that I am. If I can come to the wrong conclusion, so can others. Fancy my having to tell a diplomat of your caliber that appearance matters more than reality."

"Fine. Consider me suitably chastened."

Yorin shook his head at her. "The Queen will see you this morning for breakfast in her chambers. Get an hour or two of rest to prepare. Meanwhile, his grace is reflecting on the advice he's received from Calan and yourself. I'll do my best to sway him."

"Is there anything else I should know?"

"Only that you look like you slept in a stairwell. We'll have your other uniform ready for you by noon, so you can change then."

"Very good." An unexpected rush of gratitude prompted Rema to give Yorin her brightest smile. "Thank you, Yorin."

Yorin bristled his eyebrows, lifted a few fingers in farewell and left the chamber. Rema stretched on the bed, tensing and relaxing her legs until the soreness left. As her head sank into the pillow, weariness stole over her. More sleep was required. She stumbled across the room, locked the door and returned to the bed. A wavering half-sleep came over her, and she dozed until the sound of activity in the hallway made it clear the day had begun.

As she was pulling herself up from the mattress, somebody tapped at the door. "Come in," she said, and the handle rattled. "Oh, sorry!" She crossed the room and unlocked the door. Alys stood in the corridor, smiling so widely that her small eyes crinkled at their corners.

"You slept on the floor," she said. "Gosh, Rema."

Rema pursed her lips. "Do all the servants know by now?"

"Only some. The woman who helped you move there was chatty, but Yorin shouted at her. She's not telling anyone anymore." Alys frowned. "Rema, I don't want you to be sent away. Whenever a girl becomes too friendly with Lady Elise, she gets sent away."

"Don't listen to gossip, Alys."

"I won't. I'm here to take you to the Queen for breakfast. Come on, quick! She whips me behind the ears when she's angry."

Alys hopped nervously from foot to foot while Rema locked the door behind her. Together they hastened through the waking palace to the upper level. As they entered the corridor leading to Talitha's chamber, they slowed at the unexpected sight ahead—Elise, waiting outside the door. Her hair was more unruly than ever, spilling and tangling over her gold-edged white dress. A painful emotion tugged at Rema's heart.

Elise looked up as they approached. "Alys, you can leave us," she said.

"Yes, my lady." Alys hesitated a moment before scampering off.

"She's worried because she's supposed to announce us." Elise gave a tentative smile. "But I think my mother will forgive her."

Rema kept her tone formal in an attempt to prevent her voice from shaking. "Good morning, Elise."

Elise's smile faltered. "So it's back to Elise now." She turned her head, and her earrings jangled. Their dangling silver threads were beautiful against Elise's dark hair. If only Rema were able to tell her so.

"I'm sorry. I didn't mean anything by it."

"I suppose I don't mean anything either. Tell me why you blew me a kiss. Was it just to mock me?"

"Just a harmless joke." Rema's throat tightened, and she took a quick breath. Time to change the subject. "Are we both invited to breakfast, then?"

"Well spotted, Remela. Perhaps my mother has realized that when making a decision regarding my future, I should be present."

"If you're going to call me Remela, at least say it right. You have to roll the *r* with your tongue."

"If only you were this interested in my tongue before." Elise's voice became suddenly urgent, her face naked with a desire for consolation. "Rema, did you read my letter? Did you feel anything at all?"

Rema opened her mouth, but all she could think of was Yorin's warning. "Let's go in," she said. Elise's lips quivered, and a hot sickness flooded Rema's heart. She hurriedly opened the door, and they both trudged into Talitha's chamber, a chill distance between them.

"Sit down, both of you," said Talitha, beckoning to the women. She seemed to have aged half a decade since Rema had last seen her. Her eyelids drooped, veiling her murky eyes, but there was still energy in her voice, and her fingers played nimbly upon the spine of the book in her lap.

"Odd," she said. "I'd have imagined you both would get on, yet here you are as cold as morning's frost."

"I have things to do," said Elise. "Can we not take care of this quickly, Mother?"

"We've yet to even get the food in, Elise. Our guest must be fed." Talitha tapped her nails on the cover of the book. "Where is that girl?" On cue, a servant woman knocked and entered, bringing a tray of small cakes. They looked like nothing more than little bundles of flour and sugar, and even a hundred would be unlikely to satisfy Rema's hunger.

Talitha waited for the servant to leave before biting into a white mouthful. "Very well." She wiped her mouth with a napkin. "Talk to me."

Rema's cake was already halfway to her mouth, and she put it back on the tray. Presumably Talitha, not confident of her own ability to defeat Rema, had summoned Elise for reinforcement. Rema would have to restrain herself for fear of seeming callous, while Elise would be given opportunity to cut through Rema's arguments and expose the cruelty of the demands. It was a clever stratagem, and it might have worked on a lesser diplomat.

Rema took a measured breath. "Let's start with Calan." Talitha blushed and glared at her book. "He's made demands upon the Emperor to which I can't possibly concede."

"He's a little foolhardy, I'll admit."

"An understatement if I ever heard one," said Elise. "Get to the point, Remela."

"Calan wants to change the terms of the agreement. Instead of ending the war, he wants it to continue until Lyorn is utterly defeated. The wealth will be split between Ormun and himself. Do you know what this would mean?"

"Rhetorical question, I assume," said Talitha.

"It would mean further years of war and death. It would mean ruling over a people who resent you and will revolt at the least provocation. It would mean imperial provinces at your doorstep, garrisoned with Ormun's restless armies."

"That sounded like a threat," said Elise. "Is that how you steal princesses? Bully their mothers into submission?"

"Elise, dear, you'll have your say," said Talitha, lifting her fingers in a gesture of reproach. "Rema, continue."

"If you follow Calan along his mad path, what I've described is only the most fortunate outcome," said Rema. "It's just as possible that the Emperor will take offense at the renegotiation and withdraw his support, leaving you at the whim of an outmatched warmonger."

"Enough about Calan." Talitha's voice expressed a deep fatigue tinged with grief. "It's the fate of Elise that I'm concerned about. My daughter, Rema."

"Let's talk about her, then. If my terms aren't accepted, Lyorn will destroy you, and Elise will suffer the fate of all princesses taken through conquest rather than marriage. If you accept my offer, she will at least live at my court in Arann."

"If you can call that living," said Elise with simmering temper.

"Be clearer," said Talitha. "What is the difference between Lyorn someday breaking these walls and snatching her, and my giving her to a man who breaks walls the way other men break their bread?"

Rema swallowed. Gods help her speak these cunning half-truths. "She'll be his twentieth wife. He's only one man. There'll be indignities and suffering, but she'll have the freedom of the palace."

"The freedom of the palace!" said Elise. As before, she was beautiful in her outrage, her round cheeks livid with color. "So I'm free to move about in my cell. Thank you, Remela, for that generous concession."

"There's little time to negotiate. If you don't accept my terms as they are, then you may find that it is too late. Calan will act with all the impetuousness of youth. Your kingdom will suffer, and Elise will be no better off for it."

"Hmm." Talitha ran her tongue across her teeth. "Elise, think clearly now. What do you make of our situation?"

"I won't respond until she looks at me," said Elise, and Rema reluctantly faced her again. Elise's lips were parted in fury, and the temper in her eyes was as controlled and steady as a lance. A prickling heat crept across Rema's face. To think this frozen land could produce a woman of such ardor...

"Remela is telling the truth. The war will consume us, and Calan's way will lead to butchery and suffering. But Mother, Ormun is wrong to ask this of us. He isn't offering us aid but an insult, not only to us but to all women. We must seek other allies, other options—"

"You don't have time," said Rema. "There's no—"

"Don't you dare interrupt me. My entire life I've had to endure being interrupted, and you have no more right to do so. I'll admit that I'm being selfish. I have a strange desire not to be sent away to marry a tyrant. But this isn't only about my desires, Rema. We have to prove that Ormun can't just take whatever woman he wishes." Elise leaned forward. Her voice, though angry, was melodic, and it washed over Rema's body like a shiver. "There will be a better way. Yes, sometimes sacrifices have to be made, but this is only cruelty disguised as benevolence. I don't see a peace offer. All I see is a kind heart closing itself to kindness and a woman who knows right willingly doing wrong."

Rema's face burned as she inhaled deeply and looked into Elise's eyes. Anger, pain and sorrow seethed in those silver depths, but so too did love, distant and longing. Finally Rema understood: it was by love, and love alone, that she would reach Elise. For this trade to take place, Rema would have to offer something of her own in exchange, the sacrifice she had never given another. And for this defiant lover of women, this healer of the sick and forgotten, this furious goddess who had stared down her brother and set the court ablaze—for Elise, Rema would gladly give it.

She took Elise's hand into her own. Elise's eyes widened, and Talitha raised an eyebrow. "My father was a poet," Rema said. "He told me that the gods give every poet a riddle, and they must devote their lives to solving it. His riddle was peace. He believed that someday the world would no longer know war and suffering. He tried to describe how that might feel—to evoke an understanding of peace so powerful that it could become real. He dreamed that anyone who heard his poems would never raise a hand in anger again."

Rema pressed Elise's hand tighter, and her anger faded, replaced by a look of bewildered affection. "As a little girl, I played around his feet while he wrote. Sometimes he'd look down to me and say, 'Remmy!

Tell me what makes you happy.' And with the innocence of a child, I would name him those things that brought me joy. The sound of laughter. The warm night air of the savannah. My pet lion cub. One night, he asked me that question, and I thought longer than before. Finally I said that my truest happiness was watching him hold my mother. He wept and kissed me."

She swallowed, her throat squeezed by emotion. "My father was the reason I went to Arann. I wanted to make his dreams real, but I knew that it would take more than poetry to do it. My parents helped me pack and farewelled me with tears. Neither doubted that I could become a diplomat." She could see their faces now, clearer now than they had been for years. "I dressed as a boy and went to the palace, where I claimed to have an important letter and acted dumb when they asked me who it was from. As I hoped, the guards took me to one of the diplomats. He knew straightaway that I was a girl in disguise, but I begged him in every language I knew to let me stay."

Talitha remained still and attentive, while Elise continued to stare at Rema with intensity. "There was no law against women being diplomats," said Rema. "Only a common belief that they lacked the intelligence for the role. I was allowed to enroll in the school, and I went through the training with the boys. The diplomat who had first helped me was young, and we grew close. I valued his friendship, but I broke his heart when he learned I had no interest in men."

Elise's face trembled, but Talitha nodded. "I understand," she said. "Too busy with your studies." Despite her emotion, Rema was unable to keep back a smile. Thank the gods for naive hearts.

"Before long, Emperor Togun learned there was a girl among his junior diplomats. He was Ajulese, like my father, and I spoke his native tongue, a lyrical language called Ajulai. I used to read poetry to him, a slight young woman kneeling at the feet of a living, laughing mountain. He was a conqueror too, but conquest brought him no happiness. I dared to read him my father's poems, and he came to share my faith in their vision." Rema blinked, and a tear spilled from her lashes. "We became friends and achieved much. When Ormun killed him, I was left hollow. I've done what I can since, but it's been war after war, the dead stretching across the plains."

Rema exhaled softly, keeping the ache of her old grief in check. "A year after Togun's death, my father and mother visited me in the city. They saw pain and consoled me. Father read me his latest poem, his truest work, he said. I've learned it by heart. It goes as thus." She closed her eyes and recited the poem in Ajulai, the language of her father. The sounds were mellow in her mouth, light on her tongue and ethereal in her breath. Each verse resonated into the next, and the words hung in the air like lyrical smoke. As Rema concluded the final verse, the tears pressed hard to her eyes, and her throat squeezed shut with grief.

"How pretty that sounds," said Talitha. "I would like to understand the words, however."

"Do you speak Annari? It's easier to translate to."

"The language of the Empire. Of course we do. We're educated women."

"It loses its poetic form, but this is the closest I can manage." Rema closed her eyes and recited again.

"Beneath the wing of despair,
I drift, feathered with tears.
Shadow wreathes my every bone,
Sorrow seeks my soul.
But then I fracture, falling broken,
And the darkness breaks with me.
I feel that I am light again
And know that I am saved.
Now drift to me, twin of my heart,
Toward this certain bliss.
For love has lain a path for you,
And you will find me waiting."

The short silence that followed was broken by a confused snort from Talitha. "I don't understand what this has to do with our situation."

Rema ignored her—Elise, for whom the message had been meant, had clearly understood it. Her grip had tightened, and her eyes shimmered with unshed tears. She turned her face away and pressed her other hand to her lips.

"Sometimes we must lay down in darkness if we hope to see the dawn," said Rema, her voice soft. "But you won't be alone, Elsie."

Elise tugged her hand free, leapt to her feet and hurried from the room. Talitha jumped in her seat as Elise slammed the door behind her.

"Well!" Talitha said. "That was unexpected. Did you intend to scare her away with that story? Were you trying to persuade her by clutching her hand like that? Your manner of diplomacy is very odd."

"Talitha, please do this terrible thing." Rema closed her eyes for several seconds, searching for comfort in the blindness. It was as if all her unhappiest years were pressing upon her heart at once. "Tell your husband that you accept my conditions, and do so before Calan can destroy untold lives."

"I was expecting her to talk me out of it." Talitha stared in disbelief at the empty chair. "That was why I asked her here. I don't want to be persuaded, damn you. Yet Yorin has been at me day and night, and now Calan is causing trouble. If Elise won't stand up for herself, what am I supposed to do?"

"You know there's no choice. I think Elise has just indicated that she knows it too."

Talitha bowed her head. "Please leave me. I have to reflect."

"Thank you for your hospitality." As Rema departed, she glanced back. Talitha sat hunched, her eyes sightless and her mouth compressed to a tight line. As quietly as she could, Rema shut the door.

CHAPTER TWELVE

Rema took a seat in the front court. Peasants trudged past her, their faces smudged with dirt, their nails ragged and their backs bent from labor. Few things were as despicable as feudalism. Even Ormun, who had reinstated the slavery laws Rema had fought so hard to abolish, made no pretense to rule by divine blood. Not like here, where the serfs beyond the city walls were doomed to menial toil while the aristocracy elevated their sons to greatness and damned their daughters to forced matrimony.

In Arann, Elise could have lived and loved as she willed, and the great city would never have paused in judgment. She and Rema could have been lovers, perhaps even living together in Rema's mansion by the sea. It was impossible not to envision returning home to find Elise waiting in the front archway, her eyes heated with a consort's welcome, her lips relaxed in a smile, the seductive curves of her body silhouetted beneath loose silk…It was madness, yet Rema could think of no way to escape it.

She needed to clear her head. She followed the winding corridors to the gardens. Trembling crystals of dew hung on the grass and leaves, and as she walked through the hedges, a bird gave a shrill cry. Rema passed by a row of short trees, running her fingertips over gnarled patches of bark, and stopped at an elaborate bed of flowers near the furthest wall. She inhaled the elusive scent of the petals, tasted the thick aroma of damp soil. A butterfly perched on her nose, tickling her with its wings, and she laughed. It was as her father had told her: the sun knew when to rise.

A dry rustle rasped nearby, as of several sticks being broken at once. Rema looked up to see a tall figure slip through a weave of trees and into the dark grove. Though the tall figure had moved quickly, it had appeared to be one of the Narandane, perhaps one of Domyr's servants—if not Domyr himself. Her curiosity piqued, Rema entered the trees. The foliage hung heavy with moisture, and as she walked, the soil sunk beneath her step and wet leaves clung to her boots. She stood in the middle of the grove but saw no one.

"Hello?" she said. "I only want to talk."

A freezing pain pierced her chest, as if somebody had touched ice to her skin. Instinctively she reached for the sensation: Elise's pendant, now colder than any frost. She stepped forward, propelled by fear, and a line of pain scorched her back. Overwhelming nausea crumpled her knees, and she dropped to the mud, landing on her hands. As a disorienting mist tugged at her sight, she twisted her head. One of the Narandane servants stood behind her, holding a short sword. Its end was stained with blood.

The nausea intensified, and a tremendous sucking sound filled her ears as darkness flooded her vision. The Narandane stepped forward and raised his sword. Just as he seemed about to strike, an impossible creature radiated into being, an angel of countless colors, and collided with him. It was too much to comprehend. Nothing existed but the mud beneath her hands, the churning sickness in her stomach and the line of agony drawn across her back.

"Rema," said a voice somewhere in the fog. Loric. Sweet, kind Loric.

"She's hurt," said another voice. Muhan. Strange old Muhan. "Help her. I have my hands full."

Hands gripped Rema beneath her arms, and her body swayed. Her back throbbed—no, her coat! Could it be ruined? Gods, not her coat…She opened her mouth to speak, but only managed a groan. Ashamed, she decided never to open her mouth again. She focused instead on breathing, which was something that still seemed to make sense. If she breathed slowly and yielded to the dizziness, even the pain seemed to slip away.

The fractured darkness clung to her for some time, tormenting her with agonies and half-thoughts, until a hand touched her cheek and brought her back to the world. She opened her eyes and struggled to understand where she was—nothing but shapes and blurred outlines. "It was the Narandane," she said, determined that the world know her attacker. "He ruined my coat."

"Hush, sweetheart," said Elise. "We know. Lor, get me the box from that high shelf. Rema, drink this. It'll clear your head." A sweet liquid touched Rema's lips. She sipped, and warmth spread through her body. "There, doesn't that feel better?"

Rema nodded, and Elise took the flask away. "I have to get to the wound now. Be brave, dearest. This will sting."

Suddenly the jumble of impressions before Rema made sense. She was lying on Elise's bed, turned awkwardly on her side, with a cool pillow beneath her head. Loric was fumbling through the mess in the corner, and Elise was sitting at Rema's side, her face gentle with concern. "Elsie," said Rema. "I'm sorry."

"Hush now." Elise leaned forward, and the loose strands of her dark hair tickled Rema's nose and face. Elise began undoing the buttons of her coat, and Rema shifted her torso to make the task easier. Every movement brought pain, but she was determined to help, and soon she was free of the coat. She raised her arms, allowing her undershirt to be pulled over her head. The fabric was plastered to her back, and Rema bit her tongue as it peeled away from her skin. Her back burned, and she inhaled deeply, struggling to stay conscious.

"Loric, hurry up with that box and then give her some privacy."

"Will she be okay?" said Loric, his eyes averted.

"I believe so. Don't worry. Just go keep an eye on things downstairs." Elise gently took hold of Rema's waist. "I'm going to lift you up now, sweetheart. It shouldn't hurt too much." Rema cooperated as Elise moved her upright. A torrent of dizziness struck her, but she breathed her way through it.

"Elsie…" There was a mirror opposite the bed, and Rema winced as she caught her reflection. Thick beads of moisture glistened across her sharp features, and her bare torso was similarly sheened with sweat. Elise's pendant still rested against her collarbone, and Rema touched it lightly with her finger. It no longer burned.

"I'm going to clean this wound now." Elise climbed onto the bed and crawled behind Rema. "I'll make it hurt as little as I can."

"Thank you." Was it possible that this weak voice was her own?

"Hold your breath." Something stung her back and wiped across her skin. Despite the pain, it left her feeling cleaner. Elise put the soiled cloth aside, took a little bottle from her medicine box and unscrewed the lid. "This is for the pain." Her fingers traced the wound, spreading an ointment that left Rema's skin numb. "Oh, Rema, you poor thing."

"Is it bad?"

"It was a glancing blow, and the wound is shallow. You'll feel very queasy, but no harm is done."

"I took a step forward as he struck." Rema gripped the black stone at her neck. "I felt the pendant you gave me, and I moved. If I hadn't…"

She watched in the mirror as Elise tipped clear fluid onto a fresh cloth. "This is to prevent the wound from fouling." Rema's back was so numbed that she barely felt the pressure of the cloth. "I'm glad the pendant helped you, Rema, but…"

Why had she fallen silent? "What's wrong?"

"This is my fault." Elise's voice shook. "This happened because of me."

Rema tried to turn, but Elise stopped her. "Elsie, how could it be your fault?"

"I know what that man was." Elise began to rub another cream on Rema's back. "We'll all know soon. He was a Lyornan spy."

"How do you…"

"Because I'm a traitor. When we learned that an imperial diplomat was coming, I let Lyorn know too. I was afraid and angry, and I didn't trust that my mother would protect me forever. So I acted stupidly, treasonously. Imagine my horror when instead of some loathsome diplomat, they sent you. Every day you've been here, I've been terrified that this might happen."

Rema shifted to face her. She was sitting cross-legged, her hair pooled on the bed behind her, and her face was puckered with misery. "Look at me," Rema said, and Elise looked up, her eyelashes glistening with tears.

"If anyone finds out, it's the end of me. I'll be sent to Ormun if I'm lucky. Calan would want me executed." A tear slipped down Elise's cheek. "But I don't care about that. I'm crying because I've lost every chance of making you love me."

"You don't know how I feel." Rema touched Elise's damp face with the back of her hand. "I know I've seemed cold at times, but that's because I'm a diplomat. My manner and my feelings are rarely allowed to coincide."

Elise glanced down at Rema's bared breasts, and a blush warmed on her cheeks as she quickly looked up again. "I tried so hard to hate you this morning. I thought of how you let Calan insult me in front of everyone, and I remembered the way you turned your back on me after our dinner. But when you told me your story and recited that poem, I understood why you'd done those things to me. I saw the secret in your eyes and heard the whisper between your verse, and I knew that you were sorry."

"I am sorry. More than even poetry can express."

"There are two things I now know for certain. I can't escape this marriage, and I'm in love with you. I can't fight either. I'm doomed, and you've doomed me."

"Love is a strong word. You don't know me."

"Love is a feeling. It's not about knowing. This is one enchantment I can't break, and I'm glad. I want to live beneath your spell, even if it destroys me. You're my disaster, my damnation...my diplomat."

The compassion in Rema's chest blazed into something deeper. Gods help them both. She touched Elise's face, traced the curve of her cheekbone and stroked the smooth skin beneath her ear. Elise began to breathe quickly, her lips open with anticipation, and Rema leaned in to grant their wish.

Before their mouths could meet, a heavy knock shook the door. Elise leapt to her feet, her eyes blazing. "Who is it?"

"It's Calan." The satisfaction in his voice was audible even through the door. "I'm coming in."

Rema grabbed a pillow and pressed it to her chest. The door opened, and Calan ducked beneath the frame. He glanced at Elise before giving Rema's bare shoulders a lingering examination. "How's our little ambassador?"

"She'll live." Elise smoothed the front of her dress and flicked her hair from her face. "What are you doing here, Calan? You're getting in my way."

"Don't be so quick to chase me off. Remela is surely curious to know more about her assailant, don't you think?" Calan looked around the room and laughed. "I was going to sit, but there's nowhere to in this mess. You not only have the figure of a pig, sister, but you live like one."

"Get on with it. I have to tend to her."

Calan licked his lips. "So be it. Her attacker is one of the Narandane servants. I asked Domyr about it, and he insisted he knew nothing about the man. He'd employed him back in Narandor, had asked no questions about his background, and has no issue with us meting out judgment however we please. He also passed on his well-wishes to the victim."

"I'm sure you don't believe any of that," said Rema.

"Of course not. So I spent some time with our would-be assassin. I asked the usual questions. Who had employed him? Why had he tried to kill an imperial diplomat? How did he even know that an imperial diplomat was here? He was very sullen at first." Calan's lips moved in a thin smile. "Then I found ways to persuade him."

"Bannon." Rema clutched the pillow tighter. "You tortured him."

"You've met my pale-eyed friend, have you?" Calan chuckled. "To get to the point, our assassin was working for Lyorn. They've learned about the Emperor's offer, and they reasoned that if his diplomat died under our protection, it would both disrupt the negotiations and reflect poorly on Danosha. The Emperor would certainly be reluctant to send any more diplomats."

"Did this man implicate Domyr? Or anyone else?"

"Domyr is surely complicit, but the prisoner hasn't admitted it yet. What I'm interested to know is how he learned that we had a diplomat coming. These Narandane arrived only the day after you, so it was clear they knew exactly when you were arriving. But nobody's seen the Emperor's letter except Yorin and our family."

His implication was obvious, and Rema swallowed hard. "What about the servants?"

"Don't be an idiot." Calan picked a plant from the wall and began to pull it apart. "Servants can't read. No, I'm sure the truth is far more interesting, and I'm very eager to learn more. Little sister, you're very quiet."

"Rema needs her rest," Elise said, her voice calm. "Why don't you go back to your sick interrogation? And damn you, leave my herbs alone."

Calan tossed the mangled plant to the floor. "She's a lucky thing, that Rema. If Loric and the foreigner hadn't been taking breakfast in the gardens, she'd be in ribbons." He stepped forward. "I'm curious to see this wound of yours."

Squeezing the cushion close to her chest, Rema wriggled backward. Elise stepped between them. "Get the hell away from her!" she said, her voice wild with fury. "Take your leering eyes with you. She's not a spectacle for you to gape at."

"Ooh, such teeth!" Calan grinned. "Don't worry, we all have her best interest at heart. That's why we won't rest until we bring this traitor to justice. Isn't that right, Elise?"

"Get out!"

"How unfair. Here I am, working hard to defend us, and all you can do is berate me. Oh, don't bother opening your nasty mouth again, I'm leaving." Calan walked to the doorway, where he stood with one hand pressed against the frame. "Sister, perhaps you can clarify something for me. You aren't still being stubborn about this marriage proposal, are you?"

Elise remained silent, her fists clenched.

"I've been trying to think of a way to convince you to be gracefully wed and leave this court in peace." Calan winked. "Perhaps something will come to me." He shut the door with enough force to shake the glass jars on Elise's workbench.

The scowl Elise had worn for Calan collapsed into a look of frightened petulance. "He knows. He's going to blackmail me with it."

"Even if he suspects it, he can't yet prove it," said Rema. Her stomach still churned from disgust at Calan's unwelcome intrusion. "Don't worry. I won't let him hurt you."

"You're going to help me, even after what I've done? Are you saying I'm forgiven?"

"You were desperate. Of course you're forgiven." Rema hugged the pillow closer to her body. "Can you find me something to wear? I need to get to the prisoner quickly. With enough time, Calan can make him say anything."

"The truth is already bad enough." Elise sank onto the bed. "And I was serious when I said you need to rest. The wound isn't serious, but your body is badly shaken."

"Even if I wobble a little, I'll be fine."

Elise touched her fingertips to Rema's shoulder. "Can't we just go back to where we were before?"

Their lips had been so close…what would have happened without Calan's interruption? "We'd best not."

Elise sighed and began to rummage through the clothes tossed about the room. She smoothed the rumples out of a purple blouse and handed it to Rema, who pulled the garment over her head. "It smells like your perfume," said Rema, wriggling her arms through the sleeves.

"It's so baggy on you." Elise placed her hands upon her stomach. "Perhaps I really am as fat as a pig."

"Don't speak that way. You're perfect." Rema rose to her feet, grimacing as her back and knees complained together. "Does Loric know what you've done?"

Elise shook her head.

"And the Lyornans. Did you send them the information anonymously?"

"I didn't sign the letter, but they're not stupid. I'm sure they figured it out." Elise coiled a strand of hair around her fingers. "You do realize that if you turn me in, my parents will wash their hands of me and sign your treaty. Then you could go home."

"You'd have to endure terrible shame. I couldn't do that to you. When you leave this kingdom, it will be with your head high."

"Rema." Elise put her arms around Rema's waist and held her close. Elise's body proved alluringly soft, as one might expect of a woman so voluptuous, and Rema fought the desire to push them both to the bed. "There's a message in your eyes that gives me hope. But I want to hear you say the words I'm longing for. I want to know we're thinking about the same thing."

"One thought at a time." Rema slid out from the embrace. "Did you want to come with me to confront Calan? You're every bit as fierce as me."

Elise laughed, and the low, sensual sound quickened Rema's pulse. "I'm flattered, but I'd be more valuable here. There's something I can arrange that might help us."

"If nobody is harmed, then do it."

"I don't want to see anybody hurt, most of all you. Please be careful."

"I always am." They lingered for a moment longer, gazing upon one another. As Rema finally retreated to the door, Elise opened a book on her desk and began traversing the room, picking through her flasks and vials. What manner of sorcery did she have planned? After the painful warning from the black pendant, it was clear Elise was capable of some uncanny enchantment.

As Rema descended the stairs, her back itched, and she struggled not to touch it. It was rare she endured such violence. Yet despite what the Narandane had done to her, Rema felt nothing but pity in return. Diplomats were taught early what to expect from torturers, the numerous techniques they used to impose their cruelty upon both mind and flesh, and Bannon's eyes had suggested a man who knew them all.

CHAPTER THIRTEEN

The front court had been cleared, and the palace doors shut and sealed by a heavy wooden bolt. Yorin, Muhan and Loric stood engaged in a lively discussion. The moment Rema's boots struck the flagstones, they broke off their conversation. "Rema!" Loric dashed forward and clutched her hands. "Should you be up?"

"I'm fine. Just a little shaken. Muhan, Loric, it seems I owe you my life."

Muhan smiled. "Perhaps, but I'm too modest to lay claim to it. Let us hear the story from our prince here."

"It really was more him than me." Loric scuffed the flagstones with his heel as a new shyness stole over him. "We were breakfasting in the corner of the gardens. I noticed you following the Narandane moving into that nasty dark grove, and I mentioned it to Muhan, who said that we ought to check on you. We were just in time. But honestly, it was Muhan who saved you. He just grappled the man to the ground. It was amazing!"

"I trained as a wrestler when I was a younger man," said Muhan. "I painted my chest, stood shirtless in the marketplace and challenged passersby to throw me to the ground. So as not to go hungry, I became quite good at it."

"You're a man of many skills," said Rema. "But don't downplay what you did, Loric. You're a hero."

Loric lowered his scarlet face. "I'm just glad you're alive. When we told Yorin what had happened, he was so worried for you that he pulled his remaining hairs out."

Yorin coughed and turned his head away. The sight of his embarrassment was so uncharacteristic that Rema was unable to resist a giggle, which mortified her in turn—the great Remela, giggling?

"Look at your faces," said Muhan with evident satisfaction. "Even I couldn't produce a more striking red."

"Never mind that," said Yorin. "The end result is that Calan has the prisoner in the dungeons, and he's wringing secrets out of him. I don't want to know how."

Rema grimaced. Just as she had anticipated. "Can you take me to the dungeons? Someone else needs to be there, if only to make sure that this man isn't ill-treated."

"Are you serious?" said Loric. "He tried to kill you! He deserves everything he gets."

"Diplomats by their very nature resolve injustice without violence. In any event, we should be merciful even toward assassins. Who knows what kind of pressure that man was under? I want to talk to Domyr too, if possible."

"He's under guard," said Yorin. "We're being very polite about it, just in case he really is who he says. We don't need to make an enemy of Narandor."

"Wise of you. Now, the dungeons, if someone will be so kind?"

"Yes, yes." Yorin waved his hand in a frustrated gesture. "But if you falter even for a single step, I'm having you taken straight back to your room."

Rema followed Yorin through an archway and into an unfamiliar corridor, which was lit by a series of torches casting an uncertain glow across the irregular stone walls. The carpet running the hall's length was worn right to the stone. It ended at a cracked archway, behind which a deep stairwell dropped into shadow.

Yorin took a torch from a bracket, and he and Rema descended into the darkness. Her back ached, but she concealed her discomfort. A far greater pain was presently being visited upon another, and as her father had taught her, she held only mercy in her heart.

They emerged into a grey-bricked corridor lined with cell doors. Yorin lifted his torch ahead of them, sending a wavering finger of light into the hall. Several dim lanterns lit the hallway further along. "The dungeons," he said. "Usually empty, as prisoners of war are kept in the forts."

Rema didn't need to be told where Calan and Bannon were; the prisoner's wails were audible. "I'll continue alone. You inform the King and Queen that I was attacked and barely escaped with my life. Use this incident to argue that the deal must be signed before Lyorn makes another attempt. Stress that this proves your enemies fear what our alliance will bring."

"I admire the way you turn every little thing to your advantage. Be careful as you go. There's rats down here."

A howl echoed down the corridor. "There's much worse than rats."

Rema followed the prisoner's shrieks until she reached a wooden door at the end of a row of cells. The door was ajar, and torchlight shone red behind it. She descended a short flight of stairs and entered a torture chamber, as chilling and unpleasant as every other of its kind. Sinister devices jutted from the shadows, and chains hung from the ceiling in macabre loops.

The Narandane hung from two boards arranged in the shape of an X. He had been stripped to the waist, livid wounds striped his chest, and meat hooks had been embedded in the flesh of his shoulders. A chain ran from the hooks, around a pulley and to a handle, where Bannon stood waiting.

Calan was before the cross, his face expressionless. He inclined his head as Rema entered. "Ah, it's you. Wanted the satisfaction of seeing your attacker suffer, I suppose."

"Nobody should find satisfaction in this." Sickened, Rema found herself unable to move from the final step into the oppressive gloom of the chamber. "What are you doing to him?"

"A simple device," said Bannon. "I turn the lever, like so." He spun the handle and the chain tightened. The Narandane's skin pulled, taut and grotesque, and he screamed. Sweat and tears flowed down his cheeks.

"Stop it!" said Rema. "For the love of the gods…"

"There's only one god in these parts, and he's a real bastard." Bannon grinned and released the handle. The chains sagged, and the man whimpered as his flesh snapped back to his body. "This is actually one of the tamer methods at my disposal. I think Calan's gone soft."

Calan only grimaced. Looking from one man to the other, Rema frowned—nothing in Bannon's demeanor suggested he considered himself a subordinate. He was working for the promise of money or power, surely, not from any sense of loyalty. She put the observation aside for later. "Calan, there's no point torturing him. People under torture will say anything."

"Better than nothing," said Calan. "Are you telling me that your Emperor doesn't condone torture?"

"Ormun isn't here. I am, and I don't."

"You just don't want me to confirm that your beloved is a traitor. Bannon, turn the handle."

Bannon shrugged at Rema and gave the handle several quick twists. Rema covered her mouth as her nausea rose. In her service to Ormun she'd seen several more terrible sights, but this was still a vile torment by any measure. It seemed as if the prisoner's flesh would tear at any moment, yet the hooks continued to rise.

"Tell me," said Calan. "Who leaked the information to you?"

"I don't know," said the man, staring at Rema with vacant eyes. "Please."

"Keep turning." The chains clanked, the hooks lifted and the man screamed. "Answer again."

"The letter wasn't signed! We don't know who sent it!"

"Oh? You must have some idea." Calan stroked his chin, watching with indifference.

"Why would we care who sent it?" The man's breath came in short gasps. "All that mattered was the message."

"Possibly true, but we'll punish you anyway. Bannon."

Rema moved over to Calan and grabbed his arm. "Calan, stop this."

"Don't touch me," said Calan, pushing her away. She stumbled, still uneasy on her legs, and slipped to her knees. The stone floor stung her hands, and she was unable to hold back a hiss of pain. Calan laughed. "Ah, the weakness of women. You might dress like a man, but you'll never be more than your sex. I can only imagine how much you must envy me."

"Oh, yes." Rema used the gaps in the masonry to pull herself up. "When I return to Arann, I'll put on clothes of pure silk, sit in the parlor of my mansion, pour priceless wine into a sapphire goblet and stare out over the golden sea. And I'll think, if only I were Calan, prince of the dung heap." As she spoke, she watched Bannon, who gazed back with comprehension in his pallid eyes.

"You won't be smiling in a moment." The tight vein at Calan's temple pulsed, and he turned back to the Narandane prisoner. "Did you happen to see the letter?"

"Yes, lord," said the prisoner. "Yes, I saw it."

"Good man! And would you recognize the handwriting?"

"I'm not sure…"

"Bannon." Calan lifted his hand.

"No! Don't! I would! I would!"

"Excellent. Let me show you something." Calan took a piece of paper from his pocket and held it toward Rema so she could see the eccentric, looping handwriting.

"It was you." Rema's stomach twisted. "You went into my room. You took that letter from my trunk."

Calan lifted the corner of his mouth in a sardonic grin. "What a mad accusation. But I suppose I should expect madness from a woman who sleeps in stairwells like a homeless peasant." He held the letter before the suffering prisoner. "Do you recognize this hand?"

The man opened his mouth, and his lips began to form a word. No sound emerged from his throat except a long, dry whistle. The prisoner seemed as astonished by the result as everyone else, and Calan growled. "I said, do you recognize it? Tell me!"

The prisoner wheezed again, his eyes stretching with fear. "Bannon!" said Calan. "Encourage him."

The hooks strained the meat of the man's back, yet instead of crying out, he issued a plaintive gasp of empty air. "I don't think he's faking," said Bannon. "There's no man that can stop himself screaming."

"Keep turning. Make him speak!"

Bannon turned the handle again. The man's back had become so distended that Rema had to look away, yet still the prisoner only produced the same brittle silence. "He's lost his voice," said Bannon. "You'll just kill him if I keep doing this."

"Fuck it. Release the handle." The lever whipped in circles as Bannon let it go, and the man dropped heavily back into the cross, tears and sweat pattering on the stone beneath him. "Talk to me!"

The prisoner rolled his eyes, opened his mouth and wheezed.

"Nod, then! Nod if this was the letter!"

Rema saw the muscles in the man's neck flex as if he were trying to nod, but nothing happened. He opened and closed his mouth in silent incomprehension.

"My sister has done this!" Calan thumped the wall with his fist. "With her sorcery, that fucking witch!"

"You said yourself her magic was useless," said Rema. "It's clear to me that the pain you put this man through has robbed him of his faculties."

Calan turned his head to look at her. Sweat glistened on his furrowed brows, and in the dim light of the chamber his eyes were like pits. "How stupid do you think I am? My sister is a traitor and you're in it with her. You're like her, an unnatural, cunt-lusting half-woman."

"And why would I be involved in a plot to kill myself?"

Bannon laughed, and Calan glared at him. "You think you're very clever. I'll expose you, Emperor's bitch."

"I'd be curious to know how."

"This letter. I'll show my father."

"It suggests no impropriety between us. Affectionate language is hardly a crime, and I doubt it's a secret in the court that Elise is fond of me."

"You're a vile little snake, aren't you?" Calan moved closer, clenching his hands into fists. "I can't stand the disgusting confidence that oozes from your face, your voice, even the way you stand. You should tremble before me, you warped shadow of a man."

"You're the one who lacks perspective, boy." Rema stared back at him, undaunted. Far more powerful men had tried to bully her, and in the presence of Calan's atrocities, defiance came easily. "In three weeks I will be in Arann, helping to manage the affairs of an Empire over a hundred times larger than your kingdom. You will be cleaning manure from your boots in a field somewhere north of here, waiting for the soldiers that I will send you."

Calan's nostrils flared, and the muscles in his forearms swelled as he raised a fist.

"Strike me, then," said Rema. "Demonstrate your impotence. You know that you can't outwit me, you're frightened of the influence I wield, and so you'd succumb to your cowardice and try to subdue me with your fists. It would prove nothing except that in place of wit you have empty brutality, like any other dumb and sullen beast."

Bannon whistled. "I like her."

Thick tendons pumped beside Calan's jaw as he ground his teeth. "The letter means nothing? In that case, you won't mind if I send it to your Emperor."

Rema smirked. If that was his final gambit, she had won, and it merely remained to claim the spoils. "If you want to play with Ormun, little prince, you'll have to do better than that. He'd only demand your head for impertinence." She turned her back to him and put her foot on the stairs. "Bannon, let this man down."

With a grunt, Bannon walked to the cross and began to undo the man's shackles. "What?" he said, as Calan turned to stare at him. "She's right. There's no point torturing a man who can't talk back."

The prisoner settled against the floor and sat there, barely moving. Papery wheezes issued from his chest, each sound peculiarly flat. If this was the result of Elise's magic, then Rema had underestimated her yet again. She had never seen anything so uncanny.

"You think you've won," said Calan. "Nothing could be further from the truth."

"Bannon," said Rema, meeting Bannon's pale eyes. "You'd best hope that you picked the right master. If this kingdom falls, you'll be the one strapped to a cross."

She returned through the dungeons and ascended the tall stairwell. Yorin was waiting at the top, his fingers tugging anxiously at his sleeves. "Why are you so agitated?" Rema said, swiping a cobweb from her hair.

"It's been done." Yorin clutched at her wrist. "When she heard of the attempt on your life, Talitha agreed to your terms. They couldn't dare risk stalling any longer, and they understand now you'll never leave empty-handed. And so she and Cedrin are waiting for you to sign the agreement. It's as you wanted: the marriage of Elise and cessation of hostilities once our provinces are regained, in exchange for soldiers and supplies."

Rema released a breath held long in check. So it was over, then. "You've done well. Where are they waiting?"

"In the throne room." Yorin plucked a web from Rema's shoulder. Despite the weary circles beneath his eyes, he was beaming, and Rema's heart stirred. Undoubtedly he was thinking of his son. She could be proud of that good deed, if nothing else.

"Let's hurry, then, while Calan is busy stomping furiously down below."

They hastened through the hallways, Yorin so eager he seemed at risk of tripping on his robes. Rema's pleasure, however, was tempered by guilt. How could she take any satisfaction from this? There had been too many bitter conquests, too many victories written in blood and tears.

As she approached the throne room, Rema closed her eyes for several seconds, stilling an old grief. The dream was still there, tinged with incense, warmed by the desert sun. But its intensity had faded, and she was weaker than ever.

CHAPTER FOURTEEN

Talitha and Cedrin stood at the foot of the throne, their heads and hands moving as they held a quiet conversation. Yorin cleared his throat. "May I announce Rema, ambassador to Emperor Ormun of the Pale Plains."

"Very good," said Cedrin. "Come in, both of you."

Rema and Yorin approached the throne. Talitha's eyes were red from weeping, and though her hands were buried in the folds of her gown, the movement of the fabric betrayed their trembling. Cedrin's large body was hunched almost double, and the corners of his mouth drooped low. "My boy believes that we can win this war without you," he said. "Do you assure me this is not the case?"

"I assure you," said Rema.

"I can assure you as well," said Yorin. "You know I'm well apprised of what happens in the field. It's a war we cannot win."

Talitha nodded. "Then we need help, and we need it before the bloodshed is too great for our people to endure. We accept your offer. May we note that we are grieved beyond words at your cruel request to surrender our daughter."

"We ask that Ormun treat her with respect and compassion," said Cedrin. "That he be attentive to the fact she is not only a woman, but a person of talent, someone who would be of great service to his court.

"Tell the bastard that if he rapes my daughter, I will cross the seas to cut off his balls."

Rema bowed her head in contrition. "I'll do whatever I can to protect her, when I can and where I can, from the worst of his excesses."

"I believe you, though I know you can likely do nothing." Talitha gave a mournful smile. "You're a clever woman. It has been a surprise and a wonder to have been extorted by you, and if the Empire has any sense, they'll place you someday upon that wretched throne."

"I have the document." Cedrin took a furled scroll from his robe. "There's quill and ink on the table here. We'll sign it, all four of us—Talitha and I to give our seal of approval, Rema as authority of Ormun, Yorin as our trusted witness." He stared at the scroll for several seconds, as if having forgotten its purpose already, before sighing. "I'll do it first."

He flattened the paper against the table, wet the quill and scratched his name. Talitha did the same and passed the quill to Rema, who remained numb as she inked her name to the page. Yorin wrote his name last, and after signing he dropped the quill back into the inkpot. Even his handwriting looked harried.

"Forgive us if we don't hold a banquet to celebrate," said Talitha. "Somebody will have to deliver the news to Elise. Give us enough time to find a way."

"I understand," said Rema. "Shall I take my leave, then?"

"Please do," said Cedrin. "I apologize if I have been an uncivil host. I was ashamed to learn that you were attacked under my roof, and it does my heart good to see you well."

The monarch who had attempted to confront her in a guise of pride and authority had been shattered, leaving only a defeated old man. Talitha had likewise been broken, barely recognizable as the intelligent, acerbic woman Rema had first met. These people were suffering, and she was the cause of it. It was time to leave.

"Until later, then, Your Graces." She bowed and turned, only to shudder. Elise and Loric were standing together in the doorway.

"It's true, then," said Loric, his voice unsteady. "You've given her up."

"I'm sorry for what we've done," said Talitha. "But both of you know we had little other choice."

"You had all the choice in the world!" Loric stormed into the throne room and stood before Rema. His eyes were filled with tears. "You could have said no. Mother, what happened? You said you'd fight for her!"

"I became fearful, that's what happened. Fearful for my sons, fearful for our home and fearful for our people." Talitha stared at the stone floor. "I fear for my daughter, too, but what choice did I have? We had to take this chance for peace while we still could."

"I can't believe it." Loric looked at Rema with such hatred that she took a step back, stunned. "You deceived me. You've taken away everything that's good and beautiful about this place and left us with nothing but our grief. You're a duplicitous wretch."

Rema glanced toward Elise, who remained in the doorway, her expression too distant to be readable. "Loric—"

"I don't want to hear it! I really thought…" Loric's voice cracked. "I really thought you cared about her. About both of us."

"I do. And I warned you from the beginning that I intended to sign this agreement."

"I wish your ship had sunk on its way here!" Loric's voice had risen high, becoming almost childish, as his temper boiled over into rage. "I wish you'd been torn apart by sharks, and that not even your bones had survived to wash up on the shore! I should have let you die in the garden!"

"Enough!" Cedrin slammed his fist on the table, and the inkpot jumped, nearly spilling on the newly-signed document. "This decision has been made. Do you think a single person in this room is happy about this marriage?"

"She is." Loric pointed to Rema. "She has what she wants, while we have nothing."

An aching pity grew in Rema's breast. He was only a child, suffering the first great loss of his life and taking out his anger on the sole target he had. "You now have a future," she said as gently as she could. "And I believe that what you do with it will make your sister proud."

"You always have a clever reply." Loric gave a choking sob. "Not like the rest of us mortals, who feel so much pain we forget how to form words, even how to form thoughts. I hope that one day you know what it's like to try to swallow your anguish only to feel it caught in your throat, to be suffocated by it…"

"Loric, be at peace." Elise walked to her brother's side, swaying with a casual grace. Her face was solemn, her silver eyes clear. "Rema knows very well what that feels like."

Loric turned, weeping freely now, and wrapped his arms around his sister's neck. "Elsie, just refuse to go! Tell them. You know what will happen to you."

"Yes, I do." Elise set her gaze on Rema, whose heart skipped a beat. Elise's somberness concealed defiance and adoration, mixed by some alchemy of her heart to form love. "But even this darkness will break. She's promised me so."

Cedrin and Talitha exchanged confused glances, while a rush of shame, sorrow and affection exhilarated Rema even as it twisted her insides and left her raw. "Elsie, I'm sorry."

Elise smiled. "I know."

Yorin nudged Rema in the ribs. Time to go. "I'm intruding," she said. "I'll leave you all to discuss this." Shame had sapped her breath, and she waited only for Talitha's nod before hurrying toward the door. As Rema passed the siblings, Loric turned his face away. Elise, however, touched Rema on the shoulder, and their eyes met. A melancholy passion blazed through Rema's soul—no sight, no dream, no vision had ever expressed such beauty as did Elise's forgiveness—and she strode from the throne room as if fleeing.

In the front court, she stopped and gasped for air. The sun poured through the high windows as if nothing were wrong in the world.

The court was empty but for Muhan, who was reclining on a bench. "You should sit," he said. "You look very pale."

"I hate myself." Rema stood before him, slumped in defeat. "I've done what I came for, but it would have been better had that man killed me in the gardens."

"You love her. Of course you feel this way."

"First Yorin, then Calan and now you. I'm not even going to bother denying it anymore."

Muhan swung his legs off the bench, and she sat beside him. "Often those who observe us know us better than we know ourselves," he said. "For example, I used to believe that I was a very good singer until my wife persuaded me otherwise."

Rema laughed, though she still felt swollen with restrained grief. "At least I know there's one thing you can't do."

"I swear there are many. Selling dye, conjuring, and wrestling. Those are my only skills. Well, I can also build ships, because I did that for a while as a young man. And I can draw very well. But besides these things I have no talents at all."

"I'd be glad to have no talents." It was strange to sit in the empty court; it was as if the palace's activity had stopped to mark this moment. "My talent is for convincing others, and today I used it for evil."

"I suspect you have done a great deal of good to balance the scales."

"Does it work that way? Or is one act of evil enough to undo a lifetime of good deeds?"

"Will it really be that bad for her? With Ormun?"

"His twelfth wife refused to sleep with him. She was a lively, witty woman, and when she arrived in the palace, she was certain that she'd take charge. Her face isn't even recognizable these days. She refused him for a month, and each time you could recognize her less."

Muhan hissed. "Ah…and why do you still work for this man?"

"See, now you're judging me too, despite all the good on my scales." How far was her voice traveling through the hushed palace? "Muhan, a warlord without a peacemaker is nothing more than a wild animal. I'm the only one who still dares to question him, to give him better advice…the gods help me, I've known him since I was seventeen. Ormun's wickedness has grown over time. There was a time when I even had such love for him as one would have for a brother. He's not like Calan, who sounds like he was rotten from the womb. Ormun found only later in life that it was easier to take what he wanted."

"But you couldn't question him on this marriage?"

"No." Rema stared at the court wall until its stones blurred together. "He believes that these brides are his to take. I did fight him for a time, until the pain of doing so became too great. Yet I should have kept fighting until he killed me. That would be better than this."

Muhan patted her on the shoulder. "Evil men have short lives. Who knows what the future holds?"

"Who knows indeed." Rema raised her head and straightened her back. She had dwelt enough in pity. "Do you know where Domyr and the Narandane servants are being quartered?"

"Of course. Like you, I pay attention. It'd be easier to show you than to describe. Shall I lead the way?"

"Please do."

They left the echoing court behind them. After a short walk, Muhan took her to a hall that ended at a doorway flanked by two armed men. "In there."

"Thank you. I'll be sure to see you again before I leave."

"Perhaps at dinner. I imagine you have no desire to dine with the royalty at present."

Rema clasped her hands in a sign of farewell, and Muhan copied the gesture before returning the way they had come, the ends of his colorful tunic drifting through the air. After a pensive pause, she continued down the corridor.

"Good day, my lord," said the shorter of the two guards.

"Lady," said the other guard. "It's that imperial diplomat, you oaf."

"Ah." The first guard scratched at his beard. "My apologies."

"Don't mention it," said Rema. "I'd like to speak to Domyr, if that's allowed."

The guards glanced at each other, and the first shrugged. "I suppose there's no reason why not. Diplomats talking to diplomats. Makes sense."

"Thank you." Rema pushed the door open. The wide chamber beyond was furnished with several worn but well-padded chairs, all of which circled a low, flat table. Domyr was sitting in one of the chairs, while his two remaining servants waited in the corner of the room.

Domyr raised his head. "Most honored Remela. I was distressed to hear that my man attacked you. I am pleased you survived."

"I'm quite pleased as well." Rema settled into the armchair with the closest view of Domyr's stern features. "You'll excuse me if I get right to my point."

"Nobody with wisdom can object to brevity."

"I want you never to reveal the identity of the Danoshan traitor." Rema leaned forward, staring into Domyr's depthless eyes. "And when you get back to Lyorn, I want you to burn the letter that you were sent."

It was no wonder Domyr had been chosen to impersonate a diplomat; Rema had seen statues betray more emotion. Still, she had little doubt he comprehended her.

"I know you won't confirm a single word I'm saying," said Rema. "That doesn't matter. I also know that in a day or two you'll leave the capital on your way back to Lyorn. We both understand there's no evidence to link you to the attack on my person."

"Lyorn? You are confused. I am a Narandane." Domyr's lips betrayed the barest hint of a smile.

"A Narandane from Lyorn. And when you return home, you and your servants will be very rich people." Rema took out her purse and spilled its contents across the table. Golden coins bounced and clinked together. Domyr's eyes lowered to take in the wealth before him, but his face remained impassive. "In either Narandor or Lyorn, I'm sure I don't need to tell you what even a fifth of this could buy. All you need to do is burn the letter and never speak a word of this affair again."

"Your words are nonsensical and bewilder me." Domyr half-closed his eyes as he reclined in his chair. "You also appear to have spilled money on the table. Perhaps this is some consequence of your injury."

"That's right. I've injured myself, I'm rambling and I've spilled my coin purse, but I'm far too rich and lazy to pick the coins up. If you gather them for me, I'll reward you by letting you keep them all."

Domyr glanced at his servants, and a smile finally broke the sullen cast of his face. "I see now why my people fled the West. The heat there has a terrible effect upon one's senses."

"You should be grateful. Calan wanted this war to last a generation. If he'd had his way, you'd have seen many villages destroyed and buried too many dead. I've taken away your victory, and in return I've given you peace. Savor it for some time before you decide to break it again. You might just find that it appeals to you."

Domyr chuckled, deep and guttural. "While your words are nothing but strange fancies, I will do what I can to appease your whims."

"That's all I request."

Rema bowed, pushed the empty coin purse back into her pocket and left the room. She nodded to the guards before returning down the hallway. Much had been resolved, but her work in Danosha was not quite done. There remained one loose thread, the one most liable to cause her agreement to unravel—and before she confronted it, she needed a moment's respite.

The kitchen was abandoned but for a few dour-faced servants. Alys was in the pantry, crouching by a sack of grain and chasing out weevils. "Hello, Alys," said Rema. "I'd like to take some food back to my room. Do you have time to help me?"

"Yes!" Alys shook a weevil from her fingertip and dashed to the pantry with Rema in tow. "We have honey today, Rema, and there's a loaf just about to come warm out of the oven."

"Lucky me. I've also become fond of that cheese."

"You'll get fat." Alys wagged her finger. "And then you won't fit into your magnificent trousers anymore. What a shame that will be. Here, have these grapes too. I'll put them in this bowl."

"Grapes as well? I will get fat." Rema ducked as a servant walked past carrying an enormous leg of lamb, and Alys laughed. "It's certainly quieter than usual. Usually the kitchens seem hectic at this time of day."

"Well, of course! Everyone knows the news. First you were attacked, and everybody was worried for you. I'm so happy to see you safe. Then we all find out that our beloved Lady Elise is going away, so nobody's in much of a mood to smile. Who's going to tend to our bunions now?"

"Let's hurry. I want to get back to my room, and I'm hungry." They began their journey to Rema's chamber, Alys carrying the tray while Rema clutched the bowl of grapes to her chest. With all her recent distractions, she had almost forgotten about the fresh wound on her back, but now the insistent pain returned. If only she had some of Elise's numbing ointment on hand.

Upon reaching for her bedchamber door, Rema hesitated—damn it all, the key was still in the pocket of her ruined coat. "I don't have my key. Elise has it."

"Don't fret," said Alys. "I'll go get another."

She darted away, leaving Rema to guard the food. The wound gnawed at her, made worse by her exhaustion from walking the palace—she would likely dream for weeks of walking these bleak halls. It was unfair. Injured and tired as she was, she ought to be in bed with a beautiful woman feeding her these grapes by hand. Perhaps Jalaya, her sweet singer, so tender with her affections...and what would Elise make of that?

After some minutes, Alys returned triumphantly waving a key. As they entered the room, Rema noted her clean outfit folded on the bed, just as Yorin had promised. It was just as well she'd remembered to bring a spare; it would have been shameful to return without a uniform.

"Here you are." Alys placed the tray on Rema's bedside table and, after a moment's indecision, dropped the bowl of grapes on her bed. "You sleep and get well! You look very pale."

"I'll try." Rema sat on the bed, sipped water from a flask and crunched a grape between her teeth. As Rema ate, Alys hovered in the doorway.

"Will you be leaving us soon, Rema?"

"I'm afraid so, but I'll say goodbye before I do."

"Don't tell anyone, but I stole some trousers from one of the servant boys, and I've been wearing them in secret. They're so comfortable, and I feel tough! I don't know why we're not supposed to!"

"There's no sensible law that says we can't. People will stare at you and sometimes poke fun, but that's their problem, not yours."

"You're so wise. I wish all women could be like you. You don't take lip from anyone, and you're just as smart as Yorin. I thought he was the smartest person in the world until I met you."

Rema forced a smile. As sweet as the compliment was, it left her heart heavy. As a servant woman in a feudal kingdom, Alys would always struggle against an inescapable tyranny that enfolded her life with cruelties. Perhaps Loric would set things right; he was a gentle boy and would become a good man. But then, Rema had once thought the same about Ormun. An old sorrow moved in her soul, and she banished her unhappy thoughts. "Don't flatter me. I've too much pride as it is."

Alys danced out of sight, closing the door as she went. Rema picked at her food, and when it was gone she lay on her side, waiting. If she remained still, the wound didn't seem to bother her, and she found that when she breathed slowly, she could even relax. Unfortunately, such relaxation caused her thoughts to drift inevitably to Elise. The voyage home was certain to be a nightmare. Every day Elise would be taken closer to the fate she'd feared her entire life, and Rema would be there to watch her fall deeper into despair, unable to console her…

The sound of the door opening woke Rema from a drowsy, feverish slumber. "I've been waiting for you," she said, sitting upright.

"You're a sly one," said Bannon, closing the door behind him and pulling back his hood. He scrutinized the room with his pale eyes. Apparently satisfied, he reclined against the door and pushed his thumbs into the loop of his belt. "For someone who was almost killed today, you've accomplished quite a bit, haven't you?"

"You understood my message then."

"You knew that I would. By the way, Calan was livid when you left. He took it out on the prisoner, which I'm sure will hurt you to know."

Nausea touched Rema's throat—the brutality never ended, it seemed. "I'm sure you did everything you could to stop him."

"Not my responsibility. I will say, though, watching the two of you go at each other was entertaining. You made it very clear who is the top dog."

"I can see we comprehend each other. How much?"

"Thirty thousand gold imperials, property—nothing fancy—and safe passage to Arann. Lyorn is very eager to get their hands on me, and every day their claws get closer. Calan's too dumb to see it, of course."

"Agreed. You'll travel back with me, and upon our return I'll pay you the money. You should understand that I loathe you and everything that you've done."

"My heart breaks." Bannon chuckled. "I'm curious. How could you be so sure I'd understand your intention and come to you?"

"Believe it or not, Bannon, but you're not the first greedy, ambitious mercenary I've met."

Bannon's mellow laugh was an odd contrast to his unfeeling eyes. "You're a subtle operator. A few hints about your wealth, cutting Calan down to size, all the while trying to coax me into realizing that I've put my money on the wrong cock."

"I hope you're talking about roosters. Otherwise, I have some surprising news for you."

"I do enjoy that wit of yours." Bannon flashed a mouthful of even teeth. "You know, the worst thing about Calan is that he has no sense of humor. Well, he thinks he does, but it all comes down to crude jokes about women. Me, I know the rougher corners of the world, and I've met plenty of women who could break Calan over their knee."

"So I take it you won't lose any sleep over your betrayal."

"No man alive sleeps sounder than me. At any rate, you're lucky I came. Now Calan's been denied his precious war, he's told me to execute our bloody little backup plan. An hour after midnight tonight, another assassin and I will dispatch certain targets. Loric, Cedrin, Talitha. You too. Calan would love to do you himself, but he's afraid to spill the blood of an imperial diplomat. The steward survives, because Calan knows the court would collapse without him. As for his sister, he intends to kill her with his own hands."

Rema maintained her composure, but it was hard to keep the horror from her voice. "And then?"

"And then I go to Calan's chamber with this other assassin, who believes we're about to receive our payment. I kill the poor bastard right there, make it look like a struggle. In the morning it appears that Calan, alone of everyone, has escaped death by waking just in time to cut down his assailant. I pocket some money and wipe my blade clean."

Rema stared at him in disgusted fascination. "And you'd have done it, too, wouldn't you?"

"I've done so much worse, believe me. But I got your hint and understood it very well. You can cut me a better deal, and Calan's an idiot who will get me killed eventually. You're a clever woman, Rema."

"I do my best. And now you'll earn my money by making it seem to Calan as if the plan is going ahead. I'll take care of the rest."

"I'd hate to be on your bad side." Bannon gave an amused snort. "Well, that's a stupid thing to say. I am on your bad side." He threw a salute before opening the door. "We'll talk again tomorrow. Oh, and try not to look at me with so much revulsion, it's ever so hurtful."

"Get on your way. I've had enough of the sight of you."

Bannon sauntered away, leaving the door open. Rema tried to stand, but her knees had stiffened again. She rubbed them, and when the pain eased she tottered to her feet, scarcely able to stay upright. It seemed her work would never be done.

She found Yorin haranguing maids in the kitchen. He peered at Rema, sighed and dismissed the maids with a gesture. "Be off with you, and don't do it again," he said as they scattered. "Rema, you were prudent to leave the throne room when you did. Loric continued ranting, the Queen became very upset, the King shouted at them both and then Elise shouted at him. It's a good thing nobody was armed."

The image was amusing, but Rema was too tired to laugh. "Poor Elise."

"She's in your hands now. I'm sure you'll think of something."

"And how do you feel about the state of affairs?"

"There's a decent chance I'll see my boy alive again. You can't imagine what that feels like. I've become so cheerful I even gave the head cook the night off, and now of course we're all far behind for dinner."

"I'm afraid I'll have to delay you a little more." Rema frowned at the servants moving around them, their hands filled with food and utensils. "We need to speak in private, Yorin."

"Well, that's easily done." Yorin clapped his hands. "Get out of here, all of you! And don't come back in until I say so!" The servants milled for a moment in confusion before filing through the doors, looking with curiosity at Rema as they went. "Why walk to a private location when you can make one?"

"I wish there were more stewards with your practicality." Though the room was now empty, Rema still pitched her voice low. "Calan intends to kill everyone tonight. Me, Elise, Loric, the King and Queen. Everyone except you, as it happens, so I suppose your hard work does have its rewards."

Yorin's eyebrows curled. "Are you certain? I knew he was vicious, but that's wholesale slaughter. How did you find out?"

"Never mind that. I have a plan, but I need you to arrange it. Get Muhan and Cedrin to come to my chamber just before midnight. Explain to Cedrin what I've told you. You also need to find Elise and ask her not to sleep in her tower tonight. Invent a reason if you have to. It's your palace, remember."

"What are you planning? Don't keep secrets from me, Rema."

"Calan intends to kill Elise in her sleep. I want Cedrin to see what kind of man his eldest son really is. I'll take Elise's place, and Cedrin will witness everything."

"Shouldn't I post some guards?" Yorin's cheeks had grown ashen. "You can't be counting on Muhan to subdue him. Both you and the King will be in grave danger."

"It'll work out as I intend, don't worry. Just make these arrangements and quickly."

"God above, and here I was thinking the worst was behind us. Yes, yes, I'll arrange it. I trust you. I just hope Elise listens. She was in quite a sulk after the fight in the throne room."

"If not, I'll talk to her. Don't worry, this will soon be over."

"We should just arrest him now—no, you're right, they'd never believe it without evidence. They don't even believe that he beats Elise. Damn it all." Shaking his head, Yorin hurried out of the room.

Rema tried to steady her thoughts. Her body throbbed with the day's exertions. If she didn't take the opportunity to rest for a few more hours, she'd be incapable of doing anything by the time midnight arrived. According to the large, dirty clock that hung in the kitchen, it was eight hours past noon—maybe. An accurate sense of time was among the many things she missed about the imperial palace, the halls of which breathed with the ticking of precise clocks crafted by the Arann's finest tinkers.

Upon returning to her chamber, she froze, her chest constricting. Elise was sitting at the end of the bed with a bundle in her lap. "Don't just stand there staring at me," she said. "It's your room. Come in."

Rema closed the door behind her. She sat on the edge of the bed and scrutinized Elise, whose clear expression suggested no signs of sulking. "I've brought you some more medicine," said Elise as she raised a little bottle from the bedside table. "To ease your pain and soothe your head. I also brought you back this wreck of a coat. I was touched to see you were carrying my most recent letter in your pocket."

"It's not a very happy letter. And yes, I did feel something reading it."

"But you won't admit what that feeling was." Elise sidled closer. "You're so coy. What are you afraid of?"

"If Ormun learns we might be more than friends, then we'd both have plenty to fear."

"Rema, dearest! Was that a confession?"

"You have an overactive imagination." Rema rested her fingertips lightly on Elise's knee. "Elsie, I have to ask you not to sleep in your tower tonight. It's better if you don't know why."

"Tell me it's because you want me to sleep here with you instead."

Rema laughed. Even this short time in Elise's presence had lifted her spirits and chased the shadows from her soul. "There's that imagination again."

Elise pursed her lips. "I suppose this is something to do with Calan. Well, it's about time I became accustomed to not sleeping in my tower. Fine." She waved the bottle. "Come on, drink your medicine."

Rema took the bottle, uncorked it and sipped it dry. The warmth drifted through her body and dissolved the pain. "That helped."

"Of course it helped. I'm very good at healing. And other things." Elise's smile radiated mischief. "So, when do you plan on dragging me away?"

"The ship that brought me here should still be around for another three days. The sooner we leave, the sooner we can get aid to your people."

"I have so many belongings up in my tower. Books and other things priceless to me. What will become of them?"

"We'll take it all. Anything that doesn't fit, you can put in my cabin."

"Your cabin? Can't we share a cabin?"

"The sailors would gossip, and in Arann gossip has a habit of spreading all the way to the palace itself."

"So, let me get this clear. You do want to share a cabin with me, but you won't because you're afraid of getting caught?"

Rema smiled. "I'm not saying anything. You're the one talking about cabins when I'm trying to keep our attention on serious matters."

"Very well! You win, wily diplomat. I won't sleep in my tower. But tell me the truth, are you putting yourself at risk for me again?"

"I always put myself at risk. It's part of my job."

"Rema." Elise shifted closer still. "Loric told me about the night you spent in my stairwell. He couldn't understand how you could do that for me yet still take me away to Arann."

Rema tried to meet Elise's eyes, but an uncooperative force drew her gaze instead to the seductive curves of Elise's mouth. "He no doubt exaggerated. I was only on the stairs for an hour or so. I didn't sleep there."

"You're such a liar." Elise hesitated, and her cheeks flared red. "What else have you done for me that I don't know about? Be honest. Do you love me?"

"I really should rest." Rema looked away, her heart hammering a disorderly beat. "I'm wounded, as you know, and I have some business to attend to later."

Elise sighed. "If you want me, you'd better say so before it's too late." She stood and brushed several fallen hairs from the bed. "I fear you're so used to playing games that you've lost sight of what you're gambling with. Our hearts are entirely alike in conviction, both committed to righteousness and compassion. It's only proper they be together."

Rema chewed on her lower lip, not daring to respond. Elise paused in the doorway, a hand on her hip. "I love you, and I want you to be careful tonight."

"I will be." A memory jolted Rema from her longing reverie. "By the way, did you make that prisoner unable to talk?"

Elise gave a deep, satisfied laugh. "If you're going to keep secrets from me, I'm going to keep secrets from you." She left the room, drawing the door shut behind her. Rema stretched on her side, closed her eyes and inhaled the lingering sensuality of Elise's perfume.

CHAPTER FIFTEEN

Rema was woken by a low, insistent tapping. She brushed the hair away from her eyes before opening the door. Muhan was waiting in the corridor with a lamp. His face was tense, and his eyes were black under the lamplight. Cedrin stood behind him. Despite his bulk, he seemed somehow diminished, and he played nervously with a gold ring on his finger.

"Your Grace," Rema said. "Muhan. Did Yorin explain why I called for you?"

Cedrin nodded, still turning the ring. "I can't quite believe it. Why would my boy plan something like this?"

"You know why. He doesn't want this war to end, and once word of our agreement reaches Lyorn, they may concede even before the first ship lands on your shores. He has no time to act but now."

"If you are correct, you have saved my kingdom twice over." Cedrin squared his shoulders and frowned at her, a shade of defiance returning to his eyes. "If you are not, then I will expect you to leave and not return here again."

"I understand. Muhan, I suppose you know what I need you to do."

"Juggle?" said Muhan, his teeth tinted by the lamplight.

Rema joined the men in the corridor. "Let's not waste any time." They walked through the hall and into the front court, where the night had transformed the familiar space into something foreboding. Silver luminescence lit the walls, and thin fingers of shadow lay between the benches and the flagstones. The shimmering pall of moonlight recalled Elise's eyes, and Rema permitted herself a smile. Nowadays, everything reminded her of Elise.

The trio ascended to the palace's top floor, Rema and Muhan treading lightly and Cedrin struggling behind them. Darkness enveloped the hallways, a gloom pierced rarely by the weak sputtering of a torch. After several minutes of travel, Muhan's lamplight caught a familiar archway, and the group stopped before the stairwell to Elise's tower.

Rema climbed first, her fingers brushing against the curved stone wall. Cedrin wheezed from the effort, and he exhaled in relief as they reached the top. Rema opened the unlocked door and ushered them through. Starlight shone over the arcane clutter of Elise's room.

"Your Grace, if you would seat yourself in the corner," Rema said, closing the door behind them. The chair was in a pool of darkness, and when Cedrin settled himself on it, only someone looking closely could detect the way the shadows bent against his large body.

Rema turned to Muhan, whose colorful robes were washed pale by the silver light. "Muhan, if you stand beside the door, you'll be in a perfect position to surprise Calan." Muhan nodded as he stood sentinel. His tall, lean body was a reassuring presence. Contemptible worm or not, Calan was a physically daunting man, and this little adventure carried real dangers.

Rema pulled back Elise's blankets. "And I will take my place in the bed."

"You're using yourself as bait?" said Muhan. "Dear daughter of traders, are you afraid of nothing?"

"I'm afraid of only one man, and he's in Arann." Rema lay on the bed and drew the blanket over her face. The mattress was cool, and Elise's fragrance permeated the sheets. Rema took a deep breath to dissolve her tension before pressing her cheek to the pillow. Elise had promised to spend the night in one of the guest chambers, and it was a pleasant distraction to imagine her sitting awake, wondering what was taking place in her tower.

Rema waited for so long—entertaining herself with thoughts of Elise—that she might have fallen asleep if not for the anxiety clawing up the sides of her stomach. The stretch of time became immeasurable in the darkness, and visions formed and fell apart in the recesses of her mind. Finally the door opened, and a heavy step was followed by another. Her skin crawled—a dagger might be seconds from her heart.

She rose, casting off the blankets. Calan stood poised in the incriminating light of the moon. He held not a dagger but a shortsword, and his face was pale against the black of his tunic. His look of lethal composure slipped, and his mouth fell open. "You?"

"So it's true," said Cedrin. Calan started, and he looked about the room before locking his eyes on the shadowed form of the king. "Why are you doing this, son?"

"Why?" Calan laughed with an edge of hysteria. "Where do I begin? This is the kingdom I am intended to inherit, and by the time it passes to me it will be little more than a whipped dog. If we do not revenge ourselves on Lyorn, rip their lands asunder and take their wealth, then we will remain weak, backward, impotent!"

Calan brandished his sword at Rema. "This bitch knows I'm right. To her, Danosha is a joke. She sees us as provincial, unimaginative swineherds, happy to rule a pit of mud until the end of our days. A traitor you may think me now, Father, but like you, I want to improve the lot of our people. With the wealth and lands of Lyorn, we could improve the towns, enrich our farms and open up new ports of trade. The great powers would finally take us seriously. No longer would diplomats like her laugh at us as if we were still children building towers with rocks."

A strident plea entered his voice. "Father, listen. This woman intends to neuter us. Ormun isn't offering us anything but irrelevance. The terms you signed talk of parity between us and Lyorn, as if there were only our two nations in this world and not a host of other enemies already swelling in size and power! If we let Ormun hobble us, we will fall prey to Dantium, Kalanis, perhaps even the Empire of the Pale Plains itself." His voice grew steadier. "Think to our legacy. I chose to act as I did because I believed, yes, truly believed, that you were not ruling in the interests of the kingdom. Your death would have brought me no pleasure, but once it became clear you had ignored my counsel, I could see no other way. You would have died for Danosha."

An impressive speech, wasted in the service of savagery. "Perhaps you would have lamented killing your father and mother, though I doubt it," said Rema. "But Elise—I've no doubt you would have relished her murder. You imagined you'd finally triumph over the woman who has never shown you the fear and submission you crave. Instead, here you stand, bested utterly by the sex you so despise."

Calan steadied the shortsword. "My consolation in the grave will be that I took you with me."

Before Calan could move more than a step, Muhan lunged from concealment and caught him around the waist. As Calan grunted and struggled, Muhan turned his narrow shoulders, and they both spiraled to the ground, Calan landing with Muhan's knee pressed into his stomach.

"She will live a thousand years while you will die the death of traitors," said Muhan as he gripped Calan's arm and forced it behind his head. "Rema, he cannot move now until I choose to let him."

Rema stood above Calan. As he struggled, his eyes twitched, and his muscles worked in pointless exertion. She could taunt him with impunity now, but what was the point? "I believe we should fetch the guards."

"No need." Yorin entered the room with two colossal guardsmen behind him. "Don't look so startled. I had Calan trailed, and when I knew that he was in the tower I brought the guards with me."

Did this irrepressible steward have to be involved in everything? "Yorin, really! I told you to let me take care of it."

"Don't be petulant, now." Yorin frowned at Calan, who turned his head away. "So it's true. It wasn't enough that you couldn't give your sister a moment's peace throughout her poor life. You aspired to kill her too. I should have smothered you in the cradle, you venomous, detestable, loathsome—"

"Yorin," said Cedrin, and Yorin's brows jumped.

"Your Grace." Yorin bowed with haste. "I didn't see you there. Forgive me."

"Please have your guardsmen escort Calan to the cells. Talitha and I will need much time to decide what is to be done."

Yorin gestured to the guards. "You heard the King! Take Prince Calan to his new quarters. Don't bother dusting them this time."

Muhan yanked Calan to his feet—Calan's face contorted with the ache of constrained violence, but he seemed unable to break free—before shoving him to the guards. They took him by either arm and dragged him toward the door.

As he was forced into the stairwell, Calan held his gaze on Rema. "Enjoy fucking my sister from here to Arann. There's a death sentence over both of our heads." As the sound of his boots scraping down the stairs faded, Rema shivered. Rarely were parting words so frighteningly true.

"Forgive Calan his vulgarities," said Cedrin. "I must go now and tell Talitha what has transpired. It will be a shock to her, as if she had lost two children in one night." Weariness clouded his eyes. "We owe you a great debt."

"Not so," said Rema. "I've stolen Elise from you. No act can compensate for such a loss."

"I was dubious when I first saw you." Cedrin struggled to his feet. "A female diplomat was well beyond my understanding. Now I begin to see the error of my thinking. Please take care of my daughter. She is difficult and audacious."

"Those are strengths, Your Grace." Rema's power returned as she spoke, for the first time, in open defense of the woman she secretly loved. "Your daughter is one of the finest women I've ever met. Her courage has moved and inspired me. Her words of indignation are like a fire amid the snow. You should have nothing but pride in her."

"I never was an easy father." Cedrin crossed to the window and stared into the night. "I judged her as wicked. I ignored her pleas to remain unmarried. I knew she was suffering, but I told myself that it was only proper, given her crimes against nature. Now the sound of her laughter will no longer ring through my palace. I will never again pass by her pouting on the stairs, nor find her sporting with Loric in the gardens, nor watch the light play across her hair as she tends to the soreness of my heels. And I cannot even pray to our God to help her, for he despises her kind." He inhaled deeply, and his old body shivered. "I will carry this shame to my death. I put my faith in my son instead of my daughter, and he has betrayed me as I betrayed her." He shuffled from the room, and his heavy tread echoed in the stairwell.

Yorin collapsed into the nearest chair. "Tell me that's the last of it. These have been the most stressful days of my life. And that includes the week the palace was overrun by beetles."

Rema sat on the edge of the mattress. Cedrin's parting words had left her melancholy, and it was impossible to feel any triumph. "So much has happened in such a short space of time. It feels as if I only arrived this morning."

"Ah, well." Muhan pulled his mustache to its full length. "It's like the steam beneath a pot lid. It builds slowly, but when it reaches its limit, how suddenly it bursts." He released his mustache so that it flicked back into its curl. "In any event, I'm pleased to have played my small part in this performance."

"You should both stay a day or two more," said Yorin. "You deserve to rest at least a little. You'd make an excellent steward, Rema. You've endured so much, yet you've remained in control throughout."

"We'll need to stay tomorrow at least, to pack Elise's belongings," said Rema. "I want to her to be able to take as many of her possessions as possible."

"That can be arranged." Yorin gazed at the moon, which hung full and pensive beyond the tower's wide window. "It's the paperwork I'm dreading."

"As soon as Domyr reaches home, Lyorn will know their victory is lost. Your son will be home sooner than you expect."

Yorin seemed a decade younger as he smiled. "Perhaps I'll celebrate your visit by permitting the servant women to wear trousers. Alys will be delighted. She thinks I don't know she's been stealing them and trying them on."

"As for myself," said Muhan. "It's been some time since I visited Arann, and there are far worse places to sell dye."

Delight drove away some of Rema's malaise. "You'll come with us? Your company would be very welcome." Not least because of the corrupt presence of that other companion she had agreed to bring with her. She imagined Bannon skulking aboard ship, smirking at her with his fishlike eyes. Could even Muhan subdue a man who seemed so sure on his feet?

"Well," said Yorin as he stood. "I'm going to catch my precious few hours of sleep."

"So you do sleep. I'd been wondering."

As Yorin and Muhan descended the stairs of the tower, Rema paused in the doorway and looked back into the pale emptiness of Elise's bedroom. This had been Elise's home and sanctuary for much of her life, a world that she had fought to build and keep. Now she had resigned herself to losing it, and all for a covert understanding between them, a promise concealed in poetry. Though Elise's future seemed grim, Rema would remain by her side, loving her and sustaining her through the darkness of her sorrow.

PART TWO

CHAPTER SIXTEEN

In her youth, Rema had never experienced a sea voyage. She had spent her life traveling across Amantis's famed expanses, and her feet had been trained for sand and stone, not hardened wood. The ocean had proven a cruel revelation. On her first journey as a junior diplomat, headed to the silk-trade city of Molon, she had failed to keep a single meal in her stomach, and the sailors had laughed about her all the way back to port.

Now, of course, she was as tough as any sea-dog. It had been a fortnight since the coast of Danosha had vanished from sight, and her spirits remained high. As a rule, she never wore her uniform when at sea, preferring loose garments—pantaloons, harem garb, anything that might allow the cool breeze to rest between the fabric and her slender body.

She stood on deck, her hands placed upon the sun-warmed timber of a wooden rail. The great waters around her reflected the glare of the afternoon sun, but the limitless clasp of sea and sky was nonetheless beautiful to behold.

A measured step rang out against the planks. Rema knew without turning that it would be her princess-prisoner; the sailors thudded and clattered, Muhan always walked while humming, and Bannon—well, that creature crept without sound.

"I hate the smell of the sea," said Elise in Annari. She spoke the language imperfectly, but Rema had impressed upon her the need to polish it. "That briny odor. And the sailors are always bringing those awful nets of fish up from the deeps."

"They're merely ensuring that we don't go hungry."

"Speak for yourself. With that stink on everything, I can't eat a bite." Elise stood beside Rema and squinted at the horizon. "Have you seen any porpoises today?"

Elise's fickleness was an endless source of amusement to Rema and Muhan both. Seagulls she loathed, sailors she barely tolerated and the captain she thought one of the most abominable people alive. On the first day aboard, he had scolded her for carrying about in skimpy dresses, and she had stridently denounced him as a hypocrite, given that most of his crew worked shirtless. In her fury, she had forced him up against the mast, insulting him while Rema drew upon all her diplomatic reserves not to laugh.

Porpoises, however, she seemed quite fond of. "I saw two yesterday," Elise said, shading her eyes. "And Muhan tells me he spotted another. He says if I'm vigilant and fortunate, I may someday see a white one."

"Sailors do tell tales of white porpoises. Though they can never seem to decide whether they're an ill omen or an augur of good fortune."

"I'm certain it's neither. They're simply beautiful."

"I suppose you should know, being a sorceress."

Elise laughed. "Actually, none of my books say a word about porpoises. Apparently wizards pay them very little attention."

As Elise continued her hunt for porpoises, Rema covertly appreciated Elise's choice of dress: a red garment slit on either side to the upper thigh, baring Elise's legs and concealing only her essential modesties. Its low bodice exposed her shoulders and her cleavage, which was a particular source of anxiety to the captain, who believed such an ample bosom posed a risk to his crew. That may or may not have been true, but it was certainly dangerous for Rema.

A sailor stumbled onto deck, and Rema quickly returned her attention to the waves. The seaman crouched, bent his muscular back and began to scrub the tributes of the gulls from the planks. If the crew suspected Rema of paying more attention to Elise than was proper, they gave no indication of it. Muhan, on the other hand, seemed to notice every covert glance, and each time he responded with a low, chiding sound intended only for her ears.

Time to find a new diversion. "How are you this afternoon?" said Rema to the sailor.

"As cheerful as a man can be wrist-deep in birdshit." The sailor dipped a cloth in a bucket. "I'll be happier when evening comes. I've got a plan to conquer that friend of yours."

"Oh?" Rema didn't have to ask who he meant. Muhan had proven a sensation among the crew from the moment he had walked aboard, slapped the mast and declared this to be the finest ship he had ever had the privilege of standing upon. He had further won their admiration through juggling shows, acts of conjuring and his enthusiastic participation in the difficult labor that operated the ship. His chief claim to fame, however, had been his wrestling.

"Aye, it's a fact. You see, I've noted he favors his left side. True, he sometimes conceals this weakness by favoring his right instead, but I think I've him figured nonetheless."

"So the prize is as good as yours?"

"Just you watch, my lady. He'll hit the deck in under a minute."

It seemed unlikely. After Muhan had issued his challenge to the crew—that if they could pin him to deck, they would have all the wealth he had accrued in Danosha—there had been no shortage of contenders, yet even the immense first mate had proven incapable of moving the dye merchant from his feet. Because Muhan cannily asked each sailor to stake a few coins before each match, he had only increased the riches on offer, which made the prospect of battle all the more enticing. It was the kind of bold scheme Rema's mother would have admired.

Rema gestured toward Elise, whose face was sulky as she scoured the waves for her beloved porpoises. "Perhaps you should ask Elise for a token of favor."

"The captain's forbidden us to talk to the princess." The sailor sighed as he plunged the cloth back into the bucket. "But if you'd like to arrange something on my behalf…"

"Believe me, I'm in no position to share any luck. I need all that I have." Rema nodded. "I'd best not occupy more of your time. Good day, sailor."

She rejoined Elise, who seemed irritated by the break in conversation. "Why must you avoid me?" she said. "It's me who should enjoy your talk, not these sweaty brutes."

"I'm not avoiding you, Elsie. I'm simply trying not to consume your time."

Elise's lips moved in the flirtatious, mischievous smile that Rema had come to dread. "I wish you would consume me. I think about it night and day."

"Elsie!" Rema peeked over her shoulder. Fortunately, the sailor seemed too distant to hear. "You mustn't talk so candidly around the crew."

"But there's crew everywhere. They crawl all over the ship. If you don't like their presence, come to my cabin and we'll talk there."

"You know I can't do that. Not without cause."

"You do have a cause, though. And I wore this dress specifically to remind you of it." Elise slid her hand down her stomach and rested it just above her thighs, fingers suggestively parted. "If you come to my cabin, I'll remind you in more detail."

Such performances were Elise's revenge, and an effective revenge at that. In return for the ignominy of capture, she seemed determined to flirt with Rema at every opportunity. Ordinarily, Rema would have thrilled at the discovery Elise possessed such a carnal mind, but under the circumstances, her lewdness was nothing less than terrifying.

"I recall a timid woman who tried to make me blush by asking questions, only to turn crimson in an instant herself." Rema frowned at the grinning, unrepentant Elise. "What happened to her, I wonder?"

"She realized she no longer had anything to lose by audacity." Elise shook her wild hair over her shoulder. "If you aren't going to help me look for porpoises, and you aren't going to converse with me, you could at least lighten my day with a smile."

Rema could hardly deny the request, and when Elise returned the smile in kind, Rema's anxiety broke in an instant. Though the last two weeks had been stressful, Elise had also proven a perfect companion who never tired of stories of foreign lands, courts and cities. Her deep laughter and husky voice had become quickly beloved to Rema, and whenever Elise listened in her wondering reverie, her face became especially beautiful, lips parted in rapture, eyes more mystical than ever.

"Rema!" Muhan's voice came from the top step of the staircase that led below decks. He looked resplendent in his colored garments; he had redyed his mustache a vivid yellow, and his eyebrows were stained a startling blue. "May I have your company a moment?"

"Won't you join us here?" asked Elise. She had grown fond of Muhan, despite an initial aversion to his fakery, as she called it. She admired his wisdom and geniality, and he, in turn, enjoyed her quick temper and incisive questioning.

Muhan shook his head. "It concerns our fellow traveler."

"Ah!" Elise reacted as if somebody had touched her with a wet fish. She despised Bannon to the point she refused to even acknowledge his presence, and Rema could hardly blame her. "Then go on with you, Rema. I'll tell you if I see anything interesting."

"Please do."

Rema followed Muhan to the lower deck, where they stood in the shade of a sail. Sailors worked around them—and one above, too, in the rigging—but they paid no attention to Rema and Muhan. It was impossible to enjoy such privacy with Elise present, for no matter where she stood, she drew the attention of every man on deck.

"What's Bannon done?" said Rema. From the moment of boarding, Bannon had been as elusive as he was menacing. He had a cabin but never seemed to be in it, and sailors complained he roamed the deck at night, scaring them with his unblinking eyes. He never helped on deck, ate alone, and was often seen aft at evening, gazing in the direction of the land they'd just fled.

"Nothing more than is usual. I merely have mustered the courage to ask you a question that has long dogged me." Muhan pressed his hands together as he spoke, a typical Ulati custom when broaching a sensitive topic. "Rema, are you threatened by this man?"

"Threatened? How do you mean?"

"I understand you won him from his former master with promises of wealth, but do you fear reprisal if you abandon him?"

Understanding dawned. "Are you offering to dispose of him for me?"

"Accidents can happen at sea. I am not disposed to lethality, but I fear for you when I see the way he stares. Violence has marked that man as its own."

"His appearance is a mere accident of nature. I've known many a good soul with an unhappy visage. Whereas Calan could be said to be handsome, but he was as squalid a person as any I've met."

"He and Bannon are not the same manner of fiend. I have encountered men like Bannon throughout this world, and women too. Though he has never spoken to me, I know it is not from malice but simple disinterest. And I have learned to fear the kind of man in whose company I might spend a fortnight, yet will never once be bid a good morning. They are the kind who never tremble, show mercy or even understand human goodness. The kind whose lives are decided only by the edge of a blade."

"I understand, but I have to fulfill my obligation. Just ignore him. When we arrive in Arann, he'll simply become one of many mercenaries."

"There are mercenaries, and then there are devils." Muhan shrugged. "As you wish. Merely remember my words to you. How goes the princess? Does she still torment you?"

Rema chuckled. "Yes, she does. I suppose I deserve it."

"She has expressed to me an almost frantic desire to have a private conversation with you. It frustrates her immensely, and I don't believe her thinking to be entirely lustful. She has many fears to share, Rema, and very little time in which to share them." Muhan smiled. "Thus I have arranged a conjuring act for this evening. The crew will be in attendance, bar an unlucky few. Take opportunity of it to give her the comfort she craves."

His point, though discreetly put, had a bite to it. It wasn't as if Elise would forcibly ravish Rema, after all. If she remained vigilant and remembered her purpose, why should she fear a little intimacy? Wasn't it only right that she offer Elise solace and reassurance?

"I take your meaning," said Rema. "Thank you, Muhan."

"I wish only the best for you, poet-born." Muhan bowed with his hands clasped to his chest. "I must now offer my assistance to the crew. How fortunate for them that I am here, given they lost three hands in Danosha."

"I'm only amazed that any sailor would choose to abscond to Danosha, of all the ports in the world." Rema returned the farewell gesture. "Take care, Muhan. And don't mind Bannon."

"I can no more ignore him than I would ignore a viper inside my own tent." Muhan strode across deck, rubbing his palms together.

After a moment's consideration, Rema returned up the stairwell. Elise remained where she had stood before, but she had slumped against the railing, her cheek pressed to the wood. "Elsie."

It turned out that Elise was half in slumber. She murmured as she opened her eyes fully. "I thought I'd try dozing."

"Why not read in your cabin?"

"My cabin is too hot. And if I read on deck, the gulls befoul the pages." At the mention of gulls, Elise bared her teeth. "They're hideous rodents."

"I have an invitation for you. Come take the air with me this evening. We'll meet here and watch the sun set. I have reason to believe the crew will be distracted elsewhere."

"Oh!" Elise stood bolt upright. "How romantic. Will there be more of your tales, or may we finally talk candidly?"

"Candidly." It was a tough concession, yet Elise's delight made the word worth uttering. "At sunset, remember."

Elise laughed. "How could I forget? Well, now you've told me this, I'll keep watching the waves. Given my sudden luck, perhaps a white porpoise truly is near."

"I thought you said they weren't lucky or unlucky."

"I can't know, though, can I? I'm willing to be proven wrong." Elise clutched the railing as she leaned forward to look more intently at the ocean. Rema resisted the urge to pull her back to safety; the one time she'd done so, Elise had thrown a spectacular tantrum. "I'd be even happier to see a whale, but Muhan says there are none in these waters."

"Did he now? I've heard of whales being spotted in these seas."

"Truly?" Elise's smile widened further. "Then I'll watch for whales as well. Do you know what I like about the ocean, Rema? It's unconquerable. Warlords like Calan think they can have dominance over all that there is, but they forget this. The lands beneath the sea, the odd animals that call it home. My books say that people live down there, walking in cities of coral, staring up at a shimmering canopy of water they call the sky."

"Perhaps someday, my business will take me there." Rema touched the back of Elise's hand briefly, the most contact she dared. "I shall see you soon."

"Yes, yes." Elise sighed as she slumped back to the railing. "But already I'm bored again."

To shake thoughts of Elise and Bannon, Rema retired to her cabin. Its single porthole was obscured by a piece of netting, and it reeked of varnish. She checked on her trunk—still safely stowed in the corner—before reclining on her hammock with a book. This was one of the titles from Elise's great library, but a book on history, not magic. It detailed the Danoshan nobility, dwelling especially on the royal Danarian line. It had been written some decades ago, and it ended its timeline with the young Cedrin Danarian, who had apparently come to reign at the age of ten.

As fascinating as the subject of Elise's forebears was, weariness found Rema somewhere amid the pages. She awoke under a reddish glow. Not quite sunset, but near enough that she risked missing her appointment. Without a single twinge from her knees, she rose, put her book safely away and stepped into the hall outside her cabin.

The ship was riddled inside with narrow halls, the floors of which often tilted with its movement. Rema navigated with as much certainty as she could—her cabin had been changed from the first voyage, and she had spent some time reacquainting herself with a new route to the lower deck. She passed by a galley occupied by sailors, and soon encountered three more walking together. Two of them appeared animated, full of mirth, and a quick glance revealed why—they were supporting the sailor who had boasted that he would defeat Muhan. It appeared he had instead secured himself a bruised forehead and a look of despondency.

"No luck?" she said.

The sailor only muttered. His companions sniggered, and one gave Rema a friendly smile. A few of the sailors still held to the superstition regarding women on deck, but in the eyes of most, an imperial diplomat was not a female at all. Besides, Rema's appetites were no secret in Arann, and most of the crew were aware that Rema had bedded more women than any of them. Oddly, that fact seemed to win her a certain amount of respect.

The lower deck was abandoned. The sun had dipped to the horizon, caressing the ocean with the last of its light, and a faint sprinkling of stars decorated the sky above it. As Rema walked by the mast, a board creaked to her left, and she turned. She had half-expected Elise, impatient to see her. Instead, she met Bannon's malignant gaze as he emerged from around the corner of the wheelhouse.

His hood was down, and he wore a leather cloak that trailed behind him. The dagger in his belt seemed to have been placed there deliberately as a reminder—it was not quite in its sheath, exposing a meaningful hint of metal—and his smile, as ever, was charming in design but utterly cold. "Your princess is at the prow," he said. "Looking as expectant as a maiden in a moonlit garden."

"I suppose you want me to thank you for not pushing her over the edge."

"It'd be a hell of a splash."

Rema scowled. Her patience was considerable, but this man had a unique knack for testing it. "I don't care for your jokes, Bannon."

"Tell me a better one, then. What did that Ulati want from you earlier? Is he angling to break my neck?"

"Muhan didn't mention you."

"Then why did he say my name?" Bannon smirked. "I can read lips, Rema. You don't get to be the kind of man I am without mastering a few covert arts."

"And what kind of man is that?"

"A still-breathing one. Do him a favor and warn him that I'm not a sailor to be wrestled. I don't have any reason to see him dead, so personally, I'd prefer not to have to dispatch him."

Rema sighed. What was the point of lying to a man who cheerfully admitted to his own atrocities? "He was concerned for me, but I warned him off. I know very well that Muhan couldn't kill you, even if I wanted him to."

"That's perceptive of you. I suspect he knows it too, but alas, he's noble to a fault. Do you think he fancies you?"

"I very much doubt it."

Bannon took a step back and drew his cloak shut, concealing his dagger. "Lady Elise isn't dressed for ocean weather. I fancy she'll freeze up there. Unless you've plans to keep her warm."

"Why don't you go spend time sorting through the lobster nets? You might find one of your relatives."

"I bet you're fun with a few glasses of wine in you. I heard the sailors talking about how you're the most powerful woman in Arann."

"I'm hardly the most powerful woman, even at court. The Emperor's sister takes that title."

Bannon's grin spread without a trace of humor entering his eyes. "I don't believe that in the least. I have to say, I love that you can't lie to me. It disconcerts you, doesn't it?"

"You disconcert me, yes. And I have no desire to lie to you on that score. I prefer you to know it." Rema advanced, and Bannon took another step back. "Good evening."

Chuckling, Bannon returned to the shadows—somewhere he rightly belonged.

Elise was waiting, her body outlined by radiance of the setting sun. Rema held her breath as she drew near. She had experienced the company of so many women, one would think her capacity to be infatuated might have lessened, yet Elise still made the air shiver in her lungs. Her silhouette against the sky defined those captivating curves that Rema longed to traverse, as well as the untamed hair that matched Elise's temper so well. Her face was upturned, and she seemed lost in thought.

"You've come," she said, before Rema could speak a word. "And look, no sailors."

"No sailors." Rema leaned against the railing and examined Elise in profile. "Your diplomat has arrived, as promised. What troubles you, Elsie Danarian?"

"I'm in love." Elise gave Rema a coy sidelong look. "If you can call that trouble."

"And who are you in love with?"

"A very handsome individual. I'd daresay the most handsome being alive. But they tell me it's a scandal, because the object of my heart's desire is a woman." Elise ran her finger along the grain of the rail, tracing a splintered line. "But I refuse to believe my heart can be wrong."

The cool breeze fluttered over Rema's blouse, cooling the skin of her neck. She put her hand over Elise's, and Elise reddened. "It's not wrong."

"The way you act toward me, one would think you find it shameful."

"Never. I assure you, it's only your diplomatic importance that sees me so hesitant. I'm proud to love women. All in my court know it."

"It's hard to believe."

"But true. Certainly some disapprove, but none can argue the subject against me without seeming a fool. Arann is kinder to us women than many other cities. There are even taverns where we can flirt freely with one another."

Elise pressed her hand to her lips as she looked away. "Don't tell me this. It hurts my heart knowing such impossible things will be on the other side of my prison."

"Please keep hope."

"You do so well at discouraging me from it, though." Elise's blush spread. "Will you tell me how you came to know about yourself? How young were you when you understood what your heart and loins most wanted?"

"I might have a tale. But first, let me ask the same of you."

"I've known forever. My mother would point to a prince and tell me how handsome he was, and I would only stare at him in the way a fly might look at a frog. But every time I saw a pretty woman, my body would jolt. The maids who attended me, the servant girls who I passed in the corridors, the visiting princesses I was forced to play with…I wasn't attracted to all of them, of course, but I had many, many longings left unfulfilled."

"And those you did fulfill?"

"I only ever dared to lay with servant girls. I was fourteen when I first kissed the handmaid who always seemed to linger when she bathed me. She was sixteen, a girl from the city. Curly brown hair, a sweet mouth always fixed in a playful smile, gentle blue eyes. Small-breasted, like you, but ample-hipped. The way she responded when I kissed her…" Elise laughed, her blush flaring all the way to her neck. "I awoke hunger in her. I felt powerful. Yet, when we were done, she cried and wept for forgiveness. She thought I would tell my parents, that I would have her dismissed. She was so confused."

"What happened to her?"

"She didn't return. It was always the same. I would befriend some girl from the court, flirt with her, win her affection, kiss her, bed her, and then either Father would find out or the girl would lose her nerve. Once, a girl swore she loved me, and I was overjoyed. A month later, she married a young blacksmith. She told me that our love wasn't 'real love,' not like the love one held for a man. I still don't know whether she spoke in sincerity or fear. In any case, she was soon with child."

It was clear Elise was bringing herself near to tears. The light shimmered in her eyes, and her voice struggled to express memories still capable of causing pain. "Don't burden yourself any longer," said Rema. "I'll tell you my tale. It's far sweeter."

Elise gave her a grateful look. "Please do."

"I was seventeen."

"Really? So late?"

Rema pinched Elise's hand. "Don't interrupt. I was seventeen, and I'd just passed the final diplomat's exam. There were six or seven boys who'd graduated as well. We chose to celebrate at the Azure Lion, a tavern popular among the men of Arann for the many attractive women who dance, serve and entertain there. I wore my best pair of silk trousers and a loose blouse."

"I can picture you in it now."

"What did I say about interrupting?" Rema laughed. "Come, now, attend to what I'm telling you. We arrived just before nightfall. Our party sat upon a circle of cushions in one corner, laughing and drinking, while the incense drifted and settled about us. It was all very lively."

"I'm going to interrupt you again, because I must know. How did the boys treat you?"

"When I first joined the college they were very unsure about me. In time, I won them over. Some of them fell in love with me, I suspect, but that sort of thing happens to me all the time."

"You make my adoration of you sound so commonplace."

It was hard not to feel courageous beneath the waning light, kept company by creaking timber and lapping waves. "Believe me, you are far from commonplace. Many have sought my hand, but none compare to you."

Elise giggled. "You have no idea how sweet those words sound to me."

"Back to the story. A young woman was there that night, moving among the patrons. She had long, tan legs and eyes as dark and intense as smoke. It was her business to flirt briefly with the men, whisper something sweet into their ears, convince them to buy a drink and move on. Every boy was excited for her to reach us, because each was convinced that she would see him and fall madly in love."

"Go on. I'm quivering in anticipation."

"When the woman came to us, she looked at the group before picking whom she thought was the prettiest young man there. She sauntered up to me, draped her arms over my shoulders and dropped into my lap. The moment my chest met hers, she realized her mistake. But when I felt the heat of her body, I knew I didn't want her to leave. So I held her, gazed into her eyes and said, 'Don't fly away, my dove.'"

"Did she melt?"

"She was nervous and confused. As I talked to her and flirted with her, however, she grew comfortable in my lap. The other boys giggled like children and nudged each other, while the tavern owner glared at her, wishing she'd move on to the next customer. But she remained, laughing at my jokes and smiling as our heads brushed. By the end of the night she was caressing my shoulders, nuzzling my neck and whispering in my ear."

"Keep going!"

"Night grew long, and the customers began to leave. The incense thinned, the dancers slowed and some of my companions made their farewells. Finally, the tavern owner came to our group and said the girl was needed elsewhere. She pouted, pressed her lips to the back of my neck and excused herself. I sat there hardly able to breathe. I couldn't smell anything but her perfume or feel anything but her heat. The remaining boys teased and congratulated me, while I sat dizzy, only gradually understanding what these feelings meant for me. What they told me about the woman I am."

Elise issued a dreamy sigh. "How lovely. Is that the end?"

"Not quite. I stayed for some time longer before bidding my friends farewell. She was waiting for me in the humid night. Without saying a word, she took my hand and led me down an alley, where she pressed me to the wall and began to embrace me. At first I stroked her face, but then I moved my attentions to her breasts and thighs. We both wore loose clothing, nothing to impede exploring hands."

Elise's shoulders moved with the quickness of her breath. "Every last detail. I mean it."

"She had obviously never had a woman before. She touched my body tentatively, as if amazed by what she was doing. But I yearned to please her and refused to be timid. I squeezed her buttocks as tight as I could. I cupped her breasts and held her nipples between my teeth, teasing them with my tongue. I slid my fingers inside her, gasping as I felt her wetness. I kissed her anywhere that could be kissed—"

"Stop," said Elise, her voice shaking. "If you aren't going to make love to me the second this story ends, you'd better just stop it now."

"I thought you wanted all the details."

"I'll be frustrated all night imagining it now, visualizing myself in that girl's place."

"Then let's spare you further misery by changing the subject. Now I've shared this tale with you, return me a favor in kind. Tell me about magic. How did you learn it?"

"Give me a moment to cool." Elise exhaled. "Right then. When I was seventeen, a magician came to court. I convinced him to part with some of his books and apparatus, and I set myself the task of understanding it all. To be honest, I wanted to find ways to hurt Calan. I worked for months, following instructions, and succeeded in giving him the itching plague. Him and half the people in the palace. That was my first lesson in magic."

"And that's why you don't use it to harm others?"

"Exactly. I prefer to help them. There were many healing recipes and spells in the books, and collecting the various reagents proved a pleasant diversion. It was gratifying to see people cured, to know that I was the one who had brought solace to them. That kind of magic is the work of simple nature combined in little known ways. Some people wouldn't really call it magic at all."

"Explain it to me."

"Natural magic involves manipulating the relations between things in this world. It took me some time to understand it, but when it became clear, it didn't just explain magic—it explained life. We're all part of something greater, all joined to one another. The correspondences are stronger in some unions than others, but all return to the same source. You, me, Calan, Ormun, all the good and bad."

"And failed Lyornan assassins, I assume. How did you make that man lose his ability to respond to questions?"

"With subtlety, care and understanding. Everything from words to minerals has power and resonance. Think of it as a piece of string joined to millions of other pieces of string. If I pull one string, I can make the others tremble, but it takes a very skilled hand to control which strings respond and which stay still."

"And you have those very skilled hands?"

It had been a gamble, but Elise's low, delighted laughter was sufficient compensation. "Innuendo? Really, Rema. Tell me, how is it you don't already have a lover back in Arann?"

Now that was a topic best delayed. Elise would not react well to the knowledge that Rema was accustomed to loving many women, promising them nothing, and that one woman in particular—Jalaya, sweetest Jalaya—shared her bed most nights. It was, at least, a one-sided problem, for Jalaya would surely not begrudge Rema this passion; as much as they enjoyed each other's bodies, jealousy could hardly exist between two people who made no claim over each other's hearts. But Elise was different, though Rema still struggled to articulate to herself how.

"I try not to have lovers," said Rema, speaking slowly. "That is, anyone who expects me to be at their side for long. I travel much."

"Which suggests you will abandon me too, not long after depositing me in this tyrant's clutches." Elise's voice trembled. "Don't you understand that what keeps me alive is the hope you love me the way I love you? I need to believe that even while you feign defeat, in your head you're scheming ways for us to be together."

It was tempting to end the conversation now, walk away and attempt to patch the wounds later, but Muhan had been right. Elise needed this chance to clear her heart. "I understand."

"Then give me a sign! Let me know that I'm not throwing my heart into a well with nobody waiting to catch it. I've played it your way. I think I've read your hints, but I'm never certain. All I want is some confirmation that I'm not just deluding myself. You do love me, don't you?"

The lie reached the tip of Rema's tongue, but she stilled it there. The suffering she had brought to Elise meant she deserved to only ever hear the truth, even if that truth might damn them both. "Yes, Elsie. I do love you." The confession left her weak. "I'll do whatever I can for you. But there's no way we can be together. Not the way you want."

Elise crept closer, still holding Rema's hand. "You're wrong, my love. We will find a way. I just need to know that you'll be waiting for me."

Yet again a lie came to mind, only for Rema to stop it. She put her arms around Elise's waist, braving the warmth of that tantalizing body. "Even if we can only be together in mutual yearning, then it will be so. I owe you that much."

"Rema, my beloved." Elise released a shuddering breath. "I don't want this embrace to end. I hate what Ormun has done to both of us. We're so near to happiness, and he's the only thing standing in our way."

"He stands in the way of many more happinesses than our own. But he's a difficult, complex man. You'll understand when you meet him."

"I'm going to free you. I'll rescue you from hating yourself for the things you have to do in his name. Your father was right. There's no power greater than virtue, and I'll prove it to you."

Rema pressed her cheek against Elise's fragrant hair. She wanted to undress her, to kiss her and love her. Instead, she held her for as long as she dared, this woman who was both her captive and the captor of her heart.

CHAPTER SEVENTEEN

On the twentieth day of travel, the navigator spotted land, and a delighted cry rose from the deck. Rema stood at the ship's edge and watched as sheer white cliffs broke the horizon. The line marked the coast of Lastarel, the seaboard kingdom that neighbored the Pale Plains. The sight told all on board they were mere hours from home. Some distance to the west, beyond where the water struck against the cliffs, Arann's southern flank met the Sea of Red Winds—the great ocean passage between burning Amantis and frozen Ostermund. Rema had spent the last few days describing the imperial capital to Elise, though her words could offer only a faint image of the city under whose weight the world bowed.

The ship sped through the water as if even the sails were encouraged by the nearness of their destination. The captain rampaged above deck, bellowing orders that nobody needed, while Elise, Rema and Muhan watched the unfolding coast. As the land slipped by, Elise marveled aloud at the colors of the cliffs and the white trees that perched atop their peaks.

The voyage had tanned Muhan even more deeply, and his face was now a rich shade of brown. "It has been six years since I laid eyes on Arann. They say it still grows."

"Endlessly. We should divide it into two cities to make it easier to administrate, but that would require more capable urban planners than we have."

"What kind of people can I expect to meet at your court?" said Elise. "Surely not everyone is as wicked as Ormun."

"Many good people didn't survive the coup." The cliffs began to dip toward the sea, introducing a dazzling line of beach. "But yes, I have friends at court, and enemies too."

"Enemies? Why?"

"I'm powerful, I have Ormun's ear and I've been around a long time. And I have certain ideals. For some people that's enough."

They admired the passing coast until the sight lost its wonder. Muhan disappeared below deck to play cards while Elise returned to the book that she was reading, her hair shining in the sun. Rema walked across the broad deck, curious to see the view from the stern.

"You must be excited." Bannon's voice startled her, and she tried to regain her composure as he emerged from behind the wheelhouse. He rested his weight against a post and grinned at her, his blond hair ruffled by the breeze. "Not long now until you're back at that mansion of yours. You made it sound awfully pretty."

"I haven't seen you for days. I was beginning to think you fell overboard."

"And yet you sent nobody to search for me." Bannon curled his lips into a comical pout. It was an unfortunate consequence of Rema's career that she was forced to consort with murderers and villains; such was the price of a diplomat's pragmatism.

"I assumed you can swim, and I suspect you're half sea creature anyway."

"You're bold to be cheeky while you still owe me money. Knowing what I do about you and the princess, I might fathom a way to make you owe me more still."

"I doubt you'd blackmail me. I can't imagine you have any appetite for a crime that sees nobody killed."

"You read me well." Bannon spat on the deck and scuffed the saliva with his boot. "I'm disappointed. I was hoping to see a shiver of fear in that steady face of yours."

"You'll get your money and your property, so stop blustering. I've already fulfilled a third of our bargain by getting you here."

"Hell, I think you should have her. He's got nineteen wives, more than enough for any man. One is more than enough, some'd say." Bannon directed his unnerving gaze toward the coast. "I'll be glad to get off this ship. The sailors are beginning to spin legends about me. Apparently I bit the head off a teething infant just to stop him crying."

"What are you intending to do in Arann? Is there any chance you'll live a decent life, bring no harm to others?"

"The richer I am, the less harm I'll have cause to do. Unless I get bored." Bannon shrugged. "I admire that you stand up for your principles, because I respect anyone who shows spirit. But I don't have principles, Rema. I have goals, and in the way of those goals are sometimes obstacles, and when there are I remove them."

"It haunts me that I've rewarded you for the damage you've done. There's no chance that any good will come from you, is there?"

"If there's money in it, I'll do good, bad, whatever. You can't understand me any more than a mountain can understand a fish. You see someone in pain, you feel sorry for them. Me, I feel nothing. I'll hurt them, save them or kill them depending on what needs doing. I'm a man of brute facts."

There were few things less appealing than listening to Bannon's unsettling chatter. "Enjoy your lurking," Rema said, turning her back on him.

She returned to the midship and sat on a stool near the mast. On the subject of unsettling personalities, it wasn't long now until she had to face her master. There was no way to know when Ormun would want to hold the marriage, but likely he would be as taken with Elise as Rema herself had been. Her features would seem exotic to him—her white, rounded face, her arched lips and mysterious eyes. He would certainly want her in his bedchamber as soon as possible. The idea of that was too terrible to contemplate, and Rema shut her mind to it completely.

A hand touched her shoulder. It was Elise, beaming as usual. The confession of love had changed her demeanor for the better, impressing a serene assurance upon her words and actions, and every smile she gave Rema seemed to carry a subtle complicity. "That awful captain says it won't be long now. What will happen when we arrive?"

"You'll be met at the docks. Then I'll take you before Ormun and give him my final report. I'll need to change soon into my uniform."

"Do you need help getting dressed?"

It was odd to think of the confidence with which she'd fended off Elise's first clumsy advances. Now, as Elise looked at her with ardent eyes, Rema trembled with frustration in the very places that most desired an enchantress's touch. She smiled with difficulty. "You'll have to watch what you say to me in Arann."

"I dreamed about you last night. You kissed me on the lips and then I kissed you back. But a little lower."

Gods, she was bold. Rema checked to be sure nobody was standing near them. "You'll have to watch what you dream too."

"I'd love to perform that act upon you. I'd make your whole body shiver until you lose that admirable self-control in a fit of moaning. And then I'd sit astride you, my mound pressed to yours, and with every thrust of my hips, you'd surrender yourself a little more to me…"

Rema's heartbeat gathered pace. "Elsie, you're going to get us into trouble."

"Nobody's listening. Let me talk frankly while I can. I have to keep my mind away from what's coming." A forceful ocean breeze swept across them, tossing Elise's hair into the wind. "I wish I had a moment alone with you. Just one more."

Given how near they were to Ormun now, it was hardly an unfair request. "I'm sure we could find pretense to retreat to your cabin. You'll need help packing, for one thing."

"You sly thing." Elise's face lightened beneath a giddy smile. "Then let's go quickly, before your usual tact returns and you change your mind."

With the spectacle of land to distract the sailors, the women managed to retreat below decks without attracting notice. Entering Elise's cabin was much like walking into a library that had recently exploded. Books were everywhere, jumbled in tangles of paper and leather, and the musty odor of their pages seemed to have become a permanent fixture. Clothing spilled from trunks, various trinkets and vials were piled upon the sole table, and ink had been spilled across the floorboards.

"Your brothers were right," said Rema. "You are messy."

"A brilliant mind like mine has no time for cleaning." Elise took a biscuit from a bowl at her bedside. She bit into it, tentatively at first but then furiously as it became clear the biscuit had no intention of being broken. "I hope there's real food in Arann. If I must be a slave wife, I intend to be the fattest slave wife the Empire has ever seen."

"Banquets are among the few things I can guarantee you. The imperial court eats to excess."

"And its master weds to excess. With so many wives already, will I be expected to bear him children?"

"You'll be expected to share his bed. As you must know already, with your medical books, there are ways to avoid becoming with child. Ormun has so many at this point he won't even notice if you fail to bear him any."

"The thought of sharing his bed makes me shudder." Elise twirled her hair around her fingers. "What if I marry you first? Then Ormun won't be able to marry me, because I won't be an unwed princess anymore."

"You're already betrothed to him. Your parents agreed." Rema smiled. "Not that I wouldn't love to marry you."

"Think of it. We'd live together in this mansion of yours. Neither of us would do any domestic duties, so the whole house would overflow with my rubbish."

A warm rush of pleasure moved through Rema's body. Imagine that—the windows of her mansion obscured by a mountain of books. "I wonder how the master of unions would react. I don't think he's ever been called upon to marry two women."

"In Danosha, people would think the idea was lunacy. Only the church or the king can approve marriages, and the priests all think I have a forked tongue and a lizard's tail. My father's a little irreligious, but he'd never offend the church by letting two women be married."

"Ormun doesn't care for churches, and neither did his father. Religion carries a different meaning in Amantis. Our people have many faiths, many different gods. We don't get on our knees before them, but let them walk among us and share our lives."

"Tell me about them. It'll be a pleasant distraction."

Rema sat on the bed with her legs crossed, and Elise knelt opposite her. "The most sacred street in Arann is the Road of the Moon. There are temples to every god and demon there, some shaped like spires, others like grand cathedrals. The most beautiful in my estimation is the shrine of Tolos. It's an ivory tower covered in fountains."

"Tolos. That's the strange cult that worships a half-man, half-woman god, correct?"

"Your books have taught you well. But they're a gentle sect, rejecting violence and even the consumption of meat, and Tolos is not half-man, half-woman, but neither of the two. Like several of Arann's philosophers, Tolosians reject that there are only two sexes, claiming that every person has a unique sex of their own."

"What a beautiful idea. Our priests would be impatient to burn them all alive."

"They'd be even less impressed by the Church of the Six Suns, whose members worship a pantheon of spirits that walk unseen among the living. Their oracles stand at street corners and shout exaltations every hour of the day. Then there's the followers of Lameth and Lamella, the Twins of Judgment. It's said that after we die, Lameth weighs our good, Lamella our evil, and together the siblings determine our fate. Their petitioners and prophets are some of the gloomiest in the city, draped in black and waving censers wherever they travel..."

As Rema described the faiths of the city she loved, Elise listened with rapturous eyes. It was as if her heart already beat to the pulse of Arann, the White Rock of the Plains, the City of Fallen Stars, the Stable of a Thousand Horses...Rema had once wandered Arann's streets as if intoxicated, seeing in every street and building the promise of her father's dream. The day Togun died, a blight had set upon the city. But now, gazing at Elise, Rema remembered those feelings anew.

It was as Loric had suggested: there were prayers that one no longer knew how to speak, yet one's soul still ached with the need to speak them. And perhaps such prayers could be spoken with lips as well as words.

With gentle fingertips, Rema drew Elise's face toward her own. Their noses grazed, and Elise's glazed eyes closed in expectation. As their breath mingled, their lips nearly touching, somebody knocked at the door.

Elise leapt up in a comical explosion of temper. "Not again! Door-knocking should be a crime punishable by death!"

Rema gave an unsteady laugh, still dazed by the near-kiss. Elise stamped across the cabin and opened the door. "Go away!"

"I think it might be for the best that I don't," said Muhan. He smiled apologetically at Rema. "My dear friends, the captain tells me that in the merest of moments we will be drawing into port. He requests both of you prepared and on deck."

"I still haven't put on my uniform." Rema glanced down at her entirely undiplomatic clothes. "I'll have to hurry."

"Muhan, you horrible man," said Elise. "Knocking on doors is a vile and intrusive thing to do."

"Don't take your temper out on him," Rema said. "We need to get packed and ready. Anything you want to take with you directly, put in a single trunk. Everything else will be moved to the palace over the next few days."

"You're both monstrous." Elise stalked back across the cabin and stood beside her books. "I don't want to see either of you. Shoo!"

Rema hurried to her own cabin, where she unfolded her clean uniform and began the cherished process of getting dressed. Yorin had done a fine job with the cleaning, and she admired her reflection as she fastened the silver buttons. The coat's angular cut made her more imposing, and its high collar accentuated the sharp contours of her face. Her fingers had become steady by the time she clasped the seal at her neck.

She strode to the upper deck, her boots ringing on the planks and her luggage rattling behind her. Many of the sailors were busy at work hauling on the sails and eyeing the waters, while the others watched Arann as it passed by without end. It was a city of slums and mansions clustered together in unlikely companionship, of innumerable towers and spires. It had crawled from its valley of birth onto the high sides of the mountains, so that entire streets ran at crazed angles along the cliffs, where tall houses teetered from pale rocks overlooking the sea. If Rema strained her eyes, it was possible to see the immense golden walls of the palace, each cornered with a dome-tipped spire.

The ship sailed by a wide coastal marketplace, and the scent of spices and fruits carried on the humid air. Rema looked about for her companions. Muhan stood nearby, watching the city, while Bannon waited at a distance from the crew. The wide berth they gave him would have been amusing if it weren't so richly deserved.

After some minutes, Elise's head rose into view from below deck. Her dress was more modest than usual, loose-fitting at the front and with a wide black skirt that disguised the shapeliness of her hips and legs. She walked toward Rema with a trunk clutched in her arms. Her unhappy face broke into fresh wonder as her gaze met the sprawling city. "It's larger than I imagined."

Sailors shouted, sails turned and the ship made its lumbering way toward the broad inlet of one of Arann's many ports. Numerous galleons and ships waited at dock, their bright wooden sides reflecting the fierce sun. Small boats drifted by with sailors hunched at their bows, and Rema returned a friendly wave while the captain guided his vessel to an empty pier.

Even from deck, it was exhausting to see the activity of the docks; merchants shifted cargo, fishermen unbundled netting, sailors relaxed on the sun-soaked grass and horses pulled carts up the cobblestone road that wound into the city. The imperial escort was waiting among the confusion: a large covered wagon, several guardsmen wearing burnished gold helms, and an imposing man in a long cape—Artunos, one of the court's two captains of guard.

"I suppose that's for us," said Elise, pointing to the imperial party.

"Yes, it is," said Rema. She rested her fingers on Elise's shoulder. "Wait here, and I'll have a word with Muhan and Bannon."

Elise nodded, her eyes not moving from the escort. Rema left her luggage and dodged the sailors to reach Muhan. "I'd like to invite you to come visit me at court," she said. "If you mention my name to the guards at the palace gate, they'll let you in."

"I look forward to it," said Muhan. "I suspect you will need some time to settle, so perhaps I shall come visit tomorrow?"

"That would be best." They both looked to Elise, and when their eyes met again, Rema saw her own discontent reflected in Muhan's face.

"The poor woman," he said. "She's been rare company. Do take care of her."

"I intend to. I'll see you tomorrow, then?"

"Yes, it's so." Muhan clasped his hands and bowed. "Tomorrow, Rema."

"Good day, Muhan."

After a deep breath, Rema walked over to Bannon, who paused from picking at something on his boot. "Big city," he said. "And it's hot as hell."

"You ought to know. I can't conclude our arrangement today, but I can talk to you in the palace tomorrow. Just ask for me at the door."

"It would help to have a little coin to spend the night in a pleasant tavern. I don't know these streets at all, and I don't fancy rotting away on them."

Rema frowned; she'd given all her money to Domyr, the Lyornan spy. Reluctantly, she took a ring from her finger and tossed it to Bannon. He gave her a lazy salute and crossed the deck as sailors shuffled in a panic to get out of his way. With a final insolent grin in Rema's direction, he skipped cat-like down the plank and was soon lost in the crowd. What had she just unleashed upon the city she loved?

The captain detached himself from the muscular pack of sailors. "Well, we're here," he said to Rema. "I'm glad to see you brought back everything you needed."

"Has payment for you and your crew been arranged?"

"Aye, we'll be paid this evening. The crew are looking forward to being back with their families."

"I hope all your future voyages are as calm as this. All the best to you, Captain."

The distant imperial guard shifted impatiently under the sun. Rema returned to Elise's side. "It's time," she said, brushing a long hair from Elise's cheek. Elise nodded and clutched her trunk close.

They crossed the gangplank and joined a mass of sailors, merchants and fishermen chattering in many languages and weaving around one another as they conducted their day's affairs. Rema had lost sight of the escort, and she peered through the crowd, trying to remember from where on the ship she'd seen them.

The crowd parted to reveal Artunos approaching with two golden guards at his flanks. He halted and bowed, sweeping his cape before him. As he straightened, his gaze moved to Elise. "She's an odd-looking one. Do all their women appear so surly?"

"Watch out. She speaks Annari." Rema smiled. It was typical of Artunos to begin by making a prig of himself. "And I happen to think she's very attractive."

"My apologies!" Artunos bowed to Elise, who scowled at him. "Weariness has impaired my discretion. We've been waiting for hours, and were beginning to think this would be the wrong day for your arrival."

"Fortunately, the voyage went as predicted. How are you, Artunos?"

"Intact. The wise men ask for proof of miracles, and here I am."

Rema inspected her old friend and found him much as she'd left him. He was tall and dark-skinned, and his black hair was held in a high ponytail that fell in thin strands to his waist. His golden tabard bared his muscular arms, and a flanged mace with a leather grip hung from his belt. It was his preferred weapon, or so he claimed; Rema had never seen him use it. It matched his blunt temperament, however. He also had an unfortunate tendency to sullenness, not unlike someone else that she knew.

"Elise, this is Artunos, captain of the guard and one of my closest friends. He served Togun too, before the coup."

Artunos raised a thick eyebrow. "You've been telling her all about us, have you? Princess, I extend my warmest welcome to the city of Arann."

"Don't call me princess," said Elise. "My name is Elise. May I ask why Ormun let you live? Because I certainly wouldn't have." She gave an indignant sniff. "Odd-looking indeed!"

"Please, I already apologized! To answer your question, it was by Rema's intervention. I owe her my life, and I'm not the only person who can make that claim." Artunos's voice grew solemn. "Elise, I have been commanded to take you back to the palace in this wagon. Do you have any objections?"

"Yes. Why do I have to travel in the wagon? I'd like to walk the streets and see this city for myself. I've been on the sea for three weeks, and once I've married this infernal beast, I've been assured that I'll never leave the palace for the rest of my life. To hell with your wagon."

"Let her walk," said Rema, laughing at Artunos's stunned expression. "Take the wagon yourself, if you like. It'll spare us the sight of your grim face."

"Her sharp tongue recalls your own." Artunos grinned. "We've all missed you, but none so much as your little songbird. She's been pining so badly that I was beginning to worry she'd never sing again."

Elise gave Rema a puzzled look. Time to move the conversation along. "Shall we start moving?" said Rema. "I'd like to be back in the palace before the sun sets."

"Very well. The Emperor is awaiting you with great anticipation. Guardsman, take the lady's luggage." Artunos turned with a flourish of his cape and led them to the wagon. "We won't require you after all," he said to the driver, pressing a coin into his hand.

He had brought six guardsmen in total, five of them holding spears and one now carrying Elise's trunk. Artunos arranged them in two files, giving orders quietly and without ceremony, as his was habit. His organization concluded, the group began their journey to the palace—and to the man whose shadow loomed over Rema, permitting her no refuge even as she traveled every corner of the world.

CHAPTER EIGHTEEN

The paved streets of Arann were nothing like the cobbled roads of the Danoshan capital. Narrow and winding, they followed hills that descended so steeply horses trembled to follow them. Where the stone houses parted, their elevation allowed a dizzying view of the valley and the city tangled in its depths.

The group pushed through countless marketplaces—some that crowded the streets, others that occupied plazas—and passed between stalls that seemed to grow on buildings like clinging vines. As they navigated these bazaars, merchants assailed them, tugging on sleeves and proffering vivid fruits, while an immense noise swirled: pots clattering, fat sizzling in griddles, dogs baying and monkeys chirping, and the cries and countercries of vendors each selling identical wares and yet all expecting the undivided loyalty of passersby.

Elise stared at the faces around her, astonishment driving the pout from her face. All the people of the Empire and many of those from the wider world were represented in Arann, and their many-languaged conversations formed a dense and unintelligible hum. There were jet-skinned Lastar, tall Tahdeeni with olive skin and wide eyes, tanned Ulati wrapped in rough cloth, bare-chested Molonese with bundles of silk in their arms, and sallow Goronba leading broad-backed donkeys.

There were foreigners, too: pale-skinned Lyornans and Kalanese in opulent garments, unhappy red-haired Harothen sweating behind their armor, Narandane towering above the crowds, Erellan women in conical hats and even a Danoshan merchant pulling a cart laden with apples.

Elise seemed particularly taken with the golden-skinned, sharp-featured Ajulese. She stopped to watch a company pass by, a lively mingling of men and women. "They look like you. But you're a touch fairer, and all of them have black hair."

"My father was Ajulese," said Rema. "My mother was a Nastine, hence my red hair and slightly lighter skin."

The group descended a curved street that ran between two tall rows of houses. Clotheslines spanned the buildings, casting thin shadows across the street. Excited children ran about their group chasing a cat, and a woman emerged onto a step and beat dust from a tapestry. "I met a princess from Nastil once," said Elise. "She didn't have red hair."

"Nastine don't all have red hair. It's not like every Danoshan has silver eyes."

"I know that. If you insist on treating me like a child, I'll act like one and bite your foot."

Artunos frowned. "You shouldn't speak to Rema in that way."

Rema laughed. "Artunos, it's nothing. You'll have to excuse Elise if she says inappropriate things. She merely announces what she's thinking."

"She'd better break that habit before she meets the Emperor." Artunos spoke without a trace of humor. Elise sneered at him before turning to stare at a zebra that stood patiently in a stockyard among horses and camels.

Their path took them through a large public garden filled with aromatic trees. A river coursed through its center, and the road passed over it by way of a small cobbled bridge. Elise stopped to gape at the huge, many-colored birds that stretched their plumage from crooked branches and sang in tremulous warbles.

Rema took Elise's arm and pointed to the horizon. "Do you see that golden shine up there on the hill, so bright it hurts to look at? That's the palace."

"Does it really have walls of gold?"

"It's gilded. Not solid gold. But it's an impressive waste of wealth all the same."

They passed through a grove and into the caressing shade of the leaves. "Is it far to your mansion?" said Elise.

"Quite far. It's in the southeast of the city, low against the coast and overlooking the sea. The city there isn't so dense, and olive and palm trees grow in the streets."

"It's all so beautiful." Elise inhaled the scented air, and her eyelashes fluttered. "Can't we just stop here for a while longer?"

"I'm afraid not. There are gardens inside the palace, though, much larger than this. Take heart."

Judging from the impatient look in Artunos's eyes, he was waiting for a chance to speak with her. As Elise stumbled along, gawking at the birds and the trees, Rema slowed her pace so that he could fall into step alongside. When Elise was some distance away, he cleared his throat. "You've befriended this one, haven't you?"

Curse his shrewdness. "It'd be impossible for me not to like her. You've seen how lively she is."

"Things aren't going well for us lately. You've been gone almost two months, and Haran has been quick to take advantage of it. You need to spend time rebuilding our position."

"You're afraid I'm going to be reckless."

"You have that old look in your eye." Artunos swiped a fly from his cheek. "I won't say that I haven't missed it, but there is a time for conviction and a time for caution."

They caught up to Elise, who had stopped to marvel at a beetle crawling across a tree. Its gleaming blue back wobbled as it slid its belly across the bark. "Look at it," said Elise. "I never thought I'd see a scarab. It's as big as my hand."

"Careful," said Rema. "They spit terrible venom." Elise pulled back in fright and tripped on her feet. Rema caught her before she could fall, and they both giggled.

"You lied to me," said Elise, still tangled in Rema's arms. "I'll have to think of a way to punish you."

Stricken by embarrassment, Rema avoided looking at Artunos. "We should hurry along. The later it gets, the more likely it'll be that Ormun is ill-tempered."

"It sounds to me as if he's always ill-tempered." Elise adjusted Rema's scattered hair, tapped her on the nose and wandered further into the garden, still captivated by the scenery. The guards marched to keep up with her, ever expressionless.

"Very close friends," said Artunos tonelessly.

"I'm not at my best. I'm distracted. She has an effect on me."

"I can tell. Be sure that Ormun can't."

Before long they were back in the city streets, this time among extravagant marble houses and wide streets paved with smooth, neatly interlocked flagstones. After perhaps twenty minutes of strolling, they arrived at the great thoroughfare to the palace. Squat mansions lined the path, their gardens redolent with jasmine. The palace loomed, and they slowed as they entered its great shadow. Its colossal gem-studded doors were ajar. Six guardsmen stood outside on duty, their taciturn faces relaxed. Noticing Artunos, they pulled themselves upright and saluted.

"At ease," Artunos said. "You can return to your daily duties." The guards clasped their spears to their chests, banged the shafts against their golden breastplates and filed into the palace. The guard with the trunk waited, his eyes uncertain. "I'll take that from here." The guard offered up his cargo and hurried to join his comrades.

Rema and Elise followed Artunos through the doors and into the marble outer court. It had been designed to awe visitors, and even Rema still sometimes paused to admire it. Fountains on the walls surged into broad basins below, and the center of the court was dominated by an immense pool of swirling water. A painted scene of nature decorated the domed ceiling, depicting leaves and twining vines studded with blossoms, and sunlight streamed through the perfectly circular windows cut around the dome's circumference. Dignitaries, traders and entertainers wandered among the columns and fountains, rested upon velvet-cushioned benches, stood on high balconies and chatted beneath the shadows of white-limbed trees.

"You can marvel at it later," said Rema to Elise, who had walked over to one of the trees and was examining its pale leaves, her eyes quick with curiosity. "We don't want Ormun to learn we've been dallying."

"Trees growing indoors! We had trouble enough to get them to grow outside." Elise ran her fingers along the bark. "And to think this will be my home, and I only have to share it with nineteen other women."

A sudden affection took hold of Rema. Surely Elise's resolute demeanor masked a deep anxiety. "Elsie, I'll keep my promise."

Elise smiled. "You'd better."

"Let's go." Rema guided Elise across the court to the archway where Artunos waited. They followed him through winding corridors decorated with stylized murals of waves, forests and predatory animals. The air was rich with incense, and interior windows opened into sunny inner gardens, where trees splayed crooked branches, and high-stemmed flowers raised their blossoms toward the sky.

"Rema!" There was no mistaking that beautiful voice, and it inspired an equal measure of delight and dread. Jalaya bounded down the hallway, her every step made musical by the jingling of her jewelry. Her exquisite lips parted with joy as she wrapped her arms around Rema's shoulders.

"Careful," said Rema, unable to hold back a laugh as Jalaya kissed her nose. "You'll break my neck."

"You've been gone so long, I forgot that you're a frail old woman." Jalaya caressed Rema's face with both hands before kissing her on the mouth, her tongue sliding between Rema's lips. Her small body pushed close, and Rema struggled not to grip those hips and stroke those buttocks she'd touched without guilt so many times before.

Jalaya lowered her lashes in exaggerated coyness. "I've been saving that kiss for you. Was it worth the wait?"

"Jalaya, I don't..." Gods, she'd missed Jalaya, but this wasn't the time. "I have to see Ormun. We can talk later."

"Talk?" Jalaya's laughter was as light and musical as her voice. "What's this about talking? You have two months of lonely nights to make up for!"

Elise was staring as if stunned. "This is Elise," said Rema, apprehension weighing heavy in her stomach. "Ormun's latest victim. Elise, this is Jalaya, my best friend."

Jalaya slipped free from the embrace and approached Elise. "Oh, you poor thing." She tentatively reached for Elise's hand. "No wonder you look so upset."

It was no surprise that Elise showed such consternation. Jalaya was short and slender, and her features were sublime—high cheeks, wide eyes, a rounded nose and delicate ears laden with heavy golden hoops. Her silken black hair fell, without a single curl or wave, to rest above her bare shoulders. A gossamer wrap covered her small bust, exposing every other inch of her smooth olive torso, while her loose skirt stopped at her thighs and shifted suggestively as she moved. Yet as gorgeous as she was, her greatest beauty lay in her voice. Every sound and note was rich with sweetness, and her laughter was enough to make toes curl.

"I'm not a poor thing," said Elise, lifting her head. "Don't be so condescending. Who are you, anyway?"

Gods, had two women ever been more different? Elise was plump, pale and tall, whereas Jalaya was slight, dark and a full head shorter; Elise's eyes were as frightening as they were entrancing, whereas Jalaya's honey-brown eyes were lustrous with gentle affection. Jalaya had none of Elise's seductive melancholy, and Elise had none of Jalaya's gentle lightness.

Jalaya smiled uncertainly. "I'm Jalaya. I entertain the court with my love songs. Perhaps I can sing for you sometime?"

"I doubt it. Not if your singing is as irritating as you are."

Jalaya turned to Rema, her eyes more confused than hurt. "Did I say something wrong?"

"Elsie, please," said Rema. "Be nice to her."

Artunos coughed loudly. Rema had forgotten he was there, and embarrassment wracked her again. "We should really keep moving," he said. "There'll be time later for reunions and…explanations."

"I'll let you go, then," said Jalaya, her lips still bent in a tiny frown. "I'm sorry if I offended you, Elise."

"I'm sorry if you did too," said Elise, crossing her arms and staring down the corridor. Jalaya gave Rema a parting kiss on the lips before padding down the corridor. Rema tried not to watch her leave, but it was hard not to be captivated by the movement of her hips beneath that skirt. Diplomat or not, she'd have trouble getting out of this one.

Artunos coughed again, and they resumed their procession through the ornate splendor of the palace. Elise had stopped marveling at her surroundings and instead glared into the distance as she walked. Rema reached tentatively for her arm, and Elise twisted away. Damn it all— didn't she see that this was no time for childishness?

After much walking, they emerged into a small courtyard. Two grey trees stood beside a pale wooden door, the entrance to Ormun's meeting chambers. "Is he expecting me?" said Rema.

"More or less," said Artunos. "He has company, but you'll take precedent, as always."

"I'll let you get back to your duties. Thank you for the escort, Artunos. We'll talk later."

"Yes. We will. What shall I do with this trunk?"

"Place it by the door, and I'll carry it out when we're done. If you want to do me a favor, you can take my own luggage to my chambers. Here's the key."

"You'll let me touch your precious luggage? These are strange times then." Artunos bowed to both women, pulled his cloak around him and wandered away with Rema's luggage trundling behind him.

Rema sighed as she returned her attention to the petulant Elise. "Ormun is on the other side of this door. Are you ready?"

Elise hummed noncommittally and inspected her nails.

"I'm sorry, Elsie," said Rema. "We'll talk about Jalaya later. I just need to know you won't say anything reckless."

Elise put a hand on her hip. "I'll say what I please, Remela."

Anxiety tightened around Rema's heart. "Please try to be restrained. Don't talk back to him. In fact, don't talk to him at all unless he initiates it. Keep your answers short and civil."

Elise tossed her hair and looked away. Rema hesitated, every part of her now heavy with dread. "Please, Elsie," she said, and she opened the door.

CHAPTER NINETEEN

The meeting chamber was one of the most pleasant rooms in the palace. Its circular walls were broken by numerous slanted windows that let in light, fresh air and the fragile scents of the gardens, and it was bare of furniture but for two crescent tables. At the far end of the room, various petty officials stood with their heads down while Haran, the imperial judge, argued with Sothis, the minister of war.

Ormun was between them, looking back and forth with each exchange. He always dressed plainly, and that day he had chosen a simple brown tabard over red breeches. He was not especially tall, about Rema's own height, and though he was powerfully built, his features were delicate; his lips seemed always on the edge of a smile, and his light blue eyes were deceptively suggestive of sensitivity. He appeared a little less than his thirty years, though his closely-cropped brown hair receded nearly to the top of his head. As always, the sight of him made Rema shiver, the way she would if a spider writhed unexpectedly near her face.

"We have to send a message," Haran said, beating his fist into his palm. He was a tall man in his fifties, long-chinned and sunken-cheeked, with pale green eyes alive with fury and intelligence. His opponent, Sothis, was an ailing man of similar age, shrunken through chronic illness. Rather than temper, his expression showed only a tired patience.

"Then write them a letter," said Sothis. He leaned against a table for support as he spoke. "Our best legions are still in Molon, recovering from our most brutal conquest in recent memory. Half the cannons broke down on the march, and there's only enough gunpowder to load half again of the remainder. We need weeks to forge more swords and spears, some of our best captains died on the field, and if we leave the Molonese now, they're liable to rebel."

"Urandal was conquered once. Are you telling me you can't send some troops in there to remind them? They hardly have a military or government of their own anymore."

"They were once a republic. Your dictatorial heart knows nothing about such polities. They survive on the will and fury of their people's militia, and at present they are very furious indeed."

Ormun yawned. As he stretched his neck back, he noticed Rema in the doorway. "Rema!" he said, interrupting Haran's spirited rebuttal. "Haran, Sothis, go stand silently in the corner. We'll deal with your nonsense later. Rema, dear, come in."

Rema strode into the chamber. "Ormun. Has everything fallen apart in my absence?"

Ormun responded with a mellow laugh and met her halfway across the room. "It's good to see you again. I tire of these toadies always agreeing to everything I say."

"If you weren't so quick to punish dissenters, you wouldn't have so many sycophants."

"As quick to scold as always." Ormun pressed a finger to his lips as he examined Elise. "Rema, Rema, Rema. What an odd gem you've brought me. What's her name again?"

"Elise. As you can see, the agreement with Danosha was successful. We should send troops immediately—"

"Yes, yes, that. Sothis can take care of that later. For now, let's take a look at this unusual creature. Elise, you say? What's her house again?"

"Danarian. By the blood of her father Cedrin and mother Talitha, the thirty-fourth monarchs of the Kingdom of Danosha, she is a princess of true and pure lineage." Elise rolled her eyes, but Ormun seemed not to notice. Rema battled the urge to reach out to Elise and pinch her. Damn that childish petulance.

"Let's hear her talk. Elise, how do you like my palace?"

"I was disappointed," said Elise, insolence worming through her voice. "Apparently your walls aren't really solid gold at all."

"Interesting." Ormun stroked his chin. "She's quite tall for a woman, isn't she? Just as tall as you, Rema. Good handfuls of flesh on her too. We'll have to get that mess of hair cut, but those eyes, though. Quite special. Not one of my other wives has silver eyes."

"My eyes are grey. It's hardly unusual."

Rema waited for Ormun's anger. "My dear," he said. "Please wait your turn." His gaze had grown colder, but there was no sign yet of the twisting muscle in his cheek that always marked the beginning of his anger. He turned his attention back to Rema. "This court has been a mess since you left, dear. Haran skulks about day and night, trying to turn me against you. Don't you, Haran?"

"Not in the least," said Haran, raising his head haughtily. "I have nothing but respect for our most esteemed diplomat."

"Ah, how he loathes you!" Ormun grinned, revealing his chipped front tooth. "And your own friends are very noisy too, Rema. It's back and forth, back and forth like barking dogs. I'm so glad you're here. Now you can respond to Haran's accusation last week that you're a... what was it? Tenderhearted little idiot?"

"That's fine," said Rema. "I've called him much worse."

Haran licked his dry lips. "Remela, you can't deny you were unwise to deprive us of your expertise for so long and on such an insignificant errand. The fate of a mean little kingdom is nothing to us—"

"Did you just imply that our Emperor's future bride is insignificant, Haran?"

"I...of course not."

Ormun clapped Rema on the shoulder. "Ah, how I'd missed your gift of making Haran seem like a fool."

"He needs no help in that regard," said Rema, smiling at Haran, who returned the smile with venomous insincerity.

"How fun things will be here again." Ormun rubbed his hands together. "Now, the matter of my future bride. Look at you, Elise, you peculiar vision. How old are you?"

"Ninety," said Elise. "It's amazing what cosmetics can do."

"You can tell jokes. Well, I suppose I can excuse one or two. How old is she, Rema?"

"Twenty-six," said Rema, her heart aching from the shock of hearing Elise speak so irreverently.

"Very late to be married. Very late indeed. Is there a reason for that? Is she barren? Skin disease?"

"Both," said Elise. "And my feet are webbed. At night I turn into a frog and flop about everywhere, shrieking at people and chewing on furniture."

"Another joke. Elise, you should understand that I don't need my wives to be witty."

Elise opened her mouth, and Rema interrupted quickly with the first thing that came into her head. "Elise had never seen a scarab before, and she saw one on the way here, in the city gardens."

"How grand that must have been for you, Elise!"

"I was so excited I just screamed and rolled on the ground," said Elise, her voice radiating scorn. "In my giddiness, I couldn't stop screaming, and Rema had to stuff leaves in my mouth to keep me quiet."

"That..." Ormun raised his finger, his mouth open. "I don't think that's true. Rema, am I going to have trouble with this one?"

Haran gave a broad smile. Nothing would have given Rema greater pleasure at that moment than to cross the room and bang his head into the table. "Surely not," she said. "In the time I've spent with her, she has proven to be a demure and charming companion."

"She doesn't seem very demure to me." Ormun lifted a strand of Elise's hair and stared at it. "Elise, you must be thrilled to come here to all this splendor. You'll live in luxury, eating only the finest food and drinking only the finest wines, as befits my wife."

"It must be hard to split the food and drink among twenty," said Elise. "Do you pass around a glass and we each take a tiny sip?"

Ormun's cheek twitched. "You're quickly becoming tiresome with your chatter. I want you to appreciate that a wife is an ornament to her husband, not a jester. You are very ornamental. Don't give me reason to change that."

"If I'm so ornamental, perhaps you should have me framed and hung on a wall."

Ormun sighed as his eyes clouded. "How tragic. I've had to discipline many of my brides, but rarely within minutes of meeting them." He reached for his belt and unhooked a mahogany rod. From its end dangled five short, knotted whips. "I'd hate to damage your face so soon. Take off your dress."

Rema's insides spasmed, and a cold sweat broke on her body. Haran smirked, Sothis looked away and Elise took a step backward, her eyes wide. "You can't be serious. I was only joking."

"That's why I'm punishing you." Ormun's tone conveyed more regret than anger. "Don't run, please. Then I'd have to whip you for that as well."

"Brother, stop," said Rema, her pulse racing. Ormun turned to her, his mouth rounded in surprise. "This is my fault. I didn't properly inform her how to comport herself in front of an Emperor. As I'm responsible for her actions, it is only proper that you whip me instead."

"That sounds improbable, sister. We should confer with our torturous legal mind. Haran, does it seem appropriate that Rema be punished for the indiscretion of my bride?"

"Her argument is sound," said Haran. "Due to a lack of proper care in her duty, the punishment should be meted to her. I agree with the verdict."

"How it pains me to do this. Rema, I'll ask you to remove your coat and shirt."

"My Emperor," said Sothis, taking a step forward. "This is truly not necessary."

"But she herself argued to me that it's necessary." Ormun stroked the hilt of his whip. "I am persuaded. Rema, off with it."

Rema nodded and unbuttoned her coat with numb fingers. "No!" said Elise. "Don't hurt her!" She stepped between them, and Ormun lifted his whip.

"You've misbehaved again. I told you, don't talk until spoken to. As Rema is responsible for your misdeeds, that means I'll now have to strike her twice." Anger finally broke through his composure, and his voice seethed. "I'm very fond of Rema, whereas I don't give a damn about you. If I have to punish her any further for your stupidity, I'll be very displeased."

"It's fine, Elise," said Rema. She faced the wall and pulled her shirt over her head. The worst part of it was imagining Haran watching her, his face twisted in a triumphant leer. She fixed her eyes on the wall, lowered her head and tensed her fists. Ormun stepped close behind her, and the muscles in her body tightened in anticipation.

Just at the moment she expected the blow to land, she heard his voice again, tender and curious. "Why, your back has a fine red mark on it. Whatever happened to you?"

"An accident on the ship. I was clumsy around a hook."

"Poor dear. I truly hate to see you get hurt." The cords shrieked, and her back burst into five fingers of pain that quickly became one raging line of agony. Her teeth clenched tight, barely missing her tongue, and she stifled a scream in the back of her throat.

"One more." The second blow was far worse, a pain wrapped in further pain, and for a moment Rema's vision went black and she swooned on her feet. She stumbled forward, hands meeting the wall, and blinked the tears from her eyes.

"There," said Ormun. "It's all over. I'd ask you to put your clothes back on, but I imagine the pain would be a little much right now."

Rema sank to her knees, an arm around her breasts. It felt as if she were wearing a cloak of wildfire. "I suppose you'd better get your back looked at. I'll send you off to the healers, and Elise and I can talk."

"No." Despite the pain, Rema managed to stand. She turned with her arm still across her torso. Haran watched in amusement, but Sothis kept his face averted. "I'll stay. If she misbehaves again, you'll need me here to receive her punishment."

Ormun laughed, and his delight echoed through the chamber. "Once you commit to something, you never let go, do you? And that's why you're better than any of these spineless lackeys." He frowned at Elise. "But here, she's crying. Why are you crying, Princess?"

"She's never seen anyone punished," said Rema. The pain permeated her lungs, lending a quivering ache to her voice. "Naturally, it's frightened her."

"Understandable. It's grotesque, though."

It was clear that Elise was trying to restrain her sobs, but with little success. Tears ran freely down her cheeks, and her shoulders shuddered.

"This is supposed to be a happy moment." Ormun frowned at his whip, as if surprised to find himself holding it, before returning it to his belt. "Rema, can I trouble you to take her away until she's recovered from her fright? I have matters to attend to, and poor Sothis is looking quite distressed. Perhaps we might attempt this again tomorrow."

"Of course." Rema shivered despite her best attempts to compose herself. "I'll return to you tomorrow with a much happier bride."

"Good! Don't forget your clothes." Ormun raised Elise's hand and pressed his lips to her knuckles. She stared at him, her eyes blank behind her tears. "You're a striking woman, Elise, and I look forward to the day we are man and wife. But do take care to listen to Rema as she explains to you how to properly behave. You will give her that explanation, won't you?"

Rema nodded. She was capable of nothing more. Her limbs were weak, and it felt as if she might collapse at any moment.

"You're smarting, aren't you? Please get those wounds seen to, I'd hate for them to fester. Well, you may go. It's such a joy to see you again, you have no idea!" Ormun turned and spread his arms. "Haran, Sothis, you scoundrels, where were we?"

Elise hurried to gather Rema's clothes, and she steadied Rema as they moved into the courtyard. As Elise closed the door, Rema lurched toward a stone bench intended for visitors. She lay across it and closed her eyes. Her back sang a chorus of suffering.

"I'm so sorry," said Elise, her voice broken and shaking. "I did this to you, I should have listened…"

"Yes, you should have." Rema pressed her cheek to the stone, hoping that the chill might distract her from the pain.

Elise knelt beside Rema and clutched her hand. "Do you want me to take you to the healers?"

"Forget them." It was a wonder Rema could still speak, given the sharp-clawed monster hunched on her back. "You're my healer, Elsie. Did you bring medicine in your trunk?"

"Yes, a little."

"Then numb this pain so that I can put on my shirt." There was no way to know if Ormun took a carnal thrill from stripping women and subjecting them to pain—that mind was beyond deciphering—but there was no doubting Haran had found titillation in it, and that fact magnified her indignation a hundredfold. And it could so easily have been Elise naked and screaming under that whip…

Rema's anger settled into cold determination. She would never let that happen.

Elise spread an ointment over the wound, and a welcome coolness extinguished the worst of the flame. "I'm so stupid. It was all because I was jealous that woman kissed you. I dream night and day of kissing you, and she did it as if it were the easiest thing in the world."

Rema lifted her head as Elise held a vial to her mouth. She sipped the liquid, and a tingling sensation entered her limbs. "Is there much bleeding?"

"The second strike drew a little. Ormun was very precise."

Rema sat upright and struggled into her shirt, grimacing as the fabric flattened against her tender back. "The blood never washes out. That's two shirts ruined."

"I don't even know what to say." Elise settled beside Rema on the bench. "You suffered so that I wouldn't have to. I'm an idiot and a coward."

"Don't blame yourself. Blame him."

"I do." Elise tightened her hands into fists. "He'll pay for that. He'll suffer like no man has ever suffered."

"You can vent your wrath later." Rema touched Elise lightly on the cheek. "For now, let's just catch our breath and be glad that we're still alive."

"I was so cruel to that beautiful little woman. Her exquisiteness made me feel so homely, and you gave me no warning that you had a lover."

"You're every bit as beautiful as she," said Rema, glancing into the corridor as she spoke. "We can't talk here, not like this. We should go to my chambers. They're not far."

"There's just one thing that confuses me. You called him brother, but surely that can't be…"

"That's a long story that requires a clear mind to tell. Will you help me up?"

Elise nodded, and she aided Rema to her feet before taking the handle of the trunk. They walked together, Rema often stumbling and pausing to regain her balance. "It's so quiet," said Elise as they moved down an echoing hall decorated with curling sandstone columns.

"It becomes quieter by the day. After the coup, many of the officials were never replaced. Their families, assistants, students, all of them gone. Ormun believes he can make do with his own delusions and a handful of advisors who are always at each other's throats."

"What about servants?"

"There are few, mostly kitchen staff and errand runners. The majority of the work is done now by slaves, who work in the early morning while the court sleeps. Ormun likes the palace to seem as if maintained by an invisible hand. Up this little flight of stairs here, come."

Each marble step was wrought with patterns reminiscent of clouds, and at the head of the balustrade rested a marble sculpture of a lion's head, its lips curled in a snarl. "There's nothing plain in this place, is there?" said Elise, following Rema up the stairs.

After navigating another ornate corridor, they reached a broad door within a thin marble arch. "My chambers," said Rema. "It should be unlocked, if Artunos has been here already." She tested the handle and exhaled in relief as it turned. "Here we are."

The window of Rema's bedchamber overlooked one of the palace's inner gardens, and dwindling evening light filled the room. Her large bed was heaped with velvet pillows, and a thick, intricately-styled rug covered much of the stone floor. One wall was taken up by a fireplace stocked with fresh logs. "Do you ever have to light that?" said Elise, peering up the chimney. "It's so warm here."

"I find I need it, but you'll probably be able to walk about naked in our winter."

The cicadas began their shrill chirping in the garden below. In less than an hour, the air would be thrumming with the noise of insects. Rema crossed to the window and inhaled the blossom-steeped taste of the evening. Even though the afternoon had long waned, the day's heat still lingered in the air, bringing with it pleasant memories of hours spent idle under the sun. Her back pulsed again, and she steadied herself against the sill.

"I have to lie down," she said, retreating to the bed and reclining on her side.

Elise sat among the pillows and lifted Rema's head into her lap. "We need to get the rest of my luggage here, with all my books and supplies. Not just to treat you, but to take care of him."

"I'd be careful what you do." Rema pressed her cheek against the soft, warm curve of Elise's stomach. Now here was a sufficient compensation for so much pain. "Ormun has a court magician of his own. I still don't understand how this magic of yours works, but I expect he has ways of protecting Ormun from whatever you have in mind."

"There must be something we can do. Rema, this is ridiculous. You want us to see him again tomorrow and curtsy? We're better than that, my love. We have to fight."

"I know. And my back hurts again. Make it stop."

"Endure a little." Elise stroked the back of Rema's ear. "Too much medicine at once won't be good for you."

Rema closed her eyes, and drowsiness spiraled toward her. The pain became a memory and faded, replaced by a sense of being held and comforted, and for a moment she glimpsed the faces of her mother and father—they were afraid for her, but proud, too, of the stand she'd taken. The images washed away, and her mind faded with it.

CHAPTER TWENTY

Rema opened her eyes. The room was suffused by a dim red light. A chorus of insects piped outside the room, whirring their wings and celebrating the coming night. The warmth of Elise's body was still behind her head. How long had she slept in her lap?

Footsteps echoed in the corridor, their sound mixed with a familiar jingling. The door swung open to reveal Jalaya's frightened face. "Rema! Haran has been telling everyone you were whipped... oh, hello..."

"Come in, Jalaya," said Rema. "I'm well enough for visitors."

Jalaya sidled into the room and closed the door, her bright eyes switching between Elise and Rema, whose head was still in Elise's lap. A single wrinkle of bemusement appeared between Jalaya's eyebrows. "Elsie is a healer," said Rema. "She's taking care of me."

Jalaya smiled as if that were explanation enough. "I hope you're not badly hurt." She eyed the bed, clearly trying to determine how to appropriately involve herself, before finally sitting cross-legged beside Elise and placing a hand on Rema's shoulder. In response, Elise began to defiantly stroke Rema's hair.

"Maybe I should lie across both your laps," Rema said, smiling at the absurdity of the competition. "It would seem fairer."

"As your healer, I advise against being across more than one lap," said Elise, and Jalaya replied with a peal of melodious laughter. Elise's frown wavered—unsurprisingly. It would take a stern soul indeed to be immune to the sound of Jalaya's merriment.

Rema sat upright and winced as her back straightened. "Are you in much pain?" asked Jalaya.

"I'll be fine. Elsie has cared for me well."

Jalaya took one of Elise's hands and pressed it to her chest. "Thank you for treating Rema. I hope you don't blame yourself for what happened."

Elise's cheeks colored, and Rema's chest panged with unexpected jealousy. Jalaya was so very beautiful, after all, and much younger—but no, those thoughts were absurd…

"Of course I blame myself," said Elise. "I should've kept my mouth shut."

"Haran said he thought you very amusing. Even though it was unwise to talk back to Ormun, everyone is impressed by how brave you were to do so. I don't know anyone except Rema who has the courage to do that."

"She'd better not do it anymore," said Rema. "Or my back will be nothing but scar tissue by the end of the month."

"Don't worry about your back." Elise stared at her hand, which was being held very close to Jalaya's left breast. "I know what I'm doing."

Jalaya rested her other hand on Elise's knee. "You look a little flushed yourself. Was it a difficult voyage?"

"Very difficult." Elise's gaze moved down Jalaya's body. "A painted man knocked on my door exactly when he shouldn't have."

Jalaya wrinkled her forehead. "How terrible of him."

Rema frowned. She was starting to feel left out. She stretched across Elise's lap and poked Jalaya in her small, soft stomach. "If you want to be useful, you could fetch me some water and perhaps something for us both to eat."

"Of course, beloved." Jalaya leant forward and, oblivious to Elise's scowl, planted a kiss on Rema's lips. She smiled again at Elise and left the room, her skirt shifting as she moved.

"I can't stop her kissing me," said Rema, taking Elise's hand. "She's too quick."

Elise moved her lips in a rueful smile. "It still hurts to see her kiss you, but she's so sweet, isn't she? And even prettier than I remembered."

"Many reckon her to be the most beautiful woman at court. Though now you're here, I'm sure plenty will reconsider."

"Oh, I think she keeps her title. Perhaps I should be jealous of you instead!"

Rema frowned as doubt prodded her heart once more. She'd been so concerned that Elise would envy Jalaya, it had never crossed her mind the two might be attracted to each other. That possibility seemed so obvious to her now. With her wild looks and passionate heart, Elise was exactly the kind of woman liable to leave Jalaya smitten.

"Now we're alone, enlighten me," said Elise. "Have you truly been hiding a lover from me, or is this not what it appears?"

"It's a little of both. At court and in the city, there are many women with whom I enjoy sleeping. Among those, Jalaya is the dearest to me. We kiss, touch and caress each other with the ready intimacy of lovers, but there are no vows between us. My heart is unsworn to anyone."

"So you live in indiscriminate lust. Why did you never tell me?"

"Did you honestly believe me to be chaste?"

Elise's chuckle did a great deal to ease Rema's apprehension. "I suppose you have a point. You were even seen flirting with the servant women, Loric told me."

"These handsome trousers rarely stay buttoned for long. I enjoy women too much to ignore their interest. But when I swore I loved you—that was unlike anything I've ever done."

Elise exuded satisfaction, and Rema relaxed further. Perhaps the worst of this matter was now behind them. "Tell me how you met her," said Elise. "This lovely Jalaya of yours."

"It was five years ago, when I was visiting a brothel—don't raise your eyebrows like that, I was on business."

"What kind of business could you possibly have in a brothel? Apart from the obvious."

"Togun and I were trying to reform them. Too many prostitutes in Arann were held against their will, shipped about from city to city like slaves."

"Sorry." Elise laughed. "Don't look so offended. Go on."

"I was interrogating the owner when I heard a beautiful voice lifted in song. I demanded to know who the singer was. Reluctantly, the man showed me to Jalaya, who was sitting among silken pillows and crooning a sad melody to herself." Rema sighed, remembering. "She was only nineteen. I asked her why she was there, and she told me that her father had sold her against her will. A few days later I had her installed at court in the much happier life of a palace entertainer."

"Poor Jalaya. Did she…I mean, did anyone…"

"She'd been there three weeks, and she'd fought like a cornered animal. The one time they tried to force her to sleep with a patron, she bit him on the nose. But though she managed to escape that indignity, she didn't evade the torment of being repeatedly punished. She was bruised all over, the poor thing, and her lip was split."

"And when did you two start…?"

"Not straightaway. At first she was lost and frightened, and it would have felt as if I were taking advantage of her. I comforted her and let her dine with me. I enjoyed those innocent nights together, basking in her sweetness, and we quickly became true friends. About a year after she'd moved to court, we had our usual dinner together, and afterward she kissed me. Now we share our bodies as well as our joys and sorrows."

"Are you going to tell her about me? About us?"

"I have to, don't I? But it feels dangerous to talk openly about that in the palace, even to her."

"I think your friend suspects something, that rude man in the cloak. Are there many people here that we can trust?"

"Artunos and Jalaya would never betray me. You saw the minister of war earlier, Sothis. He's a friend of mine too. He and I have differences, but we both agree that the wars need to end. There's also Calicio, the spymaster. He's a good man. He's a fierce opponent of slavery, like I am, so we get along well."

"So who are your enemies? That Haran was a slime. And Ormun… he was worse than I'd anticipated, but also different. I was thinking he'd be like a gigantic Calan, but he was nothing like that at all."

"Apart from Haran, I often clash with Ferruro, the imperial treasurer, and Lakmi, the captain of the house guard. Then there's Betany, Ormun's sister. She despises me."

"What about this court magician you've mentioned?"

"His name is Melnennor. He's a mystery to me. He doesn't take sides or even talk politics."

"He has a very wizardly name. I don't believe that's his real name at all."

Rema laughed. "Possibly not."

"Your court is so much more complex than my own. You should dismiss everyone and replace them with a cranky, overworked steward."

"I liked Yorin. I suspect your kingdom would have fallen to pieces by now without him."

"Secretly, I'm fond of him too." Elise gave a round-cheeked grin. "I like to think of him as a beloved uncle, one who's tremendous fun to tease. I was hell on him as a child, always disobeying him and escaping my tutors. I was a wilful thing."

"Was?" Rema tickled under Elise's arms, and Elise yelped in surprise and flopped to the bed.

"You beast." Elise pouted at Rema through a veil of black hair. "I'll destroy you!"

Before Rema could be destroyed, Jalaya returned with a tray wobbling in her arms. "I don't know how to keep this balanced," she said, staring intently at a quivering jug of water. "There's cherries, olives, cream and strawberries, and I'm about to get it all over myself—"

Elise helped Jalaya steady the tray, and together they placed it by the bedside. Jalaya pounced onto the bed beside Rema, dipped a strawberry in cream and lifted it toward Rema's mouth. Rema shook her head, and Jalaya ate the strawberry herself.

As Elise returned to her place, she took Rema's hand. After a moment's consideration, Jalaya took Rema's other hand. "I'm going to need a hand to eat with," said Rema, laughing. "Give them both back."

Jalaya giggled as she surrendered her grasp. "Is it much colder than this where you come from, Elise?" she said, talking through a mouthful of strawberry.

"Oh yes." Elise's hands were full of olives, which she stared at suspiciously. "People die during our winters, and there's nothing we can do about it." She put an olive in her mouth, and her face contorted. "It's salty!"

"Have a strawberry instead." Jalaya held one before Elise's lips, and Elise smiled before taking it with her teeth. "It'll sweeten your tongue once more."

Even though she should have been pleased to see them bonding so quickly, Rema felt a surge of ill-temper. Did they have to prove so fascinated by each other? "We were talking about weather," she said, as if that had been the most intriguing topic imaginable. "I suppose it snows often in Danosha."

"Yes," said Elise. "It makes collecting herbs impossible. I can't stand snow."

"I'd love to see snow," said Jalaya. "I've seen paintings of it, and it seems beautiful."

Elise sniffed. "It's disgusting. So cold and slushy. But I suppose it's a shame to have never seen snow at all."

Jalaya laughed and clapped her hands. "You're so grumpy!"

"I have reason to be."

Jalaya slithered across Rema's lap and startled Elise by clambering over her as well. After much wriggling, Jalaya arrived at the far side of the bed, where she crouched by Elise and gazed at her with compassionate eyes. "This must be dreadful for you," she said.

"You have no idea."

"You should let me sing for you." Jalaya smiled as she touched Elise's shoulder. "It might bring you some happiness. I sing love songs, and I write them myself." She took a few strands of Elise's hair in her fingers. "You have such wonderful hair. Are all women as beautiful as you in Danosha?"

Elise's eyes heated. "You're a flirt."

Jalaya giggled, her little shoulders shaking. "I didn't intend to be. If I were to flirt, I'd remark upon your tempestuous gaze, like a captivating argent flame…"

"Now I see why Rema likes you so much." Elise drew back her neck and shook her head, allowing her hair to fall more neatly about her body. "Is there anything about you that isn't perfect?"

Usually, Rema was amused by Jalaya's effortless ability to charm women; she'd seen countless fall prey to her lyrical tongue, expressive eyes and endearing smile. Somehow, it was less entertaining when the object of the seduction was the first woman Rema had seriously fallen in love with. She bit her lip, trying to ignore the anxiety in her stomach.

Jalaya arranged herself cross-legged and straightened her back. "Would you like to hear me sing?"

Rema shifted uneasily. "I don't know if we have time."

"Let her sing," said Elise. "The singers in Danosha are dreadful."

"I don't often write songs in Annari, because it's not very pretty," said Jalaya. "But this one is nice enough." She closed her eyes and inhaled. Her eyelashes trembled, and her next exhale carried her poetry, borne on the melody of her breath.

"O lover mine, where are you now?
Does sea-wind bear you home?
I fear the ocean breaks its vow,
And claims you in its foam;
O lover, come home now.

O lover mine, is your heart well?
Does it beat sound and true?

I dread that in it, some plague swells
And saps the life from you.
O lover, please be well.

O lover mine, do you see land?
Do white cliffs now draw near?
And do you see me on this sand,
Where I wait every year?

O lover, come home now,
O lover, please be well…"

The sad song faded. "I wrote that while thinking of you, Rema."
Jalaya lowered her gaze. "I missed you."

Elise stared at Jalaya, a deep emotion turning in her eyes. Rema's
own chest ached with the intensity of the poem, imbued as it had
been with Jalaya's sweet sorrow. It was time to force a change of topic.
"Ouch," Rema said, feigning pain. "My back is sore again."

"You poor thing!" Jalaya put her arms around Rema's shoulders
and nuzzled her nape. Elise watched, but her face remained calm.

"I suppose you can have some medicine now." Elise shifted to the
side of the bed and fetched a bottle from the trunk. She returned to
Rema's side, pressing close. "Just a little sip." With Jalaya embracing
her and Elise leaning over her, Rema experienced the not unwelcome
feeling of being suffocated under attractive women.

"Rema's greedy," said Jalaya. "Good luck getting her to take just a
sip. Whenever we share a wineglass, she drinks most of it."

"I can believe that. She's bossy and stubborn too."

"That's right. She's such a tyrant, I don't know why I find her so
attractive."

"I know how you feel."

Jalaya glanced sidelong toward Rema. Her brown eyes contained
no trace of envy or alarm, only gentle concern.

Before anyone could speak again, the door shook under a series
of knocks, and Rema frowned. It wouldn't do to be caught covered in
women. "Off," she said, and Elise and Jalaya scattered. "Enter."

Artunos walked into the room, seeming smaller without his cape.
"Is it true? Did Ormun have you beaten?"

"Yes. Fortunately, I have a remarkable healer, so I'm feeling much
better."

"What happened?"

"We can talk about it later. All of us, tomorrow night."

"Very well." Artunos motioned to Elise, who had retreated to the back of the bed. "Elise, I have arranged you a large bedchamber for your own. If you come with me, I'll settle you in, and then we'll see to giving you a fine dinner."

"I'm happy here with my friends," said Elise. "And Rema's hurt. She needs me to look after her."

"That wouldn't be wise. Ormun will be very sensitive to how you behave yourself in here. There are plenty of people walking these halls who would like nothing better than to tell him that you went into Rema's room and didn't reappear until morning."

"But I'm healing her! Why should it be scandalous?"

"Because Rema has a well-known disposition, and when women spend the night in her room, people assume things. Speaking frankly, and with apologies to you, Rema."

"Don't be rude, Artunos," said Jalaya. "You should let her stay as long as she likes."

"No, he's right," said Rema. "Elsie, it'll be fine. Artunos will look after you, I promise you. I'll come visit you first thing in the morning."

Elise's voice rose in indignation. "And who's going to take care of your back if it hurts during the night?"

"Don't you remember how my back got hurt in the first place? Please go with Artunos. If he's worried, he has good reason to be."

"Haran is already spreading insinuations," said Artunos. "How interesting, he says, that Rema would take such a punishment for this woman. And then he adds that perhaps people can grow very close on a long ship voyage…"

Elise tugged on Rema's sleeve. "Rema, tell this stupid man to go away."

Rema shook her head. "I'll see you first thing in the morning, I promise."

"Fine." Elise pouted as she flung herself from the bed. "I'm going. I don't really want to spend any more time with you anyway. There's still medicine in the bottle, but don't drink any more unless you wake up in the night and you're hurting. Goodnight, Jalaya." She joined Artunos by the door and stood glaring at the floor.

"Jalaya, have a word with our colleagues," said Artunos. "Make sure they're invited to dinner tomorrow. Rema, Elise will be in the spare chambers opposite my own. I look forward to you telling me what idiot thing you did to provoke Ormun this time. He hasn't struck you in years."

Rema gazed at Elise with helpless anxiety building in her chest. That temper may have been attractive back in Danosha, but by the gods, it was liable to get them all into a lot of trouble here. "Look after her, Artunos. I care a great deal about this woman."

Any hope the admission would placate Elise was quashed when she turned away, still scowling. Artunos escorted her from the room.

The moment the door was closed, Jalaya put a hand on Rema's forearm. "Tell me what's happening between the two of you."

"We fell in love," said Rema. "And it's hard, Jalaya. I feel responsible to her, and she feels like she needs me to keep living."

"Oh, Rema. I don't blame you. She has the same proud spirit that you do." Jalaya ran a finger down Rema's cheek. "Is this why you look so troubled? Let me help you." She kissed Rema on the forehead and the lips, and Rema shivered as she looked into Jalaya's understanding eyes. What was it she wanted? Could she really forfeit Jalaya's tenderness? Elise could be so temperamental and aloof, so oblivious to the feelings of others…

Jalaya undid her top and dropped it to the bed. Rema caressed Jalaya's dark-nippled breasts and the smoothness of her belly, while Jalaya pressed her tongue against her teeth as she tugged at Rema's shirt.

"Leave it on," Rema said. "Please." She still felt vulnerable beneath the thin garment, reluctant to bare her torso again and conscious of what must be an ugly mark on her back.

"I understand. And I know you must be conflicted, bound by your feelings for her. I don't expect you to make love to me." Jalaya touched the silver button that kept Rema's trousers closed. "If you want, you can close your eyes and forget your troubles while I pleasure you. If not, I'll just hold you in my arms and sing you to sleep."

Rema closed her eyes. For the last four years, Jalaya had been her refuge, their nights together Rema's only respite from her terrible complicity in Ormun's reign. Jalaya's expert fingertips caressed away anxiety and guilt, and her lips eased the aching grief. Yet the sorrow always returned.

"Jalaya, you don't understand. When I say that I love her, I don't mean a relationship like we have, one where we make no claim over each other. I promised that I would be with her. Only her."

"I do understand that you're hurting, and to see you in pain is more than this heart can bear." Jalaya popped the button. Caught between desire and doubt, there was nothing for Rema to do but wait for the pleasure she knew was coming.

Jalaya pushed Rema back to the bed and leaned over her. They kissed, and Jalaya slipped her hand into Rema's undergarment. With light pressure and steady motion, she began to provoke that incomparable, frustrating, breathtaking sensation, and Rema moaned. No doubt it had been audible in the gardens below, but she was beyond caring. She went limp, letting herself be guided toward oblivion.

Her pleasure swelled, mounting to a consuming intensity, and fled with a desperate gasp of breath. She was freed, emptied, satiated; the shadow had retreated. Jalaya extracted her hand and kissed Rema gently on the nose. "All I want is for you to be happy."

"Then sing to me."

Carried upon the haunting sound of Jalaya's lullaby, Rema sailed into slumber. Her final thought, before the beautiful, melancholy song pulled her away from the world, was of Elise.

CHAPTER TWENTY-ONE

Ormun was chasing her. His eyes were Bannon's, a pair of hateful, slick and bulging orbs, and he carried his whip, the cruel cords of which were alive and wriggling. They writhed through the air and wrapped around her legs. As Rema fell, she realized that Elise was already dead.

Rema woke to a room full of thin morning light. Jalaya was nestled in the crook of her arm. A bird in the garden beat its wings, and Jalaya stirred and mumbled some nonsense. Rema touched her cheek, and she opened her sleepy, tranquil eyes.

"Good morning," said Rema, lifting herself up on her elbow.

"I'm so glad you're back." Jalaya stretched her toes toward the sunlight. "I always dream nice things when I'm with you."

"What do you dream when I'm not here?"

Jalaya only smiled and pressed her tired lashes together. Rema sat upright and poured some water into a ceramic mug, while Jalaya tilted her head to watch Rema as she drank. "Rema, I want to ask you something, but I don't want to make things harder for you."

"When have we ever had secrets?"

"We've been best friends for so long." Jalaya caressed Rema's neck as she spoke. "Every moment I'm not by your side, I'm thinking of you. I know and adore everything about you. But though you've known Elise for only the tiniest while, you say you must love only her. Why not me too?"

"You know how fond I am of you." Rema kissed Jalaya's fingertips. "I've never met anyone who can speak straight to my heart the way you do."

"Isn't that love?"

"I don't know. Perhaps."

"I love you, Rema." Jalaya turned her head, and the morning sun lit the side of her delicate face. "Whenever I've said it before, you've laughed like I'm just being affectionate. But I meant it. I've always meant it. And I've always thought that maybe you loved me too."

Rema took an unsteady breath. "I always thought…love means a commitment, and we never committed to…We've both seen so many other women in the time in which we've known each other, whereas my love for Elise is different. It's not something that can be shared."

"I don't see why. Even when I slept with other women, I was still in love with you. To me love means caring, not belonging."

A beetle whirred through the window and settled on the bedside table, its wings still vibrating. Rema stared at it, avoiding the torment of meeting Jalaya's eyes. "It's not like that for me. Maybe it's because my father and mother were so devoted to each other. I've always believed that true love is reserved for only one other. I don't know, Jalaya. It's hurting my heart just to think about it."

Jalaya held out her hand and watched the light steal between her fingers. "She must be very special."

"She's so intense, so full of wild conviction. When I first met her she was nervous and lovesick, but only because she understood sooner than I did that we need each other."

"What does she give you that I can't?" Jalaya said the words without a trace of bitterness, as only she could.

"Ormun killed something in me. You can ease my pain for a night, but you can't give me back that missing part. I think she can. If I were the woman I used to be, the woman she now is, I would never have followed Ormun's orders for these four years. I would rather have died."

"But your diplomacy saves lives. You're doing good things."

The reasoning was as familiar as it was false. "I help Ormun win nations and abduct brides. I could save a hundred thousand lives and still wake up grieving."

"I'm going to lose you, aren't I? And I'll lose you though I love you, because I love you."

"I don't deserve you." Rema cupped Jalaya's cheek in her hand. "And I never meant to hurt you. You have a heart so clear that I can't even comprehend it. I need you as my friend, I don't want our lives to ever be parted, but I can't make love to you again."

Jalaya closed her eyes and smiled as Rema cradled her face. After several seconds of tranquil stillness, she brushed aside Rema's hand and slipped from the bed. "Don't feel guilty about last night. What we do with our bodies doesn't dictate where our hearts belong."

Rema pointed to Jalaya's bare breasts. "As for you, don't forget your top."

Jalaya giggled as she tied her flimsy upper garment around her chest. "I hope your back is feeling better."

Rema touched the skin at the small of her back. A raised line, but no sensation. "I don't feel any pain at all. Elise is a remarkable healer."

"I like to think it was my singing." Jalaya lowered her lashes. "I'm going now, my love, to a strange new life, one where you belong to a woman who can finally match your melody. May I kiss you one last time?"

"I…" Rema hesitated. If she had no choice but to make this sacrifice, it was better not to waver. "Let's not."

Jalaya remained silent for a moment before sighing. "Thank you, Rema. Thank you for saving me from silence and returning music to my heart." She trod softly to the door, her golden hoops jangling, and paused with her fingers on the handle. "I'm glad that I'm still your dearest friend. Take care of your Elsie." She looked away as she began to croon, low and soft:

> *"Her love has held my grief at bay,*
> *And now she sets me free,*
> *To drift upon my lonely way,*
> *Like mist across the sea.*
> *But in my breast still burns the gift*
> *Of her sweet mystery;*
> *My lips will always feel her kiss,*
> *Her heart remains with me."*

There was something final about the way Jalaya closed the door, and Rema buried her head in her hands. Had she lost her mind? She was forfeiting everything—her career, her lover and potentially her life—for a woman she'd just met and who was perhaps forever out of reach. The ache of desolation reached for her heart, and Rema rose out of bed in an attempt to banish it.

She stood by the window. The garden beneath her was walled by marble, and the palace roof stretched beyond it, punctuated by courtyards. Behind the palace's golden barrier, the city spread to the horizon, stone buildings and towers that carried all the way to the endless sea. For the first time in years, the sight stirred determination rather than resignation. Jalaya's parting poem had been a promise not of sorrow, but of hope; that old courage was still within her, waiting to be brought forth again.

Rema fixed her hair in the mirror, washed her face over the basin and swapped her shirt for a clean one. She put on fresh underclothes and trousers before buttoning up her coat. Had it really been thirteen years since she'd first donned this uniform? As she patted her face dry, her thoughts turned to Elise. It had been considerate of Artunos to place her next to his own chambers, though she was in no danger until the wedding, as Ormun never touched a bride until marriage. He played by certain inscrutable rules.

Once more in her diplomatic finery, Rema set off for Elise's chambers. The cunning design of the palace allowed for windows in almost every corridor, carved even into the ceiling where necessary, so that a visitor almost always found themselves in sunlight. No two passages were alike. One hallway was lined with exquisite arches; another contained paintings of hypnotic vividness stolen from cities throughout the Empire. Others corridors were alive with fountains, the waters of which poured down the walls and vanished into unseen pipes. It was a telling commentary on Ormun's reign that some of the water fixtures had run dry—the imperial engineer had died in the coup and never been replaced.

She turned a corner and stumbled into Ferruro, the imperial treasurer. He was immense, easily the tallest and largest man Rema had ever met, and was the terror of bureaucrats throughout the court. Few people were brave enough to ask him directly for money. Instead, they delegated the task to attendants who accepted their fate the way prisoners resigned themselves to execution.

"It's you," said Ferruro, stepping back and looking down at her. "Our flame-headed diplomat returned from the wilds."

"Ferruro. Did you miss me?"

"Oh, it was a relief not to have you underfoot. I didn't have to worry so much about treading on you."

Ferruro was new to the court, one of Ormun's appointments. He had aligned himself with Haran despite being openly contemptuous of the imperial lawmaker and his tyrannical excesses. Rema found him infuriating and likeable in equal measure. He was frustratingly deadpan and immune to even the most biting gibes, and more than once their regular sparring had ended with Rema impaled upon a barb quicker than her own.

"If you weren't so clumsy, such things wouldn't happen," said Rema. "So what mischief have you been getting up to?"

Ferruro chuckled, a sound like rocks shifting. "Merely counting coins. Tell me, what is the twentieth bride like? I know nothing about this Danosha, save that it's the kind of kingdom where every winter the king is forced to eat his horse."

"And why are you so interested in her?"

"If I want to know the quality of a wine, I ask a wine taster. If I want to know the quality of a woman, I ask Remela."

Rema laughed. "You're in good form today."

"One has to be, under the circumstances. Oh, I heard about your mishap yesterday. Haran was gloating about it."

"No doubt. I expect it was the closest he's ever been to seeing a woman undressed."

Ferruro rumbled in delight. "This is a wonderful arrangement. I tease you, and in return you tease Haran."

"I may as well. You're two sides of the same coin."

"Oh, cruel. And untrue. Believe me, I know a great deal about coins." Ferruro's eyes glittered with good humor. "While it has been a delight to see you again, I must hurry off on business. Even now there may be people trying to spend my money."

Rema stepped aside and gestured to the hallway behind her. "Don't tread on anyone I know."

"Oh, don't worry about what I might do to your friends. Haran, however, has found himself a zealous streak lately. Keep your little eyes sharp." Ferruro strode past her, ducking to avoid a stone arch.

Her heart troubled by his parting words, Rema continued down the hall until she reached a spiral staircase, the walls of which were pebbled with an intricate mosaic. The stairs ascended into a low corridor lined with slender golden rods joining in a latticework across the ceiling. Rema passed the door to Artunos's quarters and knocked on its nearest neighbor. After a long moment, the door opened. Elise's head appeared in the gap, and affection swelled in Rema's chest.

"Good morning," Rema said. A simple welcome, but her knack for romance had failed her.

Without replying, Elise opened the door and gestured Rema in. Her bedchambers were modestly sized and lit by a large, crescent-shaped window. The bed was a mess, covered with tangled blankets and tossed pillows, and Elise had already pulled half the contents of her trunk onto the floor. She appeared as disorderly as her room, with a sullen pout on her lips and hair tangled wild around her face.

"You're such a scruffy thing," said Rema. "Aren't you happy to see me?"

"As happy as I can be, given I'm required to grovel piteously before the most horrible man in the world."

Rema touched Elise's shoulder, but the contact provoked no change in expression. "I know you resent it. But it's important to keep him in a good mood so that I can convince him not to marry you right away."

"Is that possible? That he'd marry me today?"

"Yes. The master of unions lives here in the palace, and he's hardly likely to tell the Emperor that he's overscheduled."

"I imagined there'd be a wedding ceremony. Something imperial-sized."

"Ormun got tired of that fifteen wives ago. Now he only cares about getting ink on the document." Rema gave a smile without managing to elicit one in return. "Elsie, is something wrong?"

"I can't stop thinking about how he hurt you. I'm terrified he's going to do it again."

"He won't if you just nod and say the right things."

"That's not who I am, Rema. The moment I saw you, I threw myself at you. The moment Calan came home, I rushed to the door to berate him. I'm not like you. I can't play along with his cruelty and pretend that I don't care."

Rema sucked in her breath. Though the words reflected what she herself had been saying to Jalaya that morning, it still hurt to hear it. "You'll be fine," said Rema with careful calmness. How ironic—her reaction to being accused of concealing her emotions had been to bury them even deeper. "Let's make haste. Ormun is most amenable in the mornings. One of my little tricks is to bring him important things to sign before dawn."

"Not to mention unimportant women who are being married against their will."

"Elsie, I never even implied that you were..." Rema trailed off in exasperation. There had been genuine venom in her voice, but why? Gods, had she really given up Jalaya's sweetness and wisdom for a spoiled, stubborn princess incapable of seeing beyond the fog of her own misfortune? "If I've insulted you, I apologize. Now please, let's go."

Elise trudged slowly in pursuit, her head kept low. As she and Rema entered the courtyard that acted as antechamber to Ormun's meeting hall, Rema found herself on the verge of wild laughter. Here they were again, in exactly the same circumstances as the day before. The gods enjoyed their sport.

"Remember what happened last time," said Rema. "I can tell you're angry, but please behave yourself."

"You think I'd say something to get you hurt?" Elise's voice was feverish with indignation. "I would rather die than see you endure that again."

"I'm sorry, Elsie. For everything and anything." Rema sighed. "Are you ready?"

"It seems like a simple enough task. Let's get it over with."

Rema reached for the handle. As her fingers met its cool bronze surface, she shivered despite the early heat—thinking of that dream she'd had, the way the whip had moved—but before despair could take hold, a new resolve rose within her. Today she had broken the heart of her truest friend, who in return had offered neither tears nor recriminations, only blessings. Rema owed it to her to see this matter through.

She opened the door.

CHAPTER TWENTY-TWO

Ormun was standing alone in the chamber, his gaze fixed on a window. Rema cleared her throat. "Yes, I know you're there," Ormun said. "I'm just watching a parrot. Wonderful creatures…and there, it's gone." He swiveled to face her. "I have to say, Rema, if this is your idea of a happy bride, you and I must talk."

After a moment of tense silence, Elise offered a weak smile. Rema tensed. Would the feigned pleasure be enough?

"That's better," said Ormun, and Rema relaxed. "Come closer, into the sun."

Rema and Elise joined Ormun by the window. From the audience chamber, it was possible to see much of the westward basin and into Arann itself. Splashes of color marked where markets and festivals were being held, the dark shapes of people and animals coursed through the streets, pale smoke rose from smithies and bakeries, and beyond it all lay the sweeping mountain that enveloped Arann on its western side. Even the mountain was not impervious to the city, which crawled all the way up the mountainside and stopped only at the sheerest cliffs.

"This city is ours, dear bride," said Ormun. "Aren't you happy?"

"Yes," said Elise without tone or expression.

"Good!" Ormun patted Elise's shoulder. "All I want is for you to be at home here. I may have many wives, but I care for each of them." He lifted Elise's hand and examined her fingers the way a trader might inspect the teeth of a horse. "I'd like us to be married soon. I'm sure you'll agree that a big event is a tragic waste of time and expense. It's enough to know you'll be living in all of this grandeur. Am I right?"

"Yes."

"That's what I thought. And once we're married we can finally become intimate, as husband and wife are. But I won't talk about that in front of Rema, who is a very chaste and pious woman." Ormun winked at Rema. It was the same way he'd winked as an adolescent whenever he'd told her some bawdy joke. She hated how he could entangle familiar playfulness among his wickedness, reminding her of the boy she'd known.

"I don't believe we should rush into the wedding," Rema said. "Elise should have time to enjoy the palace. She needs to understand what she is to inherit if she is to be as excited as possible to be your bride."

"That's a good point. I'd have ordered the marriage for this afternoon, but you're right, dear, why not allow her some anticipation? Has she seen the imperial gardens yet?"

"Not at all. I can show her today. Perhaps the day after, I can take her to the galleries. Then another day to take in the beauty of the great hall and your throne room—"

"Three days." Ormun snapped his fingers. "Three days to see the palace and then marriage. It's a strain on my patience, but done! Imagine the smile on her face when the day finally comes, knowing all that is to be hers."

Did he believe his own words or was it all part of his game? "I should begin the tour as soon as possible. I wouldn't want a single sight to be missed."

Ormun offered Elise a curt bow. "My bride, it has been a joy to see you again. And please do fix your hair before the ceremony, sweetling, you look like a walking hedge."

"Yes," said Elise.

"Now, Rema." Ormun turned his back on Elise as if she no longer existed. "I need a word alone. Do you have the time?"

"Of course," said Rema. "Elise, if you wait in the courtyard, we'll begin our tour shortly."

Elise trotted obediently from the room. Only three days in which to save her? It seemed impossible, but perhaps—Rema broke off her thoughts as Ormun put an arm around her shoulders. "I noticed she said nothing but yes."

"And I noticed you'd forgotten her name again."

Ormun gestured to the window. "The city is in an odd mood lately. People are having trouble forgetting the disorderly ideas of my father. Everyone remembers that only a few years ago, a man might work himself free of slavery or a woman might divorce her husband for adultery. Silly little memories."

"It's foolish to give rights and then take them away. What did you expect for it, praise and adoration?"

"Now, now, don't bite. Haran has been agitating, dear. He's brought to me a proposal that I'm obliged to consider seriously. He believes that people in the streets talk ill of me and instead speak fondly of my father. The appropriate response, according to our judge, is to declare such speech a crime punishable by death."

"Why even raise that barbarity with me? You already know what I'll say."

"I know. But I'd like to hear the way you have to say it."

Rema hardened her tone as much as she dared. "I've traveled to most cities in the world. There are none as diverse and vital as Arann, and it's a city I have no shame in calling my home. Haran's proposal would banish the life from it. Yes, we need laws to condemn citizens when their actions do harm, but thoughts are something else entirely. Do you really want to end all debate, stifle thought and create a condition under which there'll never be any reform or progress?"

Ormun made a brisk, dismissive gesture with his hand. "Progress is a dangerous thing. Look at the rebellious people of Urandal. They once had a king. They overthrew him. Now they rule themselves—or did, until I came along. Everyone referred to that regicide as progress and reform, but it seems to me the king came off rather poorly."

"Your father didn't want to command the people. He wanted to unify them and organize in them the power to direct themselves. He wasn't any less effective an Emperor for that."

"He came to your notions late in life. He built all of this the same way I'm building the further Empire, on the backs of slaves and at the tips of swords."

"Were you asking my advice, or did you just want to gloat?"

"Dear Rema." Ormun tightened his grip on her shoulders. "Not everyone appreciates your candor as much as I do, alas. You should know that Haran and Betany are calling for your head."

"And how is your sister?"

"Unhappy, as always. She's a peculiar one. She wants me to make sexual deviation a crime punishable by death, and she even has Haran putting the idea to me formally. I think Haran is enamored with my sister, isn't that a funny idea?"

Rema frowned. "And what exactly is a sexual deviation?"

"You, dear. And your male counterparts."

"Is she really such a prude, or is this just another convoluted way of getting me executed?"

"A little of both, I suppose." Ormun dropped his arm and leaned forward on the sill, squinting into the sun. "If Haran keeps lobbying me unopposed, I'll have to do what he says. So you'd better get back into the game! More time at your desk, less time playing with your pretty toys."

"I'll see to it."

"Go on then! Take my bride on a tour."

Rema walked toward the door, filled with the tense certainty that he had something left to say. Sure enough, when she was halfway across the room, he spoke again. "Are you in love with her?"

Keeping her face still required all the diplomatic discipline in her possession. "Why are you asking?"

"Ugly rumors spread by our ugly lawmaker. Nothing but the products of his scaly little mind, I'm certain! It's interesting, though. I've been told there are rumors from her own court that she is…well, to borrow from my sister, a sexual deviation. Do you think so?"

"I've seen no indication." Fear rattled Rema's heart, and she took a slow, calming breath. He was only playing with her. He knew nothing.

"I suppose you'd be able to tell. There must be a trick to it, mustn't there, identifying those women who are amenable to your advances?" Ormun rubbed his hands, a dark satisfaction in his eyes. "I'll have to make sure my wedding night is vigorous. No offense to yourself, Rema, but I need my wives to have a healthy lust for men. She'll understand the virtue of masculinity by the time the night is through."

"Is that all?" Rema was no longer able to keep the coldness from her voice.

"You've been offended. A thousand pardons." Ormun rested his hand on the whip at his belt. "I shouldn't have raised Haran's dirty innuendos. Unlike him, I'm not about to pry into the secrets of your heart, dear sister."

"Good day, Ormun."

The moment she was in the courtyard and away from his gaze, her hands began to shake, and she clasped them together to keep them still. How could it be that she'd once sat at Ormun's desk and helped him struggle through his lessons? How he could be now so unlike the boy who'd crept with her into the orchards to pick apples, figs and oranges, and who had laughed and joked as they feasted on them late into the night? She'd been delighted when Ormun had first called her "sister." The two of them had once conspired to court lovers, thinking of ways to win the heart of an elegant harpist or kitchen maid. Now he tormented women, and she had grown to fear him.

Her reverie broke as she made a realization—the courtyard was empty. Where was Elise? Rema entered the hall and found her standing further down the corridor, inspecting a portrait of the Emperor Togun. It was a painting from late in life—not by chance, as Rema had arranged for the older, more warlike portraits of him to gradually disappear from the palace. He'd been depicted in one of the gardens, a hand on a stack of books and the other on the head of a child. It was a close likeness, faithful to all of Togun's muscular presence. The artist had made his face stern, but with some magic of the brush had captured the witty kindness in the eyes and the corners of his mouth. Yet the quality she had loved the most, his sonorous voice, was forever beyond the painter's brush.

"That's him, isn't it," said Elise. "The good Emperor. The one who believed in you."

"I still miss him, Elsie." Rema's eyes blurred as she gazed at the painting, and she blinked several times to clear them. "Especially on days like this."

"Did you sleep with her last night? Jalaya?"

For once, Rema's experienced tongue proved perfectly inept. "I… Elsie, I, ah…"

"Don't stammer at me. I left you and that impossibly exquisite woman huddled together on your bed. Don't tell me nothing happened."

"What do you mean?" Rema grimaced at her own clumsiness. Of all the stupid, inadequate responses.

"I know it's idiotic of me to be jealous. I know it's pathetic of me to care. Whatever you do with her is your own business. After all, she's sweet, beautiful and kind, and I'm just a stubborn, selfish bitch who wants what she can't have. All I do is get you beaten."

So Elise wasn't oblivious to her shortcomings, but felt them as acutely as Rema did. She softened her tone. "Stop blaming yourself for that. It's my fault you're here, enduring this terrible marriage. Protecting you was the least I could do."

"You're so stupid sometimes!" Temper blazed in Elise's eyes, a silver fire. "You think that's supposed to console me? I'm terrified that what you feel for me is guilt, not love. You say you love me, you protect me from danger, but I fear it's because you want redemption for what you've become: a cold-hearted schemer, like everyone else behind these gilt walls."

"Elsie…"

Elise slumped as if the flame in her were nearly extinguished. "Last night, you let me be sent away as though I were a child past her bedtime. It was my first night in this monstrous palace, the home of a man who wants to hurt me and who did hurt you. I was bereft, Rema. I needed you. I was alone. You brought me here, you gave me your promise…and you chose to be with her…"

Rema pushed Elise to the wall, holding her face in one hand and pinning her wrist to the marble with the other. As their bodies met, Elise's soft breasts pushed against Rema's chest, a contact thrilling enough to warrant tempting death—and to finally meet those pouting lips, which proved as soft and heated as Rema had anticipated. After a second of surprised submission, Elise returned the kiss with greater passion while stroking Rema's neck and face.

Their heads tilted, and Rema kissed more deeply still, touching Elise's tongue and feeling the delicate tips of her teeth. She could see nothing but those eyes, their silver glinting behind half-lowered lashes. By the time Rema pulled back, Elise was breathing rapidly, her cheeks in full blush and her gaze bright and wondering.

"I love you," said Rema. She kissed Elise again, harder than before, and her hip pushed into Elise's groin. Elise moaned as she clutched Rema's behind and pulled her closer still. They were moments away from losing control, and Rema broke the kiss while she could. Elise was still shaking, her full breasts heaving, and the desire to return to her lips was near unbearable.

"Don't stop," Elise whispered.

"You have to trust me." Rema touched a fingertip to Elise's mouth. "I won't lie to you. Last night I was hurting, and Jalaya consoled me. But this morning, I told her we couldn't love that way again. I want you, as fiery and moody as you are. I want to know what I may yet become if I have someone like you at my side."

Elise blinked, and tears fell from her lashes. "Why are you telling me this only now?"

"Because I've realized my fear of him is nothing beside my fear of losing you." Rema laid her fingers against Elise's damp cheek. "Elise

Danarian, our breath is one breath. Our heart is one heart. Our life is one life."

"More poetry. I wish I could say something pretty back."

"It was my parents' wedding vow." Rema took Elise's hands and twined their fingers together. "I'm yours, my love, from this day until the last."

Footsteps rang in the corridor, and the women disentangled and turned in disarray. Artunos was standing midstride, bewildered. "Have you both gone mad?"

"Yes, and I'm glad for it," said Rema. "And don't look at me like that. You have no right to."

Artunos glanced behind him. "What if somebody sees you? Rema, you should know better!"

Rema moved a sweaty strand from her forehead. "I suppose I'm a little disheveled."

"Not nearly so much as she is."

It was true enough; Elise looked exactly like someone recently ravished in a hallway. Her hair was stuck to her flushed cheeks, and her dress had ridden up nearly to her thighs—how that had happened, Rema couldn't even remember. "What do you want me to say? I love her, Artunos. I'm not going to let that madman have her."

"Rema, he'll have you killed!"

"So be it. At least I'll have died for the sake of something I believe in."

Artunos's voice, usually so strong, now trembled with agitation. "This isn't the time to chase martyrdom. Our position is tenuous. We need you clear-headed, to direct and guide us…"

"I've guided us nowhere. I've only helped us bleed out rather than die on our feet." Rema smiled, unable to share in his fear—the truth of love was with her now, Jalaya's parting gift. "This is the right path to follow, old friend. Trust me."

"Whatever conversion you believe you've undergone, we can discuss it tonight. I came to tell you that a man is here in the palace to see you. A colorful trader by the name of Muhan."

In the drama of the last few hours, Rema had forgotten, and as the magician returned to her thoughts, an elegant, implausible plan began to form. "Of course, Muhan. Where is he?"

"The outer court. I had someone bring him a flask of wine." Artunos continued to glare at her. "I still can't believe you were so reckless. There are countless beautiful women in Arann. Why throw your life away over this sour-faced foreigner?"

"You've either forgotten that I can understand you, or you're ruder than I thought," said Elise. "Have you never loved anyone?"

"Love isn't as simple as you think. I have two wives, and one of my wives has another husband. Does that surprise you, easterner?"

"Do you think that because I come from over the sea, I'll be shocked by every little thing you say? You just caught me kissing another woman. Do you really believe I'm scandalized by you having two wives?"

"I don't have time to listen to you two fighting," said Rema. "Elsie, did you want to come with me to see Muhan?"

"Send him my greetings. I have something else to attend." Elise tugged down her skirt and adjusted her hair. "You," she said, pointing to Artunos. "Fetch me my belongings from wherever they are now, as many of my books and crates as you can. They need to be here by this afternoon." She hesitated before adding, with obvious reluctance, "And can you show me the way back to my room?"

"Whatever you say, Princess," said Artunos. "Rema, I'll see you this evening. For the love of the gods, tread carefully."

Elise winked. "And for the love of me, tread however you please. I'll count every breath from now until I see you again."

Artunos strode away, and Elise sauntered in pursuit, a satisfied wiggle to her hips. Rema closed her eyes and collapsed against the wall, still dazed by the audacity of their kiss and the feeling of liberation that had followed. It was as if she had thrown herself over a terrifying edge but fallen into happiness rather than death. And had her father not told her this would happen?

"I feel that I am light again," she said in a murmur somehow not her own. "And I know that I am saved."

CHAPTER TWENTY-THREE

The outer court was crowded but quiet. An emissary from Kataris was sitting cross-legged at the edge of the fountain, his hands folded in his lap as he listened to two of Rema's junior diplomats. Beside a column, a musician plucked the strings of a silver-necked lute. Some distance away, a handful of traders whispered together under an ornamental tree. They would be at court to seek favors from Ferruro, either to mitigate some levy or impose one on some competitor.

Rema found Muhan sprawled on a wrought-iron bench, his eyes closed and his mustache puffing into the air as he breathed. "Good morning," she said.

Muhan opened his left eye and smiled. "There you are. I had a most excellent breakfast this morning. Grapefruit. You've no idea how many years it's been."

"And wine, I'm told. Arann is spoiling you."

"Yes, well." Muhan stretched his arms back while yawning. "Luck is a finite thing. No doubt you're here with a warrant for my execution."

"On a charge of cruelty to monkeys." Rema sat beside him. "Is this your first time in the palace?"

"Indeed, and before you interrogate me, I've a question. I have a keen interest in colors—you may have noticed—and I observe there are two colors of guards here, some silver and some gold."

Rema nodded. "The golden guards are protectors of the imperial officials—that is, me. The silver guards protect the house—that is, you."

"So if you were to attack me, the silver ones would join my defense, and the golden ones would leap at their throats?"

"Something like that. We can find out, if you like. I'm feeling savage today."

"Oh?" Muhan raised his colored brows. "Is there a reason for your bloodlust?"

"Your brothers who were killed in the invasion of Ulat Province." Rema spoke in Ulat, the curling melodies vibrating easily off her tongue. "Do you think of them often?"

Muhan's smile vanished. "Why do you ask?"

"Are you a vengeful man, Muhan?"

"I would hope not."

"I'm not usually a vengeful woman. But I can't go on like this. Ormun will marry Elise three days from now. This whole farce of his, the wars, butchering and stolen wives. I've endured it too long, thinking that I can do some good by remaining at his side. And I've endured too much."

Muhan bent closer. "Are you sure nobody around us speaks Ulat? These are dangerous words."

"Nobody in this palace speaks it but me. Ulat Province is only so much primitive soil in the eyes of the Empire. Your language isn't taught, your people are rarely welcomed. There's a prejudice against the Ulati, as I hardly need tell you. But I learned your languages and customs as a child when we traded among your people. I remember drinking handfuls of goat's milk and eating from steaming bowls of lentils while listening to the Ulati singing and talking around me."

Muhan exhaled. "Tell me what you need."

"I want you to meet with some of my friends tonight, here in the palace. If you return to this court in the late evening, someone will meet you here. What I'm planning will be dangerous, but if we succeed then your homeland could be free again. No imperial garrisons to plunder your herds and harass your women."

"I'm not so provincial as to be moved only by the plight of my native people, or, least of all, to be concerned about the fate of herds." Muhan leaned back, his fingers clasped against his chest. "I'm a traveling magician and dye trader, not some brave Ulati rebel or irate shepherd. But—" He raised his hand to interrupt Rema's objection.

"I'm also a man who can recognize when fate is beckoning him to become something larger. For you and the lady Elise, I will do this."

"If we succeed, you'll never have to trade dye again."

"Gods forbid. How drab a life that would be!"

Rema smiled. "I can't talk to you much longer. Those around us will wonder why I'm speaking at such length in an unfamiliar tongue."

"Then we've spoken enough. I'll be here tonight, as requested. Shall I trouble to have dinner first?"

"There'll be food, if you want it."

"I'll wait to gorge myself up to the very tip of my mustache." Muhan rose and clasped his hands. "Give my regards to our enchantress. Has that brute laid his hands on her yet?"

"I've stood in his way." Rema returned to her feet and copied the gesture, her fingers locked in respect. "She's fierce and undaunted. We'll survive this together."

Muhan gave his mustache a pensive stroke. "The Ulati forbid women to lie with women. As do Danoshans, I believe."

"As do many other people, but it is permitted in Arann. There were laws, but they were rarely enforced, and Togun and I repealed them."

Muhan nodded. "I only mention it in order to note that, to my great surprise and wonder, I believe you two were intended for each other. That's the joy of being a traveler: every day your eyes open a little wider." He bowed and walked to the gates, his lean body swaying as he hummed beneath his breath.

Rema took a deep breath and adjusted her collar. Now to deal with the skulking beast she'd seen from the corner of her eye. She walked around a thick marble column and confronted Bannon. "How long have you been hiding here?"

"Not long. I was only admiring this pillar. Crafty detailing, isn't it?" Bannon lowered his hood, revealing his downy blond hair and protruding ears. If it hadn't been for those unnerving eyes, he might have had a boyish charm. "I'm surprised you saw me. I thought you were tied up in conversation with the Ulati."

"You're not as sly as you imagine."

"Oh, no, I am." Bannon flicked a speck of dirt from his fingers. "You're just a very clever woman."

"If you've come to serenade me, it won't work."

"Believe me, I know." It was unnerving how Bannon's gaze gave the impression he was watching somebody else through her. "Shall we take this discussion to your office?"

"Fine. This way."

Rema directed Bannon toward an archway and between two silver-suited guards, who scowled as Bannon passed. "Everybody always assumes I'm guilty of something," he said in a low tone of amusement.

They entered a corridor decorated with alcoves containing jade and onyx statuary. Bannon admired the chiseled objects as he walked by them, at one point stopping to run his finger along the engraved wings of a bird captured in flight. "Why do I have the feeling this statuette will be gone in the morning?" said Rema. Bannon responded with an expression of mock innocence that could have made her smile, had its owner been anyone else.

Their path took them into a small garden courtyard. To Rema's irritation, Haran and Betany were sitting on a bench beside an artificial lake. Perhaps sensing Rema's animosity, Betany lifted her head and glowered. The movement startled Haran, who had been talking closely into her ear.

Rema approached them, forming her most insincere smile. Betany looked very much like Ormun, with the same short brown hair, delicate features and long, thin-tipped nose. She was a year older than Rema and attractive, if she was considered without regard to her personality. When that was taken into consideration, she was nothing short of repulsive. Her smile in particular was repellent—a bitter curl with no warmth whatsoever.

"You shouldn't be in the garden," said Betany. "A face like yours will scare away the birds."

"It seems I've already scared a pair of lovebirds."

Bannon chuckled, and Haran drew himself to his full height, his lips pursed. "Lady Betany and I were in rational and sensible discussion," he said, rubbing furiously at his wrist. It was a common tic when he was annoyed; Rema had fond memories of the day she'd frustrated him so much he'd broken the skin. "She is the sister of our Emperor, and you'd be wise to treat her with respect."

"Oh, so that's who this woman is! For years I'd believed she was some poor beggar who had wandered into the palace and gotten lost." Rema bowed. "My apologies. I'll stop telling the guards to watch for you."

"What have you brought in with you?" said Betany, pointing an indignant finger in Bannon's direction. "Some kind of ogre?"

Bannon stepped forward before Rema could answer. "My name is Bannon." He gestured dramatically to himself with both hands. "As for what I am, dear sister of the Emperor, I am the monster that ogres flee from in their nightmares."

Betany looked as if someone had thrown water over her, while Haran tucked his hands into his sleeves, becoming a slender apparition of disapproval. "I would like to know the business of your visitor." His peevish eyes blinked. "For my official records."

"Bannon helped me in my diplomatic mission, and I promised to compensate him," said Rema. "May I now inquire about your business here in the garden, for my official records?"

"I dislike your tone."

"Let's not start listing things we dislike about one another. We could be here until evening."

"Damn you, Remela," said Betany. "How you can continue to be so insolent and keep your head is beyond me."

"I believe I keep my head precisely because of my insolence." Rema widened her smile—nothing infuriated Betany more than people smiling, especially those people she detested. "Speaking of which, I've heard that you're again agitating to have me executed. I can't understand this obsession of yours. Are you secretly in love with me? If so, come out with it already."

"You're disgusting." Betany wrinkled her nose. "You shame this court, cavorting so openly with that singer of yours."

"I'd rather cavort openly with her than with Haran. I mean, really. You might as well be consorting with a hyena."

Bannon snickered. "Laugh while you can, merchant's girl," said Betany. "The world you know is almost ended."

"We finally agree on something. Good day, turtledoves."

Her adversaries remained silent. As they exited the courtyard, Bannon bid them farewell with a low, mocking bow, and Rema frowned. Amusing as Bannon could be, it wasn't an entirely pleasant feeling to have him on her side.

Upon returning to the palace's decorated corridors, Bannon fell into a relaxed saunter. "That man, the one who looked like he was talking through a lemon. What's his story?"

"That was Haran, imperial lawmaker and supreme judge of the Empire."

Bannon gave an exaggerated gasp. "I do hope I behaved myself!"

"Here." Rema stopped by a solid mahogany door. She unlocked it and directed Bannon into her office, which was among the largest in the palace. Its front half was a comfortable meeting area, strewn with large cushions, while her study took up the rear half, the floor of which was slightly raised. Behind her desk, a large window oversaw one of the prettier sections of the gardens. The view was a mixed blessing, as being near the scent, splendor and teeming color also meant enduring the endless surging of the waterfall and the irritated calls of the wildlife that lived in the menagerie.

Bannon explored the room, admiring the paintings and carvings that decorated its walls. He rested his hand on a marble bust. "Lots of naked women in those paintings. Breasts or buttocks, what's your preference?"

"It's art. Appreciate it, don't leer at it." Rema sat behind her desk and gestured to the low seat before it. Bannon swaggered across the rug, glancing down once to inspect its intricate overlapping pattern, and dropped into the seat. His limbs hung loosely, and he tilted his head lazily back, looking like a discarded marionette. Rema folded her hands on the desk and watched him with—she hoped—contempt in her eyes.

"I mentioned to you once that my job is solving problems." Bannon swung a boot up on her desk, and Rema held her tongue. She'd put her own boots up there often enough. "You've a lot of problems, Rema."

"Is that so?"

"Let's see." Bannon extended a fist to count with. "One, you want that woman for yourself. Two, you don't much like this Emperor of yours. Three, you have to watch your back from that charismatic couple we met earlier. Four, whatever it is you spent so long talking to the Ulati about."

"And you make number five. Are you just showing off how clever you think you are, or is there a point?"

"There's a point. You just have to tell me who to stick it in."

So it was going to be that kind of game. At least Rema knew the rules. "And then you'd sell me out just like you sold out Calan. Haran could pay you as much as I. Ormun even more."

Bannon grinned. "Difference is, Calan was an idiot. I never knew if I was going to get paid or if he was going to get us both killed. And I doubt I'll improve my chances by working for a mad Emperor or a lawman. But you? You'd stick to your word, you'd keep my throat intact, and you're tougher than any man I've met. Working for you would be a pleasure."

Rema frowned. A compliment from a man like Bannon was worse than an insult from a friend. "We both know that I don't approve of your methods. I'm hardly about to give you more money to reward your butchery."

"Still, let's hypothesize. I've explored the palace a little and talked to a few people since I got here. Oh, yes, I got past the guards, don't raise your eyebrow like that. First interesting fact: Ormun is rarely guarded. In his meeting chambers, no guards. At dinner, no guards. Even walking the palace he's rarely guarded. He only has guards in his throne room and one outside his bedchamber. How does a man with so many enemies stay alive?"

"Fear, I suppose. Even if he dies, the law will outlive him, such as it is. Where can an assassin flee to when the Empire controls two-thirds of the continent? And even if they escaped, the end result would still only be that Betany takes charge, a prospect that appeals to nobody except Haran."

"Many assassins are fearless." Bannon drummed his fingers on his knee. "But let's move on. I think it interesting that one of the captains of guard is a friend of yours."

"I see where you're going, but no. Just because he's captain doesn't mean he can order the guards to do something treasonous. There are a lot of ambitious men serving in the palace guard, and they'd happily turn Artunos over to Ormun if they thought he was plotting a coup."

Bannon's laughter was improbably charming, coming as it did from such a vile source. "When I backstab a friend to get ahead, they call me a monster. When someone does it at court, they call it ambition!" He chuckled again before sobering. "Fine, fine. Tell me, why don't you just walk out of here with the woman on your arm? Nobody could stop you."

"Because without me, my friends here will die. Don't think I haven't been tempted."

"Then do the noble thing and arrange for her to be smuggled off. Remain here without her."

The challenge in his eyes was obvious, and to her shame, Rema found herself unable to meet it. "Selfish, selfish," Bannon said as she stared at the table. "Yes, it's true. I could escort her to safety and you might never see her again. Is it worth it?"

"How long would she survive?" Rema picked up an onyx paperweight and turned it in her hands. "She'd be alone and in an unfamiliar city. She's resourceful and clever, but she's spent her entire life in the one room of a palace. The world is bigger than she can comprehend. She needs me."

"An implausible response. I could take her to a safe house in the city where you could visit her."

Damn his relentless logic. "No use. The moment she's gone, Ormun will suspect I'm involved, and it'll likely end up with my execution."

"It's no wonder you don't get anywhere. You're a terrible pessimist."

"Unlike your jolly self." Rema forced herself to look again into his unsettling eyes. "Tell me what I've overlooked, then."

Bannon leaned closer. "You don't think I started out working for Calan, did you? I've been around. Danosha was a refuge from a bounty I picked up in Lyorn, and I was in Lyorn because I managed to stir up some trouble in Kalanis. I'll admit Arann is bigger than I'm used to, but I'm a quick learner. You've overlooked me."

Rema dropped the paperweight with a wooden thud. "I've written you a letter of credit." She slid a piece of paper across the desk. "I'll start discussing property with those who can arrange it—that'll take time. As far as I'm concerned, after that, we'll no longer need to deal with each other."

Bannon's smile widened. "Your tongue and eyes disagree with each other. You're so desperate to help her, it's driving you mad. If it helps, think of me as a tool. Better a good woman direct me than a bad man. I'll only hurt those you direct me to. I don't get pleasure from killing, you know. Just pleasure from a job well done." He gave another pleasant chuckle. "And sometimes, well, that means killing."

Rema lowered her head, letting his words play through her mind. The late morning sun warmed her back, and the mingled odors of the garden drifted through the window. If not for the fiendish presence opposite her, she could almost be at peace. "You should be in jail in at least three different kingdoms."

"But I'm not."

The plan Rema had in mind could easily fail, and to think of the consequences of that failure set her insides trembling. Still, she was tired of scheming and appeasing. It was time to be clear of heart and conscience once more, so that she could look into Elise's eyes without guilt. Perhaps such moral clarity was an infantile dream, and Elise's grand tantrums merely naivety stamping its foot. But even if that were true, Rema would love her all the same, for her strange magic, her wild appearance and her furious and undaunted will.

"I haven't decided on anything," said Rema. "But I doubt you'll hear from me again."

Bannon shrugged as if he'd never expected any other response. "I'll be around. Skulking, as you all put it. Even if you turn down my offer, there's profit to be made here. I see many people with many problems. Be sure you hire me first, Rema."

"I'm sure you can show yourself out." Rema gestured to the door.

"Indeed!" Bannon took the letter of credit from the desk and leapt to his feet. "A pleasure doing business with you. Our debt is almost settled."

"I'll be sure to arrange you a house with no mirrors, lest you frighten yourself."

Bannon was still laughing as he closed the door. Rema sighed and poured herself a glass of wine from the cabinet beside her desk. She felt old today, every bit of her thirty years. And wasn't she going to be thirty-one in only five months? She needed a distraction from her worries. An image of Jalaya immediately came to mind, and she sighed again. A different distraction. She reached for her quill. Two months of paperwork seemed as effective a diversion as any.

First she had to write a report of her trip to Danosha, including any observations that might be of interest to Calicio, the spymaster. Following that was a request to Sothis to arrange troops and provisions; an accompanying letter to Ferruro, adding her name to the request for funds that would be necessary for such an endeavor; and another letter to Ferruro requesting her pay for the previous two months, as well as the bonus she was entitled to for a successful diplomatic mission. After some thought, she also wrote a letter to Haran formally protesting his proposal to criminalize speech. Only at the last line did she realize that, regardless of the failure or success of her plan, the letter would never be necessary. She grumbled and filled the rest of the page with scribbled pictures of Elise and half-remembered lines of poetry.

By the time she was done, she had gone through half an inkwell, her fingers were clenched and weary, and the light behind her had faded into dullness. She splashed her face with water from a bowl, and the cold touch shivered her into alertness. Seeing Jalaya and Elise together had made Rema conscious of her age, and now she peered closely at her reflection, frowning at the lines on her forehead. Her slim wrists and forearms were concerning. Was she eating enough? She'd forgotten to have lunch yet again, and soon she'd have to start thinking about dinner.

At least there was still time to visit Elise before the evening's conspiracies began. The thought was cheering, and Rema whistled as she walked through the winding corridors. It was all this traveling that made her so thin, surely, always marching from one room of some court to another. Perhaps Elise would be willing to take an early dinner somewhere in the palace. They would eat a grand main, followed by dessert—yogurt, perhaps, with honey and cinnamon. Elise would get some on her cheek, and Rema would lick it off...

Rema knocked on Elise's door as if in a dream. The door opened, and she smiled into Elise's round, untidy features. "Rema!" said Elise, her eyes lighting. "Come in, you divinity."

So she was in a good mood, thank the gods. Amazing what one could achieve with a passionate kiss, a fervent declaration and a clever tongue.

CHAPTER TWENTY-FOUR

Elise's room was a catastrophe of books and open crates. Scattered among the tomes was an indecipherable assortment of odds and ends, eldritch crystals and powders of every conceivable color. Elise—strangely enough—had changed into a tight silver dress slashed at the right thigh to reveal most of her leg. Most unexpected of all, however, was Jalaya, who was sitting on a side table swinging her feet. She grinned at Rema and fluttered her long lashes.

"What are you doing here?" said Rema. Even now, the sight of that gentle little face provoked a whirling mingle of guilt, regret and jealousy that was entirely outside Rema's comprehension.

"I'm keeping Elsie company," said Jalaya. "I know you're as busy as the breeze, and I couldn't let her sit glumly by herself."

"Well, I had work to do." Rema closed the door and stared at the room around her. "Where can I sit in all this mess?"

"That pile of books looks like a good Rema-seat." Jalaya's tone grew sly. "I heard you kissed her for the first time today. I was shocked."

Rema's cheeks warmed. Gossiping little imps. "And why did that shock you?"

"Three weeks at sea, and you never even touched her once? I don't think I could have had your restraint."

During their exchange, Elise had returned to her desk and grown busy again with her work. Hearing Jalaya's words, she drew back her unruly wave of hair to reveal a smile. "Jalaya's been good company," she said, sifting a powder through her hands. "We gossiped for a little, and she helped me unpack. She became excited when she saw my dresses, so I put some on for her."

Jalaya put a hand over her lips as she giggled. "Don't look at me like that, Rema. I covered my eyes while she was changing."

It was a typical Jalaya prank. Rema willed back her creeping envy. "And you never once peeked between your fingers?"

"Not once." Jalaya spoke with absolute solemnity—the surest sign that she was lying.

"In other words, more than once."

Jalaya laughed again, and Elise turned red. "You said you wouldn't! Jalaya, really!"

"I only peeked a little, I swear." Jalaya winked. "She also asked me countless questions about lovemaking. I've never met someone so interested in the subject. She's prurient."

"Try to see it from my perspective," said Elise. "You two are the only women I've met who are like me. For all I know, my servant women were pretending in order to satisfy me. You can't imagine how it feels to see you two traipsing about unashamed with nobody even stopping to comment. It's wonderful. I want to know everything I've missed out on."

Rema spotted the promise of a space on the bed and began to clear the books about it. As she shifted the heavy tomes, Elise continued talking. "Jalaya's father is even worse than mine, it seems. He sold her to a brothel because he discovered her with a woman."

"Yes, a sad story." Rema settled between two precarious walls of books. "Most women in our situation have sad stories. Not so me. When my parents first visited me in Arann, my father asked if I'd been seeing any young men. I told him that I'd discovered something far more interesting. He asked if I meant literature, poetry, religion…and I told him no, that I meant young women. Gods, how they laughed. My mother was delighted. She told me I'd be better off with a woman. That they have more sense."

"I'll never forget my own meeting with them," said Jalaya. "Rema's father and I exchanged verse after verse, and her mother made me sing until my voice was tired. She told me she wished she could bottle my voice and sell it. It was a blissful evening. I seated myself in Rema's lap, the two of us entangling as lovers will, and her parents showed no perturbation at all. Only the deepest affection."

Elise bowed her head. "My parents couldn't have been more different. I still remember my father's words when I first got caught. 'Get her married off quickly, Talitha, before anyone finds out.' That's what he said."

"Try to be at peace with them. It's in the past now, and they've learned their error. What else have you two been up to?"

"Elsie told me a little about magic," said Jalaya. Irritatingly enough, her attention remained entirely on Elise, whose dress tightened suggestively across her body every time she stretched for some new reagent. "It's complex. I only understood a little."

"I suppose your thoughts were elsewhere."

"Are you implying something?" Jalaya widened her innocent eyes. "There's nothing improper happening in this little head. Oh, Elsie, I think you dropped something under the desk there…"

"Really?" Elise dropped to her knees and pressed her cheek to the floor, peering beneath the desk. As Elise's behind wiggled in the air, its owner oblivious, Jalaya covered her lips and her body shivered beneath countless giggles. Rema found herself smiling as well. She liked Jalaya's playful way of flirting, which was often more silly than erotic, and it had been thoughtful of her to keep Elise company.

Elise returned to her feet, her face puzzled and suspicious. "I didn't drop anything."

Jalaya widened her artless eyes further. "No! Really? Are you sure you don't want to look again?"

"Oh, you demon." Elise played with a loose strand of her hair. "I see what you're doing. Stop ogling me and let me get on with my work."

"And what is your work?" said Rema.

Elise lifted a vial, and it bubbled goop over her wrist. "I'm working on a solution. You're going to tell me not to, I suppose."

"No, but it would nice to know exactly what you have in mind."

"I won't tell you yet. Mostly because I'm not sure I'm doing this right, and it may not turn out as I expect it to." Elise poured the bubbling mixture into another, and the combination wailed and emitted a puff of wavering green smoke. "Your horrible friend Artunos was very rude to me earlier. When he left me here in my chambers, he warned me not to keep tempting you astray."

"You're tempting me, but not astray. Don't worry about him."

"It took you so long to visit me." Elise laid down her tools and turned toward Rema. "I want to hear your excuses. How is Muhan?"

"He's well. He says hello. I had to deal with Bannon as well, and paperwork."

Elise scrunched her nose. "Bannon. Well, so long as you were properly occupied." She left the desk and climbed into Rema's lap. "I missed you."

Rema slipped a hand into Elise's forest of hair, feeling for the slender shape of her neck. As she did so, she glanced at Jalaya, who watched with a serene smile. If her face could be so untouched by envy, what excuse did Rema have? Yet it was hard not to be jealous of the way Elise had blushed when she'd learned that Jalaya had watched her dressing—but there, she was doing it again. Was this incessant envy part of being in love, or was it a flaw of her own?

"You're tense." Elise squeezed Rema's shoulders. "I wish there was room on the bed."

"Do I need to leave you two alone?" said Jalaya. "Or shall I stay here and watch? I could write a scandalous song about you."

"Don't you worry. There'll be no fun for us yet. I have to get this work done. I just wanted to hold my Rema a moment." Elise played with a lock of Rema's hair. "You're so serene, Jalaya. Aren't you going to miss her now that I've stolen her from you?"

Jalaya smiled, but there was something forlorn in the tilt of her lips. "No matter what I've tried, she's always been unhappy. For her, I'd have given up any other lover and spent every moment at her side. Yet if she had chosen me, she would have stayed unhappy, always yearning for something I couldn't give her." Tears glistened at the tips of her lashes, and a painful regret gripped Rema's heart. "I can't stand up to people the way you two do. I hate conflict. I don't know magic or diplomacy. I was happy being her little songbird, but she doesn't need me like she needs you."

"Jalaya," said Elise. "Oh, sweetheart, please don't cry."

Jalaya brushed the tears from her lashes. "Silly me. I didn't think I would."

It was unendurable, hearing that beautiful voice so suffused with sadness. "Jalaya—"

"Don't say a thing, or I'm going to fall to bits." Jalaya took a deep breath before returning to her feet. "It's time for me to fly away. Don't forget the meeting, Rema. Goodnight, Elsie. I hope I didn't misbehave too much."

"Goodnight," said Elise, her voice uncharacteristically subdued. The moment Jalaya shut the door behind her, Elise tightened her arms around Rema. "I feel so sorry for her. She seems so calm, but it's obvious she's missing you terribly inside. I'm trying to imagine how I'd feel if someone took you from me. I'd rip off their face."

"I have to confess I've felt a little jealous lately. You two look charming together."

"She's the loveliest person I've ever met. I enjoy it when she looks at me, and the naughty way she teases me is tremendous fun. But she's not you." Elise raised Rema's chin and drew their lips together in a brief but searching kiss. The moment their mouths parted, Elise wriggled to her feet. Rema made to pull her back, missing the warmth of her body, but Elise shook her head.

"I have to get back to my work. Believe me, you have no idea how hard it is for me to refuse you after I've waited so long to have you." Elise returned to her desk and dropped a crystal into a vial. The result was a hissing puff of dark yellow smoke, and she looked disappointed.

"I have a plan of my own. It may not work, and for now, it's safer if you don't know about it."

"I trust you. I always knew you wouldn't sit by while Ormun married me."

"If only I'd always known that myself. Until a few days ago, that was honestly what I was prepared to do."

Elise shrieked as she dropped the vial. "Hot!" She shook her hand, her expression rueful. "You may think that, but I know better. Your heart wouldn't have let you. You're the woman who took a whipping for me and who slept in my stairwell to protect me from Calan." Elise mingled two dusts and squeaked in delight. "They changed color! I knew they'd do that!"

"Now I understand why Jalaya was so enrapt. I could watch you do this for hours."

"You mean you could stare at my behind for hours. You're both shameless."

"Bannon offered me his help." Rema stared into her palms. Even the name was haunting her. "I sent him away, but I wasn't brave enough to refuse him outright. Once I wouldn't even have breathed the same air as a man like that."

Elise put down her tools again and folded her arms. "Rema, I know you agonize over whether your life has been good or bad. Stop worrying and look at the people around you. Jalaya adores you. Loric loved you, and once we're done, he'll love you again. My mother admired you and even my father spoke well of you. As for Yorin, I've never seen him soften to anyone the way he did to you. And I can't even put into words the way you make me feel."

Rema nodded slowly. "When this over, I'm making this empire right again. I'm going to finish the work Togun and I started. I'm going to end these senseless wars and I'll send these women home."

"It's serious, then, this plan of yours."

"It's this or death, and I have two days in which to succeed. Losing you would be no different than dying for me."

"I can't wait until we're able to wake together as lovers do. Every morning, before sense returns to me, I'm stricken by the thought that you must be a dream. I want to be able to open my eyes upon waking and see you there, the articulate, passionate woman who returns the full measure of my love."

"I'll tell you I love you so many times you'll get sick of it. But whatever you're doing, Elsie, be careful. Don't forget Melnennor."

Elise opened her eyes wide. "I did forget about the magician! I'd like to meet him."

"You're bound to, if you keep up what you're doing." Rema stood beside Elise and kissed her neck. "I'm off now for a meeting with my friends. Don't forget to have some dinner."

"That awful Artunos said he'd bring me some." Elise murmured as Rema's kisses reached her ear. "God. I want you for dinner."

Rema laughed as she squeezed her. "Hold that thought."

"I asked Jalaya what you were like as a lover. She was very candid, but I won't tell you what she said. It'd make you blush."

"I think I'm blushing now." Rema kissed Elise once more before pulling away. "Good luck with your mixing."

"Mixing is only the beginning." Elise snapped a stick in her hand, and it released a steady stream of soot. "Ooh, that stings my eyes…"

Before leaving the room, Rema stopped to admire Elise, who was staring into the boiling depths of her alembic. Whatever it was that swirled in her concoction radiated a green light, illuminating her round cheeks. Was this the sorcery that had silenced Calan's prisoner? What would Melnennor make of it, that enigmatic member of court whose craft nobody had ever witnessed firsthand? Rema drew the door shut and cleared her thoughts. Some elements in this struggle were beyond her comprehension and best left there. The meeting with her friends drew nigh, and it was time to call upon her own gift for enchantment.

CHAPTER TWENTY-FIVE

Rema drifted through the silent, darkening corridors, still lost in thoughts of love. As she passed by a courtyard, the crying of a nocturnal bird startled her into alertness. Love was dangerous to the concentration, it seemed.

She arrived at a kitchen and passed through the long rows of ovens into its pantry. A trapdoor rested in one corner, partially hidden by barrels of dried fruit. Rema lifted the trapdoor's corroded ring and pulled. The door swung before landing with a resonant thud, revealing a flight of stairs. Rema took a tinderbox from her pocket, ignited a nearby torch, lifted it from its bracket and descended into the shadows.

As she reached the bottom, the baleful torchlight outlined the hunched shadows of wine casks and the pointed ears of sacks of grain, most of them no doubt filled with mold or beetles. In one corner, several crates had been upturned and arranged in a semicircle. An imaginative onlooker would have correctly guessed them to mark some secret meeting place. Rema placed the torch at the base of the stairs, took her place, crossed her legs and waited.

Sothis was the first to arrive, his high-collared robe gathering cobwebs as he tottered down the stairs. He walked with a limp, the result of a war injury, and Rema winced in sympathy as he struggled from the final step. His face was ill-humored and sallow, and his heavily-pouched eyes indicated both exhaustion and illness. Rema waved her fingers, and Sothis managed a sickly smile.

"How was your trip?" he said, in his reedy, breathless voice. He was only forty-one, but his health had been poor for as long as Rema had known him.

"Memorable. Would you like me to find you something easier to sit on?"

"No, I'll survive a few hours." Sothis settled onto a crate beside her. His labored breathing began to ease to a more measured rhythm. "How are your knees?"

Rema and Sothis often exchanged stories of woe, he complaining about his lungs and she about her aching joints. "They've been a little better since I got back to Arann. I think it's the warm weather."

"You should take care of them while you're young. Have a healer look at you."

"I know, I know, but it's like admitting that I'm growing old."

Sothis rasped a thin chuckle. "You are growing old."

The sound of brisk footsteps heralded the arrival of Artunos, who descended with Muhan walking close behind him. Artunos directed Muhan to a crate and sat beside Rema, his arms folded. "I hope we can trust this man," he said.

"Have faith in my judgment." Rema pressed her palms together, and Muhan returned the gesture. "Muhan, I'm glad you joined us this evening."

"I don't see the food," said Muhan, his colorful grin eerie in the flickering light. "A good thing I stuffed myself with suckling pig."

"Don't tell me about suckling pig," said Sothis. "Anything more than liquid makes my stomach ache."

"Don't talk about pigs at all," said a clear voice at the top of the stairs. Jalaya stepped into view, her cheeks bronzed by torchlight. "Whatever did the poor things do to you?" For no clear reason other than her natural tenderness, Jalaya held the unwavering conviction that harming animals—even to eat them—was a grave sin. Rema, who had grown up among hungry merchants, had at first been doubtful such a diet was possible, but Jalaya had worked hard over several years to persuade her, producing endless fragrant dishes filled with spiced roasted vegetables, intensely-colored lentils and nutty yellow rice. Eventually Rema had conceded Jalaya could be right, though she had insisted, to Jalaya's dismay, that a fish was not an animal.

"Have you heard anything interesting tonight?" Rema said as Jalaya trod softly down the stairs.

"Well, a musician friend told me that Haran and Ferruro are very drunk."

Artunos's frown deepened. "A good mood for them means trouble for us."

"Or they're drinking to avoid their sorrows," said Rema. "Jalaya, don't sit yet. Let's bring some food down. I haven't eaten for hours."

"But I just walked down all those stairs," said Jalaya, teetering on the last step. "You bully."

Rema took Jalaya's hand and pulled her up the stairs to the pantry, where they scoured for food. Jalaya began to fill a basket with fruits and cinnamon loaves, while Rema foraged several lengths of cured meat for the others, ignoring Jalaya's look of gentle reproach. "Jalaya," she said. "I'm sorry about earlier. I never realized you felt so strongly about me."

Jalaya hesitated, her small hand still midreach for a vivid yellow apple. "I should be apologizing. I left in such a sulk."

"You call that a sulk? You should see how Elise sulks."

"I'm half in love with her myself." Jalaya finally snared the apple and dropped it into her basket. "She's grumpy and she's strange, but her heart is animated in a way I've only seen before in you. I've never forgotten how you shouted at that brothel owner until he started to cry. I was in love with you from that moment. I can only imagine how you must have dazzled her."

"I was fortunate enough to have a gentle father and a ferocious mother to demonstrate what should be obvious. Women have every right to be strong and to claim their equality."

Jalaya held a pear to her nose, her eyes bright with appreciation. "You always say such serious things. I love how you think, but you never find time to stop." Her smile grew wicked. "Though I was once able to pause your thoughts by running my fingers across your skin and breathing my passion upon your lips…"

A pleasant shiver ran through Rema's body. "Jalaya, don't tease. Come on, let's take this food."

"Look at us, the women serving the men. How subservient we are!"

Rema pinched Jalaya on her cheek, and she shrieked and danced away, her eyes sparkling. They returned to the cellar to discover that Calicio had somehow appeared in their absence. He stood some distance from the others, and the torchlight barely reached him, enveloping much of his body in shadow. He was the imperial spymaster, a reclusive and intelligent man; despite being an easterner—the only one among the court's officials—he spoke Annari like a native. He also kept a male lover at court, and it was only by Rema's hard work that it was permissible for his consort to be publicly known.

"How did you creep by us?" said Rema, staring at him. "We were up in the pantry the whole time."

"You were preoccupied. One doesn't survive twenty years as a spy without being able to sneak past a pair of giggling women."

Rema shook her head, laughing. "We're lucky you're on our side."

After giving Calicio a quick wave, Jalaya perched atop a wine cask and crossed her legs, exposing for a moment her bare thighs. Muhan lowered his head as if embarrassed, but none of the other men appeared to notice.

Rema placed the tray of food in reach of the group and stood before them, meeting each of their eyes in turn. "I'm glad you all came. This is Muhan, a friend of mine. Muhan, this is Artunos, captain of the official's guard. To his left is Sothis, minister of war, and over there is Calicio, spymaster. The radiant woman is Jalaya, my dearest friend." Muhan smiled as Jalaya beamed at him.

"Before you say whatever is on your mind, Rema, let me speak," said Artunos. "You need to know exactly what's taken place in your absence." There was a touch of aggression in his voice, and he cracked his knuckles before continuing. "At some point in the last month, Haran and Betany began working together very closely. Betany obviously wants to be rid of us and is beginning to push Haran to more extreme measures. They're crafty about it too. They've lobbied for a law against dissident speech that could also be used against us."

"Haran trying to pass cruel laws is nothing new," said Rema. "He managed to overturn Togun's slavery act last year, remember."

"Yes, but now he's combining repressive laws with laws that undermine our group. Though I doubt it's Haran's mind at work. It seems more Betany's approach."

"That reminds me. Ormun told me that Betany is pushing for new laws against supposedly improper sexual activity. That would make three of us here criminals." Rema spoke with a bitterness she couldn't conceal. She had once been sent on an errand to Kalanis, where the law held that no love could be allowed but that between a man and a woman, and while there, she had intervened in the execution of two men. An official complaint had been written to the Emperor, but Togun had torn it to pieces in front of her. Betany would reject her father's tolerance and destroy uncounted lives, all to take out her petty revenge.

"I was aware of the new law," said Calicio. "But only you have the power to influence Ormun to join us in opposing it. Haran simply overrules us by citing his legal authority."

"It's Betany, not Haran, who is our real enemy," said Rema. "She knows that Ormun won't listen to her, so now she's trying to beguile Haran to disguise her vengeance as lawmaking."

Sothis cleared his throat, and the group waited patiently for him to struggle through a series of short wheezes. "But there's nothing we can do about her. She has no rank or office. We can't agitate for her to be dismissed."

"What about a scandal?" said Artunos. "She could be disgraced. She must have somebody in her bedchamber."

Old friend or not, sometimes Artunos was appalling. "I find it distasteful that a woman might be disgraced merely for making love. But I'll humor you. What do our spies have to say?"

"There are no love letters circulating for her," said Calicio. "No mysterious gifts. Obviously, she has Haran infatuated, but there is no indication she's returning his affections."

Rema looked to Jalaya, who shook her head. "I'm sure she sleeps alone," Jalaya said. "The window of her room opens to one of the lower courts, where anything could be heard. The only gossip is that Haran is in love with her."

"Thank you," said Rema, and Jalaya squashed her face into her palms. She was beloved among the court entertainers, and every dancer, musician, actor and poet in the palace jumped to share their daily observations with her. For years, Haran and Ferruro had attended performances with no idea that their every word and action was passed along a chain of whispers that ended at Rema, and Calicio often quipped that Jalaya was a better spymaster than he. The compliment always delighted her to no end.

"Haran and Betany could become a scandal," said Artunos. "One that might dispose of the both of them."

"Forget about scandals! Ormun doesn't care about scandals. Or perhaps he will one day and not the next. He has no direction except an animal one toward bloodshed and dominance. I'll plead reforms while Haran shouts for new capital punishments, and Ormun will decide based purely on who most entertained him. He's completely outmatched by Ferruro, who has been siphoning imperial money into his own coffers for years. It's a disastrous regime. All we do is chase more wars while the city and its palace fall into disrepair and disorder."

"It's true that the wars have to stop," said Sothis. "There needs to be a period of peace and consolidation. Yet every time I try to suggest it, Haran turns Ormun the other way, advising him to punish our enemies." He coughed, his hand pressed to his chest. "And the Empire is spread too thin. We've only just conquered Molon, and he wants us back in Urandal before we can even set up some form of civil governance."

"The people of Arann are unhappy," said Calicio. "You don't need a network of spies to see it. Togun gave them new amphitheaters and gardens, made their lives easier and kept the streets safe. Ormun is neglectful to the extent that many doubt he's even alive. Slavery is worse than ever. Forced prostitution has returned, and I've had to withdraw spies from the brothels because of the dangers there." He exhaled a long, troubled sigh. "I don't enjoy reading my morning correspondences."

"Don't forget about his wives," said Jalaya. "He'll take one to dinner with him, and we'll have to keep singing and dancing while he beats her or tears off her clothes. Nobody ever sees them outside their rooms anymore. They're too afraid to leave and too bruised to show their faces. Lakmi has a guard posted at every bedchamber, and he says it's for their protection, but the women feel terrorized." She rested her troubled gaze on Rema. "I don't want that to happen to Elsie."

Artunos groaned. "Yes, I get the point. Ormun is a bad emperor. How am I to argue with that litany of sorrows? But there's nothing that we can do about him. Our only target with any kind of vulnerability is Haran. Remove him, and Betany will lose her mouthpiece and Ormun won't be exposed to his ramblings."

"No," said Rema. "The time has come to grasp the problem by the root. Ormun must be deposed."

A reaction was to be expected, and she was not disappointed. Artunos twisted his mouth in sour disapproval, Calicio's eyebrows leapt, Sothis sagged, Jalaya opened her mouth wide and Muhan, who had been until then seemingly bemused by affairs outside his understanding, inhaled deeply.

"You can't be serious," said Artunos. "Even if we could, the throne would go to Betany and things would be even worse than before."

"Generations ago, the Empire was ruled by a council of the wise and learned. Then a general—the first Emperor—returned from victory and deposed them. We'll refuse Betany her throne and return to the old way of rule. It's not yet a democracy, but at least we'll not be ruled by dictators."

Calicio shifted against the wall, an uncertain light in his eyes. "There is precedent for it. But we can hardly persuade Ormun to step down."

"No. We have to remove him."

The anger in Artunos's expression faltered into disbelief, and Jalaya leaned forward, her eyes liquid under the torchlight. "You're not a murderer, Rema. None of us are."

"Put that aside for later. The first step is to take Betany's support away from her. We can't have her assume power afterward. I don't think we can convince Haran, but I suspect that Ferruro would be amenable. He cares only for his treasury."

"If anyone should talk to Ferruro, it's you," said Calicio. "You're the only person at court he has any respect for."

"Sothis and I will both talk to him. I think we could persuade him that Ormun's endless wars are more costly than a few freed slaves and better living conditions."

Sothis nodded. "That much is true." His hands trembled. No doubt he was thinking of his family sleeping in their mansion on the other side of Arann—a wife and three daughters, all of them endangered by their father's actions.

"With Betany out of the picture, there will be nobody else to take control. Ormun's infant children aren't of age, and the Empire has never had the patience for regencies. None of the generals will get involved; who would want to inherit this disaster? Lakmi might support Betany, leading to a war between the guard factions, but if we win over Ferruro that outcome becomes far less likely. Where the money is, Lakmi will follow."

"Irrelevant chatter," said Artunos. "You've not yet revealed how Ormun is supposed to be dispatched. A single drop of blood will be enough for Haran to have us hung. Ferruro isn't going to stick his neck out for assassins."

"That's why it has to appear like an accident."

Calicio rubbed his chin. "Slow poison? Impossible to trace, if done properly."

"No. We have to do this within two days."

Sothis gasped, and Artunos rose from his crate, his eyes black with fury. "Even if I did agree to this suicide pact, we can't win over Ferruro and rid ourselves of Ormun in merely two days! We need time to plan, to prepare…"

"Two days."

Artunos laughed, a quick, bitter bark, and turned to face the others. "Do you know why she insists on this? Because in two days Ormun marries his new bride, and Rema is infatuated with her. That's what all of this is about. Not the betterment of the Empire, not rescuing us from tyranny, but because she's fallen for Elise Danarian."

"She's not the only one," said Jalaya, a quiet anger in her voice. Rema looked up, surprised. Jalaya, angry? "If Rema says we have two days, then we have two days."

"And what do you have at stake? You're just a singer. You could flee the palace in the night, and a week later nobody would remember you. It's our heads that will adorn the palace gate."

"Still your tongue, Artunos," Rema said, with such roughness that Artunos flinched. "You'll not talk to her that way. She's worth a hundred of us, and if anything happened to her, many pillows in this palace would never again be dry."

Artunos sank back to the crate, his face slackening, and extended his hands with his palms upturned. "I'm sorry. Jalaya, I didn't mean to insult you. I'm just overwhelmed by all of this. Go on, Rema."

Jalaya's eyes smoldered with gratitude, and Rema looked away to keep herself from blushing. "I'm going to persuade Ormun to impress Elise by arranging a performance. The show's highlight will be an exotic magician from distant lands, a master of colors and an invoker of mysteries."

Muhan's mustache quivered. "My dear Rema. I see now why you required me, but this is rather more than I imagined."

"You won't be at any risk. You'll wear a mask, and you'll be out of the palace well before anyone notices what we've done." Rema softened her voice. "He killed your brothers, Muhan."

Muhan scratched his cheek and said nothing.

"That trick you did with the monkeys. Will you tell me how it's done?"

"At the cost of my livelihood, but very well. The box is much larger than it seems from the view of the audience. It has a false interior wall. A long pedal near my foot rotates it in the middle so that I can reveal various compartments."

"Are larger devices possible that could accommodate a man? A box with two compartments, one front and back?"

Muhan nodded. "Easily adjusted. I would need a skilled mechanic in the city to construct it, however."

"That can be arranged. It will need to be finished tomorrow, however, so that it can be ready for the performance the next day."

Artunos grunted. "This plan gets better and better. And how do you propose to get Ormun involved?"

"I'll coax him. He trusts me, the gods help him. When he gets into a playful mood, he can almost be like the boy he once was…" Rema shook away the sadness before it could steal over her. "The beauty of the plan is that if Ormun doesn't cooperate, no harm is done. I'll volunteer in his place and nobody will suspect a thing."

"So Ormun is to enter my cage," said Muhan. "And then?"

"Jalaya steps out in his place. Everyone is tremendously amused, there is great applause, and Jalaya, you'll then sing for everyone. A very long song with a loud musical accompaniment, so that Muhan can step behind the cage, open its rear compartment and knock Ormun out cold. I assume you can do that."

"Yes. There are several ways to strike an unsuspecting man and send him to sleep, and I know them well."

Artunos gave another weary shake of his head. The tiresome man seemed determined to naysay everything, but then, that was his nature. "Eventually someone is going to wonder why he's taking so long to emerge. He's the Emperor, Rema. Every second he's out of sight the guards will grow more nervous."

"True," said Rema. "Jalaya, do any of the entertainers resemble Ormun? I seem to remember this one actor…"

"Yes!" Jalaya clapped her hands. "I know who you mean. We joke about it all the time. He's the same build and hair color and has a similar pointy nose. You wouldn't mistake the two up close, though."

"It doesn't need to be close. We'll have this actor dress up in clothes like those that Ormun is wearing on the day, and we'll cut his hair the same. When Jalaya is done singing, the actor emerges on a balcony and waves. I shout in recognition, everyone points, cheers and stares. Dancers move on to the stage while Muhan and Artunos begin to remove his props, including the box that now contains Ormun."

"So we've effectively made Ormun disappear," said Muhan. "You'd make a good magician."

"I suppose we're then meant to kill Ormun," said Artunos. "Dispose of the body. Nobody can figure out what's become of him, and the magician at that point has disappeared. But won't people suspect Jalaya?"

"Of what? Of being Ormun magically transformed? Artunos, everyone will know we're responsible, but nobody will be able to prove it. Haran can't turn his courts against us without evidence, Ferruro won't care so long as he keeps his position, and Betany can howl from now to the end of time."

"I hope you realize this is the most ridiculous plan I've ever heard, if not one of the more ingenious."

"It is a bit far-fetched," said Calicio. "And all in two days, Rema. Nobody could question your imagination or your intelligence, but this seems fanciful."

"All conjuring tricks sound fanciful when described in their details," said Muhan. "You think to yourself, can an audience truly overlook that? And yet every time they do. To those watching it would be certain that Ormun had departed from the balcony. None will consider that he might still be in the box."

Calicio tapped the side of his nose. "You don't need to tell an old spy about the art of illusion. So in this plan Jalaya sings, Muhan conjures, Artunos moves props, Sothis wheedles…what role is there for me?"

"We don't all need to risk our lives," said Rema. "It's best if you keep your hands clean."

"Speaking of clean hands," said Artunos. "Ormun can hardly stay unconscious forever. Who here is willing to spill imperial blood?"

"Leave that to me."

Artunos nodded at her, his brow indented with worry. "Very well, Rema. Tell me my entire part in this farce."

"You must know the best smiths. Take Muhan to the city tomorrow and help him construct the prop. Then you'll take your place in the performance tomorrow as a stagehand or otherwise send your most trusted guards."

"You're lovesick and pigheaded, Rema. I wish you'd rethink this."

Rema sighed. Even if he was right, it was too late to heed his advice. "What do you think, Sothis?"

Sothis peered back at her, his eyes tired. "I think you're gambling everything. And if what Artunos says is true, all for the sake of some woman."

"For her, yes, but also for all of us. There are aspects of Ormun's evil that will never change but only worsen. The longer this farce continues, the more responsibility we bear for all the blood and suffering." Rema grimaced. "Look, it's late. Let's either agree to do this, or you can all abandon me and I'll end up doing something even madder by myself."

"I'll do it," said Muhan. "It should be a performance to remember."

"As will I," said Jalaya. "You know I'd die for you, Rema."

"I suspect we all will." Artunos shrugged. "Damn you, Remela. I'll do it."

Calicio and Sothis exchanged glances. "I'd like to help," said Calicio. "Let me see if my spies can't find something we can use as leverage against our enemies."

"And I'll help you talk to Ferruro," said Sothis. "But that is all. I have a family to worry about."

"Thank you all." Cold sweat beaded the back of Rema's neck. She had expected to win over the group in the end, but even so, their support was moving. Especially that of Muhan—a man she hardly knew, yet still prepared to risk his life for her. Would the day ever come when she no longer had to gamble with the lives of innocents?

"I've certainly an appetite now," said Artunos. "Muhan, let's share some wine. It's the least I can offer you."

"I need my rest." Sothis staggered to his feet. "The air is dry down here, not good for my lungs. Could someone be so kind as to aid me up the stairs?"

"I'll come with you," said Rema, moving to his side. "Jalaya, Calicio?"

"I'll stay," said Jalaya. "I want to talk to Muhan too."

"And I'll stay as well," said Calicio. "To gather intelligence." Rema smiled and squeezed his hand. Doubt mingled with determination in his eyes. It was clear he was doing this not only for her, but to protect the man he loved.

"Goodnight then," said Rema. "We can get to work tomorrow."

"Say goodnight to Elsie for me," said Jalaya, and a sharp, unfamiliar emotion pierced Rema's chest. "May you both float through honeyed dreams."

Rema attempted a smile but only managed to make her lips tremble. "Come on, Sothis." They ascended through the trapdoor and into the dark kitchens.

"We should try to catch Ferruro at his breakfast," said Sothis as he steadied himself against a shelf. "We're all early risers."

"That sounds wise. I'll find him first and invite him to one of the inner gardens. Perhaps that one with the jade inlay on the benches?"

"I know it. I'll wait for you both there."

"Goodnight, then."

"Goodnight." Sothis gave a slight, stiff bow, pulled his robes around his body and limped from the kitchen.

Rema lingered for several minutes, to avoid their being seen together, before beginning the long walk toward Elise's chambers. The palace shone tonight, illuminated by ghostly light pouring through the many windows and carved openings. As she passed by moon-soaked outdoor courts, she paused to inhale the mild air and to gaze at the far-flung stars. Her plan had seemed clever in her head, but the more she had explained, the more absurd it seemed. Was it really necessary to make Ormun's fate a mystery when Bannon could simply put a knife in his back?

Of course, Rema hadn't dared voice her real motive for sealing Ormun in a box and leaving his fate unknown even to her co-conspirators. The others would be furious to learn what she intended, all but Jalaya, who would have been proud of Rema for still feeling the restraint of mercy. But Jalaya was unique in that way, a soul steeped in love and compassion.

Feeling a twinge of loneliness, Rema quickened her pace. She needed to see Elise again in order to make sense of the mad path she'd chosen. The shadows of the sleeping palace enveloped her, and her boots echoed through the carven halls.

CHAPTER TWENTY-SIX

The door to Elise's room was open, spilling a wedge of light into the hallway. Two voices in conversation were audible beyond it. One was Elise's, soft and low, and the other a male voice that Rema couldn't identify. She stood outside the door, her breath held, and peeked through the gap.

Elise was beside her desk. Melnennor stood before her, his shoulders stooped to bring his face closer to hers. Rema saw the court magician only rarely, and each time she was startled by how tall he was—the only figure at court who might look Ferruro in the eye. His Ajulese features were severe and precise; he looked, in fact, a little like one of Rema's uncles. His black silk robe was embellished by a cascade of red symbols, and he lifted its long sleeves as he talked, turning his thin hands to add some esoteric significance.

Rema leaned forward, listening. "…understand," said Elise. "But you know that…" The rest slipped out of Rema's hearing. Melnennor wagged his head in response and tucked his hands back into his sleeves.

"You know the dangers of this path." Melnennor's strong voice was the louder of the two. "See that you don't destroy the very thing you hope to preserve."

Elise said something in response, and Melnennor put his hand briefly upon her shoulder before turning to the door. His eyes met Rema's, but he continued to the doorway without pausing or saying a word. Rema stepped back as he entered the corridor and closed the door behind him. "I hope your evening is well, Remela," he said in Ajulai. The complex, fluting language came somber from his tongue. "I bid you goodnight."

"Goodnight," said Rema, too surprised to say anything more. She watched him retreat down the hall, his long shape dwindling until she could hardly discern him from the shadows. After a second's confused hesitation, she knocked on Elise's door. The door opened, and Elise smiled and waved Rema in.

The bedchamber was hot, though it was difficult to determine the source of the heat. The desk overflowed with even more apparatus than before, including a cluster of jars that whirled with odd colors and spilt smoke in every hue. The space that Rema had earlier made on the bed had long been devoured by its neighboring books.

"You should sit," said Elise. "Though I have to admit, I'm not sure where."

"Help me clear the bed." Elise's lips drooped, but she nodded. "How were you planning to sleep tonight under all of this?"

"Who said anything about sleep?" Elise grumbled as she moved a heavy volume to the floor. "I've lost the page on this one now!"

Would she mention Melnennor, or had something secret transpired between them? "It's so hot in here." Rema sank onto the bed and shook off her boots. "Why aren't you sweating?"

"It's this light dress. It's wonderful. In Danosha, I couldn't wear most of these dresses—they were meant for much warmer climates. But here, I'll be able to wear them all."

"You won't catch me complaining."

"If only Calan could see me." Elise grinned as she shook a tangle from her hair. "He once told me that women were better covered until men had need of them. I laughed until he turned scarlet. I'm sure half of these dresses were meant for courtesans, and I don't care. I enjoy my body and I don't give a damn what anyone thinks."

Rema admired Elise's smooth, bare thigh. "I'd never get away with a dress like that. I don't have your hips, and my legs are hairy."

"In truth, I have coarse black hairs all the way up to my knee. I discovered a cream that makes them turn lighter so you can only see them in the sun. I invented another one that makes them drop off, but it burns when I use it."

"You're as mad as Jalaya. She's determined to be hairless all over, so she shaves her legs with a long razor. She's always cutting herself."

"I'm sure she feels wonderfully smooth, though. If men can shave their chins, I don't see a problem with Jalaya shaving her legs."

"Who knows why men or women do the mad things that they do? I try to focus on more important things."

"Are you saying I'm trivial?" Elise gave a triumphant smile. "Well, this trivial woman just met your court magician. Melnennor."

"Oh? What did he want?"

Elise settled onto the bed, her boastful expression still in place. "He came to tell me I was up to no good. I was so startled when I opened the door and saw him standing there, ominous and grim. I had a coquettish look on my face too. I was expecting you!"

Rema laughed as she tugged Elise closer. "I hope he didn't get the wrong idea."

"I thought he'd be angry, but he wasn't at all. He accurately suspected what I was doing, and I admitted to it. He didn't seem like the kind of person it's easy to lie to."

Rema placed her hand on Elise's warm thigh, and her gaze wandered by its own initiative across the other bare parts of Elise's body. "Go on."

"Rema, I'm preparing a spell that could well kill Ormun. I admitted it to Melnennor, and he didn't even threaten me. Instead, he talked to me about magic, and told about where he was from, and described things he'd seen and learned. He told me stories I couldn't even begin to retell." Elise brushed her hair from her eyes, a silly smile spreading on her face. "I liked him. He's the first magician I've met since the clumsy one who sold me his books, and he was so much more impressive. He took me seriously and spoke to me with respect, like we were equals."

"How curious. He's supposed to be responsible for protecting Ormun's life."

"He left politics aside. We talked only about magic and mystery. I think it might have been a long time since he had anyone to talk to about such things, and he seemed as interested in me as I was in him. I don't think he'd ever met a self-taught enchantress before."

"So this spell of yours could actually kill Ormun?"

"Yes. But Melnennor reminded me of what I already know very well. That kind of magic always hurts more than its target."

It was terrifying to think that something as chaotic as magic might intrude into the careful order of Rema's schemes. She frowned, but continued stroking Elise's knee. "So what are you going to do?"

"I'm going to think. Meanwhile, let's talk about less serious matters."

"Well, there is something else we could discuss." Rema hesitated. It was embarrassing, and yet…"It's not serious at all. It's my knees. They hurt when I sit for too long, especially when it's cold."

"Why didn't you say so? Nobody should have to endure painful knees! Have they been hurting lately?"

"Not too much in Arann. It's the warmth, I think. In Danosha they ached terribly. I'm worried it's getting worse as I get older."

"Look at that sheepish face. You're shy about getting old as if it were somehow your fault."

"Well, I'm almost five years older than you. I was following my parents across dunes before you were even born."

Elise replied with her deep, sensual laugh, the sound of which set a welcome warmth moving through Rema's body. "What a foolish thing for someone so clever to say. Men routinely marry women thirty years their juniors, and that's supposed to be normal. Meanwhile, we're practically the same age."

"I know." The heat gathered in Rema's cheeks. "I've never been insecure before. Or jealous, for that matter. But then, I've never fallen in love like this before."

"You're a strange one, Remela. Let's have a look at these withered old legs. Take off your trousers."

"You just want to see how hairy my legs really are."

Elise undid the silver button of Rema's trousers. Her fingers lingered for a moment over Rema's lap before pulling away. "Take them off," she said in a commanding voice. Rema pulled the trousers free, kicking her legs so as to send the garment flying to the carpet.

Elise stared at the short-legged pants Rema wore beneath, and her lips puckered in distaste. "That is the ugliest piece of clothing I've ever seen. Horrible!"

Rema blinked. Usually, her lovers were more interested in the contents of her undergarments than in their appearance. "I suppose you wear fashionable underwear designed for courtesans."

"You'll never find out if you keep those disgusting things on. I'm going to have to insist you take them off. They're dangerous to your health."

"Is that so?" The heat spreading through Rema's body became a thrill. "I suppose I'd better do as you say." Her legs pressed chastely together, Rema wiggled off the undergarment and dropped it to the floor beside her trousers.

"Oh, Rema." Elise's face twitched, and she broke into laughter, covering her mouth. "I'm sorry. You just look so funny in your coat and nothing else. You'd better take it off as well."

With a petulant sniff, Rema undid her coat and heaved it off her shoulders. She tugged her long purple shirt down to cover her lap. "Am I less funny now?"

"We're getting there." Elise's eyes remained serious, but a scarlet line crested her cheeks. "Now let's look at these knees. Oh, here's the hair you were so shy about!" She ran her hands across the light red fuzz. "You poor ape."

"I never said I was shy about it. I like my legs, hair and all."

"I like them too." An amorous intensity shone in Elise's eyes as she massaged Rema's kneecap, her other hand resting lightly on Rema's upper thigh. "How old were you when the pain started?"

"Twenty-seven, twenty-eight, I suppose."

Elise felt beneath Rema's knee and gave it a final squeeze before lifting her hands away. "I don't feel scar tissue in there. I have an ointment that soothes joint pain, and if you apply it whenever your knees start misbehaving, it should help."

"You only checked one knee. That seems very lazy of you."

"What a difficult patient you are." Elise gave the left kneecap a similar exploration. "This one is terrible. I'll have to remove it."

Rema gasped in melodramatic horror. Elise giggled as she slid Rema's legs back to the bed. "Don't run away now." She wandered the room until she found a wooden chest, which she rummaged through while muttering under her breath. "Let's see, where is it? Yes! Here." She returned to the bed clutching a golden cylinder. Unscrewed, it revealed a thick, glistening paste with a deep aroma reminiscent of wine.

"This will relax you," said Elise. "I'm going to rub it all over your legs, and you have to promise not to kick me."

"No promises. I have a powerful kicking instinct."

Elise dipped her fingers into the paste and began to rub it into Rema's skin, her hands moving in deliberate, sensuous circles. The hair rose on Rema's arms as a tingling sensation accompanied the caress. "You'll not have to worry about sore legs all week after this," said Elise, gazing into Rema's eyes as her hands did their work. "It'll be like you had the body of a young woman again."

"Stop teasing me. As you said, I'm only four years older than you."

"You poor crone. Don't worry, your infant lover will rub ointment into your doddering legs."

Elise finished with Rema's lower leg and slid her hand higher. Rema held her breath as gentle fingertips massaged both her outer and inner thigh, moving slowly toward her groin.

"It rubs right into the skin," said Elise. "It won't leave anything behind. Clever, isn't it?"

Rema murmured in agreement. Elise's hands crept higher still, and her fingers brushed against Rema's lower lips, provoking a dizzying rush of pleasure. Elise's face was mostly concealed beneath her tousled hair, but her excitement was obvious in the rapid rising and falling of her chest.

"You're very thorough," said Rema. "It was only my knees that were sore."

"This ointment can go anywhere." Elise lifted her hands away. "How do your legs feel?"

"Soothed," said Rema, her voice as shivery as she felt.

"There's one more thing I need to do before you're better." Elise parted Rema's legs and knelt between them, her bare shoulders shifting beneath the tumbling waves of her hair. She smiled as she lowered her dark, unruly head. Her lips made contact, her tongue moved and Rema shivered as a convulsion of pleasure shot through her. She stared down at Elise and found her gazing back, her eyes blank with lust.

Elise gripped Rema's waist as she kissed deeper, and Rema gasped beneath another ecstatic surge. She was becoming lightheaded, she was losing breath, yet the sensations only continued to mount—

"Stop," she said, her hips twisting. "Not yet."

Elise raised her head. "Am I more than you can handle?" She sat upright and eased her dress off her shoulders. The garment dropped, releasing her heavy breasts and the roundness of her stomach. Rather less gracefully, she tried to wriggle out of the dress without moving from her seductive position. She ended up caught in the fabric, and with a look of displeasure she stood and yanked the dress free.

"It was a good try," said Rema. Elise was now naked, and spectacularly so, save for a brief silk undergarment tied at her hip. "So that's what enchantresses wear under their clothing."

"That sneaky Jalaya. She saw all this before you did."

"Don't remind me." Rema removed her shirt and cast it aside. "Come to me, and we'll negotiate a reward for such a remarkable display of healing."

Elise returned to the bed and embraced her. They held each other close, Rema's small breasts pressed against Elise's large ones, and shared the warmth of their bodies. Elise traced the sharp lines of Rema's shoulder blades and spine. "You skinny thing."

Rema took Elise's hand, extended her index finger and guided its tip into her mouth. She sucked while licking beneath each delicate joint—she could taste the ointment, a flavor sweeter than any fig, richer than any date—and in return, Elise cupped Rema's breast and caressed its nipple with her thumb. Rema squirmed and laughed. To lay with a woman was divine; to lay with one's true love was a joy beyond even the comprehension of divinities.

"I have an idea, but I'm going to need my other hand back," said Elise. In her amusement, Rema almost bit her.

"You'd make a bad diplomat. You're giving more than you're getting."

"Stop being clever. There are so many more useful things you can do with your mouth right now."

As they made love, their playfulness gave way to their impatience for each other. Their teasing ceased, and they fell into the intensity of focused, rapturous sex. Pinned under Elise's body, held between those soft thighs, Rema gasped one last time as the urgent pressure fled and left her senseless. She stretched back, breathing heavily and barely able to see through a drifting veil of stars. Elise collapsed beside her.

"I expected somebody to knock at the door the entire time," she said. Her face was covered in damp hairs, and she tugged a long strand from her mouth. "Oh, I'm sleepy. But I don't want you to go."

"Sleep, my love." Rema drew Elise into a tight embrace. "I'll stay with you."

"Really? You'll sleep the night with me?"

"Every hour of it." Rema plucked another stuck hair from Elise's forehead. "We'll wake together as lovers should."

"I was so lonely before you came," said Elise, her voice a dreamy murmur. "You've saved me, Rema, and now you'll save everyone else. You'll end every war, you'll put an end to ignorance. People will cease being afraid of women like us. They'll see we're in love and understand…"

In the afterglow of ecstasy, Rema could believe anything. She kissed Elise's forehead before closing her eyes. The dizziness returned, and this time, she offered no resistance.

CHAPTER TWENTY-SEVEN

Rema woke to the warmth of sunlight. Without opening her eyes, she reached for Elise and felt nothing but sheets. "Elsie?" She sat up. Elise was hunched over her desk, intent on her sorcery. "What are you doing?"

"I worked on my spell while you were sleeping." Dark impressions circled Elise's eyes, and she wobbled as she returned to the bedside. "I'm so tired."

The glow suffusing the room was dawnlight, but only barely; Rema would have to hurry to catch Ferruro at his breakfast. "How late is it?" she said, staring about vainly for a clock.

"The sun just came up. It's early." Elise toppled onto the bed and rested her cheek on Rema's breast. "Sleepy."

Rema kissed the top of Elise's head. "Did you finish your potion?"

"It's not a potion. Nothing is left over. Everything I do, the mixing, the combining, the pouring and stirring, is to harmonize myself to a certain intent. The spell is in me." Elise yawned. "It works through an emotional conduit. When I put my spell on the prisoner, for example, I used certain vibrations that joined all three of us."

"Beloved, I have no idea what you're talking about."

"He caused you pain. That's an intense emotion. Anyone who harms someone binds themselves to them. Similarly, anyone who loves someone is bound to them too. Through you, the assassin and I were strongly linked. I only had to adjust the cosmos and express my will."

"I'm still lost. How does this relate to what you were doing all night?"

"I've prepared some grotesque magic for Ormun." Elise's eyelashes brushed against Rema's skin as her eyes closed. "It's so strange, Rema. I can feel his love for you. It's not like mine, it's dark and desperate, but it's every bit as intense. We're all tangled together."

"Are you suggesting you could kill Ormun as easily as you made that man stop talking?"

"The power feels awful inside me. I don't want to use it. Not even on him. But for you, for us, I'd do anything."

"Don't use it. You don't have to. I have a plan that won't kill anybody, not even Ormun." Rema gently tipped Elise onto the bed. "You get some sleep while I'm gone."

"Mmm. Love you." Elise burrowed into the pillows while Rema stood and conferred with her mirror. She washed herself at a nearby basin, put on her uniform and combed her bangs into obedience. Her coat was covered in Elise's hair, and she spent a few minutes carefully removing the fine black strands. Before leaving, she kissed Elise on the cheek. The sleepy enchantress mumbled something incoherent in response.

Reaching Ferruro's chambers required her to navigate a gauntlet of exquisite corridors. She passed several guards on her way and nodded to each one; the gold guardsmen nodded back, while the silver resolutely ignored her. She arrived at the impressive bronze-hinged door to Ferruro's chamber and, after taking a breath, knocked twice.

The door opened to reveal Ferruro wearing an immense silk dressing gown. His broad face was at first stern, but noticing Rema, he brightened. "Why, an unexpected guest. Surely you of all people don't need to borrow money."

"Of course not, which is why you're so fond of me. I'd like to invite you to breakfast."

Ferruro smirked. "Oh? Have you changed your inclinations and now intend to court me?"

"You're much more than I could handle. Just a chance for friendly conversation, Ferruro. Or would you prefer to eat with Haran and let him gripe into your ear?"

"Oh, well, when you put it that way. Who wouldn't prefer to start the day listening to a pretty voice?"

Rema smiled. "You're referring to mine, I hope, and not Haran's. That man talks like a vulture being strangled."

Ferruro boomed in appreciative laughter. "Wait there, Remela, and I'll dress myself more appropriately."

"In other words, you'll put a hat on."

"Yes, indeed!" Ferruro retreated into his room, closing the door behind him. As she waited, Rema eyed the intricate mosaic chasing the length of the wall. A stylized spear ran toward the far end of the corridor, where it nearly touched the painted image of a running man. The less militaristic decor on the other side of the palace was far more appealing.

Ferruro emerged in a golden gown and a hat with a tassel that flopped against the side of his head. "I wasn't planning on wearing a hat, but I'd hate to disappoint you." He locked the door behind him. "I suppose you already have arrangements, so do lead the way."

"Tread lightly. You don't want to wake the palace."

They walked together through high, arched corridors until, after much turning and climbing, they came to a circular outdoor court. Orange trees lined the walls, their leaves concealing vibrant fruits and noisy parrots. Beneath the trees were arranged several benches with intricate inlaid jade patterning. Sothis was sitting on one of the benches, a breakfast tray beside him.

"What's this cadaver doing here?" said Ferruro. "Heavens, I've fallen into a ruthless trap."

"It's too late now," said Rema. "Surely you've already smelt the enticing aroma of oat and tomato soup rising from that tureen."

"Oh, my favorite. You trickster. Well, if I'm to be manipulated, I may as well get a meal out of it." Ferruro's long shadow cut across the tiled courtyard as he moved toward the bench. "Sothis. What a pleasant surprise."

"Good day, Ferruro," said Sothis. "Why don't you take a seat and join me at breakfast?"

"Oh, how curious. Remela was just inviting me to do the same. Say, the strangest idea strikes me—why don't we all have breakfast together?" Ferruro took a spoon and sampled the soup, pursing his lips with appreciation. "Very good."

Rema joined the men by the bench, though she remained standing with her back to the sun. "Be sure to leave room for all the children you have to gobble up later."

In response, Ferruro handed her a pear. "They say the pear is the most feminine of fruits. I'm sure you've bitten into a few."

Rema bit into its yielding flesh. It was a little overripe, but the juice was fresh on her tongue. "Sothis, will you have something to eat?"

"I'll be having lime juice and nothing else," said Sothis. "Believe me, I'm not happy about it." Ferruro chuckled through a mouthful of soup.

"Tell me, Ferruro," said Rema. "What exactly is going on with Haran and Betany?"

Ferruro returned his spoon to the bowl and dabbed at his lips. He lifted his mellow eyes as he replied. "They've always been close, haven't they? Oh, but they are rather cozier than usual. Can you believe that Haran's shriveled old heart might be capable of love?"

"I'd be surprised to find he has a heart at all." It was time to switch the subject to keep him uncertain. "And how are the imperial finances these days?"

"Mmmm. Well." Ferruro sipped at a fluted water glass. "Things have been better."

"I've been moving pieces on the board lately," said Sothis, his voice stronger in the sharp morning air. "Boats, siege towers, artillery, supplies. I don't know anything about money, but it strikes me as looking very costly. Swords and gunpowder aren't cheap these days, are they?"

"Quite the contrary." Ferruro's tone soured as he reflected on what everyone knew to be his least favorite subject: expenditure. "Is it quite settled that the legions are marching north again?"

"Ormun's definite. My own recommendations were pointless, of course. He likes to run the wars himself, and I often feel as if my job is only to sign off on his imperatives."

"Well, your duty would be easier if Haran weren't always whispering in his ear," said Rema, watching Ferruro's face. He knew exactly what she was doing, and everything depended upon whether his irritation at being manipulated outweighed his understanding that she was right. "He doesn't have a very long-term mind, our Haran."

Ferruro hummed and took another sip of his soup. "Oh, aren't you sly. But you've never made clear how you're going to pay for such minor things as, oh, abolishing slavery. Once we have to pay people to build things, well, you can imagine. And ending the wars—yes, they're expensive, but they also turn a profit when properly handled."

"Rema is the pacifist here," said Sothis. "I'm a man of war, which is why I know best when the time for war is over. This is our chance to trade instead of battle. To grow instead of stagnate. To invest in ploughs and scythes instead of armor that gets thrown into a grave a week later. To enjoy the barter of goods rather than raze towns as we advance."

Sothis was a canny one; his words would appeal to Ferruro's mercantile heart. But Ferruro would also resent any point being belabored. "Enough about that for now," said Rema. "I'm thinking on what you just said about Haran. Do you think Betany might have genuine feelings for our lawmaker? She's never struck me as the romantic type."

"She certainly isn't your romantic type," said Ferruro. "You should hear her complain about that singer of yours. Unfathomable, if you ask me. Such a sweet woman, and that voice! Even Haran has a soft spot for her."

"Hate is Betany's trade." Rema hardened her voice, and Ferruro's smile faltered. "If you had been here for the coup, you would understand. She forced Ormun to execute official after official, determined to purge disloyalty. Afterward, neither of them could fathom how to replace the talent they'd lost. You were appointed only because without a treasurer, we were steadily collapsing into poverty. Haran's younger brother took over the role of imperial architect. He can't even draw a circle with a compass. I've had to do all the work of a foreign minister without ever being officially appointed, and I'm overworked enough as it is."

"Well, I can hardly complain at not having to pay out yet another salary."

"Can you imagine how things would be if she'd had her way? She even tried to have Calicio executed, despite that nobody else knows the identities of his countless spies. You understand the trade advantage that they give us. And only my intervention prevented us from losing him."

Ferruro tapped his spoon against his palm. "Dear Remela, as much as I enjoy your dulcet voice, I am eagerly awaiting your point."

"Here's what keeps me awake at night. Thanks to Haran's laws, Betany would inherit the throne after Ormun. Her whims would become reality, and nobody would be safe."

Ferruro shrugged his immense shoulders. "Oh, I can't argue that Betany would be a terrible Empress, but Emperor Ormun, may he reign forever, is a hearty young man. One, I might add, who is very amenable to my suggestions."

"I think Haran finds him rather more difficult than you do. Do you ever wonder whether he and Betany might have further ambitions? As

Togun's highest-ranked general, Ormun was a useful tool for the coup, but he's unreliable. Perhaps his value to them is over."

Ferruro narrowed his eyes. "You dance very nicely, but now I'm tired of dancing. What do you want exactly? I'm not about to cuddle up to your ragtag party of the pity-hearted. Oh, Haran is an idiot, but profit and law run hand in hand. Our mutual friend taxes and fines however I tell him to, and then I click my fingers and Ormun fills my purse with gold. This court has been very good to me."

"Let me put it plainly. Betany wants revenge, and Haran may be lovesick enough to be her instrument. How will you profit from civil unrest? If she really does kill all of us—me, Sothis and Calicio—what will that mean for this sorry Empire?"

Ferruro leaned back, a stocky index finger pushed against his temple. "Honeyed words from our cleverest tongue. Yet witty as you are, you forget that my opinions count for very little on subjects unrelated to finance. I can hardly grovel before Ormun on behalf of your weak-kneed notions. I can coax him to spend or save, nothing more."

Rema and Ferruro glared at each other, though their animosity was tinged with admiration. A gentle breeze swept through the court and shook the leaves, startling a fat parrot that burst cackling from the foliage. "Let's consider a hypothetical question," said Rema. "Imagine if you had a choice: rule by Betany or rule by a council."

"And who would comprise this council?"

"You. Sothis. Me. Haran. Calicio. And whoever we appoint to fill the vacant roles."

"You'd include Haran in such an arrangement?" Ferruro rocked the bench as he laughed. "Oh, how fair-minded of you! I can taste the viper venom of treason in this discussion, and I want nothing to do with it." He raised an eyebrow. "If, on the other hand, there was a choice between Betany and anything else, no, I would not support her. That's what you wanted me to confirm, isn't it, you little schemer?"

"Fortunately, Ormun is so very robust that this conversation is only academic." Rema extended her hand. "May I have another pear?"

"You may have them all." Ferruro stood and settled the tray on the bench behind him. "I am quite satiated. Oh, but don't think I didn't appreciate our little conversation. As you know, I rarely see eye to eye with anyone, giant that I am. This time, however, you've given me much to cogitate." He bowed to Rema and Sothis in turn. "I'll leave you mice to squeak to each other. Good day."

"Good day," said Rema, and Sothis mumbled in assent. Ferruro strode out of the court, playing with his tassel as he moved.

"I think that went well," said Sothis. "At least, he saw our point of view."

"He's always seen our point of view. The challenge was to make him realize his own point of view is no longer worth clinging to."

"It was beautiful to see you and Ferruro dueling. You're both masters of the art. Nobody in this court can touch either of you." Sothis sipped his lime juice, and his eyes watered. "You know, before I met you, I was of the opinion that women were inferior intellectually. How foolish I was."

Rema sat beside him and rested a hand on his thin shoulder. "If it were easier for women to be educated, you'd have realized your mistake much earlier."

"We clashed often during Togun's reign. The very moment a war started, you began devising ways to stop it. I resented your naivety, but I always admired your heart. You probably don't know which end of a sword is meant for sticking, but I'll be damned if you don't have more mettle than my best soldiers." Sothis laughed before pressing his hand to his side, as if the sound had pained him.

Rema gazed at his sunken face. "How bad is it?"

"The healers give me a few more years. I'd prefer to spend them with my family rather than waste them ordering more men to their deaths."

"Perhaps you should visit Elise when all this is done. She has an uncanny gift. I suspect she could add more than a few years to those estimates."

"I'll never forget how you took that punishment for her. Nor the grief on her face when you were struck." Sothis gave a wan smile. "My middle daughter recently confessed to having fallen in love with one of our maids. I told her it was inappropriate to be involved with a servant and had the maid in question dismissed. Too harsh, you may think. But I also told her that if she came to me someday as an adult, hand in hand with a different young woman who's not paid to be in our service, I'd understand. And I'd understand because I've watched you, Rema, and I've seen the dignity and courage with which you live."

As Rema sat dumbfounded, an unanticipated tear slipped down her cheek. Would that her father were here to see this: the master of war praising the mistress of peace. "You were just commending me for my speechcraft, yet here I am, lost for words."

"A good morning will suffice." Sothis stood, holding the bench until he was steady on his feet. "I hope the rest of your preparations go so well."

He shuffled from the court, and Rema lifted her hand in farewell. She shut her eyes against the sun, letting it soak her body as she inhaled the scent of ripening oranges. As she rested, a bird chuckled insistently above her head. Her next step was the one she most feared: persuading Ormun to hold the celebration, an agreement vital for their plan to continue. Though he was often pliable, he was also inexplicably unyielding on some matters, and there was no telling how he would react to her suggestion.

Reluctantly abandoning the gentle morning warmth, Rema hurried to Ormun's meeting chamber. She tried the handle—locked. It was one of those madcap days, then, when Ormun sacrificed his duties to wander the palace, visit his wives or engage in whatever else might entertain him. Rema toyed with her bangs as she pondered. There was never any predicting his movements. He could be anywhere, even in the streets for all she knew.

At a loss, she followed the corridors until she entered the grand inner court, the counterpart of the outer court in size and opulence but reserved for those who worked within the palace. Numerous skylights punctured its vaulted ceiling, and its walls were trellised with artificial vines carved from stone and embedded with fruit-shaped jewels. Around the court's pillars and benches, small pockets of human activity ensured this was the liveliest section of the place—entertainers joking over their breakfast, Ferruro's accountants gathering in gossip around ornamental trees, mournful generals sharing their meals with off-duty guards.

A pack of uniformed junior diplomats spied Rema as she entered, and their eyes expanded in awe. As she approached them, they tugged nervously at their collars and assembled themselves in postures of deferent welcome. One or two were immediately familiar, among them a dark-haired young woman. "You passed the test, I see," Rema said, smiling at the girl. "Congratulations."

The young woman babbled something unintelligibly grateful, and Rema laughed. "That's how you communicate? Perhaps they should have failed you after all."

Rema's patronage had protected the diplomatic school from the general malaise that afflicted the rest of the palace, and she had spent the last four years training a new generation of diplomats, lecturing them and mentoring the brightest. For now, they handled minor errands and amused visiting dignitaries, but each aspired to travel the world as she did, brokering treaties and ending wars. They idolized Rema as the epitome of elegance and diplomacy—a perfectly fair and accurate assessment.

"I'm sorry, mistress." The others relaxed as they realized Rema had singled out her victim. "It's just always such an honor to speak with you."

Rema admired the young woman's trim uniform. She had enlisted the girl herself and tutored her closely; the poor thing was teased for it, of course, but such was the puerile wit of children. "I remember how proud I was the day I first donned my uniform. Back then, the imperial tailor was scandalized at the thought of fitting trousers to a woman. He offered to make me a skirt, so I offered to make him a eunuch. I got my trousers. Tell me, does he still grumble?"

"No, mistress. He muttered a little as he turned the needle, but that was all."

"It fits you well." The girl blushed. "Have you by any chance seen Ormun today?"

The girl shook her head, but a lanky diplomat raised his hand. "He's in the gardens, mistress. I heard the guardsmen complaining about it."

Rema nodded. The guards disliked it when Ormun strolled the gardens, as amid its forests and groves were any number of hiding places for an ambitious assassin. Bannon was right—it was a wonder Ormun had survived as long as he had. "Thank you. Both of you. All of you. Keep up the good work."

Rema walked away from their terrified smiles and made her way toward the palace gardens. After one too many exquisitely-cornered marble stairwells, she emerged into the open light and bent to catch her breath. She had entered the garden near its forested west side, devoted to flowering trees. The trees were planted close enough to create a canopy across the garden path, busy with warm colors and shining limbs. As Rema strolled under the trees, birds screeched and chattered, sometimes emerging plump and boastful to puff out their chests. Floral aromas drifted on the warm air, and she took a moment to enjoy a deep, scented breath.

She followed the cobbled path into the depths of the garden. The sound of the waterfall built from a murmur to a clamorous torrent. It had been constructed against a miniature mountainside, and by some miracle the water returned to the top once its journey had ended. When that mechanism broke, Ormun would finally have no choice but to appoint an engineer. Rema pushed through a tightly-packed wall of pink blossoms and spotted the waterfall ahead of her, pounding into a wide and surging lake. Its spray dashed against the rocks on the shore, wetting her face as she approached.

Ormun was sitting on a rock, his head in hands, smiling at the endless tumbling water. Rema stepped off the cobbled path and onto the loamy soil. She called his name, but the waterfall snatched every word from her mouth. She moved to his side and shook his shoulder, and he lifted his head and fixed her with languorous eyes. "Rema, dear," he said. "Let's get away from this noisy thing."

He took her arm, and together they returned to the path. They moved into a stretch of the gardens dominated by exotic flowers, many of them as tall as Rema. She touched their broad petals and inhaled their dark, sweet pungency. Ormun stopped them before a tangle of tropical carnivorous plants, all of which looked unwell, clearly unable to find enough warmth even in the plain's heat. Dark blotches mottled their strange, pulpy flesh.

"Such a pleasant surprise," said Ormun. "How did you sleep?"

"Well enough. What are you doing lurking about in the gardens?"

"Escaping from Haran and Sothis. They're always after me for one thing or another. Not today. I don't want to hear Calicio's dry reports, either, or even listen to Ferruro wheedle for money, humorous as he is." Ormun pressed her hand. "But I've always time for you, dear heart. I'm sorry about having to punish you earlier. It was necessary, but still, I never like to see you in pain."

"I don't much like it myself." Rema was unable to take her eyes from the spindly teeth of an enormous flower behind Ormun's shoulder. The resemblance was uncanny. "Ormun, it wouldn't hurt to show clemency once in a while."

"No doubt, but I am what I am. So, cherished, have you sprung upon me for a reason?"

"I'd like to talk about your marriage to Elise tomorrow."

"Oh, yes. I'm looking forward to it. How is she enjoying the palace? Has she seen all of it yet?"

"We're getting around to it. There's a lot to see."

"Yes. I'm sure you're showing her many fascinating things." Ormun's eyes crinkled, as if he thought himself cheeky. Rema mastered her face and disguised her anxiety. Could he know what she and Elise had been doing? They had, after all, given up on discretion.

Rema matched his amused gaze as she spoke. "Ormun, Elise's parents promised her a wedding ceremony. She's longed for one ever since she was a little girl. You've seen how sulky she can get. We don't want her to pout on your wedding night."

"Perish the thought!"

"I wondered if perhaps, with your permission, we might arrange a little event for tomorrow. Just the court entertainers, and perhaps one or two entertainers from the city. To welcome her to Arann and make her realize the grandeur of being your bride."

"You like this one, don't you?" Ormun settled onto the grass, and Rema sat cross-legged before him. "You stopped bothering me about my wives some time ago."

Rema kept her eyes fixed on the bizarre plants that bowed and twisted around them. This was the only subject on which Ormun was liable to lose his temper and forget, albeit briefly, his affection for her.

"I can be a brute," he said. "But I do love these women. I wish they'd carry about the palace more. I'd like to see them frolic in the gardens, entertain people in the court, but instead they lock themselves away."

"Astonishing."

"You don't approve. I won't discuss it. You'll just have to appreciate the good and forgive the bad. This Elise. How badly in love with her are you?"

Rema tugged a handful of grass from the soil. "I've already told you I'm not in love with her."

"Oh, Rema, you underestimate me. I am sorry for you, I really am. But she's married to me now. You'll have to just accept that some women are beyond your clutches."

"Naturally."

"But because you're so fond of her, I'll let her have this little celebration. It will be fun, won't it? I haven't had marriage celebrations in such a long time. The last time, everybody sat with such sour faces. It sucked all the joy from the occasion."

"And the bride kept crying, as I recall."

"Let's not dwell on that." Ormun's voice remained merry, but there was no humor in his eyes. "Make sure you invite Betany. She hates seeing people enjoy themselves." A sudden breeze flattened his thin hair and whispered through the stalks. "Ah, it's peaceful." He stretched back, his arms sprawled between the plants and his face turned to the sun. "I like to lie here and imagine myself decomposing into the ground. Rotting into the soil until all my flesh is gone, and then snaking my way up again, all awful and misshapen, a mass of tangled things punching out of the earth. Isn't that odd?"

"Not in the least." Rema brushed grass from her lap as she returned to her feet. "Good day."

"It will be if you don't tell the others where I'm hiding!"

Rema retraced her steps, moving past the spray of the waterfall and into the shadow of the floral canopy. It was just as likely Ormun was trying to tease her, unaware his jests were accurate. If someone had seen her and Elise kissing in the corridor or overheard them making love, the gossip would be all over the palace. Ferruro would at least have made some reference to it. She sighed as she weaved around a bush with wide, serrated leaves. No, it was impossible that—

Calicio stepped silently from behind a bent-branched tree, and Rema's heart missed a beat. "Oh! Gods, you scared me!"

"All part of my job." Calicio extended a piece of paper. "I've dug up a little present for you. Take this to Lakmi and see what he says."

Rema unfolded it. The fussy handwriting was Betany's—she knew it all too well. "Dear Haran," she read, keeping her voice quiet. "Consider adding Lakmi to our list of undeserving appointments. It is true that he has served us adequately, but his reputation for corruption makes him an unseemly ally. Ferruro or the deviant could potentially buy him away from us. In any case, he is an illiterate toad of a man. Consider it. Yours, Betany."

Rema lowered the letter. "The deviant? Never mind. How did you get this?"

"She never sent it. It was in her desk drawer. Like Ormun, Betany pretends the palace slaves don't exist, and naturally, several of them work for me."

"I'm so grateful I could kiss you. But that'd be strange for both of us."

"I don't know, Rema. You're quite as handsome as any man I've met."

Rema laughed as she put the letter in her pocket. "I'll take that as a compliment, I suppose."

"Use this well. I'm glad I could do my part." Calicio bowed before disappearing back into the trees, his head dislodging petals from the branches.

Rema returned through the fragrant gardens, intent on finding Lakmi, the captain of the house guard and the master of the palace slaves. She moved through the halls and stopped at the first silver guard she saw. "Guardsman," she said. The man's helm inclined in recognition, but the tan face underneath remained still. The guards were aware of the factions at court and the loyalties they were expected to maintain. "Tell me where to find your captain."

"Training yard," said the guard, and he shifted his attention back to the corridor.

"Thank you." Even her gratitude failed to remove the sullen hostility from the man's face.

Rema reoriented herself and proceeded through a series of twisting narrow halls. As she approached the high archway connecting the palace to the training yard, a clamor rose of stamping boots and the shivering clang of swords striking iron. She stepped beneath the arch and was blinded for a moment by morning light reflecting off argent armor. Lakmi stood before the practicing guards, his eyes squinted. He saw her, scowled and crossed the yard to meet her.

Betany was wrong about many things, but she was right about Lakmi. He was a head taller than Rema and overweight, with a swollen, whiskery face. His leather armor was embossed with a silver fist, and a diamond-hilted sword hung bare at his belt. He enjoyed parading wealth and power; little did he comprehend such displays were signs of weakness. "Remela," he said. "What do you want?"

"Only to pass on a letter that somehow missed you." Rema offered it to him.

Lakmi paused a moment, his gaze moving mistrustfully over her face. "Fine." He read the letter, and when he finally spoke again, his voice seethed with irritation. "Illiterate. I can read as well as anyone."

"I think she meant that you don't spend much time doing so. She's an unfair woman."

Lakmi licked his wide lips. "Well. What do you expect me to say?"

"I only expect you to understand. When Betany vacates a court position, she doesn't just send the unlucky occupant back to Arann. She has their head paraded through the outer court." Rema injected a measured note of scorn into her speech. "But you know that, don't you? You saw quite a few of them paraded four years ago. Among them the head of the best Emperor our city has ever known."

"Spare me your speeches."

"If you'll spare me your sullen defiance. If you want to save your own head, start using it. Who is Haran more likely to side with, you or her?" Without a bow or a word of farewell, Rema marched from the square, leaving Lakmi standing in the dirt.

There was only one last person to speak to, futile though it would be. At this time of day he was certain to be in his office, gleefully putting ink to execution warrants. Rema quickened her step and soon stood before Haran's door. After several knocks, the door opened partway, and Haran's long face filled the gap.

"Let me in," Rema said. "Unless you're so busy you don't have time for an old friend."

Haran glowered several seconds longer before opening the door the rest of the way. His office was the size of Rema's, but even more crowded with books and papers. As she entered, Rema frowned at his decor, chilled as always by his odd taste in art. He preferred paintings of trial, imprisonment and execution, and the most prominent piece was a scene of three men hanging.

Rema seated herself before his wide desk, and Haran took his place on the other side. He sat with his hands interlocked and his lips tight with distaste. "Well, state your business," he said.

"I remember when I first met you." Rema leaned back in her chair, and Haran puckered his face in a scowl. "I was strutting along a corridor, young, pretty and pleased with myself, and you were lurking there in your spidery way. You stopped me and gave me a long look up and down."

Haran sipped a dark fluid from an ornate mug—either wine or the blood of infants. His eyes searched her own, trying to discern the reason for her visit. "You asked me why I was wearing a diplomat's uniform," she said. "I boasted that I'd just been allowed into the service. You smiled, shook your head and suggested I would be well-served getting to know you. I laughed in your face and told you that even if I were interested in men, I'd never lower myself to sleep with the hanging judge of Arann."

"Isn't reminiscing fun." Haran's tone was bitter, though that was nothing new. "And then I made the worst mistake of my career. I complained to Togun about you, he discovered your existence and you've been a thorn in my side ever since."

"You started my career. I really should thank you. Fortunately, now we're old enough to laugh about these things."

"What do you want? I can't stand the self-assured sound of your voice."

"How have you fared with Togun's successor, the young general you put in the place of a peacemaker? Do you think he really cares about your laws, or is his thought consumed with chasing war and wives?"

"I hear vaguely treasonous undertones, Remela." Haran hunched lower, giving him an appropriately predatory appearance.

"Only vaguely. I merely want to remind you that you have poor judgment when it comes to regime change."

"Yes, Ormun is challenging. For every concession he gives me, he seems to feel that he must give you one as well. Yet with him as Emperor, I at least gradually get my laws through, whereas you had such power over his father that they were blocked at every step. Justice is on my side."

"Justice is something you've been escaping your whole life. Take some advice and open your eyes. Betany is leading you into an even bigger blunder."

Haran's face livened with malice. "You sound concerned. Is she finally breaking through that famous composure of yours? You know that your time here is nearly concluded, and now you're writhing in fear for your life like a worm on a hook."

Rema kept any emotion from her voice, though as ever in the presence of Haran, her chief desire was to slap him across the face. "You're the one who should be afraid. Let's say Betany does do away with me. Will you be the one to clean up Ormun's messes and repair our reputation? We can't conquer the entire world, and even the provinces under our control are filled with free-minded people who resent being ruled from afar."

"I always thought you a poor choice for a diplomat. You speak your mind too openly. A diplomat must keep their own thoughts inside and speak only the will of the Emperor."

"If I were to speak the will of Ormun, I would speak only in violent grunts and mad laughter." Rema sighed. There was nothing expressed in Haran's long features but pride and greed. "Your entanglement with Betany does you no credit. She's using you."

"What would you know about human relationships? You consort with women and expect us to believe your union is natural."

"We don't have any say in who we love. If you knew anything about human relationships, you'd understand." Rema stood. "I've wasted our time. Good day."

"I'm not a fool. Betany wants some unreasonable things. But I can keep it all in check. She's a strong, intelligent woman who knows what's best for this Empire."

"I hear vaguely treasonous undertones, Haran." Rema opened the door and paused. "These portraits. Do you find nothing haunting about them?"

"You're so timid." Haran gave a crooked smile. "A man on the gallows is a sublime work of art, the triumph of civilization. Death isn't disturbing when it's legal."

Rema closed the door on his malevolence and paused to collect her thoughts. Her enemies had been dealt with, leaving her only to organize her friends. She had yet to consult with Jalaya regarding the entertainment, and later she would have to see if Artunos and Muhan had succeeded in creating a magic box. These were not daunting tasks, and for the first time since the meeting it seemed possible that her plan might truly work. The stage was nearly set for an improbable coup, and if all went to plan, the Empire would once more be turned to the path of peace. Rema adjusted her collar, flicked back her hair and, with a confident step, returned to the maze of hallways.

CHAPTER TWENTY-EIGHT

Rema looped her initial a final time, dropped the quill into the inkwell and flattened her face against the desk. Her fingers were stained with ink, and she felt every ache of the exhausting afternoon. She released a deep sigh and closed her eyes, relishing the bliss that always followed the end of paperwork.

It had been a tiring afternoon. Jalaya had spent an entire hour quizzing Rema on the details of the performance, wanting to know if they were to have a poetry recital, how many dancers would be needed, if it was appropriate to invite the fire-breather and how loudly the drummers were expected to beat. When Rema had suggested dancing animals, Jalaya had given her as filthy a look as was possible from her innocent eyes. "Those poor beasts," she had said before wandering away, shaking her little head. It had been hard to resist the impulse to chase and kiss her.

After taking lunch, Rema had found Artunos and Muhan in the front court struggling beneath an enormous coffin. The three of them had taken the device to the palace theater, where hours were consumed placing it upon the stage. The key, Muhan had told them, was to make it impossible for anyone to see behind the box. The wide stage made this feat a nightmare, and Rema had worn herself out running to every imaginable perspective and calling out "yes" or "no" depending upon her view.

Finally she had returned to her office. She had needed to write a formal letter of approval to Ferruro for every entertainer to be paid, and it had proven a tedious pile of documents. As she had worked, she had sought solace in the fact that for every paper she submitted to Ferruro, he would have to write another two.

The long ordeal behind her, she released another exhausted breath, vowing never to lift a quill again. A knock at the door roused her from her daydreaming. "Enter," she said, and Elise and Jalaya tumbled into the room. Their faces were flushed, and Jalaya's eyes were alight with mischief. "What's so amusing?"

"You sounded so stern," said Jalaya. She put her hands upon her hips and scowled. "Enter!"

"Don't tease me. I've had a long day."

"I forget that you're a weary old woman." Jalaya sauntered into the office with as much assurance as if it were her own bedchamber. She spotted her favorite silk cushion and threw herself onto it, limbs sprawling.

Elise followed, with somewhat more decorum, and paused to appreciate Jalaya's ungainly posture. "Jalaya, I can see up your skirt."

"How lucky for you! Whenever I sing, Haran tries to sit where he can see up my skirt, but I'm far too wily for him." Jalaya and Elise giggled together, and exhausted as she was, Rema smiled. It was good to see them in high spirits. Elise's worried talk about murder and magic had been at the back of her mind throughout the day.

"I'm glad Rema doesn't wear a skirt. We'd be able to see those ugly little trousers she wears under her impressive ones."

Jalaya cackled until her cosmetics ran down her cheeks. "Shame on you both," said Rema. "This office is for important business, not your slanderous chatter."

Elise sat on the desk and tugged on Rema's collar. "Jalaya and I want to know if you'll have dinner with us. We're bored without you. Let's all relax and forget our worries."

"Let's all look up my skirt," said Jalaya, still hiccuping with laughter.

"Now I understand," said Rema. "She's drunk. Elise, did you give her wine? She's always like this with wine."

"We only drank a little," said Elise. "It didn't affect me very much."

"It's because I'm small." Jalaya examined her left hand as if encountering it for the first time. "It makes me dizzy too fast. I shouldn't drink it at all." She bounced on the cushion and almost fell off. "Oh!"

"We'd better eat here in my office," said Rema, trying without luck to force her smile into something sterner. "She's not very discreet when she's like this."

"Good idea." Jalaya stretched her arms and legs, wriggling her toes inside her sandals. "Go get me some food."

"As you will. But I won't bring anything but smoked camel."

"No!" Jalaya leapt to her feet and straightened her clothes. "I'll do it." She wobbled toward the door, trying to wink at Elise as she did so. The wink failed disastrously, and she crashed into the doorframe. She collected herself and wandered out of sight.

Rema stacked the papers and rose from her desk. "Now you've seen drunken Jalaya, you've seen everything."

"When she was on the pillow, I almost did see everything." Elise knelt on a cushion and beckoned with an imperious hand for Rema to sit beside her.

"Yes, Princess." Rema settled onto the cushion and slid an arm around Elise's waist. "Gods, it's been a long day."

"Rema, it's about time you told me what you're up to."

"Yes, you should know." Rema put her lips to Elise's ear. "With Muhan's help, Ormun will disappear during a magic act. People will suspect me, but there'll be no way to prove it. We'll take over, everyone will be happy, and we'll make love for hours on end."

"I hope your plan works. Meanwhile, your whispering is making me tingle."

Rema kissed her. They sank into the cushion, limbs entwined and hands exploring, each touch becoming more adventurous. Just as Elise's hand was creeping into Rema's trousers, Jalaya pushed open the door. Rema disentangled herself and scurried to a neighboring cushion, while Elise stayed where she was, enveloped in the untamable sprawl of her own hair.

"That looked like fun," said Jalaya as she stumbled into the room beneath a tray of food. "I don't know how I managed not to drop this. It keeps trying to run away from me." She placed the tray on a small table among the cushions and curled up on a large, flat pillow.

"Let's see what you've brought us," Rema said. "Is there any warm food?"

"There were only two servants there, and they didn't have time to heat anything. They also mocked me because I'm so giddy. I did bring more wine, though!"

Rema tugged on Jalaya's foot, and she slipped from the pillow, squealing. "Look at the silly thing. She's a shameless drunkard."

"I don't get drunk." Jalaya poured three glasses. "I get delightful. Here, Elsie, this one is for you. I hope you become so tipsy that you decide to run away with me. You're the most beautiful woman I've ever seen."

Elise took the glass and sniffed its contents. "Seeing how silly Jalaya has gotten, I'm almost afraid to drink it."

Rema scrutinized the tray. "What is this, a giant bowl of strawberries? Is this supposed to be our dinner?"

"I'm going to bury my head in it," said Jalaya. "But don't worry. There are some cold soups and a wonderful thing made of potatoes and tomatoes. Potatoes and tomatoes. What funny words."

Rema and Elise exchanged an amused glance over their glasses. "How are the arrangements for the performance?" said Rema.

"Good! Wait until you see me singing, Elsie. Then you'll fall in love with me."

"Who said I wasn't in love with you already?" Elise tickled Jalaya's feet, provoking at first merriment and finally an outraged screech as Jalaya tucked them beneath her. "Oh, look, we've made Rema pout."

"I'm not pouting," said Rema. "You two can marry for all that I care. Is that a saffron cake?"

"I brought it just for you," said Jalaya. "Because I still love you, even though Elsie is prettier."

Elise began to giggle, and when Rema turned a sulky look toward her, she broke into outright laughter. "I'm sorry, Rema." Her eyes shone, and with more than merely wine. "I just find drunken Jalaya very entertaining."

"She's not entertaining. She's making a fool of herself." Rema scowled at Jalaya, but she proved unable to hold the frown and ended up chuckling herself. "Did you finish that glass already?"

"No." Jalaya stared into the empty glass. "It just emptied itself. Also, Elsie, I gathered up lots of sweets for you. I'm going to make you fatter." She crawled into Elise's lap, put her arms around Elise's waist and squeezed, provoking another fit of giggles. "You're so fun to hold. I could squish you forever."

"Don't crawl all over her like that. Elise isn't enjoying it."

Jalaya tried to nuzzle Elise, who laughed. "Jalaya, behave," Elise said, stopping Jalaya's advancing mouth with her fingers.

"It's your perfume," said Jalaya. "It's giving me thoughts. Rema, do you remember the night we met that merchant woman, the one who sold silks?"

"That was different," said Rema. "Elise doesn't want anything to do with your tipsy fantasies."

"Doesn't she?" Jalaya stroked Elise's cheek, and Elise blushed, her eyes dizzy with amusement.

Rema summoned her sternest tone. "Go back to your cushion!"

Jalaya gave an indignant harrumph before returning to her previous position, this time modestly tucking her skirt between her legs. "I'm not a naughty house cat, Rema. You should let Elsie decide whether she wants me to crawl on her."

"You poor thing. Tomorrow you'll apologize to her so many times, you'll wear your voice out. Do you remember the time you got so drunk you walked into the corridor wearing nothing but my trousers?"

"Give me a fig and I'll behave. And I want one kiss from Elsie. Just one."

"That seems fair," said Elise. Rema pinched her on the arm, and she shrieked. "I mean, no! No kisses!" She dissolved into a mess of wine-fueled mirth, and Jalaya immediately joined her.

As Rema looked between her friends, affection warmed her chest and dissolved her troubles. "Let's eat the saffron cake. Tell me you brought a knife."

They dined and drank until moonlight crept through the window and mingled with the warm glow of their lamp. Jalaya became too silly to do more than chuckle, and she finally fell asleep with her head in Elise's lap. "I can hardly wait to see her reaction in the morning," said Elise, running her fingers through Jalaya's lustrous black hair.

"I have to admit, some of the most enjoyable times I can remember involved Jalaya and wine," said Rema. "But I prefer her sober nonetheless. When she drinks, she becomes far too light-minded for someone so intelligent."

"I'm so fond of her, Rema. I hope there's something good waiting for her at the end of all of this."

"I wish I understood her better." Rema watched Jalaya's lashes as they flickered in slumber. "She has a strange, yearning heart. All those songs she sings about love. I've never understood half of them, but they fill my soul and make me weep all the same."

"Why is she so infatuated with me?"

"She especially loves women who are…well, hurt in some way. The unhappier I became, the more Jalaya focused her attentions on me. My guess is that she can sense the sorrow your life has left inside you like so many scars. Her own past is very sad, though you wouldn't know it to look at her."

Elise touched Jalaya's nose. Jalaya sniffed and batted dozily at Elise's hand. "She was getting very amorous. I won't lie, I enjoyed it. You're lucky I'm so devoted to you."

"She was teasing. She'd love to have the both of us, but I think she understands that it can't be that way."

"Poor thing. We'd better wake her so we can all go to our beds." Elise tugged on Jalaya's ear, and Jalaya wriggled, a dreamy smile animating her lips. "Wake up, you little goose," said Elise, tugging harder.

"Oh," said Jalaya, opening her eyes. "Rema, I've been ridiculous." She turned her head and bumped her face into Elise's stomach. "Hello, Elsie. I was just dreaming about you."

"Get up, sleepy. I'll help you get back to your room, wherever that is."

"Yes, do. Rema won't rest all night from wondering whether you invited yourself in."

"I think I've passed that particular anxiety now," said Rema. As she stood, her knees unfolded with painless ease. Elise lifted Jalaya to her feet, and they joined Rema in the doorway.

Rema kissed Elise on the lips before embracing Jalaya, whose drowsy lashes brushed Rema's cheek. "I'm glad I still get hugged," said Jalaya. "I was worried you'd only shake my hand from now on."

"Tomorrow, everything will be decided. Elsie, I'll ensure some of Artunos's guards escort you to the theater tomorrow. I'd be surprised if Ormun even talks to you."

"He'd better not," said Elise. "I've had about enough of holding my tongue."

"Jalaya, are you alert enough to tell Elsie where to take you?"

"Rema, really," said Jalaya. "I have full command of my senses. It's just my legs that want to curl up and go to sleep."

"Come on." Elise took Jalaya by the hand. "Let's put you to bed. I'm never giving you wine again."

"Good idea." Jalaya leaned against Elise's arm. "Promise you'll tuck me in."

Rema watched, her heart light, as the pair walked down the night-wreathed corridor, Elise stooping slightly to keep Jalaya from falling. Her best friend and her lover, linked together, whispering and chuckling—not a sight to inspire envy, she understood now, but gratitude.

She locked the office door and began the long walk to her bedchambers. The moonlight about her was feeble; if only she'd taken a lantern from her office. Familiar as the palace was, it was unpleasant to trace through it in the dark, feeling against the rough outlines of a sculpture or tentatively inching over the edge of a sharp step. Years ago the palace had been illuminated throughout by steady lamplight, but Ferruro had declared it to be a waste of oil and had removed most of the lanterns. It had been an unpopular move, but Ferruro seemed able to get away with anything.

Rema turned into a wide corridor that was entirely dark save for a single ray of nocturnal light cast from a thin, high window. Holding her breath, she walked into shadow. Cicadas droned beyond the window, accompanied by the rattling banter of frogs. Rema took several steps more and paused, her ears straining. Were those footsteps shadowing her own, taking advantage of the echo of her boots to mask their tread?

Rema's skin burned with a chill fire, and she touched the pendant that rested against her chest. She turned, certain that something was approaching in the dark with predatory patience. Surely it was her imagination. Surely—

Bannon stepped into the shaft of moonlight. Within his shadowed hood, two pale orbs glistened, their stare made even colder by the lunar radiance. "I said I'd come when you needed me, and now you do. It's time to make me an offer, Rema."

"First, you'll have to tell me what Betany offered you," Rema said, trying to keep the fear in her gut from slithering into her voice.

"A lot of money. But more than that, she said that she'd give me protection. You see, I've just learned that the Kalanese Adventurers are coming for me."

"Surely you're a match for them."

"Maybe I could stand against some of them. But no man alive is a match for Blackworm, Wild Eye or the Jade Ghost. I'm not about to get eaten by some bigger fish."

"If no man alive can help you, then how exactly is Betany going to offer you protection?"

"Perhaps she can't, but I'm sure you could find a way." Bannon took a slow step forward. "Look, I need a contract. A tool that's disused grows rusty. Finish our original bargain but double the sum, and I'll kill Betany for you. Double it again and I'll catch Ormun, too, while he's sleeping."

"And by their blood I would win an empire." Rema stared into his lifeless eyes. She had rarely been closer to death. "You know I won't give you another coin more, Bannon, and I certainly won't hire you to kill anyone."

"My blade's going to drip red by the end of this night regardless. Take my offer. I like you much better than I do that haughty bitch."

"The answer is still no."

"How can you refuse? If you die, that princess of yours is abandoned to her fate. Why throw it all away?" Bannon shook his head, his lips twisted. "Fine, then. You don't need to double the sum. Just offer me some small incentive. A few jewels, a good horse…"

"I'll pay you to leave, but I won't pay you to kill."

"I have to kill." Bannon shifted irritably. "It's been too long since I slit a throat. If a man doesn't kill regularly, he gets soft, and I have too many enemies to lose my edge. Your neck or Betany's. I'm letting you make the choice."

"And I'm giving you a third choice: neither. For once in your life, take the nobler way."

Bannon exhaled a soft breath that was, perhaps, a sigh. "I left the nobler way a long time ago. Far too long ago to remember how to find the path again."

Rema began to run—surely she had the advantage of distance—but she hadn't anticipated Bannon's speed. His feet were almost soundless in pursuit, and in seconds his fingers pressed hard against the flesh of her arm. Her scream was caught short by his other hand. Sickened by the taste of the sweat on his palm, she fought in vain to free herself, powerless against Bannon's might.

"Don't struggle," said Bannon. "It'll just wear you out."

Rema clawed at his arm with her free hand. Her blunt fingernails scraped ineffectually against his skin. Bannon began to tug her backward with frightening ease, and terror ran wild through her body. She flailed, caught a handful of his hair and pulled as hard as she could. Bannon grunted, his grip loosening, and she tore free. He tripped her as she lifted her feet to run, and she stumbled into a wall. She reeled, her face throbbing and wet with blood, and screamed again. Bannon's hand clenched tight around her jaw.

"I warned you. Come on, let's get this over with."

Rema wanted to kick, resist, scream, but her head was aching, her vision swimming, and the darkness and Bannon's inexorable strength were overwhelming. She gave no resistance as he dragged her through the corridors. Long tongues of moonlight and shadow stretched past her, merging into something incomprehensible: a vision of life and death. She closed her eyes to the chaos, tormented by the burning pain in her arm and jaw. Cold crept around her, then heat, and a door opened.

A familiar laugh rang out.

"Betany." Rema opened her eyes, hatred returning her strength. Bannon had hauled her to Betany's chambers, where Betany herself was standing at the far end of the room, enveloped in flickering lamplight. She was wearing a nightgown, but it was obvious from her alertness that she hadn't been sleeping.

"Well done," Betany said. "She looks subdued. Push her forward."

Bannon released Rema's arm and shoved her. Rema tottered a few steps, unable to distinguish between her left and right feet. She steadied herself and looked into Betany's triumphant face.

"I love the irony that this monster is only here because you brought him with you," said Betany. "It seems nothing but death and disaster awaited you in Danosha. I know all about you and the princess."

"If you knew it all, you'd blush as you said that," said Rema, trying not to sway as she stood.

Betany's thin lips moved in something less than a smile. "You ridiculous thing. Strutting about in your trousers and coat, so cocky and proud of your mannish ways."

"I'm not mannish." Blood trickled past Rema's ear. "I'm no less a woman than you. You just can't understand that strength isn't only for men."

"You talk so much nonsense. You always have. You should have died with the others."

"Do tell me why my life so affronts you."

"You know why. I begged him! I said to him, 'Ormun, for your love for me as a sister, execute her. She's your father's most loyal servant, she'll never forgive you and she'll never cause us anything but grief!'" Betany sneered, a remembered fury kindling in her eyes. "He laughed and said, 'Kill her? My Rema? She's more my sister than you will ever be.' I couldn't have been more shocked had it been a slap to my face."

"What do you expect? You ignored his suffering, whereas I saw the transformation happen, and I comforted him as his mind was extinguished. The whole time, you cared about nothing but your own little schemes."

"You stole my father too." Betany clenched her fists. "He treated you with more affection than he treated me, the daughter of his blood. You entered my household and replaced me! And now you scheme ways to destroy us, and Ormun turns away his indulgent eye."

"Indulgent? How many times has Ormun threatened and beaten me? I never recall him laying a hand on you."

"That's because I mind my tongue. If you weren't Rema, his dearest darling, you'd be dead a hundred times over for the things you dare say to him. He hits you because he's an animal. He has half a mind, or a fractured mind…but he's my brother! Not yours!"

"Your ranting is tiring me," said Bannon. "Order me to finish it already."

"Mind your manners, ogre! You're a henchman and you should focus on henching." Betany took a tentative step forward. Rema bared her teeth and hissed, and Betany leapt back.

"Poor Betany," said Rema. "So much hate, yet not a shred of courage."

Betany hid her shaking hands behind her back. "Ormun couldn't bring himself to kill you, but I can think of nothing more pleasurable. Your body will be found in the gardens, bloodied beyond recognition. A few tears will be shed and then life will go on much more smoothly." Excitement tightened her voice, raising its pitch and giving it a quivering edge of mania. "Oh, and before I send Bannon away, I'll have him garrote that singer of yours. An appropriate way for her to die, don't you think?"

The threat hit Rema like a fist to her gut. "No. Betany, she's never done a thing to you. Leave her be."

"It's touching you still care for her even after you've abandoned her for your new trophy. Perhaps I should have her strangled slowly instead, so that the last thing she sees is Bannon's remarkable eyes. A dying song warbling from her little throat."

"Bannon." Rema's voice shook, and her stomach churned. Her own life was one thing, but Jalaya…Gods, no, it couldn't end that way for her. "I want to reconsider my position. Please."

"I'm sorry," said Bannon. "It's far too late in the game for that. You played your hand badly, Rema. At least this employer has the bloodlust to keep me occupied."

"I'm tired of her." Betany ran a finger across her throat. "Finish it."

Bannon nodded and drew his sword. The sight of its honed iron edge sent Rema's heart into spasms. How could it all end here, ingloriously cut down at Betany's feet? She took a deep breath and squared her shoulders. At the very least she'd not give Betany the satisfaction of seeing fear.

CHAPTER TWENTY-NINE

The door opened, slamming against the marble wall so forcefully that the room's paintings shook on their fixtures. Bannon spun, his sword still raised, and the anxiety scaling Rema's stomach reached new heights. Elise and Jalaya were standing in the doorway, their faces whiter than the moonlight that drenched the hall behind them.

"How the hell did you find us?" said Bannon, swinging his sword to point at Rema again. "Don't run, or she dies."

"Elsie felt something was wrong," said Jalaya. "We thought we heard a scream, and then we found blood…" Her eyes were immense in the dark, and horror trembled in her voice. "Whoever you are, don't hurt her. Please."

Betany laughed in wild delight. "Look, her lovers have arrived to save her! Now we can kill three deviants at once. How efficient."

"Betany, how could you?" Jalaya's fear seemed to have sobered her. "You hateful thing."

"Why don't you sing a song while she dies? A touching little dirge." Betany laughed again. "And look, the foreign bitch can't even talk, she's so frightened. You should watch closely as she dies, you chubby slut. Maybe you'll learn something about the price of infidelity."

Elise remained motionless in the moonlight, her pale face framed by the unruly cascade of her black hair. Her eyes shone with an unnatural radiance both bright and forbidding.

"Come on, say something," said Betany. "Or don't you speak Annari? Should I grunt instead, in the manner of your people?"

Elise stepped forward, her long shadow stretching almost to Betany's feet, but her gaze was fixed not on Betany but Bannon. "Heed me well, Calan's butcher. I'll not let you harm the woman I love. Release her or die under an agony even your baleful mind can't comprehend."

"How absurd," said Betany. "What is she going to do, smother you?"

"The little one," said Bannon. "Get inside and close the door. Or else I kill her." Jalaya quivered as she pulled the door shut and pressed her back to it. "Now, what's this about me dying in agony?"

"Release my lover." A commanding power inhabited Elise's voice. "You've caused her pain, and now I feel your dark heart beating close to mine. I have the hand of death, Bannon, and I will close it tight around you."

"I don't know what you're talking about." Bannon spoke with a shade of uncertainty. "If you're going to threaten me, you need to do better than to give me spooky looks."

Betany clapped her hands. "Bannon! Get on with it!"

Bannon blinked, and the doubt left his eyes. He advanced on Rema. Before he could strike, Jalaya shrieked and leapt at him. She pounded her tiny fists on his back and pulled vainly on his arms. "Rema, run!"

Bannon turned and struck Jalaya across the face. She stumbled, holding her cheek. Bannon lifted her with a single hand, gripping her by the neck, and dashed her against the wall. Her small body spasmed as it struck the stone, and she fell crumpled to the floor.

Tears burned in Rema's eyes—it couldn't be, not her Jalaya, anyone but her—and she screamed as she threw herself at Bannon, ripping his face, kicking his legs, punching his chest and tearing at his fist in an attempt to free the sword from his hands. Bannon retreated, fending off her frantic, useless attacks.

Rema pulled again on his arm, and he struck her across the face with the hilt of his sword. Pain obliterated her thoughts. Another powerful blow caught her stomach, and she reeled and wheezed, falling to her knees and disappearing into a fog of nausea, breathlessness and consuming pain. Bannon's sword raised high above her, a line of moonlight defining its killing edge.

Rema closed her eyes and waited for the blow. Impossible seconds passed, yet she still lived. A slow gurgling broke the silence, and she opened her eyes. Bannon had frozen in midswing, his muscles tensed and his neck bulging. Blood trickled from the corner of his mouth.

"What is this?" said Betany. "Bannon! Kill her!"

Elise was standing behind Bannon, her eyes closed and her hands pressed together over her chest. A single tear ran down her cheek, and her lips moved without sound. As she continued her silent murmuring, her hair rose and writhed through the air, the black strands moving like feathered serpents.

Bannon twitched, and the sword dropped from his hand. Rema and Betany both flinched as it hit the marble with a sharp, metallic crack. A second tear slipped from Elise's lashes, and Bannon doubled over and coughed up blood, so much blood that Rema's stomach rolled.

"Make her stop," said Bannon, his voice raw with suffering.

"I'm sorry," said Elise. Her whisper somehow filled the room, and it was as if many other voices were contained within it, some mournful, some furious, others triumphant.

Bannon's face had become paler than his eyes, which he turned toward Rema, bemusement and fear frozen in their dying depths. He dropped to one knee, shivered and fell forward into the pool of his blood. A long groan shook his body before he shuddered into the stillness of death.

"Get up!" Betany retreated to the wall of her chamber, pressed herself against the stone and stared at Elise. "Bannon, get up and take care of this sorceress!"

Rema pushed aside her pain and ran to Jalaya, who still lay motionless in the corner. Rema lifted her and held her close, pretending not to see the blood on her head or to feel the limpness of her body. "She's hurt," Rema said. "Elsie, help her." She sobbed as she pressed her cheek against Jalaya's hair. "Jalaya, my love, please be alive. I love you, please come back…"

Elise drifted toward them, an inhuman apparition, and Rema shrank away. Elise's eyes were silver from edge to edge, and her hair was spread as wildly as if she'd been touched by lightning. "Her heart still beats," she said, her voice lit by spectral power. "I can feel her spirit still radiant within her, a soul like no other in this world. I'll save your little songbird, Rema. I promise."

"Hurry." Rema brushed away her tears and opened the door. Elise carried Jalaya out of the room and into the shadowed hallway. Rema stared for some time at the dark opening, paralyzed by concern and confusion, before the thought of Betany broke through her trance. Her fear and grief hardened into a cold hunger for revenge.

Betany was still standing against the wall, her face contorted. "Mark my words," said Rema, picking up Bannon's sword as she advanced across the room. "I'll cut you into ribbons, Betany, if you've killed her."

Betany wept—self-pity, and fear for her own life. As Rema drew closer, Betany squished against the marble as if she hoped to sink into it. Rema pointed the sword at her breast. "Tell me, why shouldn't I finish you and leave your body in the gardens?"

"You should. I would, if I were you. But you won't, because you're weak."

"Jalaya would say that sparing a life is braver than taking it, but I don't have her depth of forgiveness. If you've slain her, I will harbor a vengeance to make your own hate seem like the petulance of childhood. There is no sea or mountain range that will protect you from me."

Betany stared at the tip of the sword. "If you take what is mine, then I'll take what is yours."

"Don't threaten her again, or I swear I'll impale you against this wall."

"Look at you." Betany spat at Rema's feet. "Holding a sword to a defenseless woman. There's a little bit of Ormun in all of us, isn't there?"

Nausea rose in her stomach, and Rema turned away. She walked slowly across the room and stopped to stare at Bannon's body sunken in blood. Death had followed her from Danosha, but it would end here. She tossed the sword aside, and it clattered in the corner.

"Get out of my chambers." Betany's voice had regained its haughty calm. "If you're not going to kill me, then leave me be."

"Every time I look at you, I see the physical resemblance." Rema rested her hand on the doorframe, not turning to look at Betany as she spoke. "If only you had similarly inherited your father's compassion. Instead, your brother vanishes into madness while you burn with hatred. The only solace I can find in Togun's death is that he never lived to see what his children have become."

She slammed the door shut as she left the chamber. It was late enough for a chill to have invaded the night, and the fog in her mind receded as she inhaled a cool lungful of air. The side of her face ached, but the pain hardly mattered—nothing mattered now but Jalaya.

Rema moved as quickly as she could manage without blundering into the walls. A warm light shone ahead of her, and as she hastened her step, a guard walked into view, his golden armor gleaming under the glow of his lantern. Rema's relief turned to anger. "Where were you?" she said. "Where are the guards?"

"I'm sorry," said the guardsman, steadying her by the shoulder. "I don't understand what you're saying. All the guards are patrolling as they should be…" His eyes widened. "Mistress Remela! What happened to your head?"

"Why is it so dark? Why weren't you there?" Rema slammed her fists against his breastplate. "Damn it, my friends could have died tonight!"

"Died?" The guard drew himself upright. "What are you talking about?"

Rema caught herself. It would do her no good to prompt an official investigation—it would only expose her own machinations. "Nothing. I've just been drinking. My apologies."

"But your head. You're injured…"

"Nothing. It's nothing. I hit it on a low ceiling."

The guard's expression was a study in skepticism, but he nodded dutifully. "Well, there aren't enough patrolmen for this palace, and that's a fact. My lady, you seem shaken. Can I escort you somewhere?"

"Take me to Artunos's chambers. Quickly, please."

The guardsman walked briskly with his lantern swinging before him, and Rema followed, stewing with impatience despite their steady march. If the worst had befallen Jalaya, and Rema wasn't in time to say farewell…"Hurry up! This is important!"

"Yes, my lady." The guard quickened his walk.

They hurried through the corridors, the guard's lamplight catching the sculpted features of the halls and making them appear warped and sinister. After far too many anxious minutes, the lamp's swaying radiance touched on a latticework of gold, and Rema remembered how to breathe. She waved her hand at the guard. "Thank you. You can go back to your duties now. Go, go!" The guard stomped down the hallway, his confusion evident.

For a moment, Rema considered awakening Artunos, but no—he would only complicate this matter with his worrying. She strode instead into Elise's room, not even pausing to knock.

Jalaya lay on the bed, her head supported by a pillow and her eyes closed. Elise was leaning over her, applying something to her forehead. Rema hastened to the bedside and took Jalaya's small, warm hand. "How is she?"

"She hit her head quite hard," said Elise. "She's opened her eyes once or twice, but she couldn't say much. I'm hoping she's just stunned.

This balm will help the wound heal, and it'll also soothe what may be the biggest headache she's ever had. Poor Jalaya."

Rema caressed Jalaya's face. A subtle smile lifted Jalaya's lips, as if the gesture had touched her dreams, and grief hardened in Rema's throat. She had always loved watching Jalaya's face in slumber. "This is my fault."

"Nonsense." Nothing remained of the eldritch spirit that had animated Elise earlier. Her eyes were human once more, and her hair was messy rather than preternatural. "It wasn't you that struck her or threw her against a wall."

Rema winced. "What happened in there?"

"It was the spell I'd prepared for Ormun. I felt the life leaving his body. I'll never do anything like that again."

"You had best not," said a sonorous voice behind them. Melnennor entered the chamber, his robes sweeping across the stone floor. He moved to the bedside and touched Jalaya's arm. "Is the wound grievous?"

"I can't yet say," said Elise, while Rema wiped her eyes, hoping the magician hadn't seen her tears. She had a reputation to maintain, even now.

"I was sleeping when you exerted that force. It intruded into my dreaming, corrupting it into nightmare and forcing me awake. You didn't heed my warning."

Elise's eyes blazed with sudden temper. "I heeded it until heeding wasn't an option. Someone would have died tonight regardless. What I did saved Rema and Jalaya's lives."

"For now." Melnennor placed his fingers upon Jalaya's cheek, and sympathy moved in his narrow eyes. "These vibrations will continue for some time. There will be a reckoning soon, I believe." He tilted his head to look at Rema. "Remela, I know your plan. It will fail."

Rema gaped. "How can you...?"

"Nothing that happens evades my eye. Why do you think Ormun lured me into his service?"

"But it's your job to protect him. Shouldn't you have had us arrested?"

Melnennor smiled. "I interpret my role as I see fit. As Elise must have demonstrated to you already, only the stubborn and individualistic pursue the arcane. But let us return to the point. The events of tonight ensure that your plan cannot proceed as you had imagined."

"And why is that?" Rema looked at Melnennor with what she hoped was defiance and suspected was tearful confusion.

"Elise's spell has reordered everything. Or disordered, to be more precise. She has shaken the branch of eternity, and now its fruit will fall to rot on the ground."

"Well, I'm sorry," said Elise. "You don't need to keep going on about it."

"Indeed. In any case, you have a patient, and I am no healer. And this injured woman must live. She has a unique and brilliant heart." Melnennor closed his eyes, and the shadows of the room seemed to move. "A mighty, sorrowful presence wanders this world, turning many fates with the edge of a blade. It has never been tamed, but she will tame it. She will brave a darkness that has never been broken, and she will break it. Treat her well so that she might fulfill her purpose."

Melnennor switched to speaking Ajulai, and Elise frowned in incomprehension. "Remela, you are wondering why I am allowing you to continue on your treasonous path. My answer is your own. We both have a duty to our master, but Elise is too rare to sacrifice to the altar of his lunacy. Keep her safe. In time, her touch will change the flow of nature and bend the weave of worlds."

He bowed before leaving. Even after he was gone, Rema stared at the doorway. "I'm not used to being speechless," she said.

"That's Mel for you," said Elise.

"Mel?" Despite everything, Rema laughed. "You have a nickname for that terrifying man?"

"Melnennor is too long. Anyway, I think it's safe now to try to wake her up." Elise tipped a vial over Jalaya's mouth. A drop of liquid reached her lips, and her eyes opened.

"Jalaya?" Rema knelt beside the bed, clasping Jalaya's hands tightly in her own. "Are you awake?"

Jalaya sighed and turned her head to meet Rema's gaze. "I'm sorry. I did drink that second glass." Her eyes widened. "No! I remember! He was going to kill you!"

"It's over now." Elise stroked Jalaya's hair. "We just wanted to ensure you were well, dear heart. You can go back to sleep."

"Sleep sounds lovely. I'm not in my own bed, though. My bed has many more pillows than this."

"It's my bed."

"We're not sharing it, are we?"

"Not quite. But anything is possible in dreams."

Jalaya smiled. "Make her happy, Elsie. It's been so hard for her, and every day she seems to creep closer to that terrible darkness. You can save her. Bring her out of sorrow and into your love." She closed her eyes and turned her head.

Rema remained beside the bed, holding Jalaya's hand, until she heard the familiar sound of her sleeping breath. As Rema released her hand, Jalaya mumbled. "She always sings in her sleep," said Rema, wiping away yet another tear. "For a moment there, I thought the worst."

"It was closer than I let you know," said Elise. "I took the swelling down in time. If I hadn't, she definitely wouldn't have been singing again tomorrow. Or maybe ever."

Rema drew a blanket over Jalaya and tucked it around her shoulders. "Should we stay with her?"

"She'll be fine. Everyone needs to be rested for tomorrow. Although now Jalaya has my bed, I'm not sure where I'm going to sleep."

"That's simple enough. You can sleep with me."

"No objections here." Elise adjusted the pillow beneath Jalaya's head. "I don't want to sleep alone anyway. I can still feel Bannon's heart, wet and screaming in my hands."

"You saved our lives. I know it was hard, but you did the right thing."

Elise tilted Rema's head gently with her fingertips. "I really should treat your wound too. You took a nasty blow to the forehead."

"I'm fine. Just exhausted."

Rema gazed again at Jalaya lying tangled among the blankets. The moment she had lifted that limp body, a tragic revelation had taken hold of her; Jalaya was no mere friend and bed companion, but something far deeper, a soul inextricably bound to her own. How blind Rema had been to think Elise had been her first true love. Now Rema had sacrificed love without knowing it, and she would never again fall asleep to the lullaby of Jalaya's wise, caring heart.

"I know what you're thinking," said Elise. "I saw how you reacted when Bannon threw her against that wall."

"How is it possible that I loved her, loved her as truly and surely as I love you, yet never knew it?"

"What did I tell you?" Elise stroked Rema's cheek. "Love is a feeling. It's not about knowing."

"She wasn't like you. She didn't demand me. She simply tried to make me happy, asking for nothing in return. And so I took her for granted. How could I be so stupid?"

"You don't have to explain yourself to me. How could you not love her?"

"Elsie, I've given myself to you. I have no regrets. Come to bed. I need your solace, and you need mine."

They left holding hands, heedless of the risk of being seen. Despite her concern, Rema refused to dwell on her fears. Love was stirring in her heart, and at least until morning, it deserved to move there unhindered.

CHAPTER THIRTY

They lay beneath the blankets, their faces speckled by the moon as it shone through the branches of the tree beyond the window. Insects gathered in the garden, humming their sleepless song. Despite Elise's naked warmth, not a single lustful urge stirred in Rema's body, and by Elise's shivering it was clear she felt the same. It was dizzying to have been so abruptly tossed from merriness to pain, from sorrow to relief, and it was impossible to contemplate the events of the night without being overwhelmed.

"I murdered him," said Elise. "He begged me to stop, but I couldn't."

Rema kissed Elise's neck. "Don't think about it."

Elise turned to her side. Her eyes seemed impossibly pale under the moonlight. "I used to imagine killing Calan, yet I could never bring myself to do it, no matter how much he beat me. I knew that to kill someone would take me to an even darker place." She shuddered. "I underestimated how dark it would be."

"You're thinking about it." Rema ran her fingers along Elise's naked side. "I told you not to."

"You flinched away from me. After I killed him. You couldn't even look at me."

"It was the magic. It made you look…different. You're back to yourself now."

"It's awful. This could be our last night together, and all I want to do is curl into a ball and cry."

"Then curl into my arms and cry there." Rema pulled Elise closer. "Don't lose that strong spirit I love so well. Do you want to know when I fell in love with you?"

Rema felt Elise's cheek move as she smiled. "Tell me."

"The day you defied Calan in the front court. I'd never seen anything as beautiful as you in that instant, cloaked in your grace and fury. I ached for you, and when you turned to me looking for support, it felt as if my soul were collapsing. After that, you became the center of my every thought. I wish I'd said something to defend you."

"Not even you can be strong all the time." Elise's voice trembled. "I try to be, and I fail sometimes too. You stormed into my desolation, confident, clever and strong. I wanted so badly for you to love me. I wanted you to see in me the same things I saw in you." Dampness touched Rema's cheek, and it took a moment to realize the tears were Elise's, not her own. "Now here I am, trembling in your arms, frightened this will be the last time I'll feel your chest move against mine."

"Don't talk that way. We'll share long lives, and at their end we'll pass together in our sleep, both escaping this world in the same breath."

"Tell me about our future. I want to fall asleep thinking only of us."

Rema began to stroke Elise's back, following the sensual contour from her shoulders to her hips. "Every morning we'll wake together, still entwined from the night before. I'll kiss you on the nose, and you'll grumble at me. For breakfast we'll eat saffron cakes and berries. Then we'll read poetry together in the sun before resting in the cool grass, feeling the wind rush over our bodies."

Elise exhaled, her breath soft with emotion. "And each afternoon you'll sit at your desk, wearing that thinking frown of yours. I'll rest my shaggy head on your shoulder and watch your mind at work. As evening comes, we'll talk and laugh about all the things we've seen and done that day. Then we'll go back to our bed and love each other. Best of all, we'll never be ashamed. Everyone will know you as my lover, and they'll be glad for the joy we share."

"We'll build a new house together. I'm tired of that mansion of mine. We'll erect a tower on top to make you feel at home, and we'll have a huge library so your books don't have to be strewn everywhere."

"Jalaya will visit and sing for us. She'll have a lover of her own, a woman every bit her equal. Muhan will come to perform magic tricks, and your boring friend Artunos will join us for dinner and scowl at me. And Lor, he'll come and drink up all our wine…" Elise sobbed. "I miss my little brother. He's by himself now, he doesn't have me to look after him. I miss him so terribly…"

"Oh, sweetheart." Rema held her tighter. Why had it been so long since she thought of the pain of a sibling's separation? How easy it was to be selfish when in love.

"Please distract me. Tell me another of your father's poems."

"I could recite one he wrote for my mother. They were inseparable. I was told that when she fell sick, he died with her, knowingly contracting her plague."

"I want you to make me happy, not sad."

"I'm sorry. Let me recite it to you in Ajulai." Rema crooned the verses in Elise's ear, their harmonies shivering and rolling from her tongue. Elise's body relaxed, and her sobs subsided. She sighed as the last syllable faded from Rema's lips.

"That language makes me dizzy. But say it again in a way I can understand."

"As you wish." Rema touched her lips again to Elise's ear.

"I was born alone and parted,
Caught in neither life nor death,
Blind and without understanding,
A roaming emptiness.
But when my fingers touched your face,
My eyes began to see,
And when my body felt your heat,
My blood began to flow,
And when your breath first met with mine,
My lungs began to move,
Yet only when my lips found yours
Did I begin to live."

Elise wept, and Rema kissed away each tear as it fell. Sleep came to them in embrace, bringing dreams of Elise floating in the warm bay beside the mansion. Her hair drifted loose in the water as Rema swam beside her, supporting her and teaching her to swim. Jalaya was with them, laughing as she was splashed, her face radiant.

Rema awoke to find Elise still sleeping in her arms. It was early morning, and idle birds were gossiping to one another on the branches beneath the window. Rema sat upright, aware of a dull ache at her forehead, and touched the dried blood on her scalp. The tenderness of the skin brought back every memory of the night before, each one as articulate with terror as if she had just lived them. She shuddered, and Elise stirred and rose beside her, her face hidden beneath her hair.

"Good morning," said Rema. "I have to catch Ormun as soon as I can. Will you visit Jalaya and give her my love?"

"Mmmm." Elise brushed the hair from her face and kissed Rema clumsily on the lips. "I'll go to her as soon as I'm dressed. Why do you need to see Ormun?"

"To find out what clothes he's wearing."

Elise wrinkled her nose. "How odd. Rema, I'm sorry if I was a little overwrought last night."

"You have nothing to apologize for. We're going to share everything from now on, and that includes our sorrows."

Rema opened her wardrobe, searching for a uniform not sullied by blood or neglect. As Rema hunted, Elise drew back the blankets and stretched. Her figure was so unlike Rema's, curved where Rema was straight, round where Rema was flat. Too many of the women Rema had courted were insecure about their bodies; even Jalaya fretted about her lack of height. Not so Elise. She was all the more beautiful because of her confidence, that remarkable way she wore her body without apology.

"Stop staring," said Elise. "Go and do your important business!"

Rema smiled. "You're right. I'll have a lifetime to stare." She put on her boots, adjusted her hair and splashed her face with water. There was still dried blood on her forehead, and she sponged it off. "Ugh. There's a nasty purple bruise here. Ormun will want to know where I got it."

"Put on a hat."

Rema returned to her wardrobe and took out a perky black hat with a ball of red fuzz on its peak. She donned it and presented herself to Elise, who covered her mouth as she tittered. "It's painfully sweet on you. But it's not very Rema."

"It'll have to do." Rema peered into the mirror and straightened the hat. "I'll come visit you and Jalaya as soon as I'm done with Ormun, so we don't need to have a teary goodbye just yet."

Elise walked naked across the room and kissed Rema with such force that the hat slipped over her ear. "Tonight, we'll have to do more than sob at each other."

"Make that a promise."

Elise laughed as she fixed the hat. "Get out there and solve all our problems. Don't worry about what Mel said to you last night. I have faith in you."

"I'll be with you again soon, enchantress of my heart."

"Don't say sappy things like that. You'll get me weepy again."

They shared a lingering kiss, and Rema headed toward the door. Elise remained standing naked in the sun, her hair draped about her body and her eyes distant with thought. Though she appeared human once more, there still seemed a touch of the otherworldly upon her. What had Melnennor's strange prophecy meant? Had Rema fallen in love with a woman or a goddess?

It was early enough to catch Ormun in his chambers, but his eccentricity could place him anywhere in the palace. Some nights he never slept and instead walked through the menagerie, pulling faces at the animals. Some days he never rose. It was a relief to find a golden guard standing outside the door of Ormun's room, indicating that the Emperor was within.

"My lady," said the guard, touching his helmet.

"I need to talk with Ormun."

Other visitors might have been questioned further, but not Rema. The guard knocked on the door, and after a moment Ormun opened it, his hair in disarray. Damn it all—he wasn't yet dressed, only clad in a white linen tunic that reached past his bare knees. "Rema!" Ormun opened the door wide. "Come in, dear, come in!"

The ceiling of Ormun's chamber was supported by gilt columns, and a carved depression in the floor ran toward three arched windows that opened directly into the palace gardens. Had the palatial room been tidy, it would have stunned visitors with its austere majesty. Instead, it had become a heaping ground for Ormun's clothes, as he refused to let anyone clean his chambers and had no patience to do so himself. A woman was huddled in Ormun's bed, her face buried in the pillow. Judging by her golden hair, she was Ormun's seventh wife. The woman's breath was quiet and steady; hopefully her night had been painless.

"So, you're restless too," said Ormun, shutting the door behind them. "It's to be expected when we've such an exciting day ahead of us."

"And yet you're not even dressed. Or is that what you intend to wear?"

"No, no." Ormun opened his wardrobe and gestured to the few clothes that remained hanging. "Perhaps you can help me pick something that'll impress the court."

Rema concealed her relief. This was ideal—she could ensure the double would be able to match his appearance. "I'd be happy to. In my estimation, you should dress simply. Elise is from a simple part of the world, and it would make her feel at home."

"But she wears those fancy dresses, Rema! I've never seen anything like them outside of the most expensive brothels." Ormun lifted a sleeve and sniffed it. "Why, I wouldn't want to look plain beside her. What kind of message would that send?"

"It would show your humility and goodness. I know you enjoy wearing that brown tabard with the wide sleeves, and it pairs so well with black leggings."

"It's true, it's a fetching combination." Ormun scratched his head. "Fine! I concede! It's all too much to think about anyway." He gestured toward his sleeping wife. "Look at that thing. She's with child, I think, but the healers aren't clear on whether it'll live. I have something like five babies now. I held one for a little. It gurgled. Ugly, fat little face."

Rema had no special sentimentality for infants herself, but she wasn't willing to humor him. "I'm sure you'll grow fond of them as they age."

Ormun seemed not to have heard her, engaged as he was in wrestling with the sleeves of the tabard. Rema sighed and helped him put it on. "You still dress like a child."

"Some things stay the same." Ormun flapped his arms, his eyes lively. "Even at twenty, I'd never have any idea what to wear, and I'd stump around trying to get some button done at the back. And of course Betany was never inclined to help. But you were, dear, always you."

He chortled, clearly pleased with his reminiscences. Rema looked away. It was his brotherly love enfolded in malice that had made these four years such a torment. If he were more predictable, if he had simply been a woman-hater like Calan, she would have understood him more and feared him less.

A moment of desperate hope took hold of her. "Ormun," she said. "My brother. If I asked you to remember all the years I've served you, been a sister to you, endured your cruelties, witnessed your atrocities and abetted your wickedness—if I asked you to remember all of this and then I begged you to let her go…what would you say?"

"So it's true." Ormun tugged on his trousers. "You do love her. What's her name again?"

"Elise." Rema took a breath, and the air carried with it a wild rush of courage. "Yes, I love her. I don't want you to hurt her, and we both know that you will."

"No man is perfect, dear."

Rema took Ormun's hand and looked into his eyes, searching through his madness for a sign of her long-missing friend. "I can't keep doing this for you. You know what you are, and you know what I believe. You're intelligent enough to comprehend what you've done to me. Let me have at least this happiness."

"Rema, dear." Ormun squeezed her hand. "It cannot be. She belongs to me now." He lowered his voice. "But you've moved me, treasured one. What if I let you visit her once a week? For one night of seven, touch her and take her all that you please. You're right, after all. I have so many wives, and you have none! Why shouldn't I share one of them with my sweet sister?"

"No, you were right." Rema's words sounded as leaden as her heart felt. "It cannot be. Forgive me for asking."

"What's so special about her, anyway?" Ormun stood before the mirror and began to attend to his buttons. "I suppose she's pretty in a funny way. It's the eyes, mostly. She's got an ample figure too, but she'll be a pig in a few years. Have you slept with her? Is that why you're so giddy for the woman?"

"Of course not. That would have been an insult to you."

"Good. That would have been a bit much, dear. All the same, what is your fascination with her?"

"You couldn't understand. The nature of her beauty is among those things you've long closed yourself to."

"You're very frank today." Ormun stepped back and admired himself. "And I look positively monastic. Wonderful." He turned from the mirror, good humor still glowing in his eyes. "Rema, you say I mistreat you. It's true, it's true. I'm bleeding our empire white through war, and you're the only one who's brave enough to tell me. Sothis will only mumble and shuffle away, and Haran says, smite them! Strike them! Yet despite all your protests, I do as I please. No wonder you're miserable." His smile widened. "Haran says there are rumors that I'm mad. He doesn't mention that he and Betany say the same themselves."

"And are you?"

"You know, I often try to imagine what our empire looks like. I don't mean the land or the soldiers or the people—I mean what it truly is. Rema, it's a black octopus, all huddled and twitching over this continent of ours, one long tendril stretching out into the sea.

Suffocating. Swallowing. Everything under it mine. I don't even know what to do with it! Betany told me to take it, but why? I destroy everything that belongs to me. How foolish to give me an empire."

Ormun put his hand on her shoulder. "Yes, but there's one thing that will never be mine. You're the faithful angel that tells me when I'm wrong. I feel all the bolder when I disobey you." He pointed to the woman on the bed. "Do you think I see a woman there? I see property. Flesh. Hideousness. I warned you once what my eyes were becoming. Now there's only one thing left that's beautiful: you. You're the only thing in this world that doesn't hurt my soul to look upon. Yes, sister, I'm destroying you, for I love you. A fire can't help but long for timber."

"What am I supposed to say to that? Is that your way of convincing me of your sanity?"

"Why, I was only returning your frankness! Don't you appreciate it?" Ormun waved his hand dismissively. "Enough, enough. I look forward to seeing my bride again. Elise, that's it. Can you believe, I spent all night with this one and I can't for the life of me recall her name."

"Lassielle. She was eighteen when one of the Dukes of Kalanis offered her to you in tribute. I can tell it's her by the curly golden hair."

"Ah, yes, the Kalanese girl. They're so pale, those Kalanese. Speaking of easterners, I'd like a Narandane wife sometime. I don't have one already, do I? Or a Nastine! It'd be amusing to have a wife with your red hair."

"I'm not sure I see the humor. Pardon me, Ormun, but I have to make sure the entertainers are prepared."

"Please do." Ormun pouted. "I hope our little discussion didn't unsettle you."

Rema bowed before leaving the chamber. There seemed no point in trying to untangle Ormun's ramblings—such deranged musings were nothing new—and so she focused instead on walking to Elise's bedchambers as quickly as she could. She entered a colonnaded hall, spotted Ferruro lumbering toward her and swerved to avoid him. He frowned at her, presumably wondering why she'd deprived him of their usual morning banter. Turning a corner, she ran into a pack of Urandan diplomats. They reached for her and shouted her name, wanting to talk to the woman who had given them peace only months earlier. Rema apologized curtly and brushed them aside.

She arrived at Elise's chamber and exhaled in gratitude. Elise was chattering to Jalaya, who was sitting cross-legged on the bed. "How's your head?" said Rema.

Jalaya lifted her bangs, revealing a dark mark across her forehead. "I'm purple."

"Don't worry." Rema raised her hat to reveal her own bruise. "We can be purple together." She tried to meet Jalaya's eyes, but Jalaya peered intently at her hands.

"She's shy this morning," said Elise. "She hasn't made eye contact with me either."

"Tell me it was a dream." Jalaya's lyrical voice was clouded with embarrassment. "Tell me I didn't really sit in Elsie's lap and try to kiss her."

"You also told her that she was the most beautiful woman you'd ever seen," Rema said. "I was offended. I thought I held that title."

"Rema, I'm terribly sorry. It was the wine that said those things."

"That's not how it works," said Elise, rearranging the supplies in her medicine box. "The wine just made you speak the truth."

"Oooh." Jalaya pushed her hands into her cheeks and pursed her sulky lips. "Curse that wine, stealing all my secrets."

"We can tease you later," said Rema. "For now, I need to know if you'll be well enough to perform."

"Yes, I'm well enough." Jalaya continue to stare at her feet. "I even tested my voice by singing a song to Elsie." She began to sing, her voice ethereal and lilting. "Under light so pale and moon so bare, I touched her lips and stroked her hair…"

"Oh, that one." Rema laughed. "I hope you didn't get to the part about her breasts."

"She did," said Elise. "I was flustered. It's a good thing you came in when you did."

"Well, don't waste your voice. We'll need you to sing long enough to keep everyone distracted. When you see our Ormun double, tell him to wear a brown tabard and black leggings. Cut his hair to just above his ears, if it's not already. I assume we can trust him to play his part."

"He'd do anything I'd ask him to," said Jalaya. "He's in love with me. Poor man."

"Is there an entertainer in the palace that isn't in love with you?"

"Of course there is. You know that woman who plays the harp? I invited her to dinner once, and she looked like I'd tried to hand her a spider. I had no intention of courting her, either. I only wanted to talk about music."

"Maybe she was afraid of your cooking."

"How cruel you are. Incidentally, I've been writing a song about a diplomat who falls in love with an enchantress." Jalaya touched her hand to her chest and sang: *"Her eyes were lit with lunar fire, her abductor's heart was set aflame; theirs was a love that would not tire, two hearts that felt and beat the same…"*

"You're clever," said Elise, blushing.

Jalaya sprang to her feet. "I better hurry. I'll see you both from the stage. I suppose I'll miss most of the performance, locked in Muhan's horrible box."

"I suppose you will," said Rema. She hugged Jalaya, pressing her chin against Jalaya's head. "But when you come out you'll leave everyone dazed, as you always do."

"I want to give you something." Elise embraced Jalaya and kissed her firmly on the lips. Rema stared, envy making a return—it was one thing to kiss her, but did they really need to do it for so long and so passionately? When the kiss finally broke, Jalaya wobbled back, her eyes disoriented with pleasure.

"If that was my punishment for last night, I regret nothing," she said, touching her mouth. She gave a giddy smile and padded from the room, her jewelry jingling as she ran down the hallway.

Rema cleared her throat. "Well, then."

"She's risking her life for us. She's going to spend hours inside a giant box!" Elise shook her hair, satisfaction blazing in her eyes. "Besides, now we're even. I had to watch you kissing her, remember?"

"And what did you learn? That she kisses better than I do?"

"I'll never say. I'm proud of you, though. You're hardly pouting at all."

"Well, while you savor your stolen kiss, I should check that Muhan and Artunos have finished setting up the stage." Rema took Elise's hand and pulled her close. "This may be the last time we can speak before the performance."

As she held Elise to her chest, Rema's chest tightened with dread. What if the plan failed and she was never again able to stroke Elise's round face, touch her sensual lips or gaze into her enthralling eyes? If only she could lock all these sensations safely in her heart, never to lose them.

"This will work," Elise said. "It will, won't it? Rema, I don't know if I can let you go…"

Was there another way? They could flee the palace, and there were any number of places they might hide. Yet Ormun's specter would haunt them, and Rema would wake every morning choked with guilt. "This isn't just about us anymore," she said. "Think of Jalaya. Think of the slaves. Think of the women and men who are forbidden to love. We have the chance to rescue not only ourselves, but everyone."

"No matter what happens, I'm glad. You've already made my life worth living. I love you."

"And I love you. How powerful those words feel right now."

"Let's see if they can endure a lifetime." Elise stepped back and fixed Rema with an assertive look betrayed by the shaking of her voice. "Go now. Win us the peace we long for."

CHAPTER THIRTY-ONE

The double doors of the theater were open. Artunos's guardsmen moved back and forth through them, carrying crates and extra seating. They stopped, saluted and stood aside to allow Rema entrance.

The theater was modest by imperial standards. Three box seats rose above the stalls and were neighbored by two elevated galleries, both of which had twenty seats apiece. The walls were of smooth, polished marble, cracked with dark veins, and at either side of the wooden stage, two gold-ringed columns connected floor and ceiling. Sunlight entered through six massive round windows and touched every brick and crevice. For night performances, lanterns had been affixed to the walls, and a great chandelier hung from above.

Muhan was on stage, rummaging through a chest. Artunos stood nearby directing his men. He signaled for Rema to approach him, and she maneuvered through the guards to reach his side. "Good morning," he said. "This part is going smoothly enough. Muhan's pleased with the location of his props. How about the rest?"

"All sorted. Jalaya is taking care of the double."

"Don't you place too much confidence in her? I like her too, but she's just an entertainer."

"Are you serious? She speaks six languages and writes verse that my father would have given his hand for. You underestimate her because she's a woman." Artunos opened his mouth, but she interrupted. "Don't even try to deny it. You make an exception for me the way everyone else does, but I'll be damned if you haven't a pigheaded view of us."

"You may be right." Artunos bowed his head. "I suppose in my line of work, I don't often deal with women."

He seemed so abashed that Rema's temper faded. "That's going to change. Female guards, Artunos. Don't widen your eyes like that. I want to see it finally happen."

"And where are you going to find me a woman who can hold a sword?"

"Have you even been to the city?" Rema put her hands on her hips. "Some of the female mercenaries that come off those boats could eat you alive. There are numerous women among the Kalanese Adventurers, and the most feared of them all, the Jade Ghost, is reputed to have won alone against ten men. The Tahdeeni have women in their army, and in Coradon women are trained for war from birth."

"They're mad, though. Sothis told me that the Empire could conquer every other nation in the world and bring all their armies together, and Coradon would still beat us on the field of battle."

"And they'd win because they don't underestimate their women. So it's settled. We'll make it happen." Rema patted him on the shoulder. "Enough bickering. I'm going to have a word with Muhan."

She climbed onto the stage, where Muhan was bending over a pile of colored cloth. "Hello, my friend," she said. "Are you pleased with the preparations so far?"

"The guards have been very helpful." As Muhan faced her, his mustache lifted to reveal a broad smile. "Yes, this will be quite a show. I've never had such a large vanishing box before. Tell me, is that delightful doe-eyed woman joining us soon? I'd like to see how much room she has to move in there."

"She'll be along as quickly as she can." Rema chuckled. "I take it you like her."

"After you left the conference, the rest of us talked quite late. She kept patting my knee and calling me a brave man. I've traveled the world, but never have I heard such a voice…Ah, dear. What would my wife think?"

"I'm curious. What does your wife think about you traipsing all over the world, selling dye and vanishing monkeys?"

"I send my profits home, so she thinks of it very highly. In any case, I suspect this wondrous angel would be immune to my charms even if I were still a handsome young man. You are spoiled beyond words, Rema."

"Don't be envious. I have to work hard to hold onto my riches. Shall I leave you to prepare?"

"Yes, yes. Oh, and before I forget!" Muhan burrowed into a crate and pulled out a tear-shaped mask. Evocative stripes of color ran from its tapered tip to its round base. "I bought the mask in the city and dyed it myself. When should I put it on?"

"Honestly? Put it on now. You never know when Betany might put her head around the corner."

Muhan frowned but did as she suggested. In the mask, with his long and colored robes, he looked like the high priest of some especially cheerful religion. "It suits you," said Rema, biting back a laugh.

"I can hardly breathe." Muhan returned to sorting his rags, his narrow shoulder blades shifting beneath his colored robe.

Rema walked to the edge of the stage and gazed at the theater, visualizing how it would appear when filled. One of the box seats was traditionally reserved for the Emperor, but Ormun had declared his intention to sit in the front row of the stalls, as she had known he would. He'd told her once that the farther away he was from the performers, the less real the performance seemed to him. Rema was to sit at his left and Ferruro his right, the only company he would tolerate. Betany would occupy the imperial center box with Haran. Calicio had taken the left box, shared with his lover. Sothis had secured the right. Despite his reservations, the war minister had invited his wife and eldest daughter, knowing it would seem suspicious not to. Ormun's wives had been given the right gallery. The stalls and remaining gallery would hold the petty officials, diplomats, assistants and orderlies of the palace.

Her stomach snarled, and she glanced at the clock above the theater door. Though the tinkers of Arann were famed for their ability to shrink timepieces, this one had been built immense enough that anyone in the audience could see its hands. They indicated that an hour remained until the performance—just enough time to placate her appetite.

Rema dropped from the stage and left the theater. As she walked to the nearest kitchens, her mind wandered to Betany, or more precisely, the question of how she had managed to dispose of Bannon's body. Most likely she had unlatched her jaw and swallowed it whole. Rema claimed a salad and took it to the front court, where she relaxed on a bench and picked at her food.

A junior diplomat was sitting nearby, endearingly shy with his covert glances. Rema relented and gestured him over. She ate her meal while watching the boy explain his ideas, his hands animated with excitement. He was convinced he had the solution to the new conflict with Urandal, and his optimism was equally touching and amusing.

As the boy delved into the intricacies of his theory, people began to move from the court. "My apologies," Rema said. "But it seems as if the entertainment is starting."

"Oh!" The young diplomat stood and straightened his collar. "Yes, of course. I have a seat right at the back. I suppose you'll be up in the best seats."

"Hardly. Ormun prefers to sit at the front, and he always wants me right beside him so that he has someone to complain to." Rema waved him farewell. "Hurry to your place. You can tell me more about these ideas of yours later."

The boy departed, but Rema remained on the bench, settling her nerves. Trepidation moved restlessly through her. What if Ormun didn't feel like taking part? What if he woke up inside the box? What if Muhan failed to subdue him? What if the double was completely implausible? Rema brushed aside her concerns. It would work.

She joined the stream of people moving toward the theater. The clamor of voices and scraping seats grew in volume as she approached the double doors. She spotted Ferruro striding ahead of her, his head and shoulders towering above the crowd, and she pushed her way to his side and tugged on his sleeve.

"Is that you under that hat, Remela?" he said. He knocked one of Haran's magistrates out of his path and pulled her to his side. "There, now you won't be crushed."

"Forget about the box seats. People should sit on your shoulders."

Ferruro rumbled with amusement. "As usual, the Emperor has requested our company specifically. Oh, the misfortune of being so prized. He never stops talking during a performance."

"Ormun doesn't believe there's anyone more entertaining than himself," said Rema, and Ferruro chuckled again.

They squeezed through the door and walked past the stalls toward the front row. Ormun was already seated, staring at the drawn curtains that obscured the back of the stage. Most of the other places were already filled; Sothis's elder daughter peeped through the curtain of her box seat, her wan face brimming with curiosity, and Haran and

Betany stood together in their imperial box. Rema was too far away to make out their faces, but it was unlikely a trace of amusement graced either one.

Ferruro took his place beside Ormun, and a low curse rose from the person unfortunate enough to be seated behind him. Rema dropped into her own seat, nodding in response to Ormun's welcoming smile. It seemed only part of the theater wasn't alive with excitement or conversation: the right gallery, occupied entirely by Ormun's wives. They sat huddled and docile, the dark-skinned ones pale, the pale-skinned ones paler.

Elise sat upright and defiant among them. Her gaze met Rema's, and she blew a kiss. It was a perfect—and surely deliberate—imitation of Rema's own gesture at Muhan's first performance, and she suppressed a laugh.

"I heard there's a magician," said Ormun. "If I can see how he does his magic, I'll be very disappointed."

"Oh, I don't know much about magic," said Ferruro. "I merely do coin tricks."

Ormun snickered. "You must have an idea of what's been planned, Rema. It was your idea. What can I look forward to?"

"I wouldn't want to spoil the surprise, but I can say that there is indeed a magician," said Rema. "There will be dancers, and Jalaya will be singing. There'll also be a poetry recital in your honor."

"Poetry. Gods, hang me! Dancing sounds fine, and your singer has a lovely voice. Acrobats?"

"There might be."

"Well, well." Ormun frowned at his gallery of wives. "I hope she appreciates all of this. Ah! There she is, as surly-faced as ever. Ferruro, look at that black-haired, light-skinned woman up there. The big one. What do you make of her?"

Ferruro turned in his seat. "I think you have very little to complain about."

Rema tried to settle into her seat. The cushion had proven deceitful, appearing much softer than it really was. As she wriggled in discomfort, a grumbling rose further along the aisle, and somebody muttered an insincere apology in response—Artunos, struggling through the feet of the audience toward her. Judging from his dour expression, something had gone wrong.

"My Emperor," he said, pressing his fist to his breastplate and bowing to Ormun.

"Captain," said Ormun. "No need to stand at attention. Relax, enjoy."

"My responsibility is to keep this audience safe. I will remain vigilant, my Lord. Rema, may I have a word?"

"Surely anything you can say to Rema, you can say before me. It can't be as if you're plotting."

Artunos opened his mouth, but it was clear he had no idea what to say. Ferruro twisted in his seat to watch the exchange, his expression mirthful. "Are you a captain or a mime?" he said. "You should be on stage yourself."

"It's probably some aspect of the performance that he doesn't want to ruin for you both," said Rema. "It'll be best if I talk to him in private."

"Oh, well, in that case," said Ormun. He turned back to Ferruro and launched, with rising temper, into a complaint about the boredom of poetry.

Rema followed Artunos to the corner of the theater, as far as possible from the audience. His left eye twitched. It was a tic she'd only seen when he was under extreme pressure, and her nervousness swelled into foreboding. "What's the matter?"

"Jalaya's missing." Artunos's voice was bleak. "We were expecting her to show up at any moment. Now the performance is about to begin and she's still not here. Muhan doesn't know what to do. He needs her to get into the box."

"Missing? But I saw her only this morning. Do you know if she prepared our double?"

"No, I don't. None of the entertainers has seen her since late morning. It's not like her."

Rema glanced up at the middle box seat. Betany stared back. Despite the distance between them, there was no doubt she was smiling, and fear stirred in Rema's heart. "Artunos, this is more serious than you know. Her life may be at risk."

A drum struck behind the curtain. Its deep note vibrated through Rema and echoed in her stomach. "There's no time," said Artunos. "The entertainers are beginning the performance. You go back to Ormun, and I'll scour the palace. I'll take my five best men. If we can find her before Muhan's act, we can force an intermission. That'll give us the chance to sneak her on."

The thought of Jalaya endangered yet again inspired an equal amount of fury and despair, but Rema fought the impulse to march up to Betany's booth and demand answers; the ensuing scene would undo all their hard work. Even joining the search was impossible, for if she left the theater for any reason, Ormun would throw a tantrum and cancel the performance.

Rema cursed in Ajulai, a particularly vile imprecation, before returning to her official tongue. "Please find her. Gods, this is a disaster."

"All we can do is search. Go back to your seat. Ormun is watching us."

Rema made it back to her seat just as the curtains whisked open. Ormun smiled at her, curiosity gleaming in his blue eyes, before devoting his attention to the stage.

CHAPTER THIRTY-TWO

Three drummers sat on the stage, beating the taut leather of their instruments, while a hooded man walked to the stage's edge and bowed before the audience. He lifted his cowl, revealing his identity as one of the court's best actors, a man with a sonorous voice that always saw him cast as an emperor, king or general.

"Great court of the Empire," he said, gesturing to the audience as he spoke. "Mighty Emperor Ormun, master of the farthest reaches of Amantis. We humble entertainers today have gathered to celebrate Elise Danarian, daughter of Cedrin and Talitha, rulers of Danosha, the southern jewel of Ostermund. She is linked by passion to our majestic Ormun, son of Togun and Morga. Hail to you, Heir of the Wide Realms." A drum note quivered, and the actor folded his hands over his chest. "May we thrill your blood and quicken your hearts."

He clapped. Dancers twirled onto the stage from the wings, ribbons in their hands tracing wild patterns behind them. There were four: a graceful Tahdeeni man dancing on his toes, a Goronban woman shifting her hips to the beat of the drum, a Molonese man whose muscles rippled as he moved and a Lastar woman, her eyes bright as she twirled. The male dancers were stripped to the waist, and the women wore shimmering wraps with long, fluttering edges. Each weaved around the others, spinning with effortless grace.

The drums thudded as the dancers' movements became more frenzied. Ormun nodded his head to the beat, while Ferruro rested his face against his palm, his face bored beyond measure. A new set of instruments sang: a high, howling pipe, the shrill ring of zylls and the skittering of a rattle. The dancers began to thrust and contort like walking snakes. Rema looked over to Elise, who was watching the stage intently. This would all be novel to her. And, of course, she knew nothing about Jalaya's disappearance.

The audience gasped as a torrent of flame roared over the heads of the dancers, who spun to the wings to reveal the fire-breather, a towering Narandane woman with a shaved head and a bare chest. Her muscular breasts were slick with sweat. She tensed her shoulders, inhaled her torch and expelled another withering flame. Jalaya had once confided to Rema that despite her appearance, the fire-breather was a timid woman who was terrified of parrots. They had both laughed until Jalaya had gotten hiccups, and Rema had spent the rest of their evening coaxing her to stand on her head to cure them.

Rema gripped the armrests of her chair until her knuckles whitened. It seemed absurd to be watching this performance while her dearest friend could be dead or dying. She glanced at Ormun, who was gazing with pleasure at the fire-breather. He returned the sidelong look. Attentive to her presence as he was, she would never have a chance to leave. She sank back in resignation as the fire-breather released a last flame and sidled backward into the shadow of the wings.

A short, balding man strolled to the front of the stage. Ormun groaned. "A poem for our Emperor," said the poet in his rich voice. "And his wife most divine." He cleared his throat.

"Here sits our Danoshan daughter,
From her realm of woe and war.
A land wracked by blood and slaughter,
Ere our soldiers reach its shore.

She shall join soon with our master,
Highest lord and great protector,
He has been our surest armor,
He shall be her sweetest nectar.

We welcome her, brave child of East,
To this, the wide and sultry West,
To find her hopes and joys released,
And in her marriage long be blessed!"

A series of slow, sarcastic claps broke the ensuing silence. A backward glance confirmed Rema's fear: it was Elise producing the sardonic applause. Rema stood and began to clap enthusiastically, nudging the man on her left to do the same. From high above, Calicio shouted in approval and joined her applause, and the forced enthusiasm began to spread across the theater. The poet basked in adulation, though he gave a worried frown in the direction of Ormun, who hunched in his seat examining his fingernails.

"That was execrable," said Ormun. "Master shouldn't rhyme with armor."

Ferruro made a noise of agreement, as did Rema, who had been agonized by the poem no less than anyone else—the court poet was living proof that not everyone should be permitted to write verse. Still, Elise had been foolish to react so brashly...then again, wasn't it precisely that stubborn spirit that Rema so loved?

The poet shuffled into the wings and the drums picked up their beating. Two acrobats vaulted to the stage and spiraled in midair before landing frog-legged. Ormun seemed to cheer up, while Ferruro sunk back into apathy; he only enjoyed himself when Ormun was irritated.

As Rema watched the performers tumble, her thoughts returned to her problem. There was, at least, an obvious remedy. She could volunteer instead of Ormun, and then Muhan's substitution trick would become a vanishing one. She would then sneak from the stage, find Jalaya and arrange for Elise to be smuggled from the palace. The court's suspicion would fall on Rema, especially as Ormun knew of her feelings, but she would deal with that when it came.

The acrobats were poised for another gyrating leap when the door of the theater banged open. The audience turned in confusion at the sound of heavy boots, which preceded the arrival of a pack of silver and gold guardsmen. "Stop the performance," one said, and the acrobats rocked on their heels, faces uncertain. The audience broke into whispers.

Ormun rose. "What's the meaning of this?"

One of the golden guards approached with his helm under his arm. "My Emperor. Mistress Remela, Master Ferruro. There is a fire in the diplomat's college. We don't believe it can spread across the courtyard, but we must still remove the audience to a safer location."

Rema's heart stilled. The college was a three-story building within the palace confines. It contained the diplomatic library, the quarters of the junior diplomats, a small kitchen and dining area, and several lecture halls. It was wood-paneled, filled with furniture, tapestries and rugs, and it held innumerable books and papers…"It's a tinderbox," said Rema, rising. "How long has the fire been burning? You have to stop it before it reaches the library."

"The safety of the court is our first responsibility. Captains Artunos and Lakmi are at the fire now, arranging a defense."

A man behind them stood. "What's this about a fire?"

"Fire?" said another. "Did he say there's a fire?"

The panic spread, the dreaded word passing from lip to ear, until the entire audience was on their feet and calling out in terror. Where was the fire? Were their quarters in danger? Was there a way out of the palace? "Please don't panic," said the guard. "The fire is in the diplomat's college, and we hope to contain it there—"

There was a cry of horror from the junior diplomats, and they rushed to the door. The guards tried to hold them back, but a crowd of curious audience members joined the press, and the guards retreated. For some mad reason, people always moved toward a disaster rather than away from it. "Ferruro," Rema said. "Help me get through this crowd."

Ferruro nodded, took Rema's arm and began to force his way through the audience. Soon they were at the head of the pack. They ran through the corridors and stumbled into the wide outdoor courtyard that surrounded the school building. Flames peered from the school's upper windows. A group of guards were standing nearby, filling buckets from the courtyard well. Artunos and Lakmi were with them, their heads bowed in conference.

"What's going on?" Rema said. "How did this happen?"

"I couldn't say." Artunos's face was drawn, and his tic had worsened. "But we sent some guards in there, and they say it's already out of control. Too much smoke, and once the library goes up nobody will be able to go near it."

"We can't save your college," said Lakmi. "We're preparing to contain the fire instead. We're lucky the structure is separate."

A group had already gathered in the courtyard to stare at the blaze. Junior diplomats watched, wide-eyed and teary, as their home was destroyed, while Ferruro's face expressed the pain of seeing wealth transformed into smoke. Sothis stood well back with his daughter, holding her close, while Betany and Haran lurked together some distance from the others. Betany's arms were folded, and her eyes burned as brightly as the building.

Rema stalked across the cobbles and grabbed Betany by the shoulders. "Where's Jalaya?"

Betany laughed. "Where do you think?"

Rema stared at the burning building. It was as if her chest had been hollowed, and into the numb space had been poured a grief and fear beyond imagination. "What did you do?" said Haran. "Betany, you didn't…"

"Silence, Haran. Trust in me."

Rema felt a hand on her shoulder. It was Elise, her face even whiter than usual. "What's happening?"

"Jalaya is in there." Rema kissed Elise on the lips—Haran and Betany were staring, but damn them, what did it matter now—before running to Sothis's daughter. "I have to borrow your scarf."

The young woman unraveled the colored cloth and surrendered it. "Are you Rema?"

"Yes, but there's no time to get acquainted." Rema hurried to the well and took a bucket from the hands of a guardsman, who tried to resist until he realized who was robbing him. She drenched the scarf in the water, wrapped it around her face and ran toward the door. Artunos grabbed her by the arm.

"You're mad," he said. "You won't survive."

"You can't stop me. Jalaya is in there. I'd rather die myself than surrender her to the flames."

"Jalaya?" Artunos clutched her more urgently. "How do you know?"

"Betany did this. She understands now it's the surest way to hurt me." Rema looked into his apprehensive eyes. "If I die, I will need you to repay your debt to me. Take Elise far from here. Succeed where I failed. Save the woman I love."

His grip slackened, and she pulled free. Several voices cried her name—Ormun's was among them. He must only have arrived; that didn't matter either. Jalaya would live, or all this was pointless. Rema continued without hesitation into the lobby and ran to the stairwell. Betany, cruel as she was, would have placed Jalaya on the third floor, as far from Rema's reach as possible. But she had underestimated her rival, as she always had, as she ever would.

The heat built as Rema ascended the stairs. Upon reaching the second floor, she began to taste the smoke, and her eyes stung. The sound of fire intensified as she climbed, until the crackling and gloating of the flames became all-enveloping. To still her fear, Rema began to murmur verse beneath her breath: "Her love has held my grief at bay, and now she sets me free…"

She stumbled onto the landing of the third floor. Flames jumped across the walls and writhed about the beams while tapestries and paintings smoldered, their corners roasting to ash. Rema tightened the scarf and narrowed her eyes against the biting smoke. Elise's medallion was burning cold against her neck, a shard of ice amid the heat.

"Jalaya!" The damp cloth muffled her voice, yet how could she not call for the one she loved? She staggered across the carpet of a wide, oak-paneled room. Tendrils of fire burned along the paneling, and a support column in one corner was covered in crawling tongues of flame. "Jalaya!"

The third floor was mostly bedchambers, one after another. Rema ran past long rows of doors, glancing quickly into each room, only to falter in her step—the corridor ahead was entirely ablaze. Rema retreated from the roaring mouth of flame. Jalaya was likely to be dead by now, and new tears mingled with those already summoned by the bitter smoke. Rema ducked her head as she hurried down another corridor. A beam split and toppled, and she swerved to avoid being hit. The building hadn't been built to withstand fire, and there was real danger of the roof collapsing.

Rema turned a corner and came to a halt. Jalaya lay huddled on the floor with her face pressed against the carpet. She was dressed for her performance, and sweat soaked the gauzy fabric of her garments. Rema knelt beside her, reaching beneath her chin to lift her head. "Jalaya," she said. "Can you hear me?"

"Rema." Tears glued Jalaya's lashes, and Rema was horrified to hear a harsh roughness in her voice. "She tied me to a chair. I slipped my wrists free and escaped, but there's too much smoke, I got lost…"

"Don't talk." Rema helped Jalaya upright. As the smoke touched her face once more, Jalaya wheezed and slumped against Rema's shoulder, her breaths coming in labored gasps. Rema unraveled the scarf and tied it about Jalaya's mouth, ignoring a weak mutter of protest.

Tightening her hold on Jalaya's waist, Rema directed them back the way she'd come. The flames had built in her absence, and they seared her so intensely that it felt as if her sweat were boiling. The door to the stairwell seethed with fire, and Rema held Jalaya close as they rushed past an inferno that had spread to the stairs themselves, scorching its way down the banisters.

They had struggled to the second floor and were about to descend to the first when a tremendous groan came from above. A second later, a cascade of wood and stone broke from the ceiling and toppled into the stairwell. The rubble lay between them and the first floor, and Rema could see no safe way to guide Jalaya over it.

"Trapped," Jalaya said.

"No. There's another stairwell on the other side of this floor. Cling to me, you'll be fine."

The second floor was comprised mostly of libraries and studies, and burning paper crackled around them as they navigated the smoke-filled corridors. Rema wiped a slick sheen of sweat from her forehead as the temperature continued to rise. The smoke had stolen her vision, and her lungs struggled to find relief in the choking air.

Jalaya slipped. Rema caught her and, with much effort, lifted and cradled her. She took several unwieldy steps forward—light as Jalaya was, Rema was exhausted, and she'd never been built for carrying women in the first place.

"Rema," said Jalaya, her voice dry and feeble in Rema's ear. "I'm sorry."

With Jalaya draped over her arms, Rema continued to stagger through the deepening smoke as the fire muttered angrily about her. She pushed open a door with her shoulder and emerged into a corridor free of smoke or flames. The mouth of the stairwell lay ahead. She hurried toward it, swaying under the effort of carrying Jalaya, and stumbled into Artunos as he emerged from an adjoining corridor.

"I'll take her," said Artunos. Holding her gently, he hefted Jalaya over his shoulders. She seemed unconscious, but her chest rose with labored breaths. "Rema, I don't want to tell you this, but you'll never forgive me if I keep it from you. Elise and Ormun followed you in. As far as I know, they're still in here."

"Elise?" Rema swept her damp bangs away from her face. "Elise is in here with Ormun?"

"Nobody could stop them running in any more than we could stop you. Ormun actually commanded us to keep back. I searched the first floor, but I couldn't find them."

"Get Jalaya out of here. She needs water and a healer. I'm going back for Elise."

"You'll die, you realize. You're lucky enough to have survived in there once, and it's even more dangerous now."

"Don't scold me. Just take Jalaya to safety." Rema closed her eyes and inhaled the clear air. Would she ever taste it again?

"Here." Artunos pulled a damp cloth from around his neck and handed it to her. "Damn you, Rema…" His composure broke, and he bowed his head. It was only the second time in her life that Rema had seen him in tears, and her own eyes stung in sympathy. Without another word, he returned down the hall, moving swiftly despite bearing Jalaya's weight.

Rema wrapped the cloth around her mouth and returned to the nightmare of smoke and conflagration. The third floor would be entirely lost to inferno by now, and she could only hope that Elise hadn't been consumed with it. At the thought, a new energy found its way into her empty limbs, and she forced herself through the heat and smoke, her pulse as quick as the flames. Yet it seemed hopeless, and she quickly grew disoriented again. The decorations and furniture around her had been transformed into torches; she no longer recognized the college as her own.

Despair had tightened almost completely around her heart when she heard a sound that scattered the darkness and gave her hope again—Elise, calling Rema's name. Rema pursued her voice and found her standing behind a rubble-choked door, flushed and unkempt. Part of the floor upstairs must have collapsed, and the entire ceiling was likely to follow.

"My beloved." Elise gave a forlorn smile. "You heard me calling. I shouldn't have, but I wanted to see your face one more time."

Rema tried to shift the collapsed stones. They were too heavy, and her hands fell away, the debris unmoved. "Elsie, help me!"

"You don't understand. This is the price for my magic. I killed Bannon, and now my death will restore the balance."

"I don't give a damn about the balance. We can move this. Don't you dare give up on our love."

"I'll love you even in death." Elise's grief-stricken eyes betrayed the calm in her voice. "But there's no way for me to escape. You have to find Jalaya and save yourself."

"I found her. She's safe." Rema tugged at a chunk of masonry and only managed to scrape her hands. "Damnit! Elsie, help me! How can you be so passive?"

"Because this is my fate." Elise lowered her gaze. "I'm only relieved that I didn't hurt anyone else. Go, Rema. Your father's dream is so very near."

The smoke was building and the flames were gathering. Either the ceiling would cave in, the fire would reach them or the smoke would overwhelm them; in any event, they had little time. "Please try. You must have more strength left than I do."

"I can hear the roof above me groaning. You have to run."

Rema kicked the rubble in exasperation. "Why did you go into that stupid room?"

"Don't scold me. I was searching for you. I couldn't know the roof would fall in."

"I'm not scolding you. I'm just furious that you're so close and I can't even hold you. I need you, Elise. Without you, I'll never be—"

"There you are!" The rasping voice came from behind her, and Rema turned, her heart racing; she'd forgotten he was here. Ormun's face dripped with sweat, and his eyes were red and swollen. "I was looking everywhere, dear."

"Help me move this." Rema took his sleeve and pulled. "Hurry. Elise is trapped."

Ormun was broad and powerful, and surely possessed the strength to clear enough space for Elise to crawl free. Yet he resisted her tugging, remaining where he stood. "There's hardly time to move rocks and things. We should get out of here while we still can, sister."

"I won't leave while she's behind that debris. If you don't get her out, I'll die here with her."

A desperate spasm contorted Ormun's features. He took Rema's arm and pulled her toward him. "If you won't follow me out, I'll drag you out." She struggled and swung at him with her free hand. He caught her wrist. "Unconscious, if I have to. You don't have the luxury of death, dear. I need you."

It had to end here—his dominance, his cruelty, his manipulation. Live or die, she would never concede. "If you separate me from her, I'll die no less than if you'd torn out my heart. I'll never again speak or move. I'll remain motionless until my lungs cease and body grows cold. I love her, Ormun. She belongs to nobody, least of all to you, yet she has chosen to be with me. Even if you drag me away, my soul will remain to die with hers, and then you'll have no sister at all. You'll be alone with that dark madness."

Ormun struck her across the face. "I don't want to hear it," he said as she reached for her stinging cheek. "How do you expect me to comprehend the workings of your unclouded heart? You know that I must do as I will."

"Then will yourself to move that debris. You delude yourself if you think I'm within your reach. What stands before you is only the shell of the woman you've tormented. The part of me that was your sister, the part of me that remembers how to love and be loved…that part is with her."

"Get out of my way." Ormun approached the fallen doorway. Straining his broad arms, he heaved aside several of the larger chunks of masonry. "Go on, you fat pig. See if you can squeeze through that."

Elise pushed herself through the gap. The splintered doorframe tore her dress, drew a thin line of blood along her cheek and snagged her hair, but she managed to wriggle into the corridor. The moment she was on her feet, she kissed Rema with desperate intensity. Ormun yanked Elise away from the embrace. "Don't test me. Get moving."

Flames rolled toward them, engulfing furniture, eating decorations and capering with ecstasy among burning pages. Elise and Rema staggered, coughing, through the burning halls while Ormun followed. His brooding anger was every bit as blistering as the fire around them. Rema knew what it meant to provoke the brutal jackal that stalked the shadows of his mind, baying insanity.

They entered a long hallway, its fixtures swallowed by flame. The heat roasted Rema's skin, and the acrid smell of burning hair wafted about them. As they moved, smoke clung to their faces, and Elise and Ormun began wheezing. Rema removed her dampened rag and forced it upon the unwilling Elise. "My father raised me amid smoke," said Rema. "Have no fear."

As they neared the end of the corridor, the chill against Rema's chest sharpened into a point of frozen agony. She leapt forward, and as she did the ceiling above her howled and split. A pile of wood, stone and broken furniture tumbled into the hallway. Elise tripped, and Rema caught her arm.

"Rema," said Elise, pointing behind them. "Look."

Ormun's leg had been caught by the rubble, pinning him to the carpet. He tugged at his trapped limb, his face stretched in almost comic surprise. "Rema." His voice was as bemused as his expression. "It's fallen on me."

"Go, Elsie," said Rema. "The stairwell is just ahead of you."

"I'm not leaving you!" Elise gave Rema an incredulous look. "You just gave that heartfelt speech about never leaving me. What kind of ridiculous double standard—"

"If you love me, please do as I say. I'll join you outside. I promise."

Elise sighed. "A promise it is, then." She kissed Rema before stumbling through the smoke.

"Rema, get this off me," said Ormun. "Hurry."

Rema crouched at his side. The building was crumbling around them, beams tearing and joints splitting, and the smoke hung dense above their heads; there was no time to squander. Yet if she left this building without cleansing her soul, she would never be free. She met Ormun's dulled eyes, and as he stared back at her, he seemed to understand her intention. He relaxed, and his arms fell to his side.

"Betany told me that your performance was some kind of trap," he said. "I suppose she lit this fire to interrupt it. It seems rather extreme, even for her."

"She arranged it this way in order to hurt me." Rema reached for his hand. "She wanted to take away the things I most loved."

"How was your little plan intended to unfold?"

"I would have coaxed you to take part in a performance. You'd have agreed, relishing as always the opportunity to play the lead role. The magician would have guided you into a box. You would have waited in the dark, uncertain, until someone knocked you on the head. The box was to be smuggled away, a double was arranged to fool the crowd. It could have been hours until people realized you were missing."

"Much craftier than anything I could come up with. And then you'd have killed me?"

"I let the others believe that I would, but no. There's a tiny island two weeks off the coast, well outside any sea traveler's path. I was going to leave you there to live out your life as best you could."

"And why would you do that?" Ormun winced and pressed his hand to his thigh. "It seems to me, dear, that leaving me alive could only have created problems. Someone was bound to find me eventually."

Rema hunched lower, trying to keep her head beneath the worst of the smoke. "Do you remember my nineteenth birthday? You were still that gentle boy who accompanied me throughout the palace, consoling me when I was worried, celebrating with me when I did well. That morning, you burst into my chambers with your birthday present. It was a little golden bird. I was delighted by it and put it on my shelf. Then we sat on my bed, looking out the window and watching the real birds moving and singing in the trees."

"I remember. You were so boyish then, with your short hair."

"I told you then that I wished we could all live like birds." Rema smiled as the memory became more vivid. "I praised them for singing instead of fighting, building instead of destroying. It was the kind of silly thing a girl of nineteen might say, but I was sincere. And you began to cry. You said that some nights you laid awake for hours while a cold hatred crept through your body, as if something malign were taking over your thoughts and dreams. It was a black cloud, you said, that stole into your eyes and blocked out everything good."

"You held me. You promised to protect me. You told me to trust you. Yes, I remember. And I never did stop trusting you."

"You're sick, Ormun. Sick in a way that no healer can cure. The first time I caught you holding some poor girl against a wall, I didn't recognize you at all. There was a stranger wearing your face."

"I don't remember it too well. But I recall you were furious. You struck me about the shoulders with your little hands. I wept and told you I didn't know why I'd done it."

"After a time, you stopped weeping. You became colder, harder. You hurt others more often. You began to hurt me. When you killed your father, whom I loved as if he were my own, I realized you were lost. I'd look into your eyes hoping to see that old warmth, and I'd find nothing but your coldness."

"I remember it, but understand nothing." Ormun shook his head. "It's all so many words to me. These memories and feelings are like phantoms. They no longer have sense in them."

So he was still lost to her, even now, even with the smoke and heat rolling in to consume them both. "I've had many chances to put a knife in your back," said Rema, "yet even when you threatened to destroy the woman I love, I couldn't put the blade all the way in. I've clung so long to the belief that he's in you somewhere, the frightened boy who held me on my birthday and cried."

"I don't want to die," said Ormun in a voice thickened by emotion. "Don't leave me, Rema."

Rema released his hand and stood. "You died years ago. I loved you once, but now I have to let you go. I'm sorry it ended this way, brother." She brushed away a tear before it could fall. "I always thought you might somehow get better."

"I know what you're hoping for. That I'll say something to redeem myself. That I'll tell you to go off and love that woman. That I'm sorry for my wicked ways." Ormun grimaced. "None of that makes sense to me. But know this, Rema. You're the only person I've ever loved. Why did I hurt you? How could I hurt you? My beautiful sister. How you laughed as you held that golden bird." He groaned and tugged at his leg. "Rema, help me. I don't want to die. I command you to free me. I am your Emperor! I command you…"

She left Ormun to the flames. As she descended the stairs, a cacophony of destruction erupted behind her. Their shared suffering was over.

CHAPTER THIRTY-THREE

Rema emerged from the lobby into a circle of frightened faces. People hurried toward her, touching her and offering her water. Elise pushed through the crowd and embraced her, and Rema pressed her cheek to Elise's shoulder as she wept tears she had long forgotten she held.

"He's dead," she said. "I gave up on him. I broke my promise. I couldn't do it anymore."

Those in earshot talked quickly and in consternation. "Ormun is dead?" said Artunos. "Are you sure?"

"He was caught in debris on the second floor. I heard the ceiling give in."

Flames surged in triumph from the windows of the college's upper two stories, and the building groaned as more of its body gave way beneath the gnawing heat. Artunos gestured for the crowd to step further back. "I can't send someone in there. Not even for the Emperor."

"You've killed my brother!" Betany passed through the ring of onlookers and dragged Rema out of Elise's arms. "You lured him in there!"

"And who lured me?" said Rema, breaking free from Betany's grip. "Don't you dare blame me for this. For all I know, you expected him to follow me."

"If you mean to implicate me, then you have no evidence. But there's more than enough to prove that you and this witch have violated sacred laws of marriage. Everyone here has witnessed your tawdry embrace."

Haran moved to her side and cleared his throat. "It is true. Whatever wrongdoing has happened here, Remela is at the heart of it."

"Oh, spare me," said Ferruro, pushing aside a flock of junior diplomats as he stepped forward. "For her heroics, you want to reward her with a noose? Cynical I may be, but unlike you, Haran, I have a little blood left in my veins. Perhaps when the healers have finished taking care of the little singer, we should ask who trapped her inside the building."

"Remela's slut would say anything her mistress told her to." Betany tightened her lips and cast a cold stare at Ferruro. "You disappoint me, treasurer. I may need to reconsider your appointment now that I am Empress."

"You are not Empress," said Rema, straightening her back and regathering her composure. "And you never will be."

"The law is very clear," said Haran. "None of Ormun's heirs are of age, so Betany will take the throne." His face twitched as he looked between Rema, Betany and Ferruro, and he rubbed his hand against his wrist.

"Who said anything about the law? It's over, Haran. We aren't letting Betany take control."

"And who is we?" Haran's voice wavered. "I only see one singed, petulant woman. Who else is with you?"

"I am," said Sothis, moving to Rema's side and resting his frail hand on her arm. "Let's be done with mad rulers."

"Listen to them," said Ferruro, and Haran's face drooped at the unexpected betrayal. "You must have some shrewdness left in you. Or are you so eager to be Betany's prize puppet in a court of the dead?"

"Haran!" said Betany. "Don't listen to these vipers. They have no right. Captains, arrest these rebels."

Artunos laughed. "I don't think so."

"Lakmi!" Betany looked about for the house captain, who was beside an ornamental tree. "Will you please put this situation under control?"

Lakmi shrugged and spat on the ground. "It seems too complex for an illiterate like me. I'd prefer not to get involved."

Betany frowned and took a step back. "Haran, do something."

"Let's not be too rash," said Haran slowly. "Perhaps we should take time to talk about this."

"Traitors." Betany glared at the gathered onlookers. "Enjoy your little coup while it lasts. When you run this empire into the ground, the people will beg for me to take control. I am the rightful Empress, and when I finally come to rule I will seat your skulls at the base of my throne."

"But for now, you'll run to your room and throw a tantrum," said Rema. "Begone, Betany. Retreat with what little dignity you have remaining."

Betany lunged toward Rema, her face compressed with rage. Elise stepped between them, and Betany recoiled. "Keep away from me. You're not human."

Elise leaned forward, her hands on her hips. "Behave yourself. You know what happens to people who displease me."

Betany screeched in frustration and stalked from the court. Haran moved to follow her, but Ferruro caught him by the sleeve. "You can't be serious. Let it go, you old fool."

Haran stared after her, looking more pinched than ever. "Call me what you will, but she could have ruled. At least it would have been legal."

They all turned to stare once more at the burning school. The fire had now reached the first floor, and its fingers curled about the window frames, searching hungrily for more fuel to devour. Smoke spilled from the door, black and sinuous. "I hope you're able to contain this," Rema said.

Artunos gestured to the phalanx of silver and gold guards. They were holding buckets to their chests as they scrutinized the building with vigilant eyes. "We won't let it spread past the court. We're hoping that it'll burn itself out inside the building. I am sorry about your school, though."

"It can be rebuilt. Let this be the last good thing destroyed by Togun's children."

Artunos nodded. "Go to Jalaya. She's in her chambers with a healer. She'll want to see you both."

"Thank you," said Rema. "All of you." Sothis bowed, and Ferruro gave her a knowing smile. Haran turned away, his gaunt face grim.

The palace's corridors were flooded with wandering people, all caught in a frenzy of fear and excitement. No doubt the rumor of Ormun's death was gathering momentum. The new council would have to act soon to maintain order, but for now Rema had other matters on her mind.

"Look," said Elise, tugging Rema's hand. "There's Muhan." He was sitting on a bench in the corridor, his masked head lowered. Rema lifted the mask away to reveal his sleeping face. He rubbed his eyes and smiled.

"Do you have any idea what you've just slept through?" said Rema.

"I understand nothing in this house of madness." Muhan stretched his arms. "So I decided to rest until somebody came to educate me. You two look bedraggled but happy, so I assume everything is well. Did you find that dear little woman?"

"Yes, she's fine, and you won't be needing the mask from now on."

Muhan turned the mask in his hands. "A pity. I was becoming fond of it. So I take it that my performance is canceled?"

"Certainly not. You'll perform later this week to celebrate the change of regime. In the meanwhile, you'll get one of the finest chambers in the palace and all the grapefruit you can eat."

"Ah. I thought you'd woken me, but alas, here I am, still in a dream."

"I know how you feel," said Elise. "Come on, Rema, we can talk to silly Muhan later."

"Fine." Rema laughed as she clasped her hands. "Take care, Muhan."

They left Muhan tugging his mustache in confusion and continued to Jalaya's chambers. Jalaya was sprawled among her innumerable blankets and pillows while a wrinkled man stooped at her side, patting her face with a cloth. She raised her eyes as Rema and Elise entered.

"You're alive," she said, her voice husky. "I was worried."

Rema took her hand. "Here we are again. You can't imagine how sorry I am. Of all the people to keep being hurt on my account, why does it have to be you?"

"Well, I did promise to die for you. Fate is just determined to have me keep that promise." Jalaya winced. "Oh, my throat hurts."

"There may be harm to her singing voice," said the old healer. "Alas, she inhaled much heat and smoke."

Elise growled. "There'll be no harm if I have anything to do with it. Did you give her a mixture of honey and lemon to drink?"

"Well, no." The healer bit his lower lip. "Should I have?"

"You call yourself a healer?" Elise stamped her foot. "You abomination! Get honey and lemon for her right now!"

With a shriek, the healer dived toward the door, holding his robes tightly about him. "Hopeless," said Elise, her eyes scalding with temper. "Don't worry, Jalaya. You'll soon be singing more prettily than ever."

"Something has happened, hasn't it?" said Jalaya. "Tell me."

"Ormun is dead," said Rema. "Betany has been refused the throne. We're going to take control now, we officials of the court, and our first action will be to return Ormun's wives to their families."

"All but one," said Elise. "Let's get married, Rema."

Rema laughed and tangled a length of Elise's hair about her fingers. "Why not? It seems fitting that the first female diplomat and the first self-taught enchantress become the first married women in the Empire."

"I mean it. I'm proposing to you, Remela. Don't make me get on my knee."

"And I'm accepting. I'll marry you, Elise Danarian."

Jalaya clapped her hands and tossed a pillow into the air. "I'd cheer, but I'd hurt myself. Congratulations, you lovely things. I hope my voice comes back in time to sing at your wedding." She sank back to her bed, clearly exhausted by the short display of delight. "Rema, you're free now. Ormun's shadow has left you. You can grieve for him instead of hating him."

Rema nodded. "I want to think that the fire burned away the mad part of him, so that in whatever place the dead go, he'll be the gentle young man that I knew."

"He will be," said Elise. "The man he became is lost without redemption, but the boy he once was will remain innocent. Nature does not judge, but instead receives what is healthy and pure."

"You're a strange one, Elsie," said Jalaya. "I'll miss you both. After you're married, I've decided to leave the court." She laughed as Rema and Elise both hurried to her bedside, protesting and clutching at her. "Get off me, you brutes! There's no other way. Rema, I still love you, and Elsie, you're so much like her that my heart is dangerously close to falling for you too. I need to give you two space to grow together." She winked at Elise. "Besides, I know I'm a wicked temptation."

"You're not wrong," said Elise. "But this is cruel. I can imagine many lonely days while Rema is scratching at her paperwork, and what will I do without your company?"

Rema stared. It was as if her joy had been stolen from her, leaving her numb. "Jalaya, you can't. You don't understand how much you mean to me. We've seen through so many unhappy years together, don't you want to share the happy ones to come?"

Jalaya shook her head, jangling her earrings. "I have to leave for my own sake. Elsie was able to reach you in a way I never could, and I'll never rest until I understand why. Love is my mystery, and I have to seek it beyond these palace walls. There is a secret written in the eyes and lips of a woman who needs me, and when I find her I will croon a song of love that will wind its way through the heart of the world."

"All you poets are alike. I wanted us to grow old together."

"We will. Every day I'll think of you, and you need only do the same."

"You've been such a comfort." Elise wiped her eyes. "Don't you understand that I've never had a friend before you? Not a lover, not a brother, but a friend…"

"I've made up my mind. You two need to be together, and I need to sleep. I love you both."

"Rest well," said Elise, lowering her head. Rema was too heavy with emotion to reply. Tears blurred her vision, and she blinked them away.

They left the chamber together, hand in hand, wandering without direction through the palace. As they passed beneath the wide archway of the inner court, they paused for a moment to stare at the chaos taking place within. It seemed that all the entertainers and officials of the court had gathered to laugh and gossip, their faces animated. Calicio walked among the groups, nodding his head as he responded to questions. He spotted Rema standing in the archway and lifted his hand. She raised hers in reply.

"Where do we go?" Elise said. "I'm so tired, Rema."

"As am I. Let's go to the gardens."

It was early evening. As they entered the gardens, a warm breeze set the trees swaying, sending fragrant petals loose to the wind. The women linked arms, and Elise rested her head on Rema's shoulder as they followed the path beneath the brightly-colored canopy. Fat parrots bared their plumage to the setting sun and crooned as its last warmth touched them, while slender-beaked birds pounced among the lower branches, their heads turning to watch the lovers pass by. The air resonated with the calling of the waterfall, the cackling of animals in the distant menagerie, the hissing of wind-rustled leaves and the clamor of birds at play.

Rema led Elise off the path and toward a dense knot of pink-and lilac-flowered trees. They sat in the tall grass, and Elise laughed as a dragonfly settled briefly on Rema's head before whirring into the sky. "I just realized that you've lost your adorable little hat," she said.

"I hadn't even noticed. I hope it's content, wherever it is."

"Most likely it fell off and burned. Poor hat."

They watched as evening took shape on the horizon, a deep purple streak above the waning flame of the sun. Rema's eyes itched and her lungs ached, yet as she sat amid the murmuring insects and the aromatic petals, her discomfort was eclipsed by her bliss. She gazed at Elise, who smiled back. Though her eyes were reddened and her lashes were dried with tears, her silver gaze was clear.

"Here we are at last," said Rema, her fingertips following the rounded curve of Elise's cheek.

"Just as you promised." Elise put her arms around Rema and lowered her into the grass.

Many years before, a little girl played at her father's feet while he sat, wreathed in incense, and drifted through a poet's dreams. He knew that the world was good and prayed that his daughter would know it too, so that like him she would hope for hopeless things. So often he had asked her, *Remmy, what makes you happy?* As she lay beneath the fading sun, gazing into the enchanted eyes of the woman she loved, Rema found her answer.

Bella Books, Inc.

Women. Books. Even Better Together.

P.O. Box 10543
Tallahassee, FL 32302

Phone: 800-729-4992
www.bellabooks.com